THE FURTHER ADVENTURES
OF SHERLOCK HOLMES

Sir Arthur Conan Doyle

THE FURTHER ADVENTURES
OF SHERLOCK HOLMES

Illustrations by DAVID JOHNSON
Afterword by PHILIP A. SHREFFLER

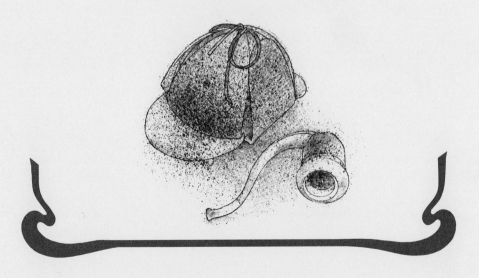

THE WORLD'S BEST READING
The Reader's Digest Association, Inc.
Pleasantville, N.Y. • Montreal

CONTENTS

ILLUSTRATIONS

I: The Adventure of Wisteria Lodge

I. THE SINGULAR EXPERIENCE OF
MR. JOHN SCOTT ECCLES

I FIND IT recorded in my notebook that it was a bleak and windy day towards the end of March in the year 1892. Holmes had received a telegram whilst we sat at our lunch, and he had scribbled a reply. He made no remark, but the matter remained in his thoughts, for he stood in front of the fire afterwards with a thoughtful face, smoking his pipe, and casting an occasional glance at the message. Suddenly he turned upon me with a mischievous twinkle in his eyes.

"I suppose, Watson, we must look upon you as a man of letters," said he. "How do you define the word 'grotesque'?"

"Strange—remarkable," I suggested.

He shook his head at my definition.

"There is surely something more than that," said he; "some underlying suggestion of the tragic and the terrible. If you cast your mind back to some of those narratives with which you have afflicted a long-suffering public, you will recognise how often the grotesque has deepened into the criminal. Think of that little affair of the red-headed men. That was grotesque enough in the outset, and yet it ended in a desperate attempt at robbery. Or, again, there was that most grotesque affair of the five orange pips, which led straight to a murderous conspiracy. The word puts me on the alert."

"Have you it there?" I asked.

He read the telegram aloud:

Have just had most incredible and grotesque experience. May I consult you?

> SCOTT ECCLES,
> Post Office, Charing Cross

"Man or woman?" I asked.

"Oh, man, of course. No woman would ever send a reply-paid telegram. She would have come."

"Will you see him?"

"My dear Watson, you know how bored I have been since we locked up Colonel Carruthers. My mind is like a racing engine, tearing itself to pieces because it is not connected up with the work for which it was built. Life is commonplace, the papers are sterile; audacity and romance seem to have passed forever from the criminal world. Can you ask me, then, whether I am ready to look into any new problem, however trivial it may prove? But here, unless I am mistaken, is our client."

A measured step was heard upon the stairs, and a moment later a stout, tall, grey-whiskered and solemnly respectable person was ushered into the room. His life history was written in his heavy features and pompous manner. From his spats to his gold-rimmed spectacles he was a Conservative, a churchman, a good citizen, orthodox and conventional to the last degree. But some amazing experience had disturbed his native composure and left its traces in his bristling hair, his flushed, angry cheeks, and his flurried, excited manner. He plunged instantly into his business.

"I have had a most singular and unpleasant experience, Mr. Holmes," said he. "Never in my life have I been placed in such a situation. It is most improper—most outrageous. I must insist upon some explanation." He swelled and puffed in his anger.

"Pray sit down, Mr. Scott Eccles," said Holmes, in a soothing voice. "May I ask, in the first place, why you came to me at all?"

"Well, sir, it did not appear to be a matter which concerned the police, and yet, when you have heard the facts, you must admit that I could not leave it where it was. Private detectives are a class with whom I have absolutely no sympathy, but nonetheless, having heard your name——"

"Quite so. But, in the second place, why did you not come at once?"

"What do you mean?"

Holmes glanced at his watch.

"It is a quarter past two," he said. "Your telegram was dispatched about one. But no one can glance at your toilet and attire without seeing that your disturbance dates from the moment of your waking."

Our client smoothed down his unbrushed hair and felt his unshaven chin.

"You are right, Mr. Holmes. I never gave a thought to my toilet. I was only too glad to get out of such a house. But I have been running round making inquiries before I came to you. I went to the house agents, you know, and they said that Mr. Garcia's rent was paid up all right and that everything was in order at Wisteria Lodge."

"Come, come, sir," said Holmes, laughing. "You are like my friend Dr. Watson, who has a bad habit of telling his stories wrong end foremost. Please arrange your thoughts and let me know, in their due sequence, exactly what those events are which have sent you out unbrushed and unkempt, with dress boots and waistcoat buttoned awry, in search of advice and assistance."

Our client looked down with a rueful face at his own unconventional appearance.

"I'm sure it must look very bad, Mr. Holmes, and I am not aware that in my whole life such a thing has ever happened before. But I will tell you the whole queer business, and when I have done so you will admit, I am sure, that there has been enough to excuse me."

But his narrative was nipped in the bud. There was a bustle outside, and Mrs. Hudson opened the door to usher in two robust and official-looking individuals, one of whom was well known to us as Inspector Gregson of Scotland Yard, an energetic, gallant, and, within his limitations, a capable officer. He shook hands with Holmes, and introduced his comrade as Inspector Baynes of the Surrey Constabulary.

"We are hunting together, Mr. Holmes, and our trail lay in this direction." He turned his bulldog eyes upon our visitor. "Are you Mr. John Scott Eccles, of Popham House, Lee?"

"I am."

"We have been following you about all the morning."

"You traced him through the telegram, no doubt," said Holmes.

"Exactly, Mr. Holmes. We picked up the scent at Charing Cross post office and came on here."

"But why do you follow me? What do you want?"

"We wish a statement, Mr. Scott Eccles, as to the events which led up to the death last night of Mr. Aloysius Garcia, of Wisteria Lodge, near Esher."

Our client had sat up with staring eyes and every tinge of colour struck from his astonished face.

"Dead? Did you say he was dead?"

"Yes, sir, he is dead."

"But how? An accident?"

"Murder, if ever there was one upon earth."

"Good God! This is awful! You don't mean—you don't mean that I am suspected?"

"A letter of yours was found in the dead man's pocket, and we know by it that you had planned to pass last night at his house."

"So I did."

"Oh, you did, did you?"

Out came the official notebook.

"Wait a bit, Gregson," said Sherlock Holmes. "All you desire is a plain statement, is it not?"

"And it is my duty to warn Mr. Scott Eccles that it may be used against him."

"Mr. Eccles was going to tell us about it when you entered the room. I think, Watson, a brandy and soda would do him no harm. Now, sir, I suggest that you take no notice of this addition to your audience, and that you proceed with your narrative exactly as you would have done had you never been interrupted."

Our visitor had gulped off the brandy and the colour had returned to his face. With a dubious glance at the inspector's notebook, he plunged at once into his extraordinary statement.

"I am a bachelor," said he, "and, being of a sociable turn, I cultivate a large number of friends. Among these are the family of a retired brewer called Melville, living at Albemarle Mansion, Kensington. It was at his table that I met some weeks ago a young fellow named Garcia. He was, I understood, of Spanish descent and connected in some way with the embassy. He spoke perfect English, was pleasing in his manners, and as good-looking a man as ever I saw in my life.

"In some way we struck up quite a friendship, this young fellow and I. He seemed to take a fancy to me from the first, and within two days of our meeting he came to see me at Lee. One thing led to another, and it ended in his inviting me out to spend a few days at his house, Wisteria Lodge, between Esher and Oxshott. Yesterday evening I went to Esher to fulfil this engagement.

"He had described his household to me before I went there. He lived with a faithful servant, a countryman of his own, who looked after all his needs. This fellow could speak English and did his housekeeping for him. Then there was a wonderful cook, he said, a half-breed whom he had picked up in his travels, who could serve an excellent dinner. I remember that he remarked what a queer household it was to find in the heart of Surrey, and that I agreed with him, though it has proved a good deal queerer than I thought.

"I drove to the place—about two miles on the south side of Esher. The house was a fair-sized one, standing back from the road, with a curving drive which was banked with high evergreen shrubs. It was an old, tumbledown building in a crazy state of disrepair. When the trap pulled up on the grass-grown drive in front of the blotched and weather-stained door, I had doubts as to my wisdom in visiting a man whom I knew so slightly. He opened the door himself, however, and greeted me with a great show of cordiality. I was handed over to the manservant, a melancholy, swarthy individual, who led the way, my bag in his hand, to my bedroom. The whole place was depressing. Our dinner was tête-à-tête, and though my host did his best to be entertaining, his thoughts seemed to continually wander, and he talked so vaguely and wildly that I could hardly understand him. He continually drummed his fingers on the table, gnawed his nails, and gave other signs of nervous impatience. The dinner itself was neither well served nor well cooked, and the gloomy presence of the taciturn servant did not help to enliven us. I can assure you that many times in the course of the evening I wished that I could invent some excuse which would take me back to Lee.

"One thing comes back to my memory which may have a bearing upon the business that you two gentlemen are investigating. I thought nothing of it at the time. Near the end of dinner a note was handed in by the servant. I noticed that after my host had read it he seemed even more distrait and strange than before. He gave up all pretence at conversation and sat, smoking endless cigarettes, lost in his own thoughts, but he made no remarks as to the contents. About eleven I was glad to go to bed. Some time later Garcia looked in at my door—the room was dark at the time—and asked me if I had rung. I said that I had not. He apologised for having disturbed me so late, saying that it was nearly one o'clock. I dropped off after this and slept soundly all night.

"And now I come to the amazing part of my tale. When I woke it was broad daylight. I glanced at my watch, and the time was nearly nine. I had particularly asked to be called at eight, so I was very much astonished at this forgetfulness. I sprang up and rang for the servant. There was no response. I rang again and again, with the same result. Then I came to the conclusion that the bell was out of order. I huddled on my clothes and hurried downstairs in an exceedingly bad temper to order some hot water. You can imagine my surprise when I found that there was no one there. I shouted in the hall. There was no answer. Then I ran from room to room. All were deserted. My host had shown me which was his bedroom the night before, so I knocked at the door. No reply. I turned the handle and walked in. The room was empty, and the bed had never been slept in. He had gone with the rest. The foreign host, the foreign footman, the foreign cook, all had vanished in the night! That was the end of my visit to Wisteria Lodge."

Sherlock Holmes was rubbing his hands and chuckling as he added this bizarre incident to his collection of strange episodes.

"Your experience is, so far as I know, perfectly unique," said he. "May I ask, sir, what you did then?"

"I was furious. My first idea was that I had been the victim of some absurd practical joke. I packed my things, banged the hall door behind me, and set off for Esher, with my bag in my hand. I called at Allan Brothers', the chief land agents in the village, and found that it was from this firm that the villa had been rented. It struck me that the whole proceeding could hardly be for the purpose of making a fool of me, and that the main object must be to get out of the rent. It is late in March, so quarter day is at hand. But this theory would not work. The agent was obliged to me for my warning, but told me that the rent had been paid in advance. Then I made my way to town and called at the Spanish embassy. The man was unknown there. After this I went to see Melville, at whose house I had first met Garcia, but I found that he really knew rather less about him than I did. Finally, when I got your reply to my wire I came out to you, since I understand that you are a person who gives advice in difficult cases. But now, Mr. Inspector, I gather, from what you said when you entered the room, that you can carry the story on, and that some tragedy has occurred. I can assure you that every word I have said is the truth, and that, outside of what I have told you, I know absolutely nothing about the fate of this man. My only desire is to help the law in every possible way."

"I am sure of it, Mr. Scott Eccles—I am sure of it," said Inspector Gregson, in a very amiable tone. "I am bound to say that everything which you have said agrees very closely with the facts as they have come to our notice. For example, there was that note which arrived during dinner. Did you chance to observe what became of it?"

"Yes, I did. Garcia rolled it up and threw it into the fire."

"What do you say to that, Mr. Baynes?"

The country detective was a stout, puffy, red man, whose face was only redeemed from grossness by two extraordinarily bright eyes, almost hidden behind the heavy creases of cheek and brow. With a slow smile he drew a folded and discoloured scrap of paper from his pocket.

"It was a dog grate, Mr. Holmes, and he over-pitched it. I picked this out unburned from the back of it."

Holmes smiled his appreciation.

"You must have examined the house very carefully to find a single pellet of paper."

"I did, Mr. Holmes. It's my way. Shall I read it, Mr. Gregson?"

The Londoner nodded.

"The note is written upon ordinary cream laid paper without watermark. It is a quarter sheet. The paper is cut off in two snips with a short-bladed scissors. It has been folded over three times and sealed with purple wax, put on hurriedly and pressed down with some flat, oval object. It is addressed to Mr. Garcia, Wisteria Lodge. It says:

Our own colours, green and white. Green open, white shut. Main stair, first corridor, seventh right, green baize. Godspeed. D

"It is a woman's writing, done with a sharp-pointed pen, but the address is either done with another pen or by someone else. It is thicker and bolder, as you see."

"A very remarkable note," said Holmes, glancing it over. "I must compliment you, Mr. Baynes, upon your attention to detail in your examination of it. A few trifling points might perhaps be added. The oval seal is undoubtedly a plain sleeve link—what else is of such a shape? The scissors were bent nail scissors. Short as the two snips are, you can distinctly see the same slight curve in each."

The country detective chuckled.

"I thought I had squeezed all the juice out of it, but I see there was a little over," he said. "I'm bound to say that I make nothing of the note except that there was something on hand, and that a woman, as usual, was at the bottom of it."

Mr. Scott Eccles had fidgeted in his seat during this conversation.

"I am glad you found the note, since it corroborates my story," said he. "But I beg to point out that I have not yet heard what has happened to Mr. Garcia, nor what has become of his household."

"As to Garcia," said Gregson, "that is easily answered. He was found dead this morning upon Oxshott Common, nearly a mile from his home. His head had been smashed to pulp by heavy blows of a sandbag or some such instrument, which had crushed rather than wounded. It is a lonely corner, and there is no house within a quarter of a mile of the spot. He had apparently been struck down first from behind, but his assailant had gone on beating him long after he was dead. It was a most furious assault. There are no footsteps nor any clue to the criminals."

"Robbed?"

"No, there was no attempt at robbery."

"This is very painful—very painful and terrible," said Mr. Scott Eccles, in a querulous voice; "but it is really uncommonly hard upon me. I had nothing to do with my host going off upon a nocturnal excursion and meeting so sad an end. How do I come to be mixed up with the case?"

"Very simply, sir," Inspector Baynes answered. "The only document found in the pocket of the deceased was a letter from you saying that you would be with him on the night of his death. It was the envelope of this letter which gave us the dead man's name and address. It was after nine this morning when we reached his house and found neither you nor anyone else inside it. I wired to Mr. Gregson to run you down in London while I examined Wisteria Lodge. Then I came into town, joined Mr. Gregson, and here we are."

"I think now," said Gregson, rising, "we had best put this matter into an official shape. You will come round with us to the station, Mr. Scott Eccles, and let us have your statement in writing."

"Certainly, I will come at once. But I retain your services, Mr. Holmes. I desire you to spare no expense and no pains to get at the truth."

My friend turned to the country inspector.

"I suppose that you have no objection to my collaborating with you, Mr. Baynes?"

"Highly honoured, sir, I am sure."

"You appear to have been very prompt and businesslike in all that you have done. Was there any clue, may I ask, as to the exact hour that the man met his death?"

"He had been there since one o'clock. There was rain about that time, and his death had certainly been before the rain."

"But that is perfectly impossible, Mr. Baynes," cried our client. "His voice is unmistakable. I could swear to it that it was he who addressed me in my bedroom at that very hour."

"Remarkable, but by no means impossible," said Holmes, smiling.

"You have a clue?" asked Gregson.

"On the face of it the case is not a very complex one, though it certainly presents some novel and interesting features. A further knowledge of facts is necessary before I would venture to give a final and definite opinion. By the way, Mr. Baynes, did you find anything remarkable besides this note in your examination of the house?"

The detective looked at my friend in a singular way.

"There were," said he, "one or two *very* remarkable things. Perhaps when I have finished at the police station you would care to come out and give me your opinion of them."

"I am entirely at your service," said Sherlock Holmes, ringing the bell. "You will show these gentlemen out, Mrs. Hudson, and kindly send the boy with this telegram. He is to pay a five-shilling reply."

We sat for some time in silence after our visitors had left. Holmes smoked hard, with his brows drawn down over his keen eyes, and his head thrust forward in the eager way characteristic of the man.

"Well, Watson," he asked, turning suddenly upon me, "what do you make of it?"

"I can make nothing of this mystification of Scott Eccles."

"But the crime?"

"Well, taken with the disappearance of the man's companions, I should say that they were in some way concerned in the murder and had fled from justice."

"That is certainly a possible point of view. On the face of it you must admit, however, that it is very strange that his two servants should have been in a conspiracy against him and should have attacked him on the one night when he had a guest. They had him alone at their mercy every other night in the week."

"Then why did they fly?"

"Quite so. Why did they fly? There is a big fact. Another big fact is the remarkable experience of our client, Scott Eccles. Now, my dear Watson, is it beyond the limits of human ingenuity to furnish an explanation which would cover both these big facts? If it were one which would also admit of the mysterious note with its very curious phraseology, why, then it would be worth accepting as a temporary hypothesis. If the fresh facts which come to our knowledge all fit themselves into the scheme, then our hypothesis may gradually become a solution."

"But what is our hypothesis?"

Holmes leaned back in his chair with half-closed eyes.

"You must admit, my dear Watson, that the idea of a joke is impossible. There were grave events afoot, as the sequel showed, and the coaxing of Scott Eccles to Wisteria Lodge had some connection with them."

"But what possible connection?"

"Let us take it link by link. There is, on the face of it, something unnatural about this strange and sudden friendship between the young Spaniard and Scott Eccles. It was the former who forced the pace. He called upon Eccles at the other end of London on the very day after he first met him, and he kept in close touch with him until he got him down to Esher. Now, what did he want with Eccles? What could Eccles supply? I see no charm in the man. He is not particularly intelligent—not a man likely to be congenial to a quick-witted Latin. Why, then, was he picked out from all the other people whom Garcia met as particularly suited to his purpose? Has he any one outstanding quality? I say that he has. He is the very type of conventional British respectability, and the very man as a witness to impress another Briton. You saw yourself how neither of the inspectors dreamed of questioning his statement, extraordinary as it was."

"But what was he to witness?"

"Nothing, as things turned out, but everything had they gone another way. That is how I read the matter."

"I see, he might have proved an alibi."

"Exactly, my dear Watson; he might have proved an alibi. We will suppose, for argument's sake, that the household of Wisteria Lodge are confederates in some design. The attempt, whatever it may be, is to come off, we will say, before one o'clock. By some juggling of the clocks it is quite possible that they may have got Scott Eccles to bed earlier than he thought, but in any case it is likely that when Garcia went out of his way to tell him that it was one it was really not more than twelve. If Garcia could do whatever he had to do and be back by the hour mentioned he had evidently a powerful reply to any accusation. Here was this irreproachable Englishman ready to swear in any court of law that the accused was in his house all the time. It was an insurance against the worst."

"Yes, yes, I see that. But how about the disappearance of the others?"

"I have not all my facts yet, but I do not think there are any insuperable difficulties. Still, it is an error to argue in front of your data. You find yourself insensibly twisting them round to fit your theories."

"And the message?"

"How did it run? 'Our own colours, green and white.' Sounds like racing. 'Green open, white shut.' That is clearly a signal. 'Main stair, first corridor, seventh right, green baize.' This is an assignation. We may find a jealous husband at the bottom of it all. It was clearly a dangerous quest. She would not have said 'Godspeed' had it not been so. 'D'—that should be a guide."

"The man was a Spaniard. I suggest that 'D' stands for Dolores, a common female name in Spain."

"Good, Watson, very good—but quite inadmissible. A Spaniard would write to a Spaniard in Spanish. The writer of this note is certainly English. Well, we can only possess our souls in patience, until this excellent inspector comes back for us. Meanwhile we can thank our lucky fate which has rescued us for a few short hours from the insufferable fatigues of idleness."

An answer had arrived to Holmes's telegram before our Surrey officer had returned. Holmes read it, and was about to place it in his notebook when he caught a glimpse of my expectant face. He tossed it across with a laugh.

"We are moving in exalted circles," said he.

The telegram was a list of names and addresses:

Lord Harringby, The Dingle; Sir George Ffolliott, Oxshott
Towers; Mr. Hynes Hynes, J.P., Purdey Place; Mr. James Baker
Williams, Forton Old Hall; Mr. Henderson, High Gable; Rev.
Joshua Stone; Nether Walsling.

"This is a very obvious way of limiting our field of operations," said
Holmes. "No doubt Baynes, with his methodical mind, has already
adopted some similar plan."

"I don't quite understand."

"Well, my dear fellow, we have already arrived at the conclusion
that the message received by Garcia at dinner was an appointment or
an assignation. Now, if the obvious reading of it is correct, and in order to keep this tryst one has to ascend a main stair and seek the seventh door in a corridor, it is perfectly clear that the house is a very
large one. It is equally certain that this house cannot be more than a
mile or two from Oxshott, since Garcia was walking in that direction,
and hoped, according to my reading of the facts, to be back in Wisteria Lodge in time to avail himself of an alibi, which would only be
valid up to one o'clock. As the number of large houses close to Oxshott
must be limited, I adopted the obvious method of sending to the
agents mentioned by Scott Eccles and obtaining a list of them. Here
they are in this telegram, and the other end of our tangled skein must
lie among them."

It was nearly six o'clock before we found ourselves in the pretty
Surrey village of Esher, with Inspector Baynes as our companion.
Holmes and I had taken things for the night, and found comfortable
quarters at the Bull. Finally we set out in the company of the detective on our visit to Wisteria Lodge. It was a cold, dark March evening,
with a sharp wind and a fine rain beating upon our faces, a fit setting
for the wild common over which our road passed and the tragic goal
to which it led us.

A COLD AND melancholy walk of a couple of miles brought us to a high wooden gate, which opened into a gloomy avenue of chestnuts. The curved and shadowed drive led us to a low, dark house, pitch-black against a slate-coloured sky. From the front window upon the left of the door there peeped a glimmer of a feeble light.

"There's a constable in possession," said Baynes. "I'll knock at the window." He stepped across the grass plot and tapped with his hand on the pane. Through the fogged glass I dimly saw a man spring up from a chair beside the fire, and heard a sharp cry from within the room. An instant later a white-faced, hard-breathing policeman had opened the door, the candle wavering in his trembling hand.

"What's the matter, Walters?" asked Baynes, sharply.

The man mopped his forehead with his handkerchief and gave a long sigh of relief. "I am glad you have come, sir. It has been a long evening and I don't think my nerve is as good as it was."

"Your nerve, Walters? I should not have thought you had a nerve in your body."

"Well, sir, it's this lonely, silent house and the queer thing in the kitchen. Then when you tapped at the window I thought it had come again."

"That what had come again?"

"The devil, sir, for all I know. It was at the window."

"What was at the window, and when?"

"It was just about two hours ago. The light was just fading. I was sitting reading in the chair. I don't know what made me look up, but there was a face looking in at me through the lower pane. Lord, sir, what a face it was! I'll see it in my dreams."

"Tut, tut, Walters! This is not talk for a police constable."

"I know, sir, I know; but it shook me, sir, and there's no use to deny it. It wasn't black, sir, nor was it white, nor any colour that I know, but a kind of queer shade like clay with a splash of milk in it. Then there was the size of it—it was twice yours, sir. And the look of it— the great staring goggle eyes, and the line of white teeth like a hungry beast. I tell you, sir, I couldn't move a finger, nor get my breath,

"Lord, sir, what a face it was! I'll see it in my dreams."

till it whisked away and was gone. Out I ran and through the shrubbery, but thank God there was no one there."

"If I didn't know you were a good man, Walters, I should put a black mark against you for this. If it were the devil himself a constable on duty should never thank God that he could not lay his hands upon him. I suppose the whole thing is not a vision and a touch of nerves?"

"That, at least, is very easily settled," said Holmes, lighting his pocket lantern. "Yes," he reported, after a short examination of the grass bed, "a number twelve shoe, I should say. If he was all on the same scale as his foot he must certainly have been a giant."

"What became of him?"

"He seems to have broken through the shrubbery and made for the road."

"Well," said the inspector, with a grave and thoughtful face, "whoever he may have been, and whatever he may have wanted, he's gone for the present, and we have more immediate things to attend to. Now, Mr. Holmes, with your permission, I will show you round the house."

The various bedrooms and sitting rooms had yielded nothing to a careful search. Apparently the tenants had brought little or nothing with them, and all the furniture down to the smallest details had been taken over with the house. A good deal of clothing with the stamp of Marx & Co., High Holborn, had been left behind. Telegraphic inquiries had been already made which showed that Marx knew nothing of his customer save that he was a good payer. Odds and ends, some pipes, a few novels, two of them in Spanish, an old-fashioned pinfire revolver, and a guitar were amongst the personal property.

"Nothing in all this," said Baynes, stalking, candle in hand, from room to room. "But now, Mr. Holmes, I invite your attention to the kitchen."

It was a gloomy, high-ceilinged room at the back of the house, with a straw litter in one corner, which served apparently as a bed for the cook. The table was piled with half-eaten dishes and dirty plates, the debris of last night's dinner.

"Look at this," said Baynes. "What do you make of it?"

He held up his candle before an extraordinary object which stood at the back of the dresser. It was so wrinkled and shrunken and withered that it was difficult to say what it might have been. One could but say that it was black and leathery and that it bore some resemblance to a dwarfish human figure. At first, as I examined it, I thought that it was a mummified Negro baby, and then it seemed a very twisted and ancient monkey. Finally I was left in doubt as to whether it was animal or human. A double band of white shells was strung round the centre of it.

"Very interesting—very interesting indeed!" said Holmes peering at this sinister relic. "Anything more?"

In silence Baynes led the way to the sink and held forward his candle. The limbs and body of some large white bird, torn savagely to pieces with the feathers still on, were littered all over it. Holmes pointed to the wattles on the severed head.

"A white cock," said he; "most interesting! It is really a very curious case."

But Mr. Baynes had kept his most sinister exhibit to the last. From under the sink he drew a zinc pail which contained a quantity of blood.

Then from the table he took a platter heaped with small pieces of charred bone.

"Something has been killed and something has been burned. We raked all these out of the fire. We had a doctor in this morning. He says that they are not human."

Holmes smiled and rubbed his hands.

"I must congratulate you, Inspector, on handling so distinctive and instructive a case. Your powers, if I may say so without offence, seem superior to your opportunities."

Inspector Baynes's small eyes twinkled with pleasure.

"You're right, Mr. Holmes. We stagnate in the provinces. A case of this sort gives a man a chance, and I hope that I shall take it. What do you make of these bones?"

"A lamb, I should say, or a kid."

"And the white cock?"

"Curious, Mr. Baynes, very curious. I should say almost unique."

"Yes, sir, there must have been some very strange people with some very strange ways in this house. One of them is dead. Did his companions follow him and kill him? If they did we should have them, for every port is watched. But my own views are different. Yes, sir, my own views are very different."

"You have a theory, then?"

"And I'll work it myself, Mr. Holmes. It's only due to my own credit to do so. Your name is made, but I have still to make mine. I should
be glad to be able to say afterwards that I had solved it without your
help."

Holmes laughed good-humouredly.

"Well, well, Inspector," said he. "Do you follow your path and I
will follow mine. My results are always very much at your service if
you care to apply to me for them. I think that I have seen all that I
wish in this house, and that my time may be more profitably employed elsewhere. Au revoir and good luck!"

I could tell by numerous subtle signs, which might have been lost
upon anyone but myself, that Holmes was on a hot scent. As impassive as ever to the casual observer, there were nonetheless a subdued
eagerness and suggestion of tension in his brightened eyes and brisker
manner which assured me that the game was afoot. After his habit he
said nothing, and after mine I asked no questions. Sufficient for me
to share the sport and lend my humble help to the capture without
distracting that intent brain with needless interruption. All would come
round to me in due time.

I waited, therefore—but, to my ever-deepening disappointment I
waited in vain. Day succeeded day, and my friend took no step forward. One morning he spent in town, and I learned from a casual
reference that he had visited the British Museum. Save for this one
excursion, he spent his days in long, and often solitary walks, or in
chatting with a number of village gossips whose acquaintance he had
cultivated.

"I'm sure, Watson, a week in the country will be invaluable to you,"
he remarked. "It is very pleasant to see the first green shoots upon
the hedges and the catkins on the hazels once again. With a spud, a
tin box, and an elementary book on botany, there are instructive days
to be spent." He prowled about with this equipment himself, but it
was a poor show of plants which he would bring back of an evening.

Occasionally in our rambles we came across Inspector Baynes. His
fat, red face wreathed itself in smiles and his small eyes glittered as
he greeted my companion. He said little about the case, but from
that little we gathered that he also was not dissatisfied at the course
of events.

I must admit, however, that I was somewhat surprised when, some five days after the crime, I opened my morning paper to find in large letters:

THE OXSHOTT MYSTERY

A SOLUTION

ARREST OF SUPPOSED ASSASSIN

Holmes sprang in his chair as if he had been stung when I read the headlines.

"By Jove!" he cried. "You don't mean that Baynes has got him?"

"Apparently," said I, as I read the following report:

"Great excitement was caused in Esher and the neighbouring district when it was learned late last night that an arrest had been effected in connection with the Oxshott murder. It will be remembered that Mr. Garcia, of Wisteria Lodge, was found dead on Oxshott Common, his body showing signs of extreme violence, and that on the same night his servant and his cook fled, which appeared to show their participation in the crime. It was suggested, but never proved, that the deceased gentleman may have had valuables in the house, and that their abstraction was the motive of the crime. Every effort was made by Inspector Baynes, who has the case in hand, to ascertain the hiding place of the fugitives, and he had good reason to believe that they had not gone far, but were lurking in some retreat which had been already prepared. It was certain from the first, however, that they would eventually be detected, as the cook, from the evidence of one or two tradespeople who have caught a glimpse of him through the window, was a man of most remarkable appearance—being a huge and hideous mulatto, with yellowish features of a pronounced negroid type. This man has been seen since the crime, for he was detected and pursued by Constable Walters on the same evening, when he had the audacity to revisit Wisteria Lodge. Inspector Baynes, considering that such a visit must have some purpose in view, and was likely, therefore, to be repeated, abandoned the house, but left an ambuscade in the shrubbery. The man walked into the trap, and was captured last night after a struggle in which Constable Downing was badly bitten by the savage. We understand that when the prisoner is brought before the magistrates a remand will be applied for by the police, and that great developments are hoped from his capture."

"Really we must see Baynes at once," cried Holmes, picking up his hat. "We will just catch him before he starts." We hurried down the village street and found, as we had expected, that the inspector was just leaving his lodgings.

"You've seen the paper, Mr. Holmes?" he asked, holding one out to us.

"Yes, Baynes, I've seen it. Pray don't think it a liberty if I give you a word of friendly warning."

"Of warning, Mr. Holmes?"

"I have looked into this case with some care, and I am not convinced that you are on the right lines. I don't want you to commit yourself too far, unless you are sure."

"You're very kind, Mr. Holmes."

"I assure you I speak for your good."

It seemed to me that something like a wink quivered for an instant over one of Mr. Baynes's tiny eyes.

"We agreed to work on our own lines, Mr. Holmes. That's what I am doing."

"Oh, very good," said Holmes. "Don't blame me."

"No, sir; I believe you mean well by me. But we all have our own systems, Mr. Holmes. You have yours, and maybe I have mine."

"Let us say no more about it."

"You're welcome always to my news. This fellow is a perfect savage, as strong as a cart horse and as fierce as the devil. He chewed Downing's thumb nearly off before they could master him. He hardly speaks a word of English, and we can get nothing out of him but grunts."

"And you think you have evidence that he murdered his late master?"

"I didn't say so, Mr. Holmes; I didn't say so. We all have our little ways. You try yours and I will try mine. That's the agreement."

Holmes shrugged his shoulders as we walked away together. "I can't make the man out. He seems to be riding for a fall. Well, as he says, we must each try our own way and see what comes of it. But there's something in Inspector Baynes which I can't quite understand."

"Just sit down in that chair, Watson," said Sherlock Holmes, when we had returned to our apartment at the Bull. "I want to put you in touch with the situation, as I may need your help tonight. Let me show you the evolution of this case, so far as I have been able to follow it. Simple as it has been in its leading features, it has nonetheless presented surprising difficulties in the way of an arrest. There are gaps in that direction which we have still to fill.

"We will go back to the note which was handed in to Garcia upon the evening of his death. We may put aside this idea of Baynes's that Garcia's servants were concerned in the matter. The proof of this lies in the fact that it was *he* who had arranged for the presence of Scott Eccles, which could only have been done for the purpose of an alibi. It was Garcia, then, who had an enterprise, and apparently a criminal enterprise, in hand that night, in the course of which he met his death. I say criminal because only a man with a criminal enterprise desires to establish an alibi. Who, then, is most likely to have taken his life? Surely the person against whom the criminal enterprise was directed. So far it seems to me that we are on safe ground.

"We can now see a reason for the disappearance of Garcia's household. They were *all* confederates in the same unknown crime. If it came off then Garcia returned, any possible suspicion would be warded off by the Englishman's evidence, and all would be well. But the attempt was a dangerous one, and if Garcia did *not* return by a certain hour it was probable that his own life had been sacrificed. It had been arranged, therefore, that in such a case his two subordinates were to make for some prearranged spot, where they could escape investigation and be in a position afterwards to renew their attempt. That would fully explain the facts, would it not?"

The whole inexplicable tangle seemed to straighten out before me. I wondered, as I always did, how it had not been obvious to me before.

"But why should one servant return?"

"We can imagine that, in the confusion of flight, something precious, something which he could not bear to part with, had been left behind. That would explain his persistence, would it not?"

"Well, what is the next step?"

"The next step is the note received by Garcia at the dinner. It indicates a confederate at the other end. Now, where was the other end? I have already shown you that it could only lie in some large house, and that the number of large houses is limited. My first days in this village were devoted to a series of walks, in which in the intervals of my botanical researches I made a reconnaissance of all the large houses and an examination of the family history of the occupants. One house, and only one, riveted my attention. It is the famous old Jacobean grange of High Gable, one mile on the farther side of Oxshott, and less than half a mile from the scene of the tragedy. The other mansions belonged to prosaic and respectable people who live far aloof from romance. But Mr. Henderson, of High Gable, was by all accounts a curious man, to whom curious adventures might befall. I concentrated my attention, therefore, upon him and his household.

"A singular set of people, Watson—the man himself the most singular of them all. I managed to see him on a plausible pretext, but I seemed to read in his dark, deep-set, brooding eyes that he was perfectly aware of my true business. He is a man of fifty, strong, active, with iron-grey hair, great bunched black eyebrows, the step of a deer, and the air of an emperor—a fierce, masterful man, with a red-hot spirit behind his parchment face. He is either a foreigner or has lived long in the tropics, for he is yellow and sapless, but tough as whipcord. His friend and secretary, Mr. Lucas, is undoubtedly a foreigner, chocolate-brown, wily, suave and cat-like, with a poisonous gentleness of speech. You see, Watson, we have come already upon two sets of foreigners—one at Wisteria Lodge and one at High Gable—so our gaps are beginning to close.

"These two men, close and confidential friends, are the centre of the household; but there is one other person, who for our immediate purpose may be even more important. Henderson has two children—girls of eleven and thirteen. Their governess is a Miss Burnet, an Englishwoman of forty or thereabouts. There is also one confidential manservant. This little group forms the real family, for they travel about together, and Henderson is a great traveller, always on the move. It is only within the last few weeks that he has returned, after a year's absence, to High Gable. I may add that he is enormously rich, and whatever his whims may be he can very easily satisfy them. For the rest, his house is full of butlers, footmen, maidservants, and the usual overfed, underworked staff of a large English country house.

"So much I learned partly from village gossip and partly from my own observation. There are no better instruments than discharged servants with a grievance, and I was lucky enough to find one. I call it luck, but it would not have come my way had I not been looking out for it. As Baynes remarks, we all have our systems. It was my system which enabled me to find John Warner, late gardener of High Gable, sacked in a moment of temper by his imperious employer. He in turn had friends among the indoor servants, who unite in their fear and dislike of their master. So I had my key to the secrets of the establishment.

"Curious people, Watson! I don't pretend to understand it all yet, but very curious people anyway. It's a double-winged house, and the servants live on one side, the family on the other. There's no link between the two save for Henderson's own servant, who serves the family's meals. Everything is carried to a certain door, which forms the one connection. Governess and children hardly go out at all, except into the garden. Henderson never by any chance walks alone. His dark secretary is like his shadow. The gossip among the servants is that their master is terribly afraid of something. 'Sold his soul to the devil in exchange for money,' says Warner, 'and expects his creditor to come up and claim his own.' Where they came from, or who they are, nobody has an idea. They are very violent. Twice Henderson has lashed at folk with his dog whip, and only his long purse and heavy compensation have kept him out of the courts.

"Well, now, Watson, let us judge the situation by this new information. We may take it that the letter came out of this strange household, and was an invitation to Garcia to carry out some attempt which had already been planned. Who wrote the note? It was someone within the citadel, and it was a woman. Who then, but Miss Burnet, the governess? All our reasoning seems to point that way. At any rate, we may take it as a hypothesis, and see what consequences it would entail. I may add that Miss Burnet's age and character make it certain that my first idea that there might be a love interest in our story is out of the question.

"If she wrote the note she was presumably the friend and confederate of Garcia. What, then, might she be expected to do if she heard of his death? If he met it in some nefarious enterprise her lips might be sealed. Still, in her heart she must retain bitterness and hatred against those who had killed him, and would presumably help so far as she could to have revenge upon them. Could we see her, then, and try to use her? That was my first thought. But now we come to a sinister fact. Miss Burnet has not been seen by any human eye since the night of the murder. From that evening she has utterly vanished. Is she alive? Has she perhaps met her end on the same night as the friend whom she had summoned? Or is she merely a prisoner? There is the point which we still have to decide.

"You will appreciate the difficulty of the situation, Watson. There is nothing upon which we can apply for a warrant. Our whole scheme might seem fantastic if laid before a magistrate. The woman's disappearance counts for nothing, since in that extraordinary household any member of it might be invisible for a week. And yet she may at the present moment be in danger of her life. All I can do is to watch the house and leave my agent, Warner, on guard at the gates. We can't let such a situation continue. If the law can do nothing we must take the risk ourselves."

"What do you suggest?"

"I know which is her room. It is accessible from the top of an outhouse. My suggestion is that you and I go tonight and see if we can strike at the very heart of the mystery."

It was not, I must confess, a very alluring prospect. The old house with its atmosphere of murder, the singular and formidable inhabitants, the unknown dangers of the approach, and the fact that we were putting ourselves legally in a false position, all combined to damp my ardour. But there was something in the ice-cold reasoning of Holmes which made it impossible to shrink from any adventure which he might recommend. One knew that thus, and only thus, could a solution be found. I clasped his hand in silence, and the die was cast.

But it was not destined that our investigation should have so adventurous an ending. It was about five o'clock, and the shadows of the March evening were beginning to fall, when an excited rustic rushed into our room.

"They've gone, Mr. Holmes. They went by the last train. The lady broke away, and I've got her in a cab downstairs."

"Excellent, Warner!" cried Holmes, springing to his feet. "Watson, the gaps are closing rapidly."

In the cab was a woman, half-collapsed from nervous exhaustion. She bore upon her aquiline and emaciated face the traces of some recent tragedy. Her head hung listlessly upon her breast, but as she raised it and turned her dull eyes upon us, I saw that her pupils were dark dots in the centre of the broad grey iris. She was drugged with opium.

"I watched at the gate, same as you advised, Mr. Holmes," said our emissary, the discharged gardener. "When the carriage came out I followed it to the station. She was like one walking in her sleep; but when they tried to get her into the train she came to life and struggled. They pushed her into the carriage. She fought her way out again. I took her part, got her into a cab, and here we are. I shan't forget the face at the carriage window as I led her away. I'd have a short life if he had his way—the black-eyed, scowling, yellow devil."

We carried her upstairs, laid her on the sofa, and a couple of cups of the strongest coffee soon cleared her brain from the mists of the drug. Baynes had been summoned by Holmes, and the situation rapidly explained to him.

"Why, sir, you've got me the very evidence I want," said the inspector, warmly, shaking my friend by the hand. "I was on the same scent as you from the first."

"What! You were after Henderson?"

"Why, Mr. Holmes, when you were crawling in the shrubbery at High Gable I was up one of the trees in the plantation and saw you down below. It was just who would get his evidence first."

"Then why did you arrest the mulatto?"

Baynes chuckled. "I was sure Henderson, as he calls himself, felt that he was suspected, and that he would lie low and make no move so long as he thought he was in any danger. I arrested the wrong man to make him believe that our eyes were off him. I knew he would be likely to clear off then and give us a chance of getting at Miss Burnet."

Holmes laid his hand upon the inspector's shoulder.

"You will rise high in your profession. You have instinct and intuition," said he.

Baynes flushed with pleasure.

"I've had a plainclothes man waiting at the station all the week.

Wherever the High Gable folk go he will keep them in sight. But he must have been hard put to it when Miss Burnet broke away. However, your man picked her up, and it all ends well. We can't arrest without her evidence, that is clear, so the sooner we get a statement the better."

"Every minute she gets stronger," said Holmes, glancing at the governess. "But tell me, Baynes, who is this man Henderson?"

"Henderson," the inspector answered, "is Don Murillo, once called the Tiger of San Pedro."

The Tiger of San Pedro! The whole history of the man came back to me in a flash. He had made his name as the most lewd and bloodthirsty tyrant that had ever governed any country with a pretence to civilisation. Strong, fearless, and energetic, he had sufficient virtue to enable him to impose his odious vices upon a cowering people for ten or twelve years. His name was a terror through all Central America. At the end of that time there was a universal rising against him. But he was as cunning as he was cruel, and at the first whisper of coming trouble he had secretly conveyed his treasures aboard a ship which was manned by devoted adherents. It was an empty palace which was stormed by the insurgents next day. The dictator, his two children, his secretary, and his wealth had all escaped them. From that moment he had vanished from the world, and his identity had been a frequent subject for comment in the European press.

"Yes, sir; Don Murillo, the Tiger of San Pedro," said Baynes. "If you look it up you will find that the San Pedro colours are green and white, same as in the note, Mr. Holmes. Henderson he called himself, but I traced him back, Paris and Rome, and Madrid to Barcelona, where his ship came in in '86. They've been looking for him all the time for their revenge, but it is only now that they have begun to find him out."

"They discovered him a year ago," said Miss Burnet, who had sat up and was now intently following the conversation. "Once already his life has been attempted; but some evil spirit shielded him. Now, again, it is the noble, chivalrous Garcia who has fallen, while the monster goes safe. But another will come, and yet another, until someday justice will be done; that is as certain as the rise of tomorrow's sun."

Her thin hands clenched, and her worn face blanched with the passion of her hatred.

"But how come you into this matter, Miss Burnet?" asked Holmes. "How can an English lady join in such a murderous affair?"

"I join in it because there is no other way in the world by which justice can be gained. What does the law of England care for the rivers of blood shed years ago in San Pedro, or for the shipload of treasure which this man has stolen? To you they are like crimes committed in some other planet. But *we* know. We have learned the truth in sorrow and in suffering. To us there is no fiend in hell like Juan Murillo, and no peace in life while his victims still cry for vengeance."

"No doubt," said Holmes, "he was as you say. I have heard that he was atrocious. But how are you affected?"

"I will tell you it all. This villain's policy was to murder, on one pretext or another, every man who showed such promise that he might in time come to be a dangerous rival. My husband—yes, my real name is Signora Victor Durando—was the San Pedro minister in London. He met me and married me there. A nobler man never lived upon earth. Unhappily, Murillo heard of his excellence, recalled him on some pretext, and had him shot. With a premonition of his fate he had refused to take me with him. His estates were confiscated, and I was left with a pittance and a broken heart.

"Then came the downfall of the tyrant. He escaped as you have just described. But the many whose lives he had ruined, whose nearest and dearest had suffered torture and death at his hands, would not let the matter rest. They banded themselves into a society which should never be dissolved until the work was done. It was my part after we had discovered in the transformed Henderson the fallen despot, to attach myself to his household and keep the others in touch with his movements. This I was able to do by securing the position of governess in his family. He little knew that the woman who faced him at every meal was the woman whose husband he had hurried at an hour's notice into eternity. I smiled on him, did my duty to his children, and bided my time. An attempt was made in Paris, and failed. We zigzagged swiftly here and there over Europe, to throw off the pursuers, and finally returned to this house, which he had taken upon his first arrival in England.

"But here also the ministers of justice were waiting. Knowing that he would return there, Garcia, who is the son of the former highest dignitary in San Pedro, was waiting with two trusty companions of humble station, all three fired with the same reasons for revenge. He could do little during the day, for Murillo took every precaution, and never went out save with his satellite Lucas, or Lopez as he was known in the days of his greatness. At night, however, he slept alone, and the avenger might find him. On a certain evening, which had been prearranged, I sent my friend final instructions, for the man was forever on the alert, and continually changed his room. I was to see that the doors were open and the signal of a green or white light in a window which faced the drive was to give notice if all was safe, or if the attempt had better be postponed.

"But everything went wrong with us. In some way I had excited the suspicion of Lopez, the secretary. He crept up behind me, and sprang upon me just as I had finished the note. He and his master dragged me to my room, and held judgment upon me as a convicted traitress. Then and there they would have plunged their knives into me, could they have seen how to escape the consequence of the deed. Finally, after much debate, they concluded that my murder was too dangerous. But they determined to get rid forever of Garcia. They had gagged me, and Murillo twisted my arm round until I gave him the address. I swear that he might have twisted it off had I understood what it would mean to Garcia. Lopez addressed the note which I had written, sealed it with his sleeve link, and sent it by the hand of the servant, José. How they murdered him I do not know, save that it was Murillo's hand who struck him down, for Lopez had remained to guard me. I believe he must have waited among the gorse bushes through which the path winds and struck him down as he passed. At first they were of a mind to let him enter the house and to kill him as a detected burglar; but they argued that if they were mixed up in an inquiry their own identity would at once be publicly disclosed and they would be open to further attacks. With the death of Garcia the pursuit might cease, since such a death might frighten others from the task.

"All would now have been well for them had it not been for my knowledge of what they had done. I have no doubt that there were times when my life hung in the balance. I was confined to my room, terrorized by the most horrible threats, cruelly ill-used to break my spirit—see this stab on my shoulder and the bruises from end to end of my arms—and a gag was thrust into my mouth on the one occasion when I tried to call from the window. For five days this cruel imprisonment continued, with hardly enough food to hold body and soul together. This afternoon a good lunch was brought me, but the moment after I took it I knew that I had been drugged. In a sort of dream I remember being half-led, half-carried to the carriage; in the same state I was conveyed to the train. Only then, when the wheels were almost moving, did I suddenly realise that my liberty lay in my own hands. I sprang out, they tried to drag me back, and had it not been for the help of this good man, who led me to the cab, I should never have broken away. Now, thank God, I am beyond their power forever."

We had all listened intently to this remarkable statement. It was Holmes who broke the silence.

"Our difficulties are not over," he remarked, shaking his head. "Our police work ends, but our legal work begins."

"Exactly," said I. "A plausible lawyer could make it out as an act of self-defence. There may be a hundred crimes in the background, but it is only on this one that they can be tried."

"Come, come," said Baynes, cheerily; "I think better of the law than that. Self-defence is one thing. To entice a man in cold blood with the object of murdering him is another, whatever danger you may fear from him. No, no; we shall all be justified when we see the tenants of High Gable at the next Guildford Assizes."

It is a matter of history, however, that a little time was still to elapse before the Tiger of San Pedro should meet with his deserts. Wily and bold, he and his companion threw their pursuer off their track by entering a lodging house in Edmonton Street and leaving by the back gate into Curzon Square. From that day they were seen no more in England. Some six months afterwards the Marquess of Montalva and Signor Rulli, his secretary, were both murdered in their rooms at the Hotel Escurial at Madrid. The crime was ascribed to Nihilism, and the murderers were never arrested.

Inspector Baynes visited us at Baker Street with a printed description of the dark face of the secretary, and of the masterful features, the magnetic black eyes, and the tufted brows of his master. We could not doubt that justice, if belated, had come at last.

"A chaotic case, my dear Watson," said Holmes, over an evening pipe. "It will not be possible for you to present it in that compact form which is dear to your heart. It covers two continents, concerns two groups of mysterious persons, and is further complicated by the highly respectable presence of our friend Scott Eccles, whose inclusion shows me that the deceased Garcia had a scheming mind and a well-developed instinct of self-preservation. It is remarkable only for the fact that amid a perfect jungle of possibilities we, with our worthy collaborator the inspector, have kept our close hold on the essentials and so been guided along the crooked and winding path. Is there any point which is not quite clear to you?"

"The object of the mulatto cook's return?"

"I think that the strange creature in the kitchen may account for it. The man was a primitive savage from the backwoods of San Pedro, and this was his fetish. When his companion and he had fled to some prearranged retreat—already occupied, no doubt, by a confederate— the companion had persuaded him to leave so compromising an article of furniture. But the mulatto's heart was with it, and he was driven back to it next day, when, on reconnoitering through the window, he found Policeman Walters in possession. He waited three days longer, and then his piety or his superstition drove him to try once more. Inspector Baynes, who, with his usual astuteness, had minimised the incident before me, had really recognised its importance and had left a trap into which the creature walked. Any other point, Watson?"

"The torn bird, the pail of blood, the charred bones, all the mystery of that weird kitchen?"

Holmes smiled as he turned up an entry in his notebook.

"I spent a morning in the British Museum reading up that and other points. Here is a quotation from Eckermann's *Voodooism and the Negroid Religions:*

The true voodoo-worshipper attempts nothing of importance without certain sacrifices which are intended to propitiate his unclean gods. In extreme cases these rites take the form of human sacrifices followed by cannibalism. The more usual victims are a white cock, which is plucked in pieces alive, or a black goat, whose throat is cut and body burned.

"So you see our savage friend was very orthodox in his ritual. It is grotesque, Watson," Holmes added, as he slowly fastened his notebook, "but, as I have had occasion to remark, there is but one step from the grotesque to the horrible."

II: The Adventure of the Bruce-Partington Plans

IN THE THIRD week of November, in the year 1895, a dense yellow fog settled down upon London. From the Monday to the Thursday I doubt whether it was ever possible from our windows in Baker Street to see the loom of the opposite houses. The first day Holmes had spent in cross-indexing his huge book of references. The second and third had been patiently occupied upon a subject which he had recently made his hobby—the music of the Middle Ages. But when, for the fourth time, after pushing back our chairs from breakfast we saw the greasy, heavy brown swirl still drifting past us and condensing in oily drops upon the windowpanes, my comrade's impatient and active nature could endure this drab existence no longer. He paced restlessly about our sitting room in a fever of suppressed energy, biting his nails, tapping the furniture, and chafing against inaction.

"Nothing of interest in the paper, Watson?" he said.

I was aware that by anything of interest, Holmes meant anything of criminal interest. There was the news of a revolution, of a possible war, and of an impending change of government; but these did not come within the horizon of my companion. I could see nothing recorded in the shape of crime which was not commonplace and futile. Holmes groaned and resumed his restless meanderings.

"The London criminal is certainly a dull fellow," said he, in the querulous voice of the sportsman whose game has failed him. "Look out of this window, Watson. See how the figures loom up, are dimly seen, and then blend once more into the cloud bank. The thief or the murderer could roam London on such a day as the tiger does the jungle, unseen until he pounces, and then evident only to his victim."

"There have," said I, "been numerous petty thefts."

Holmes snorted his contempt.

"This great and sombre stage is set for something more worthy than that," said he. "It is fortunate for this community that I am not a criminal."

"It is, indeed!" said I, heartily.

"Suppose that I were Brooks or Woodhouse, or any of the fifty men who have good reason for taking my life, how long could I survive against my own pursuit? A summons, a bogus appointment, and all would be over. It is well they don't have days of fog in the Latin countries—the countries of assassination. By Jove! here comes something at last to break our dead monotony."

It was the maid with a telegram. Holmes tore it open and burst out laughing.

"Well, well! What next?" said he. "Brother Mycroft is coming round."

"Why not?" I asked.

"Why not? It is as if you met a tramcar coming down a country lane. Mycroft has his rails and he runs on them. His Pall Mall lodgings, the Diogenes Club, Whitehall—that is his cycle. Once, and only once, he has been here. What upheaval can possibly have derailed him?"

"Does he not explain?"

Holmes handed me his brother's telegram:

Must see you over Cadogan West. Coming at once.

MYCROFT

"Cadogan West? I have heard the name."

"It recalls nothing to my mind. But that Mycroft should break out in this erratic fashion! A planet might as well leave its orbit. By the way, do you know what Mycroft is?"

I had some vague recollection of an explanation at the time of the adventure of the Greek interpreter.

"You told me that he had some small office under the British government."

Holmes chuckled.

"I did not know you quite so well in those days. One has to be discreet when one talks of high matters of state. You are right in thinking that he is under the British government. You would also be right in a sense if you said that occasionally he *is* the British government."

"My dear Holmes!"

"I thought I might surprise you. Mycroft draws four hundred and fifty pounds a year, remains a subordinate, has no ambitions of any kind, will receive neither honour nor title, but remains the most indispensable man in the country."

"But how?"

"Well, his position is unique. He has made it for himself. There has never been anything like it before, nor will be again. He has the tidiest and most orderly brain, with the greatest capacity for storing facts, of any man living. The same great powers which I have turned to the detection of crime he has used for this particular business. The conclusions of every department are passed to him, and he is the central exchange, the clearinghouse, which makes out the balance. All other men are specialists, but his specialism is omniscience. We will suppose that a minister needs information as to a point which involves the Navy, India, Canada and the bimetallic question; he could get his separate advices from various departments upon each, but only Mycroft can focus them all, and say offhand how each factor would affect the other. They began by using him as a shortcut, a convenience; now he has made himself an essential. In that great brain of his everything is pigeonholed, and can be handed out in an instant. Again and again his word has decided the national policy. He lives in it. He thinks of nothing else save when, as an intellectual exercise, he unbends if I call upon him and ask him to advise me on one of my little problems. But Jupiter is descending today. What on earth can it mean? Who is Cadogan West, and what is he to Mycroft?"

"I have it," I cried, and plunged among the litter of papers upon the sofa. "Yes, yes, here he is, sure enough! Cadogan West was the young man who was found dead on the Underground on Tuesday morning."

Holmes sat up at attention, his pipe halfway to his lips.

"This must be serious, Watson. A death which has caused my brother to alter his habits can be no ordinary one. What in the world can he have to do with it? The case was featureless as I remember it. The young man had apparently fallen out of the train and killed himself. He had not been robbed, and there was no particular reason to suspect violence. Is that not so?"

"There has been an inquest," said I, "and a good many fresh facts have come out. Looked at more closely, I should certainly say that it was a curious case."

"Judging by its effect upon my brother, I should think it must be a most extraordinary one." He snuggled down in his armchair. "Now, Watson, let us have the facts."

"The man's name was Arthur Cadogan West. He was twenty-seven years of age, unmarried, and a clerk at Woolwich Arsenal."

"Government employ. Behold the link with brother Mycroft!"

"He left Woolwich suddenly on Monday night. Was last seen by his fiancée, Miss Violet Westbury, whom he left abruptly in the fog about 7:30 that evening. There was no quarrel between them and she can give no motive for his action. The next thing heard of him was when his dead body was discovered by a plate-layer named Mason, just outside Aldgate Station on the Underground system in London."

"When?"

"The body was found at six on the Tuesday morning. It was lying wide of the metals upon the left hand of the track as one goes eastward, at a point close to the station, where the line emerges from the tunnel in which it runs. The head was badly crushed—an injury which might well have been caused by a fall from the train. The body could only have come on the line in that way. Had it been carried down from any neighbouring street, it must have passed the station barriers, where a collector is always standing. This point seems absolutely certain."

"Very good. The case is definite enough. The man, dead or alive, either fell or was precipitated from a train. So much is clear to me. Continue."

"The trains which traverse the lines of rail beside which the body was found are those which run from west to east, some being purely Metropolitan, and some from Willesden and outlying junctions. It can be stated for certain that this young man, when he met his death, was travelling in this direction at some late hour of the night, but at what point he entered the train it is impossible to state."

"His ticket, of course, would show that."

"There was no ticket in his pockets."

"No ticket! Dear me, Watson, this is really very singular. According to my experience it is not possible to reach the platform of a Metropolitan train without exhibiting one's ticket. Presumably, then, the young man had one. Was it taken from him in order to conceal the station from which he came? It is possible. Or did he drop it in the carriage? That also is possible. But the point is of curious interest. I understand that there was no sign of robbery?"

"Apparently not. There is a list here of his possessions. His purse contained two pounds fifteen. He had also a chequebook on the Woolwich branch of the Capital and Counties Bank. Through this his identity was established. There were also two dress-circle tickets for the Woolwich Theatre, dated for that very evening. Also a small packet of technical papers."

Holmes gave an exclamation of satisfaction.

"There we have it at last, Watson! British government—Woolwich Arsenal—technical papers—Brother Mycroft, the chain is complete. But here he comes, if I am not mistaken, to speak for himself."

A moment later the tall and portly form of Mycroft Holmes was ushered into the room. Heavily built and massive, there was a suggestion of uncouth physical inertia in the figure, but above this unwieldy frame there was perched a head so masterful in its brow, so alert in its steel-grey, deep-set eyes, so firm in its lips, and so subtle in its play of expression, that after the first glance one forgot the gross body and remembered only the dominant mind.

At his heels came our old friend Lestrade, of Scotland Yard—thin and austere. The gravity of both their faces foretold some weighty quest. The detective shook hands without a word. Mycroft Holmes struggled out of his overcoat and subsided into an armchair.

"A most annoying business, Sherlock," said he. "I extremely dislike altering my habits, but the powers that be would take no denial. In the present state of Siam it is most awkward that I should be away from the office. But it is a real crisis. I have never seen the Prime Minister so upset. As to the Admiralty—it is buzzing like an overturned beehive. Have you read up the case?"

"We have just done so. What were the technical papers?"

"Ah, there's the point! Fortunately, it has not come out. The press would be furious if it did. The papers which this wretched youth had in his pocket were the plans of the Bruce-Partington submarine."

Mycroft Holmes spoke with a solemnity which showed his sense of the importance of the subject. His brother and I sat expectant.

"Surely you have heard of it? I thought everyone had heard of it."

"Only as a name."

"Its importance can hardly be exaggerated. It has been the most jealously guarded of all government secrets. You may take it from me that naval warfare becomes impossible within the radius of a Bruce-Partington's operation. Two years ago a very large sum was smuggled through the Estimates and was expended in acquiring a monopoly of the invention. Every effort has been made to keep the secret. The plans, which are exceedingly intricate, comprising some thirty separate patents, each essential to the working of the whole, are kept in an elaborate safe in a confidential office adjoining the Arsenal, with burglar-proof doors and windows. Under no conceivable circumstances were the plans to be taken from the office. If the Chief Constructor of the Navy desired to consult them, even he was forced to go to the Woolwich office for the purpose. And yet here we find them in the pockets of a dead junior clerk in the heart of London. From an official point of view it's simply awful."

"But you have recovered them?"

"No, Sherlock, no! That's the pinch. We have not. Ten papers were taken from Woolwich. There were seven in the pockets of Cadogan West. The three most essential are gone—stolen, vanished. You must drop everything, Sherlock. Never mind your usual petty puzzles of the police court. It's a vital international problem that you have to solve. Why did Cadogan West take the papers, where are the missing ones, how did he die, how came his body where it was found, how can the evil be set right? Find an answer to all these questions, and you will have done good service for your country."

"Why do you not solve it yourself, Mycroft? You can see as far as I."

"Possibly, Sherlock. But it is a question of getting details. Give me your details, and from an armchair I will return you an excellent expert opinion. But to run here and run there, to cross-question railway guards, and lie on my face with a lens to my eye—it is not my métier. No, you are the one man who can clear the matter up. If you have a fancy to see your name in the next honours list——"

My friend smiled and shook his head.

"I play the game for the game's own sake," said he. "But the problem certainly presents some points of interest, and I shall be very pleased to look into it. Some more facts, please."

"I have jotted down the more essential ones upon this sheet of paper, together with a few addresses which you will find of service. The actual official guardian of the papers is the famous government expert, Sir James Walter, whose decorations and subtitles fill two lines of a book of reference. He has grown grey in the service, is a gentleman, a favoured guest in the most exalted houses, and above all a man whose patriotism is beyond suspicion. He is one of two who have a key of the safe. I may add that the papers were undoubtedly in the office during working hours on Monday, and that Sir James left for London about three o'clock taking his key with him. He was at the house of Admiral Sinclair at Barclay Square during the whole of the evening when this incident occurred."

"Has the fact been verified?"

"Yes; his brother, Colonel Valentine Walter, has testified to his departure from Woolwich, and Admiral Sinclair to his arrival in London; so Sir James is no longer a direct factor in the problem."

"Who was the other man with a key?"

"The senior clerk and draughtsman, Mr. Sidney Johnson. He is a man of forty, married, with five children. He is a silent, morose man, but he has, on the whole, an excellent record in the public service. He is unpopular with his colleagues, but a hard worker. According to his own account, corroborated only by the word of his wife, he was at home the whole of Monday evening after office hours, and his key has never left the watch chain upon which it hangs."

"Tell us about Cadogan West."

"He has been ten years in the Service, and has done good work. He has the reputation of being hotheaded and impetuous, but a straight, honest man. We have nothing against him. He was next Sidney Johnson in the office. His duties brought him into daily personal contact with the plans. No one else had the handling of them."

"Who locked the plans up that night?"

"Mr. Sidney Johnson, the senior clerk."

"Well, it is surely perfectly clear who took them away. They are actually found upon the person of this junior clerk, Cadogan West. That seems final, does it not?"

"It does, Sherlock, and yet it leaves so much unexplained. In the first place, why did he take them?"

"I presume they were of value?"

"He could have got several thousands for them very easily."

"Can you suggest any possible motive for taking the papers to London except to sell them?"

"No, I cannot."

"Then we must take that as our working hypothesis. Young West took the papers. Now this could only be done by having a false key——"

"Several false keys. He had to open the building and the room."

"He had, then, several false keys. He took the papers to London to sell the secret, intending, no doubt, to have the plans themselves back in the safe next morning before they were missed. While in London on this treasonable mission he met his end."

"How?"

"We will suppose that he was travelling back to Woolwich when he was killed and thrown out of the compartment."

"Aldgate, where the body was found, is considerably past the station for London Bridge, which would be his route to Woolwich."

"Many circumstances could be imagined under which he would pass London Bridge. There was someone in the carriage, for example, with whom he was having an absorbing interview. This interview led to a violent scene, in which he lost his life. Possibly he tried to leave the carriage, fell out on the line, and so met his end. The other closed the door. There was a thick fog, and nothing could be seen."

"No better explanation can be given with our present knowledge; and yet consider, Sherlock, how much you leave untouched. We will suppose, for argument's sake, that young Cadogan West *had* determined to convey these papers to London. He would naturally have made an appointment with the foreign agent and kept his evening clear. Instead of that he took two tickets for the theatre, escorted his fiancée halfway there, and then suddenly disappeared."

"A blind," said Lestrade, who had sat listening with some impatience to the conversation.

"A very singular one. That is objection No. 1. Objection No. 2: We will suppose that he reaches London and sees the foreign agent. He must bring back the papers before morning or the loss will be discovered. He took away ten. Only seven were in his pocket. What had become of the other three? He certainly would not leave them of his own free will. Then, again, where is the price of his treason? One would have expected to find a large sum of money in his pocket."

"It seems to me perfectly clear," said Lestrade. "I have no doubt at all as to what occurred. He took the papers to sell them. He saw the agent. They could not agree as to price. He started home again, but the agent went with him. In the train the agent murdered him, took the more essential papers, and threw his body from the carriage. That would account for everything, would it not?"

"Why had he no ticket?"

"The ticket would have shown which station was nearest the agent's house. Therefore he took it from the murdered man's pocket."

"Good, Lestrade, very good," said Holmes. "Your theory holds together. But if this is true, then the case is at an end. On the one hand the traitor is dead. On the other the plans of the Bruce-Partington submarine are presumably already on the Continent. What is there for us to do?"

"To act, Sherlock—to act!" cried Mycroft, springing to his feet. "All my instincts are against this explanation. Use your powers! Go to the scene of the crime! See the people concerned! Leave no stone unturned! In all your career you have never had so great a chance of serving your country."

"Well, well!" said Holmes, shrugging his shoulders. "Come, Watson! And you, Lestrade, could you favour us with your company for an hour or two? We will begin our investigation by a visit to Aldgate Station. Good-bye, Mycroft. I shall let you have a report before evening, but I warn you in advance that you have little to expect."

An hour later, Holmes, Lestrade and I stood upon the underground railroad at the point where it emerges from the tunnel immediately before Aldgate Station. A courteous red-faced old gentleman represented the railway company.

"This is where the young man's body lay," said he, indicating a spot about three feet from the metals. "It could not have fallen from above, for these, as you see, are all blank walls. Therefore, it could only have come from a train, and that train, so far as we can trace it, must have passed about midnight on Monday."

"Have the carriages been examined for any sign of violence?"

"There are no such signs, and no ticket has been found."

"No record of a door being found open?"

"None."

"We have had some fresh evidence this morning," said Lestrade. "A passenger who passed Aldgate in an ordinary Metropolitan train about 11:40 on Monday night declares that he heard a heavy thud, as of a body striking the line, just before the train reached the station. There was dense fog, however, and nothing could be seen. He made no report of it at the time. Why, whatever is the matter with Mr. Holmes?"

My friend was standing with an expression of strained intensity upon his face, staring at the railway metals where they curved out of the tunnel. Aldgate is a junction, and there was a network of points. On these his eager, questioning eyes were fixed, and I saw on his keen, alert face that tightening of the lips, that quiver of the nostrils, and concentration of the heavy tufted brows which I knew so well.

"Points," he muttered; "the points."

"What of it? What do you mean?"

"I suppose there are no great number of points on a system such as this?"

"No; there are very few."

"And a curve, too. Points, and a curve. By Jove! if it were only so."

"What is it, Mr. Holmes? Have you a clue?"

"An idea—an indication, no more. But the case certainly grows in interest. Unique, perfectly unique, and yet why not? I do not see any indications of bleeding on the line."

"There were hardly any."

"But I understand that there was a considerable wound."

"The bone was crushed, but there was no great external injury."

"And yet one would have expected some bleeding. Would it be possible for me to inspect the train which contained the passenger who heard the thud of a fall in the fog?"

"I fear not, Mr. Holmes. The train has been broken up before now, and the carriages redistributed."

"I can assure you, Mr. Holmes," said Lestrade, "that every carriage has been carefully examined. I saw to it myself."

It was one of my friend's most obvious weaknesses that he was impatient with less alert intelligences than his own.

"Very likely," said he, turning away. "As it happens, it was not the carriages which I desired to examine. Watson, we have done all we can here. We need not trouble you any further, Mr. Lestrade. I think our investigation must now carry us to Woolwich."

At London Bridge, Holmes wrote a telegram to his brother, which he handed to me before dispatching it. It ran thus:

> See some light in the darkness, but it may possibly flicker out. Meanwhile, please send by messenger, to await return at Baker Street, a complete list of all foreign spies or international agents known to be in England, with full address.
>
> SHERLOCK

"That should be helpful, Watson," he remarked, as we took our seats in the Woolwich train. "We certainly owe brother Mycroft a debt for having introduced us to what promises to be a really very remarkable case."

His eager face still wore that expression of intense and high-strung energy, which showed me that some novel and suggestive circumstance had opened up a stimulating line of thought. See the foxhound with hanging ears and drooping tail as it lolls about the kennels, and compare it with the same hound as, with gleaming eyes and straining muscles, it runs upon a breast-high scent—such was the change in Holmes since the morning. He was a different man to the limp and lounging figure in the mouse-coloured dressing gown who had prowled so restlessly only a few hours before round the fog-girt room.

"There is material here. There is scope," said he. "I am dull indeed not to have understood its possibilities."

"Even now they are dark to me."

"The end is dark to me also, but I have hold of one idea which may lead us far. The man met his death elsewhere, and his body was on the *roof* of a carriage."

"On the roof!"

"Remarkable, is it not? But consider the facts. Is it a coincidence that it is found at the very point where the train pitches and sways as it comes round on the points? Is not that the place where an object upon the roof might be expected to fall off? The points would affect no object inside the train. Either the body fell from the roof, or a very curious coincidence has occurred. But now consider the question of the blood. Of course, there was no bleeding on the line if the body had bled elsewhere. Each fact is suggestive in itself. Together they have a cumulative force."

"And the ticket, too!" I cried.

"Exactly. We could not explain the absence of a ticket. This would explain it. Everything fits together."

"But suppose it were so, we are still as far as ever from unravelling the mystery of his death. Indeed, it becomes not simpler, but stranger."

"Perhaps," said Holmes, thoughtfully; "perhaps." He relapsed into a silent reverie, which lasted until the slow train drew up at last in Woolwich Station. There he called a cab and drew Mycroft's paper from his pocket.

"We have quite a little round of afternoon calls to make," said he. "I think that Sir James Walter claims our first attention."

The house of the famous official was a fine villa with green lawns stretching down to the Thames. As we reached it the fog was lifting, and a thin, watery sunshine was breaking through. A butler answered our ring.

"Sir James, sir!" said he, with solemn face. "Sir James died this morning."

"Good heavens!" cried Holmes, in amazement. "How did he die?"

"Perhaps you would care to step in, sir, and see his brother, Colonel Valentine?"

"Yes, we had best do so."

We were ushered into a dim-lit drawing room, where an instant later we were joined by a very tall, handsome light-bearded man of fifty, the younger brother of the dead scientist. His wild eyes, stained cheeks, and unkempt hair all spoke of the sudden blow which had fallen upon the household. He was hardly articulate as he spoke of it.

"It was this horrible scandal," said he. "My brother, Sir James, was a man of very sensitive honour, and he could not survive such an affair. It broke his heart. He was always so proud of the efficiency of his department, and this was a crushing blow."

"We had hoped that he might have given us some indications which would have helped us to clear the matter up."

"I assure you that it was all a mystery to him as it is to you and to all of us. He had already put all his knowledge at the disposal of the police. Naturally, he had no doubt that Cadogan West was guilty. But all the rest was inconceivable."

"You cannot throw any new light upon the affair?"

"I know nothing myself save what I have read or heard. I have no desire to be discourteous, but you can understand, Mr. Holmes, that we are much disturbed at present, and I must ask you to hasten this interview to an end."

"This is indeed an unexpected development," said my friend when we had regained the cab. "I wonder if the death was natural, or whether the poor old fellow killed himself! If the latter, may it be taken as some sign of self-reproach for duty neglected? We must leave that question to the future. Now we shall turn to the Cadogan Wests."

A small but well-kept house in the outskirts of the town sheltered the bereaved mother. The old lady was too dazed with grief to be of any use to us, but at her side was a white-faced young lady, who introduced herself as Miss Violet Westbury, the fiancée of the dead man, and the last to see him upon that fatal night.

"I cannot explain it, Mr. Holmes," she said. "I have not shut an eye since the tragedy, thinking, thinking, thinking, night and day, what the true meaning of it can be. Arthur was the most single-minded, chivalrous, patriotic man upon earth. He would have cut his right hand off before he would sell a state secret confided to his keeping. It is absurd, impossible, preposterous to anyone who knew him."

"But the facts, Miss Westbury?"

"Yes, yes; I admit I cannot explain them."

"Was he in any want of money?"

"No; his needs were very simple and his salary ample. He had saved a few hundreds, and we were to marry at the New Year."

"No signs of any mental excitement? Come, Miss Westbury, be absolutely frank with us."

The quick eye of my companion had noted some change in her manner. She coloured and hesitated. "Yes," she said, at last. "I had a feeling that there was something on his mind."

"For long?"

"Only for the last week or so. He was thoughtful and worried. Once I pressed him about it. He admitted that there was something, and that it was concerned with his official life. 'It is too serious for me to speak about, even to you,' said he. I could get nothing more."

Holmes looked grave.

"Go on, Miss Westbury. Even if it seems to tell against him, go on. We cannot say what it may lead to."

"Indeed I have nothing more to tell. Once or twice it seemed to me that he was on the point of telling me something. He spoke one evening of the importance of the secret, and I have some recollection that he said that no doubt foreign spies would pay a great deal to have it."

My friend's face grew graver still.

"Anything else?"

"He said that we were slack about such matters—that it would be easy for a traitor to get the plans."

"Was it only recently that he made such remarks?"

"Yes, quite recently."

"Now tell us of that last evening."

"We were to go to the theatre. The fog was so thick that a cab was useless. We walked, and our way took us close to the office. Suddenly he darted away into the fog."

"Without a word?"

"He gave an exclamation; that was all. I waited but he never returned. Then I walked home. Next morning, after the office opened, they came to inquire. About twelve o'clock we heard the terrible news. Oh, Mr. Holmes, if you could only, only save his honour! It was so much to him."

Holmes shook his head sadly.

"Come, Watson," said he, "our ways lie elsewhere. Our next station must be the office from which the papers were taken."

"It was black enough before against this young man, but our inquiries make it blacker," he remarked, as the cab lumbered off. "His coming marriage gives a motive for the crime. He naturally wanted money. The idea was in his head, since he spoke about it. He nearly made the girl an accomplice in the treason by telling her his plans. It is all very bad."

"But surely, Holmes, character goes for something? Then, again, why should he leave the girl in the street and dart away to commit a felony?"

"Exactly! There are certainly objections. But it is a formidable case which they have to meet."

Mr. Sidney Johnson, the senior clerk, met us at the office, and received us with that respect which my companion's card always commanded. He was a thin, gruff, bespectacled man of middle age, his cheeks haggard, and his hands twitching from the nervous strain to which he had been subjected.

"It is bad, Mr. Holmes, very bad! Have you heard of the death of the chief?"

"We have just come from his house."

"The place is disorganised. The chief dead, Cadogan West dead, our papers stolen. And yet, when we closed our door on Monday evening we were as efficient an office as any in the government service. Good God, it's dreadful to think of! That West, of all men, should have done such a thing!"

"You are sure of his guilt, then?"

"I can see no other way out of it. And yet I would have trusted him as I trust myself."

"At what hour was the office closed on Monday?"

"At five."

"Did you close it?"

"I am always the last man out."

"Where were the plans?"

"In that safe. I put them there myself."

"Is there no watchman to the building?"

"There is; but he has other departments to look after as well. He is an old soldier and a most trustworthy man. He saw nothing that evening. Of course, the fog was very thick."

"Suppose that Cadogan West wished to make his way into the building after hours; he would need three keys, would he not, before he could reach the papers?"

"Yes, he would. The key of the outer door, the key of the office, and the key of the safe."

"Only Sir James Walter and you had those keys?"

"I had no keys of the doors—only of the safe."

"Was Sir James a man who was orderly in his habits?"

"Yes, I think he was. I know that so far as those three keys are concerned he kept them on the same ring. I have often seen them there."

"And that ring went with him to London?"

"He said so."

"And your key never left your possession?"

"Never."

"Then West, if he is the culprit, must have had a duplicate. And yet none was found upon his body. One other point: if a clerk in this office desired to sell the plans, would it not be simpler to copy the plans for himself than to take the originals, as was actually done?"

"It would take considerable technical knowledge to copy the plans in an effective way."

"But I suppose either Sir James, or you, or West had that technical knowledge?"

"No doubt we had, but I beg you won't try to drag me into the matter, Mr. Holmes. What is the use of our speculating in this way when the original plans were actually found on West?"

"Well, it is certainly singular that he should run the risk of taking originals, if he could safely have taken copies, which would have equally served his turn."

"Singular, no doubt—and yet he did so."

"Every inquiry in this case reveals something inexplicable. Now there are three papers still missing. They are, as I understand, the vital ones."

"Yes, that is so."

"Do you mean to say that anyone holding these three papers, and without the seven others, could construct a Bruce-Partington submarine?"

"I reported to that effect to the Admiralty. But today I have been over the drawings again, and I am not so sure of it. The double valves with the automatic self-adjusting slots are drawn in one of the papers which have been returned. Until the foreigners had invented that for themselves they could not make the boat. Of course, they might soon get over the difficulty."

"But the three missing drawings are the most important?"

"Undoubtedly."

"I think, with your permission, I will now take a stroll round the premises. I do not recall any other question which I desired to ask." He examined the lock of the safe, the door of the room, and finally the iron shutters of the window. It was only when we were on the lawn outside that his interest was strongly excited. There was a laurel bush outside the window, and several of the branches bore signs of having been twisted or snapped. He examined them carefully with his lens, and then some dim and vague marks upon the earth beneath. Finally he asked the chief clerk to close the iron shutters, and he pointed out to me that they hardly met in the centre, and that it would be possible for anyone outside to see what was going on within the room.

"The indications are ruined by the three days' delay. They may mean something or nothing. Well, Watson, I do not think that Woolwich can help us further. It is a small crop which we have gathered. Let us see if we can do better in London."

Yet we added one more sheaf to our harvest before we left Woolwich Station. The clerk in the ticket office was able to say with confidence that he saw Cadogan West—whom he knew well by sight—upon the Monday night, and that he went to London by the 8:15 to London Bridge. He was alone, and took a single third-class ticket. The clerk was struck at the time by his excited and nervous manner. So shaky was he that he could hardly pick up his change, and the clerk had helped him with it. A reference to the timetable showed that the 8:15 was the first train which it was possible for West to take after he had left the lady about 7:30.

"Let us reconstruct, Watson," said Holmes, after half an hour of silence. "I am not aware that in all our joint researches we have ever had a case which was more difficult to get at. Every fresh advance which we make only reveals a fresh ridge beyond. And yet we have surely made some appreciable progress.

"The effect of our inquiries at Woolwich has in the main been against young Cadogan West; but the indications at the window would lend themselves to a more favourable hypothesis. Let us suppose, for example, that he had been approached by some foreign agent. It might have been done under such pledges as would have prevented him from speaking of it, and yet would have affected his thoughts in the direction indicated by his remarks to his fiancée. Very good. We will now suppose that as he went to the theatre with the young lady he suddenly, in the fog, caught a glimpse of this same agent going in the direction of the office. He was an impetuous man, quick in his decisions. Everything gave way to his duty. He followed the man, reached the window, saw the abstraction of the documents, and pursued the thief. In this way we get over the objection that no one would take originals when he could make copies. This outsider had to take originals. So far it holds together."

"What is the next step?"

"Then we come into difficulties. One would imagine that under such circumstances the first act of young Cadogan West would be to seize the villain and raise the alarm. Why did he not do so? Could it have been an official superior who took the papers? That would explain West's conduct. Or could the thief have given West the slip in the fog, and West started at once to London to head him off from his own rooms, presuming that he knew where the rooms were? The call must have been very pressing, since he left his girl standing in the fog, and made no effort to communicate with her. Our scent runs cold here, and there is a vast gap between either hypothesis and the laying of West's body, with seven papers in his pocket, on the roof of a Metropolitan train. My instinct now is to work from the other end. If Mycroft has given us the list of addresses we may be able to pick our man, and follow two tracks instead of one."

Surely enough, a note awaited us at Baker Street. A government messenger had brought it posthaste. Holmes glanced at it and threw it over to me:

> There are numerous small fry, but few who would handle so big an affair. The only men worth considering are Adolph Meyer, of 13 Great George Street, Westminster; Louis La Rothière, of Campden Mansions, Notting Hill; and Hugo Oberstein, 13 Caulfield Gardens, Kensington. The latter was known to be in town on Monday, and is now reported as having left. Glad to hear you have seen some light. The Cabinet awaits your final report with the utmost anxiety. Urgent representations have arrived from the very highest quarter. The whole force of the State is at your back if you should need it.
>
> MYCROFT

"I'm afraid," said Holmes, smiling, "that all the Queen's horses and all the Queen's men cannot avail in this matter." He had spread out his big map of London, and leaned eagerly over it. "Well, well," said he presently, with an exclamation of satisfaction, "things are turning a little in our direction at last. Why, Watson, I do honestly believe that we are going to pull it off after all." He slapped me on the shoulder with a sudden burst of hilarity. "I am going out now. It is only a reconnaissance. I will do nothing serious without my trusted comrade and biographer at my elbow. Do you stay here, and the odds are that you will see me again in an hour or two. If time hangs heavy get foolscap and a pen, and begin your narrative of how we saved the State."

I felt some reflection of his elation in my own mind, for I knew well that he would not depart so far from his usual austerity of demeanour unless there was good cause for exultation. All the long November evening I waited, filled with impatience for his return. At last, shortly after nine o'clock there arrived a messenger with a note:

> Am dining at Goldini's Restaurant, Gloucester Road, Kensington. Please come at once and join me there. Bring with you a jemmy, a dark lantern, a chisel, and a revolver.
>
> S.H.

It was a nice equipment for a respectable citizen to carry through the dim, fog-draped streets. I stowed them all discreetly away in my overcoat, and drove straight to the address given. There sat my friend at a little round table near the door of the garish Italian restaurant.

"Have you had something to eat? Then join me in a coffee and curaçao. Try one of the proprietor's cigars. They are less poisonous than one would expect. Have you the tools?"

"They are here, in my overcoat."

"Excellent. Let me give you a short sketch of what I have done, with some indication of what we are about to do. Now it must be evident to you, Watson, that this young man's body was *placed* on the roof of the train. That was clear from the instant that I determined the fact that it was from the roof, and not from a carriage, that he had fallen."

"Could it not have been dropped from a bridge?"

"I should say it was impossible. If you examine the roofs you will find that they are slightly rounded, and there is no railing round them. Therefore, we can say for certain that young Cadogan West was placed on it."

"How could he be placed there?"

"That was the question which we had to answer. There is only one possible way. You are aware that the Underground runs clear of tunnels at some points in the West End. I had a vague memory that as I have travelled by it I have occasionally seen windows just above my head. Now, suppose that a train halted under such a window, would there be any difficulty in laying a body upon the roof?"

"It seems most improbable."

"We must fall back upon the old axiom that when all other contingencies fail, whatever remains, however improbable, must be the truth. Here all other contingencies *have* failed. When I found that the leading international agent, who had just left London, lived in a row of houses which abutted upon the Underground, I was so pleased that you were a little astonished at my sudden frivolity."

"Oh, that was it, was it?"

"Yes, that was it. Mr. Hugo Oberstein, of 13 Caulfield Gardens, had become my objective. I began my operations at Gloucester Road Station, where a very helpful official walked with me along the track, and allowed me to satisfy myself, not only that the back-stair windows of Caulfield Gardens open on the line, but the even more essential fact that, owing to the intersection of one of the larger railways, the Underground trains are frequently held motionless for some minutes at that very spot."

"Splendid, Holmes! You have got it!"

"So far—so far, Watson. We advance, but the goal is afar. Well, having seen the back of Caulfield Gardens, I visited the front and satisfied myself that the bird was indeed flown. It is a considerable house, unfurnished, so far as I could judge, in the upper rooms. Oberstein lived there with a single valet, who was probably a confederate entirely in his confidence. We must bear in mind that Oberstein has gone to the Continent to dispose of his booty, but not with any idea of flight; for he had no reason to fear a warrant, and the idea of an amateur domiciliary visit would certainly never occur to him. Yet that is precisely what we are about to make."

"Could we not get a warrant and legalise it?"

"Hardly on the evidence."

"What can we hope to do?"

"We cannot tell what correspondence may be there."

"I don't like it, Holmes."

"My dear fellow, you shall keep watch in the street. I'll do the criminal part. It's not a time to stick at trifles. Think of Mycroft's note, of the Admiralty, the Cabinet, the exalted person who waits for news. We are bound to go."

My answer was to rise from the table.

"You are right, Holmes. We are bound to go."

He sprang up and shook me by the hand.

"I knew you would not shrink at the last," said he, and for a moment I saw something in his eyes which was nearer to tenderness than I had ever seen. The next instant he was his masterful, practical self once more.

"It is nearly half a mile, but there is no hurry. Let us walk," said he. "Don't drop the instruments, I beg. Your arrest as a suspicious character would be a most unfortunate complication."

Caulfield Gardens was one of those lines of flat-faced, pillared, and porticoed houses which are so prominent a product of the middle Victorian epoch in the West End of London. Next door there appeared to be a children's party, for the merry buzz of young voices and the clatter of a piano resounded through the night. The fog still hung about and screened us with its friendly shade. Holmes had lit his lantern and flashed it upon the massive door.

"This is a serious proposition," said he. "It is certainly bolted as well as locked. We would do better in the area. There is an excellent archway down yonder in case a too zealous policeman should intrude. Give me a hand, Watson, and I'll do the same for you."

A minute later we were both in the area. Hardly had we reached the dark shadows before the step of the policeman was heard in the fog above. As its soft rhythm died away, Holmes set to work upon the lower door. I saw him stoop and strain until with a sharp crash it flew open. We sprang through into the dark passage, closing the area door behind us. Holmes led the way up the curving, uncarpeted stair. His little fan of yellow light shone upon a low window.

"Here we are, Watson—this must be the one." He threw it open, and as he did so there was a low, harsh murmur, growing steadily into a loud roar as a train dashed past us in the darkness. Holmes swept his light along the windowsill. It was thickly coated with soot from the passing engines, but the black surface was blurred and rubbed in places.

"You can see where they rested the body. Halloa, Watson! What is

Holmes led the way up the curving, uncarpeted stair.

this? There can be no doubt that it is a blood mark." He was pointing to faint discolourations along the woodwork of the window. "Here
it is on the stone of the stair also. The demonstration is complete. Let
us stay here until a train stops."

We had not long to wait. The very next train roared from the tunnel as before, but slowed in the open, and then, with a creaking of
brakes, pulled up immediately beneath us. It was not four feet from
the window ledge to the roof of the carriages. Holmes softly closed
the window.

"So far we are justified," said he. "What do you think of it, Watson?"

"A masterpiece. You have never risen to a greater height."

"I cannot agree with you there. From the moment that I conceived
the idea of the body being upon the roof, which surely was not a very
abstruse one, all the rest was inevitable. If it were not for the grave
interests involved the affair up to this point would be insignificant.
Our difficulties are still before us. But perhaps we may find something here which may help us."

We had ascended the kitchen stair and entered the suite of rooms
upon the first floor. One was a dining room, severely furnished and
containing nothing of interest. A second was a bedroom, which also
drew blank. The remaining room appeared more promising, and my
companion settled down to a systematic examination. It was littered
with books and papers, and was evidently used as a study. Swiftly and
methodically Holmes turned over the contents of drawer after drawer
and cupboard after cupboard, but no gleam of success came to brighten
his austere face. At the end of an hour he was no further than when
he started.

"The cunning dog has covered his tracks," said he. "He has left
nothing to incriminate him. His dangerous correspondence has been
destroyed or removed. This is our last chance."

It was a small tin cash box which stood upon the writing desk.
Holmes prised it open with his chisel. Several rolls of paper were
within, covered with figures and calculations, without any note to
show to what they referred. The recurring words, "Water pressure,"
and "Pressure to the square inch," suggested some possible relation
to a submarine. Holmes tossed them all impatiently aside. There only
remained an envelope with some small newspaper slips inside it. He
shook them out on the table, and at once I saw by his eager face that
his hopes had been raised.

"What's this, Watson? Eh? What's this? Record of a series of messages in the advertisements of a paper. *Daily Telegraph* agony column by the print and paper. Right-hand top corner of a page. No dates—but messages arrange themselves. This must be the first:

" 'Hoped to hear sooner. Terms agreed to. Write fully to address given on card. Pierrot.'

"Next comes: 'Too complex for description. Must have full report. Stuff awaits you when goods delivered. Pierrot.'

"Then comes: 'Matter presses. Must withdraw offer unless contract completed. Make appointment by letter. Will confirm by advertisement. Pierrot.'

"Finally: 'Monday night after nine. Two taps. Only ourselves. Do not be so suspicious. Payment in hard cash when goods delivered. Pierrot.'

"A fairly complete record, Watson! If we could only get at the man at the other end!" He sat lost in thought, tapping his fingers on the table. Finally he sprang to his feet.

"Well, perhaps it won't be so difficult after all. There is nothing more to be done here, Watson. I think we might drive round to the office of the *Daily Telegraph*, and so bring a good day's work to a conclusion."

Mycroft Holmes and Lestrade had come round by appointment after breakfast next day and Sherlock Holmes had recounted to them our proceedings of the day before. The professional shook his head over our confessed burglary.

"We can't do these things in the force, Mr. Holmes," said he. "No wonder you get results that are beyond us. But some of these days you'll go too far, and you'll find yourself and your friend in trouble."

"For England, home and beauty—eh, Watson? Martyrs on the altar of our country. But what do you think of it, Mycroft?"

"Excellent, Sherlock! Admirable! But what use will you make of it?" Holmes picked up the *Daily Telegraph* which lay upon the table.

"Have you seen Pierrot's advertisement today?"

"What! Another one?"

"Yes, here it is: 'Tonight. Same hour. Same place. Two taps. Most vitally important. Your own safety at stake. Pierrot.'"

"By George!" cried Lestrade. "If he answers that we've got him!"

"That was my idea when I put it in. I think if you could both make it convenient to come with us about eight o'clock to Caulfield Gardens we might possibly get a little nearer to a solution."

One of the most remarkable characteristics of Sherlock Holmes was his power of throwing his brain out of action and switching all his thoughts onto lighter things whenever he had convinced himself that he could no longer work to advantage. I remember that during the whole of that memorable day he lost himself in a monograph which he had undertaken upon the polyphonic motets of Lassus. For my own part I had none of this power of detachment, and the day, in consequence, appeared to be interminable. The great national importance of the issue, the suspense in high quarters, the direct nature of the experiment which we were trying—all combined to work upon my nerve. It was a relief to me when at last, after a light dinner, we set out upon our expedition. Lestrade and Mycroft met us by appointment at the outside of Gloucester Road Station. The area door of Oberstein's house had been left open the night before, and it was necessary for me, as Mycroft Holmes absolutely and indignantly declined to climb the railings, to pass in and open the hall door. By nine o'clock we were all seated in the study, waiting patiently for our man.

An hour passed and yet another. When eleven struck, the measured beat of the great church clock seemed to sound the dirge of our hopes. Lestrade and Mycroft were fidgeting in their seats and looking twice a minute at their watches. Holmes sat silent and composed, his eyelids half shut, but every sense on the alert. He raised his head with a sudden jerk.

"He is coming," said he.

There had been a furtive step past the door. Now it returned. We heard a shuffling sound outside, and then two sharp taps with the knocker. Holmes rose, motioning to us to remain seated. The gas in the hall was a mere point of light. He opened the outer door, and then as a dark figure slipped past him he closed and fastened it.

"This way!" we heard him say, and a moment later our man stood before us. Holmes had followed him closely, and as the man turned with a cry of surprise and alarm he caught him by the collar and threw him back into the room. Before our prisoner had recovered his balance the door was shut and Holmes standing with his back against it. The man glared round him, staggered, and fell senseless upon the floor. With the shock, his broad-brimmed hat flew from his head, his cravat slipped down from his lips, and there was the long light beard and the soft, handsome delicate features of Colonel Valentine Walter.

Holmes gave a whistle of surprise.

"You can write me down an ass this time, Watson," said he. "This was not the bird that I was looking for."

"Who is he?" asked Mycroft eagerly.

"The younger brother of the late Sir James Walter, the head of the Submarine Department. Yes, yes; I see the fall of the cards. He is coming to. I think that you had best leave his examination to me." We had carried the prostrate body to the sofa. Now our prisoner sat up, looked round him with a horror-stricken face, and passed his hand over his forehead, like one who cannot believe his own senses.

"What is this?" he asked. "I came here to visit Mr. Oberstein."

"Everything is known, Colonel Walter," said Holmes. "How an English gentleman could behave in such a manner is beyond my comprehension. But your whole correspondence and relations with Oberstein are within our knowledge. So also are the circumstances connected with the death of young Cadogan West. Let me advise you to gain at least the small credit for repentance and confession, since there are still some details which we can only learn from your lips."

The man groaned and sank his face in his hands. We waited, but he was silent.

"I can assure you," said Holmes, "that every essential is already known. We know that you were pressed for money; that you took an impress of the keys which your brother held; and that you entered into a correspondence with Oberstein, who answered your letters through the advertisement columns of the *Daily Telegraph*. We are aware that you went down to the office in the fog on Monday night, but that you were seen and followed by young Cadogan West, who had probably some previous reason to suspect you. He saw your theft, but could not give the alarm, as it was just possible that you were taking the papers to your brother in London. Leaving all his private concerns, like the good citizen that he was, he followed you closely in the fog, and kept at your heels until you reached this very house. There he intervened, and then it was, Colonel Walter, that to treason you added the more terrible crime of murder."

"I did not! I did not! Before God I swear that I did not!" cried our wretched prisoner.

"Tell us, then, how Cadogan West met his end before you laid him upon the roof of a railway carriage."

"I will. I swear to you that I will. I did the rest. I confess it. It was just as you say. A stock exchange debt had to be paid. I needed the money badly. Oberstein offered me five thousand. It was to save myself from ruin. But as to murder, I am as innocent as you."

"What happened then?"

"He had his suspicions before, and he followed me as you describe. I never knew it until I was at the very door. It was thick fog, and one could not see three yards. I had given two taps and Oberstein had come to the door. The young man rushed up and demanded to know what we were about to do with the papers. Oberstein had a short life preserver. He always carried it with him. As West forced his way after us into the house Oberstein struck him on the head. The blow was a fatal one. He was dead within five minutes. There he lay in the hall, and we were at our wits' end what to do. Then Oberstein had this idea about the trains which halted under his back window. But first he examined the papers which I had brought. He said that three of them were essential, and that he must keep them. 'You cannot keep them,' said I. 'There will be a dreadful row at Woolwich if they are not returned.' 'I must keep them,' said he, 'for they are so technical that it is impossible in the time to make copies.' 'Then they must all go back together tonight,' said I. He thought for a little, and then he cried out that he had it. 'Three I will keep,' said he. 'The others we will stuff into the pocket of this young man. When he is found the whole business will assuredly be put to his account.' I could see no other way out of it, so we did as he suggested. We waited half an hour at the window before a train stopped. It was so thick that nothing could be seen, and we had no difficulty in lowering West's body on to the train. That was the end of the matter so far as I was concerned."

"And your brother?"

"He said nothing, but he had caught me once with his keys, and I think that he suspected. I read in his eyes that he suspected. As you know, he never held up his head again."

There was silence in the room. It was broken by Mycroft Holmes.

"Can you not make reparation? It would ease your conscience, and possibly your punishment."

"What reparation can I make?"

"Where is Oberstein with the papers?"

"I do not know."

"Did he give you no address?"

"He said that letters to the Hôtel du Louvre, Paris, would eventually reach him."

"Then reparation is still within your power," said Sherlock Holmes.

"I will do anything I can. I owe this fellow no particular good will. He has been my ruin and my downfall."

"Here are paper and pen. Sit at this desk and write to my dictation. Direct the envelope to the address given. That is right. Now the letter:

DEAR SIR,

With regard to our transaction, you will no doubt have observed by now that one essential detail is missing. I have a tracing which will make it complete. This has involved me in extra trouble, however, and I must ask you for a further advance of five hundred pounds. I will not trust it to the post, nor will I take anything but gold or notes. I would come to you abroad, but it would excite remark if I left the country at present. Therefore I shall expect to meet you in the smoking room of the Charing Cross Hotel at noon on Saturday. Remember that only English notes, or gold, will be taken.

"That will do very well. I shall be very much surprised if it does not fetch our man."

And it did! It is a matter of history—that secret history of a nation which is often so much more intimate and interesting than its public chronicles—that Oberstein, eager to complete the coup of his lifetime, came to the lure and was safely engulfed for fifteen years in a British prison. In his trunk were found the invaluable Bruce-Partington plans, which he had put up for auction in all the naval centres of Europe.

Colonel Walter died in prison towards the end of the second year of his sentence. As to Holmes, he returned refreshed to his monograph upon the polyphonic motets of Lassus, which has since been printed for private circulation, and is said by experts to be the last word upon the subject. Some weeks afterwards I learned incidentally that my friend spent a day at Windsor, whence he returned with a remarkably fine emerald tiepin. When I asked him if he had bought it, he answered that it was a present from a certain gracious lady in whose interests he had once been fortunate enough to carry out a small commission. He said no more; but I fancy that I could guess at that lady's august name, and I have little doubt that the emerald pin will forever recall to my friend's memory the adventure of the Bruce-Partington plans.

III: The Adventure of the Devil's Foot

IN RECORDING FROM time to time some of the curious experiences and interesting recollections which I associate with my long and intimate friendship with Mr. Sherlock Holmes, I have continually been faced by difficulties caused by his own aversion to publicity. To his sombre and cynical spirit all popular applause was always abhorrent, and nothing amused him more at the end of a successful case than to hand over the actual exposure to some orthodox official, and to listen with a mocking smile to the general chorus of misplaced congratulation. It was, indeed, this attitude upon the part of my friend and certainly not any lack of interesting material which has caused me of late years to lay very few of my records before the public. My participation in some of his adventures was always a privilege which entailed discretion and reticence upon me.

It was, then, with considerable surprise that I received a telegram from Holmes last Tuesday—he has never been known to write where a telegram would serve—in the following terms: "Why not tell them of the Cornish horror—strangest case I have handled." I have no idea what backward sweep of memory had brought the matter fresh to his mind, or what freak had caused him to desire that I should recount it; but I hasten, before another cancelling telegram may arrive, to hunt out the notes which give me the exact details of the case, and to lay the narrative before my readers.

It was, then, in the spring of the year 1897 that Holmes's iron constitution showed some symptoms of giving way in the face of constant hard work of a most exacting kind, aggravated, perhaps, by occasional indiscretions of his own. In March of that year Dr. Moore Agar, of Harley Street, whose dramatic introduction to Holmes I may some day recount, gave positive injunctions that the famous private agent would lay aside all his cases and surrender himself to complete rest if he wished to avert an absolute breakdown. The state of his health was not a matter in which he himself took the faintest interest, for his mental detachment was absolute, but he was induced at last, on the threat of being permanently disqualified from work, to give himself a complete change of scene and air. Thus it was that in the early spring of that year we found ourselves together in a small cottage near Poldhu Bay, at the further extremity of the Cornish peninsula.

It was a singular spot, and one peculiarly well suited to the grim humour of my patient. From the windows of our little whitewashed house, which stood high upon a grassy headland, we looked down upon the whole sinister semicircle of Mounts Bay, that old death trap of sailing vessels, with its fringe of black cliffs and surge-swept reefs on which innumerable seamen have met their end. With a northerly breeze it lies placid and sheltered, inviting the storm-tossed craft to tack into it for rest and protection.

Then comes the sudden swirl round of the wind, the blustering gale from the southwest, the dragging anchor, the lee shore, and the last battle in the creaming breakers. The wise mariner stands far out from that evil place.

On the land side our surroundings were as sombre as on the sea. It was a country of rolling moors, lonely and dun-coloured, with an occasional church tower to mark the site of some old-world village. In every direction upon these moors there were traces of some vanished race which had passed utterly away, and left as its sole record strange monuments of stone, irregular mounds which contained the burned ashes of the dead, and curious earthworks which hinted at prehistoric strife. The glamour and mystery of the place, with its sinister atmosphere of forgotten nations, appealed to the imagination of my friend, and he spent much of his time in long walks and solitary meditations upon the moor. The ancient Cornish language had also arrested his attention, and he had, I remember, conceived the idea that it was akin to the Chaldean, and had been largely derived from the Phœnician traders in tin. He had received a consignment of books upon philology and was settling down to develop this thesis, when suddenly, to my sorrow and to his unfeigned delight, we found ourselves, even in that land of dreams, plunged into a problem at our very doors which was more intense, more engrossing, and infinitely more mysterious than any of those which had driven us from London. Our simple life and peaceful, healthy routine were violently interrupted, and we were precipitated into the midst of a series of events which caused the utmost excitement not only in Cornwall, but throughout the whole West of England. Many of my readers may retain some recollection of what was called at the time "The Cornish Horror," though a most imperfect account of the matter reached the London press. Now, after thirteen years, I will give the true details of this inconceivable affair to the public.

I have said that scattered towers marked the villages which dotted this part of Cornwall. The nearest of these was the hamlet of Tredannick Wollas, where the cottages of a couple of hundred inhabitants clustered round an ancient, moss-grown church. The vicar of the parish, Mr. Roundhay, was something of an archæologist, and as such Holmes had made his acquaintance. He was a middle-aged man, portly and affable, with a considerable fund of local lore. At his invitation we had taken tea at the vicarage, and had come to know, also, Mr. Mortimer Tregennis, an independent gentleman, who increased the clergyman's scanty resources by taking rooms in his large straggling house. The vicar, being a bachelor, was glad to come to such an arrangement, though he had little in common with his lodger, who was a thin, dark, spectacled man, with a stoop which gave the impression of actual physical deformity. I remember that during our short visit we found the vicar garrulous, but his lodger strangely reticent, a sad-faced, introspective man, sitting with averted eyes, brooding apparently upon his own affairs.

These were the two men who entered abruptly into our little sitting room on Tuesday, March the 16th, shortly after our breakfast hour, as we were smoking together, preparatory to our daily excursion upon the moors.

"Mr. Holmes," said the vicar, in an agitated voice, "the most extraordinary and tragic affair has occurred during the night. It is the most unheard-of business. We can only regard it as a special Providence that you should chance to be here at the time, for in all England you are the one man we need."

I glared at the intrusive vicar with no very friendly eyes; but Holmes took his pipe from his lips and sat up in his chair like an old hound who hears the view-halloa. He waved his hand to the sofa, and our palpitating visitor with his agitated companion sat side by side upon it. Mr. Mortimer Tregennis was more self-contained than the clergyman, but the twitching of his thin hands and the brightness of his dark eyes showed that they shared a common emotion.

"Shall I speak or you?" he asked of the vicar.

"Well, as you seem to have made the discovery, whatever it may be, and the vicar to have had it secondhand, perhaps you had better do the speaking," said Holmes.

I glanced at the hastily clad clergyman, with the formally dressed lodger seated beside him, and was amused at the surprise which Holmes's simple deduction had brought to their faces.

"Perhaps I had best say a few words first," said the vicar, "and then you can judge if you will listen to the details from Mr. Tregennis, or whether we should not hasten at once to the scene of this mysterious affair. I may explain, then, that our friend here spent last evening in the company of his two brothers, Owen and George, and of his sister Brenda, at their house of Tredannick Wartha, which is near the old stone cross upon the moor. He left them shortly after ten o'clock, playing cards round the dining room table, in excellent health and spirits. This morning, being an early riser, he walked in that direction before breakfast, and was overtaken by the carriage of Dr. Richards, who explained that he had just been sent for on a most urgent call to Tredannick Wartha. Mr. Mortimer Tregennis naturally went with him.

"When he arrived at Tredannick Wartha he found an extraordinary state of things. His two brothers and his sister were seated round the table exactly as he had left them, the cards still spread in front of them and the candles burned down to their sockets. The sister lay back stone-dead in her chair, while the two brothers sat on each side of her, laughing, shouting, and singing, the senses stricken clean out of them. All three of them, the dead woman and the two demented men, retained upon their faces an expression of the utmost horror—a convulsion of terror which was dreadful to look upon. There was no sign of the presence of anyone in the house, except Mrs. Porter, the old cook and housekeeper, who declared that she had slept deeply and heard no sound during the night. Nothing had been stolen or disarranged, and there is absolutely no explanation of what the horror can be which has frightened a woman to death and two strong men out of their senses. There is the situation, Mr. Holmes, in a nutshell, and if you can help us to clear it up you will have done a great work."

I had hoped that in some way I could coax my companion back into the quiet which had been the object of our journey; but one glance at his intense face and contracted eyebrows told me how vain was now the expectation. He sat for some little time in silence, absorbed in the strange drama which had broken in upon our peace.

"I will look into this matter," he said at last. "On the face of it, it would appear to be a case of a very exceptional nature. Have you been there yourself, Mr. Roundhay?"

"No, Mr. Holmes. Mr. Tregennis brought back the account to the vicarage, and I at once hurried over with him to consult you."

"How far is it to the house where this singular tragedy occurred?"

"About a mile inland."

"Then we shall walk over together. But, before we start, I must ask you a few questions, Mr. Mortimer Tregennis."

The other had been silent all this time, but I had observed that his more controlled excitement was even greater than the obtrusive emotion of the clergyman. He sat with a pale, drawn face, his anxious gaze fixed upon Holmes, and his thin hands clasped convulsively together. His pale lips quivered as he listened to the dreadful experience which had befallen his family, and his dark eyes seemed to reflect something of the horror of the scene.

"Ask what you like, Mr. Holmes," said he eagerly. "It is a bad thing to speak of, but I will answer you the truth."

"Tell me about last night."

"Well, Mr. Holmes, I supped there, as the vicar has said, and my elder brother George proposed a game of whist afterwards. We sat down about nine o'clock. It was a quarter past ten when I moved to go. I left them all round the table, as merry as could be."

"Who let you out?"

"Mrs. Porter had gone to bed, so I let myself out. I shut the hall door behind me. The window of the room in which they sat was closed, but the blind was not drawn down. There was no change in door or window this morning, nor any reason to think that any stranger had been to the house. Yet there they sat, driven clean mad with terror, and Brenda lying dead of fright, with her head hanging over the arm of the chair. I'll never get the sight of that room out of my mind so long as I live."

"The facts, as you state them, are certainly most remarkable," said Holmes. "I take it that you have no theory yourself which can in any way account for them?"

"It's devilish, Mr. Holmes; devilish!" cried Mortimer Tregennis. "It is not of this world. Something has come into that room which has dashed the light of reason from their minds. What human contrivance could do that?"

"I fear," said Holmes, "that if the matter is beyond humanity it is certainly beyond me. Yet we must exhaust all natural explanations before we fall back upon such a theory as this. As to yourself, Mr. Tregennis, I take it you were divided in some way from your family, since they lived together and you had rooms apart?"

"That is so, Mr. Holmes, though the matter is past and done with. We were a family of tin miners at Redruth, but we sold out our venture to a company, and so retired with enough to keep us. I won't deny that there was some feeling about the division of the money and it stood between us for a time, but it was all forgiven and forgotten, and we were the best of friends together."

"Looking back at the evening which you spent together, does anything stand out in your memory as throwing any possible light upon the tragedy? Think carefully, Mr. Tregennis, for any clue which can help me."

"There is nothing at all, sir."

"Your people were in their usual spirits?"

"Never better."

"Were they nervous people? Did they ever show any apprehension of coming danger?"

"Nothing of the kind."

"You have nothing to add then, which could assist me?"

Mortimer Tregennis considered earnestly for a moment.

"There is one thing occurs to me," said he at last. "As we sat at the table my back was to the window, and my brother George, he being my partner at cards, was facing it. I saw him once look hard over my shoulder, so I turned round and looked also. The blind was up and the window shut, but I could just make out the bushes on the lawn, and it seemed to me for a moment that I saw something moving among them. I couldn't even say if it were man or animal, but I just thought there was something there. When I asked him what he was looking at, he told me that he had the same feeling. That is all that I can say."

"Did you not investigate?"

"No; the matter passed as unimportant."

"You left them, then, without any premonition of evil?"

"None at all."

"I am not clear how you came to hear the news so early this morning."

"I am an early riser, and generally take a walk before breakfast. This morning I had hardly started when the doctor in his carriage overtook me. He told me that old Mrs. Porter had sent a boy down with an urgent message. I sprang in beside him and we drove on. When we got there we looked into that dreadful room. The candles and the fire must have burned out hours before, and they had been sitting there in the dark until dawn had broken. The doctor said Brenda must have been dead at least six hours. There were no signs of violence. She just lay across the arm of the chair with that look on her face. George and Owen were singing snatches of songs and gibbering like two great apes. Oh, it was awful to see! I couldn't stand it, and the doctor was as white as a sheet. Indeed, he fell into a chair in a sort of faint, and we nearly had him on our hands as well."

"Remarkable—most remarkable!" said Holmes, rising and taking his hat. "I think, perhaps, we had better go down to Tredannick Wartha without further delay. I confess that I have seldom known a case which at first sight presented a more singular problem."

Our proceedings of that first morning did little to advance the investigation. It was marked, however, at the outset by an incident which left the most sinister impression upon my mind. The approach to the spot at which the tragedy occurred is down a narrow winding country lane. While we made our way along it we heard the rattle of a carriage coming towards us, and stood aside to let it pass. As it drove by us I caught a glimpse through the closed window of a horribly contorted, grinning face glaring out at us. Those staring eyes and gnashing teeth flashed past us like a dreadful vision.

"My brothers!" cried Mortimer Tregennis, white to his lips. "They are taking them to Helston."

We looked with horror after the black carriage, lumbering upon its way. Then we turned our steps towards this ill-omened house in which they had met their strange fate.

It was a large and bright dwelling, rather a villa than a cottage, with a considerable garden which was already, in that Cornish air, well filled with spring flowers. Towards this garden the window of the sitting room fronted, and from it, according to Mortimer Tregennis, must have come that thing of evil which had by sheer horror in a single instant blasted their minds. Holmes walked slowly and thoughtfully among the flowerpots and along the path before we entered the porch. So absorbed was he in his thoughts, I remember, that he stumbled over the watering pot, upset its contents, and deluged both our feet and the garden path. Inside the house we were met by the elderly Cornish housekeeper, Mrs. Porter, who, with the aid of a young girl, looked after the wants of the family. She readily answered all Holmes's questions. She had heard nothing in the night. Her employers had all been in excellent spirits lately, and she had never known them more cheerful and prosperous. She had fainted with horror upon entering the room in the morning and seeing that dreadful company round the table. She had, when she recovered, thrown open the window to let the morning air in, and had run down to the lane, whence she sent a farm lad for the doctor. The lady was on her bed upstairs, if we cared to see her. It took four strong men to get the brothers into the asylum carriage. She would not herself stay in the house another day, and was starting that very afternoon to rejoin her family at St. Ives.

We ascended the stairs and viewed the body. Miss Brenda Tregennis had been a very beautiful girl, though now verging upon middle age. Her dark, clear-cut face was handsome, even in death, but there still lingered upon it something of that convulsion of horror which had been her last human emotion. From her bedroom we descended to the sitting room where this strange tragedy had actually occurred. The charred ashes of the overnight fire lay in the grate. On the table were the four guttered and burned-out candles, with the cards scattered over its surface. The chairs had been moved back against the walls, but all else was as it had been the night before. Holmes paced with light, swift steps about the room; he sat in the various chairs, drawing them up and reconstructing their positions. He tested how much of the garden was visible; he examined the floor, the ceiling, and the fireplace; but never once did I see that sudden brightening of his eyes and tightening of his lips which would have told me that he saw some gleam of light in this utter darkness.

"Why a fire?" he asked once. "Had they always a fire in this small room on a spring evening?"

Mortimer Tregennis explained that the night was cold and damp. For that reason, after his arrival, the fire was lit. "What are you going to do now, Mr. Holmes?" he asked.

My friend smiled and laid his hand upon my arm. "I think, Watson, that I shall resume that course of tobacco poisoning which you have so often and so justly condemned," said he. "With your permission, gentlemen, we will now return to our cottage, for I am not aware that any new factor is likely to come to our notice here. I will turn the facts over in my mind, Mr. Tregennis, and should anything occur to me I will certainly communicate with you and the vicar. In the meantime I wish you both good morning."

It was not until long after we were back in Poldhu Cottage that Holmes broke his complete and absorbed silence. He sat coiled in his armchair, his haggard and ascetic face hardly visible amid the blue swirl of his tobacco smoke, his black brows drawn down, his forehead contracted, his eyes vacant and far away. Finally, he laid down his pipe and sprang to his feet.

"It won't do, Watson!" said he, with a laugh. "Let us walk along the cliffs together and search for flint arrows. We are more likely to find them than clues to this problem. To let the brain work without sufficient material is like racing an engine. It racks itself to pieces. The sea air, sunshine, and patience, Watson—all else will come.

"Now, let us calmly define our position, Watson," he continued, as we skirted the cliffs together. "Let us get a firm grip of the very little which we *do* know, so that when fresh facts arise we may be ready to fit them into their places. I take it, in the first place, that neither of us is prepared to admit diabolical intrusions into the affairs of men. Let us begin by ruling that entirely out of our minds. Very good. There remain three persons who have been grievously stricken by some conscious or unconscious human agency. That is firm ground. Now, when did this occur? Evidently, assuming his narrative to be true, it was immediately after Mr. Mortimer Tregennis had left the room. That is a very important point. The presumption is that it was within a few minutes afterwards. The cards still lay upon the table. It was already past their usual hour for bed. Yet they had not changed their position or pushed back their chairs. I repeat, then, that the occurrence was immediately after his departure, and not later than eleven o'clock last night.

"Our next obvious step is to check, so far as we can, the movements of Mortimer Tregennis after he left the room. In this there is no difficulty, and they seem to be above suspicion. Knowing my methods as you do, you were, of course, conscious of the somewhat clumsy water pot expedient by which I obtained a clearer impress of his foot than might otherwise have been possible. The wet sandy path took it admirably. Last night was also wet, you will remember, and it was not difficult—having obtained a sample print—to pick out his track among others and to follow his movements. He appears to have walked away swiftly in the direction of the vicarage.

"If, then, Mortimer Tregennis disappeared from the scene, and yet some outside person affected the card players, how can we reconstruct that person, and how was such an impression of horror conveyed? Mrs. Porter may be eliminated. She is evidently harmless. Is there any evidence that someone crept up to the garden window and in some manner produced so terrific an effect that he drove those who saw it out of their senses? The only suggestion in this direction comes from Mortimer Tregennis himself, who says that his brother spoke about some movement in the garden. That is certainly remarkable, as the night was rainy, cloudy, and dark. Anyone who had the design to alarm these people would be compelled to place his very face against the glass before he could be seen. There is a three-foot flower border outside this window, but no indication of a footmark. It is difficult to imagine, then, how an outsider could have made so terrible an impression upon the company, nor have we found any possible motive for so strange and elaborate an attempt. You perceive our difficulties, Watson?"

"They are only too clear," I answered, with conviction.

"And yet, with a little more material, we may prove that they are not insurmountable," said Holmes. "I fancy that among your extensive archives, Watson, you may find some which were nearly as obscure. Meanwhile, we shall put the case aside until more accurate data are available, and devote the rest of our morning to the pursuit of neolithic man."

I may have commented upon my friend's power of mental detachment, but never have I wondered at it more than upon that spring morning in Cornwall when for two hours he discoursed upon celts, arrowheads, and shards, as lightly as if no sinister mystery was waiting for his solution. It was not until we had returned in the afternoon to our cottage that we found a visitor awaiting us, who soon brought our minds back to the matter in hand. Neither of us needed to be told who that visitor was. The huge body, the craggy and deeply seamed face with the fierce eyes and hawk-like nose, the grizzled hair which nearly brushed our cottage ceiling, the beard—golden at the fringes and white near the lips, save for the nicotine stain from his perpetual cigar—all these were as well known in London as in Africa, and could only be associated with the tremendous personality of Dr. Leon Sterndale, the great lion hunter and explorer.

We had heard of his presence in the district, and had once or twice caught sight of his tall figure upon the moorland paths. He made no advances to us, however, nor would we have dreamed of doing so to him, as it was well known that it was his love of seclusion which caused him to spend the greater part of the intervals between his journeys in a small bungalow buried in the lonely wood of Beauchamp Arriance. Here, amid his books and his maps, he lived an absolutely lonely life, attending to his own simple wants, and paying little apparent heed to the affairs of his neighbours. It was a surprise to me, therefore, to hear him asking Holmes in an eager voice, whether he had made any advance in his reconstruction of this mysterious episode. "The county police are utterly at fault," said he, "but perhaps your wider experience has suggested some conceivable explanation. My only claim to being taken into your confidence is that during my many residences here I have come to know this family of Tregennis very well—indeed, upon my Cornish mother's side I could call them cousins—and their strange fate has naturally been a great shock to me. I may tell you that I had got as far as Plymouth upon my way to Africa, but the news reached me this morning, and I came straight back again to help in the inquiry."

Holmes raised his eyebrows.

"Did you lose your boat through it?"

"I will take the next."

"Dear me! that is friendship indeed."

"I tell you they were relatives."

. . . Dr. Leon Sterndale, the great lion hunter and explorer.

"Quite so—cousins of your mother. Was your baggage aboard the ship?"

"Some of it, but the main part is at the hotel."

"I see. But surely this event could not have found its way into the Plymouth morning papers?"

"No, sir; I had a telegram."

"Might I ask from whom?"

A shadow passed over the gaunt face of the explorer.

"You are very inquisitive, Mr. Holmes."

"It is my business."

With an effort, Dr. Sterndale recovered his ruffled composure.

"I have no objection to telling you," he said. "It was Mr. Round-hay, the vicar, who sent me the telegram which recalled me."

"Thank you," said Holmes. "I may say in answer to your original question, that I have not cleared my mind entirely on the subject of this case, but that I have every hope of reaching some conclusion. It would be premature to say more."

"Perhaps you would not mind telling me if your suspicions point in any particular direction?"

"No, I can hardly answer that."

"Then I have wasted my time, and need not prolong my visit." The famous doctor strode out of our cottage in considerable ill humour, and within five minutes Holmes had followed him. I saw him no more until the evening, when he returned with a slow step and haggard face which assured me that he had made no great progress with his investigation. He glanced at a telegram which awaited him, and threw it into the grate.

"From the Plymouth hotel, Watson," he said. "I learned the name of it from the vicar, and I wired to make certain that Dr. Leon Sterndale's account was true. It appears that he did indeed spend last night there, and that he has actually allowed some of his baggage to go on to Africa, while he returned to be present at this investigation. What do you make of that, Watson?"

"He is deeply interested."

"Deeply interested—yes. There is a thread here which we have not yet grasped, and which might lead us through the tangle. Cheer up, Watson, for I am very sure that our material has not yet all come to hand. When it does, we may soon leave our difficulties behind us."

Little did I think how soon the words of Holmes would be realised, or how strange and sinister would be that new development which opened up an entirely fresh line of investigation. I was shaving at my window in the morning when I heard the rattle of hoofs, and, looking up, saw a dogcart coming at a gallop down the road. It pulled up at our door, and our friend the vicar sprang from it and rushed up our garden path. Holmes was already dressed, and we hastened down to meet him.

Our visitor was so excited that he could hardly articulate, but at last in gasps and bursts his tragic story came out of him.

"We are devil-ridden, Mr. Holmes! My poor parish is devil-ridden!" he cried. "Satan himself is loose in it! We are given over into his hands!" He danced about in his agitation, a ludicrous object if it were not for his ashy face and startled eyes. Finally he shot out his terrible news.

"Mr. Mortimer Tregennis died during the night, and with exactly the same symptoms as the rest of his family."

Holmes sprang to his feet, all energy in an instant.

"Can you fit us both into your dogcart?"

"Yes, I can."

"Then, Watson, we will postpone our breakfast. Mr. Roundhay, we are entirely at your disposal. Hurry—hurry, before things get disarranged."

The lodger occupied two rooms at the vicarage, which were in an angle by themselves, the one above the other. Below was a large sitting room; above, his bedroom. They looked out upon a croquet lawn which came up to the windows. We had arrived before the doctor or the police, so that everything was absolutely undisturbed. Let me describe exactly the scene as we saw it upon that misty March morning. It has left an impression which can never be effaced from my mind.

The atmosphere of the room was of a horrible and depressing stuffiness. The servant who had first entered had thrown up the window, or it would have been even more intolerable. This might partly be due to the fact that a lamp stood flaring and smoking on the centre table. Beside it sat the dead man, leaning back in his chair, his thin beard projecting, his spectacles pushed up onto his forehead, and his lean, dark face turned towards the window and twisted into the same distortion of terror which had marked the features of his dead sister. His limbs were convulsed and his fingers contorted as though he had died in a very paroxysm of fear. He was fully clothed, though there were signs that his dressing had been done in a hurry. We had already learned that his bed had been slept in, and that the tragic end had come to him in the early morning.

One realised the red-hot energy which underlay Holmes's phlegmatic exterior when one saw the sudden change which came over him from the moment that he entered the fatal apartment. In an instant he was tense and alert, his eyes shining, his face set, his limbs quivering with eager activity. He was out on the lawn, in through the window, round the room, and up into the bedroom, for all the world like a dashing foxhound drawing a cover. In the bedroom he made a rapid cast around, and ended by throwing open the window, which appeared to give him some fresh cause for excitement, for he leaned out of it with loud ejaculations of interest and delight. Then he rushed down the stair, out through the open window, threw himself upon his face on the lawn, sprang up and into the room once more, all with the energy of the hunter who is at the very heels of his quarry. The lamp, which was an ordinary standard, he examined with minute care, making certain measurements upon its bowl. He carefully scrutinised with his lens the talc shield which covered the top of the chimney, and scraped off some ashes which adhered to its upper surface, putting some of them into an envelope, which he placed in his pocketbook. Finally, just as the doctor and the official police put in an appearance, he beckoned to the vicar and we all three went out upon the lawn.

"I am glad to say that my investigation has not been entirely barren," he remarked. "I cannot remain to discuss the matter with the police, but I should be exceedingly obliged, Mr. Roundhay, if you would give the inspector my compliments and direct his attention to the bedroom window and to the sitting room lamp. Each is suggestive, and together they are almost conclusive. If the police would desire further information I shall be happy to see any of them at my cottage. And now, Watson, I think that, perhaps, we shall be better employed elsewhere."

It may be that the police resented the intrusion of an amateur, or that they imagined themselves to be upon some hopeful line of investigation; but it is certain that we heard nothing from them for the next two days. During this time Holmes spent some of his time smoking and dreaming in the cottage; but a greater portion in country walks which he undertook alone, returning after many hours without remark as to where he had been. One experiment served to show me the line of his investigation. He had bought a lamp which was the duplicate of the one which had burned in the room of Mortimer Tregennis on the morning of the tragedy. This he filled with the same oil as that used at the vicarage, and he carefully timed the period which it would take to be exhausted. Another experiment which he made was of a more unpleasant nature, and one which I am not likely ever to forget.

"You will remember, Watson," he remarked one afternoon, "that there is a single common point of resemblance in the varying reports which have reached us. This concerns the effect of the atmosphere of the room in each case upon those who had first entered it. You will recollect that Mortimer Tregennis, in describing the episode of his last visit to his brothers' house, remarked that the doctor on entering the room fell into a chair? You had forgotten? Well, I can answer for it that it was so. Now, you will remember also that Mrs. Porter, the housekeeper, told us that she herself fainted upon entering the room and had afterwards opened the window. In the second case—that of Mortimer Tregennis himself—you cannot have forgotten the horrible stuffiness of the room when we arrived, though the servant had thrown open the window. That servant, I found upon inquiry, was so ill that she had gone to her bed. You will admit, Watson, that these facts are very suggestive. In each case there is evidence of a poisonous atmosphere. In each case, also, there is combustion going on in the room— in the one case a fire, in the other a lamp. The fire was needed, but the lamp was lit—as a comparison of the oil consumed will show— long after it was broad daylight. Why? Surely because there is some connection between three things—the burning, the stuffy atmosphere, and, finally, the madness or death of those unfortunate people. That is clear, is it not?"

"It would appear so."

"At least we may accept it as a working hypothesis. We will suppose, then, that something was burned in each case which produced an atmosphere causing strange toxic effects. Very good. In the first instance—that of the Tregennis family—this substance was placed in the fire. Now the window was shut, but the fire would naturally carry fumes to some extent up the chimney. Hence one would expect the effects of the poison to be less than in the second case, where there was less escape for the vapour. The result seems to indicate that it was so, since in the first case only the woman, who had presumably the more sensitive organism, was killed, the others exhibiting that temporary or permanent lunacy which is evidently the first effect of the drug. In the second case the result was complete. The facts, therefore, seem to bear out the theory of a poison which worked by combustion.

"With this train of reasoning in my head I naturally looked about in Mortimer Tregennis's room to find some remains of this substance. The obvious place to look was the talc shield or smoke guard of the lamp. There, sure enough, I perceived a number of flaky ashes, and round the edges a fringe of brownish powder, which had not yet been consumed. Half of this I took, as you saw, and I placed it in an envelope."

"Why half, Holmes?"

"It is not for me, my dear Watson, to stand in the way of the official police force. I leave them all the evidence which I found. The poison still remained upon the talc, had they the wit to find it. Now, Watson, we will light our lamp; we will, however, take the precaution to open our window to avoid the premature decease of two deserving members of society, and you will seat yourself near that open window in an armchair, unless, like a sensible man, you determine to have nothing to do with the affair. Oh, you will see it out, will you? I thought I knew my Watson. This chair I will place opposite yours, so that we may be the same distance from the poison, and face-to-face. The door we will leave ajar. Each is now in a position to watch the other and to bring the experiment to an end should the symptoms seem alarming. Is that all clear? Well, then, I take our powder—or what remains of it—from the envelope, and I lay it above the burning lamp. So! Now, Watson, let us sit down and await developments."

They were not long in coming. I had hardly settled in my chair before I was conscious of a thick, musky odour, subtle and nauseous. At the very first whiff of it my brain and my imagination were beyond all control. A thick, black cloud swirled before my eyes, and my mind told me that in this cloud, unseen as yet, but about to spring out upon my appalled senses, lurked all that was vaguely horrible, all that was monstrous and inconceivably wicked in the universe. Vague shapes swirled and swam amid the dark cloud bank, each a menace and a warning of something coming, the advent of some unspeakable dweller upon the threshold, whose very shadow would blast my soul. A freezing horror took possession of me. I felt that my hair was rising, that my eyes were protruding, that my mouth was opened, and my tongue like leather. The turmoil within my brain was such that something must surely snap. I tried to scream, and was vaguely aware of some hoarse croak which was my own voice, but distant and detached from myself. At the same moment, in some effort of escape, I broke through that cloud of despair, and had a glimpse of Holmes's face, white, rigid, and drawn with horror—the very look which I had seen upon the features of the dead. It was that vision which gave me an instant of sanity and of strength. I dashed from my chair, threw my arms round Holmes, and together we lurched through the door, and an instant afterwards had thrown ourselves down upon the grass plot and were lying side by side, conscious only of the glorious sunshine which was bursting its way through the hellish cloud of terror which had girt us in. Slowly it rose from our souls like the mists from a landscape, until peace and reason had returned, and we were sitting upon the grass, wiping our clammy foreheads, and looking with apprehension at each other to mark the last traces of that terrific experience which we had undergone.

"Upon my word, Watson!" said Holmes at last, with an unsteady voice; "I owe you both my thanks and an apology. It was an unjustifiable experiment even for oneself, and doubly so for a friend. I am really very sorry."

"You know," I answered, with some emotion, for I had never seen so much of Holmes's heart before, "that it is my greatest joy and privilege to help you."

He relapsed at once into the half-humourous, half-cynical vein which was his habitual attitude to those about him. "It would be superfluous to drive us mad, my dear Watson," said he. "A candid observer would certainly declare that we were so already before we embarked upon so wild an experiment. I confess that I never imagined that the effect could be so sudden and so severe." He dashed into the cottage, and reappearing with the burning lamp held at full arm's length, he threw it among a bank of brambles. "We must give the room a little time to clear. I take it, Watson, that you have no longer a shadow of a doubt as to how these tragedies were produced?"

"None whatever."

"But the cause remains as obscure as before. Come into the arbour here, and let us discuss it together. That villainous stuff seems still to linger round my throat. I think we must admit that all the evidence points to this man, Mortimer Tregennis, having been the criminal in the first tragedy, though he was the victim in the second one. We must remember, in the first place, that there is some story of a family quarrel, followed by a reconciliation. How bitter that quarrel may have been, or how hollow the reconciliation we cannot tell. When I think of Mortimer Tregennis, with the foxy face and the small, shrewd, beady eyes behind the spectacles, he is not a man whom I should judge to be of a particularly forgiving disposition. Well, in the next place, you will remember that this idea of someone moving in the garden, which took our attention for a moment from the real cause of the tragedy, emanated from him. He had a motive in misleading us. Finally, if he did not throw this substance into the fire at the moment of leaving the room, who did do so? The affair happened immediately after his departure. Had anyone else come in, the family would certainly have risen from the table. Besides, in peaceful Cornwall, visitors do not arrive after ten o'clock at night. We may take it, then, that all the evidence points to Mortimer Tregennis as the culprit."

"Then his own death was suicide!"

"Well, Watson, it is on the face of it a not impossible supposition. The man who had the guilt upon his soul of having brought such a fate upon his own family might well be driven by remorse to inflict it upon himself. There are, however, some cogent reasons against it. Fortunately, there is one man in England who knows all about it, and I have made arrangements by which we shall hear the facts this afternoon from his own lips. Ah! he is a little before his time. Perhaps you would kindly step this way, Dr. Leon Sterndale. We have been conducting a chemical experiment indoors which has left our little room hardly fit for the reception of so distinguished a visitor."

I had heard the click of the garden gate, and now the majestic figure of the great African explorer appeared upon the path. He turned in some surprise towards the rustic arbour in which we sat.

"You sent for me, Mr. Holmes. I had your note about an hour ago, and I have come, though I really do not know why I should obey your summons."

"Perhaps we can clear the point up before we separate," said Holmes. "Meanwhile, I am much obliged to you for your courteous acquiescence. You will excuse this informal reception in the open air, but my friend Watson and I have nearly furnished an additional chapter to what the papers call the 'Cornish Horror,' and we prefer a clear atmosphere for the present. Perhaps, since the matters which we have to discuss will affect you personally in a very intimate fashion, it is as well that we should talk where there can be no eavesdropping."

The explorer took his cigar from his lips and gazed sternly at my companion.

"I am at a loss to know, sir," he said, "what you can have to speak about which affects me personally in a very intimate fashion."

"The killing of Mortimer Tregennis," said Holmes.

For a moment I wished that I were armed. Sterndale's fierce face turned to a dusky red, his eyes glared, and the knotted, passionate veins started out in his forehead, while he sprang forward with clenched hands towards my companion. Then he stopped, and with a violent effort he resumed a cold, rigid calmness which was, perhaps, more suggestive of danger than his hotheaded outburst.

"I have lived so long among savages and beyond the law," said he, "that I have got into the way of being a law to myself. You would do well, Mr. Holmes, not to forget it, for I have no desire to do you an injury."

"Nor have I any desire to do you an injury, Dr. Sterndale. Surely the clearest proof of it is that, knowing what I know, I have sent for you and not for the police."

Sterndale sat down with a gasp, overawed for, perhaps, the first time in his adventurous life. There was a calm assurance of power in Holmes's manner which could not be withstood. Our visitor stammered for a moment, his great hands opening and shutting in his agitation.

"What do you mean?" he asked, at last. "If this is bluff upon your part, Mr. Holmes, you have chosen a bad man for your experiment. Let us have no more beating about the bush. What *do* you mean?"

"I will tell you," said Holmes, "and the reason why I tell you is that

I hope frankness may beget frankness. What my next step may be will depend entirely upon the nature of your own defence."

"My defence?"

"Yes, sir."

"My defence against what?"

"Against the charge of killing Mortimer Tregennis."

Sterndale mopped his forehead with his handkerchief. "Upon my word, you are getting on," said he. "Do all your successes depend upon this prodigious power of bluff?"

"The bluff," said Holmes, sternly, "is upon your side, Dr. Leon Sterndale, and not upon mine. As a proof I will tell you some of the facts upon which my conclusions are based. Of your return from Plymouth, allowing much of your property to go on to Africa, I will say nothing save that it first informed me that you were one of the factors which had to be taken into account in reconstructing this drama——"

"I came back——"

"I have heard your reasons and regard them as unconvincing and inadequate. We will pass that. You came down here to ask me whom I suspected. I refused to answer you. You then went to the vicarage, waited outside it for some time, and finally returned to your cottage."

"How do you know that?"

"I followed you."

"I saw no one."

"That is what you may expect to see when I follow you. You spent a restless night at your cottage, and you formed certain plans, which in the early morning you proceeded to put into execution. Leaving your door just as day was breaking, you filled your pocket with some reddish gravel that was lying heaped beside your gate." Sterndale gave a violent start and looked at Holmes in amazement.

"You then walked swiftly for the mile which separated you from the vicarage. You were wearing, I may remark, the same pair of ribbed tennis shoes which are at the present moment upon your feet. At the vicarage you passed through the orchard and the side hedge, coming out under the window of the lodger Tregennis. It was now daylight, but the household was not yet stirring. You drew some of the gravel from your pocket, and you threw it up at the window above you."

Sterndale sprang to his feet.

"I believe that you are the devil himself!" he cried.

Holmes smiled at the compliment. "It took two, or possibly three, handfuls before the lodger came to the window. You beckoned him to come down. He dressed hurriedly and descended to his sitting room. You entered by the window. There was an interview—a short one—during which you walked up and down the room. Then you passed out and closed the window, standing on the lawn outside smoking a cigar and watching what occurred. Finally, after the death of Tregennis, you withdrew as you had come. Now, Dr. Sterndale, how do you justify such conduct, and what were the motives for your actions? If you prevaricate or trifle with me, I give you my assurance that the matter will pass out of my hands forever."

Our visitor's face had turned ashen grey as he listened to the words of his accuser. Now he sat for some time in thought with his face sunk in his hands. Then with a sudden impulsive gesture he plucked a photograph from his breast pocket and threw it on the rustic table before us.

"That is why I have done it," said he.

It showed the bust and face of a very beautiful woman. Holmes stooped over it.

"Brenda Tregennis," said he.

"Yes, Brenda Tregennis," repeated our visitor. "For years I have loved her. For years she has loved me. There is the secret of that Cornish seclusion which people have marvelled at. It has brought me close to the one thing on earth that was dear to me. I could not marry her, for I have a wife who has left me for years and yet whom, by the deplorable laws of England, I could not divorce. For years Brenda waited. For years I waited. And this is what we have waited for." A terrible sob shook his great frame, and he clutched his throat under his brindled beard. Then with an effort he mastered himself and spoke on.

"The vicar knew. He was in our confidence. He would tell you that she was an angel upon earth. That was why he telegraphed to me and I returned. What was my baggage or Africa to me when I learned that such a fate had come upon my darling? There you have the missing clue to my action, Mr. Holmes."

"Proceed," said my friend.

Dr. Sterndale drew from his pocket a paper packet and laid it upon the table. On the outside was written, "*Radix pedis diaboli*," with a red poison label beneath it. He pushed it towards me. "I understand that you are a doctor, sir. Have you ever heard of this preparation?"

"Devil's-foot root! No, I have never heard of it."

"It is no reflection upon your professional knowledge," said he, "for I believe that, save for one sample in a laboratory at Buda, there is no other specimen in Europe. It has not yet found its way either into the pharmacopœia or into the literature of toxicology. The root is shaped like a foot, half human, half goat-like; hence the fanciful name given by a botanical missionary. It is used as an ordeal poison by the medicine men in certain districts of West Africa, and is kept as a secret among them. This particular specimen I obtained under very extraordinary circumstances in the Ubanghi country." He opened the paper as he spoke, and disclosed a heap of reddish-brown, snuff-like powder.

"Well, sir?" asked Holmes sternly.

"I am about to tell you, Mr. Holmes, all that actually occurred, for you already know so much that it is clearly to my interest that you should know all. I have already explained the relationship in which I stood to the Tregennis family. For the sake of the sister I was friendly with the brothers. There was a family quarrel about money which estranged this man Mortimer, but it was supposed to be made up, and I afterwards met him as I did the others. He was a sly, subtle, scheming man, and several things arose which gave me a suspicion of him, but I had no cause for any positive quarrel.

"One day, only a couple of weeks ago, he came down to my cottage and I showed him some of my African curiosities. Among other things I exhibited this powder, and I told him of its strange properties, how it stimulates those brain centres which control the emotion of fear, and how either madness or death is the fate of the unhappy native who is subjected to the ordeal by the priest of his tribe. I told him also how powerless European science would be to detect it. How he took it I cannot say, for I never left the room, but there is no doubt that it was then, while I was opening cabinets and stooping to boxes, that he managed to abstract some of the devil's-foot root. I well remember how he plied me with questions as to the amount and the time that was needed for its effect, but I little dreamed that he could have a personal reason for asking.

"I thought no more of the matter until the vicar's telegram reached me at Plymouth. This villain had thought that I would be at sea before the news could reach me, and that I should be lost for years in Africa. But I returned at once. Of course, I could not listen to the details without feeling assured that my poison had been used. I came round to see you on the chance that some other explanation had suggested itself to you. But there could be none. I was convinced that Mortimer Tregennis was the murderer; that for the sake of money, and with the idea, perhaps, that if the other members of his family were all insane he would be the sole guardian of their joint property, he had used the devil's-foot powder upon them, driven two of them out of their senses, and killed his sister Brenda, the one human being whom I have ever loved or who has ever loved me. There was his crime; what was to be his punishment?

"Should I appeal to the law? Where were my proofs? I knew that the facts were true, but could I help to make a jury of countrymen believe so fantastic a story? I might or I might not. But I could not afford to fail. My soul cried out for revenge. I have said to you once before, Mr. Holmes, that I have spent much of my life outside the law, and that I have come at last to be a law to myself. So it was now. I determined that the fate which he had given to others should be shared by himself. Either that or I would do justice upon him with my own hand. In all England there can be no man who sets less value upon his own life than I do at the present moment.

"Now I have told you all. You have yourself supplied the rest. I did, as you say, after a restless night, set off early from my cottage. I foresaw the difficulty of arousing him, so I gathered some gravel from the pile which you have mentioned, and I used it to throw up to his window. He came down and admitted me through the window of the sitting room. I laid his offence before him. I told him that I had come both as judge and executioner. The wretch sank into a chair paralysed at the sight of my revolver. I lit the lamp, put the powder above it, and stood outside the window, ready to carry out my threat to shoot him should he try to leave the room. In five minutes he died. My God! how he died! But my heart was flint, for he endured nothing which my innocent darling had not felt before him. There is my story, Mr. Holmes. Perhaps, if you loved a woman, you would have done as much yourself. At any rate, I am in your hands. You can take what steps you like. As I have already said, there is no man living who can fear death less than I do."

Holmes sat for some little time in silence.

"What were your plans?" he asked, at last.

"I had intended to bury myself in Central Africa. My work there is but half finished."

"Go and do the other half," said Holmes. "I, at least, am not prepared to prevent you."

Dr. Sterndale raised his giant figure, bowed gravely, and walked from the arbour. Holmes lit his pipe and handed me his pouch.

"Some fumes which are not poisonous would be a welcome change," said he. "I think you must agree, Watson, that it is not a case in which we are called upon to interfere. Our investigation has been independent, and our action shall be so also. You would not denounce the man?"

"Certainly not," I answered.

"I have never loved, Watson, but if I did and if the woman I loved had met such an end, I might act even as our lawless lion hunter has done. Who knows? Well, Watson, I will not offend your intelligence by explaining what is obvious. The gravel upon the windowsill was, of course, the starting point of my research. It was unlike anything in the vicarage garden. Only when my attention had been drawn to Dr. Sterndale and his cottage did I find its counterpart. The lamp shining in broad daylight and the remains of powder upon the shield were successive links in a fairly obvious chain. And now, my dear Watson, I think we may dismiss the matter from our mind, and go back with a clear conscience to the study of those Chaldean roots which are surely to be traced in the Cornish branch of the great Celtic speech."

IV: The Adventure of the Red Circle

I

"WELL, MRS. WARREN, I cannot see that you have any particular cause for uneasiness, nor do I understand why I, whose time is of some value, should interfere in the matter. I really have other things to engage me." So spoke Sherlock Holmes and turned back to the great scrapbook in which he was arranging and indexing some of his recent material.

But the landlady had the pertinacity, and also the cunning, of her sex. She held her ground firmly.

"You arranged an affair for a lodger of mine last year," she said— "Mr. Fairdale Hobbs."

"Ah, yes—a simple matter."

"But he would never cease talking of it—your kindness, sir, and the way in which you brought light into the darkness. I remembered his words when I was in doubt and darkness myself. I know you could if you only would."

Holmes was accessible upon the side of flattery, and also, to do him justice, upon the side of kindliness. The two forces made him lay down his gum brush with a sigh of resignation and push back his chair.

"Well, well, Mrs. Warren, let us hear about it, then. You don't object to tobacco, I take it? Thank you, Watson—the matches! You are uneasy, as I understand, because your new lodger remains in his rooms and you cannot see him. Why, bless you, Mrs. Warren, if I were your lodger you often would not see me for weeks on end."

"No doubt, sir; but this is different. It frightens me, Mr. Holmes. I can't sleep for fright. To hear his quick step moving here and moving there from early morning to late at night, and yet never to catch so much as a glimpse of him—it's more than I can stand. My husband is as nervous over it as I am, but he is out at his work all day, while I get no rest from it. What is he hiding for? What has he done? Except for the girl, I am all alone in the house with him, and it's more than my nerves can stand."

Holmes leaned forward and laid his long, thin fingers upon the woman's shoulder. He had an almost hypnotic power of soothing when he wished. The scared look faded from her eyes, and her agitated features smoothed into their usual commonplace. She sat down in the chair which he had indicated. "If I take it up I must understand every detail," said he. "Take time to consider. The smallest point may be the most essential. You say that the man came ten days ago, and paid you for a fortnight's board and lodging?"

"He asked my terms, sir. I said fifty shillings a week. There is a small sitting room and bedroom, and all complete, at the top of the house."

"Well?"

"He said, 'I'll pay you five pounds a week if I can have it on my own terms.' I'm a poor woman, sir, and Mr. Warren earns little, and the money meant much to me. He took out a ten-pound note, and he held it out to me then and there. 'You can have the same every fortnight for a long time to come if you keep the terms,' he said. 'If not, I'll have no more to do with you.' "

"What were the terms?"

"Well, sir, they were that he was to have a key of the house. That was all right. Lodgers often have them. Also, that he was to be left entirely to himself, and never, upon any excuse, to be disturbed."

"Nothing wonderful in that, surely?"

"Not in reason, sir. But this is out of all reason. He has been there for ten days, and neither Mr. Warren, nor I, nor the girl has once set eyes upon him. We can hear that quick step of his pacing up and down, up and down, night, morning, and noon; but except on that first night he has never once gone out of the house."

"Oh, he went out the first night, did he?"

"Yes, sir, and returned very late—after we were all in bed. He told me after he had taken the rooms that he would do so, and asked me not to bar the door. I heard him come up the stair after midnight."

"But his meals?"

"It was his particular direction that we should always, when he rang, leave his meal upon a chair, outside his door. Then he rings again when he has finished, and we take it down from the same chair. If he wants anything else he prints it on a slip of paper and leaves it."

"Prints it?"

"Yes, sir; prints it in pencil. Just the word, nothing more. Here's one I brought to show you—SOAP. Here's another—MATCH. This is one he left the first morning—DAILY GAZETTE. I leave that paper with his breakfast every morning."

"Dear me, Watson," said Holmes, staring with great curiosity at the slips of foolscap which the landlady had handed to him, "this is certainly a little unusual. Seclusion I can understand; but why print? Printing is a clumsy process. Why not write? What would it suggest, Watson?"

"That he desired to conceal his handwriting."

"But why? What can it matter to him that his landlady should have a word of his writing? Still, it may be as you say. Then, again, why such laconic messages?"

"I cannot imagine."

"It opens a pleasing field for intelligent speculation. The words are written with a broad-point, violet-tinted pencil of a not unusual pattern. You will observe that the paper is torn away at the side here after the printing was done, so that the 'S' of 'SOAP' is partly gone. Suggestive, Watson, is it not?"

"Of caution?"

"Exactly. There was evidently some mark, some thumbprint, something which might give a clue to the person's identity. Now, Mrs. Warren, you say that the man was of middle size, dark, and bearded. What age would he be?"

"Youngish, sir—not over thirty."

"Well, can you give me no further indications?"

"He spoke good English, sir, and yet I thought he was a foreigner by his accent."

"And he was well dressed?"

"Very smartly dressed, sir—quite the gentleman. Dark clothes—nothing you would note."

"He gave no name?"

"No, sir."

"And has had no letters or callers?"

"None."

"But surely you or the girl enter his room of a morning?"

"No, sir; he looks after himself entirely."

"Dear me! that is certainly remarkable. What about his luggage?"

"He had one big brown bag with him—nothing else."

"Well, we don't seem to have much material to help us. Do you say nothing has come out of that room—absolutely nothing?"

The landlady drew an envelope from her bag; from it she shook out two burnt matches and a cigarette end upon the table.

"They were on his tray this morning. I brought them because I had heard that you can read great things out of small ones."

Holmes shrugged his shoulders.

"There is nothing here," said he. "The matches have, of course, been used to light cigarettes. That is obvious from the shortness of the burnt end. Half the match is consumed in lighting a pipe or cigar. But, dear me! this cigarette stub is certainly remarkable. The gentleman was bearded and moustached, you say?"

"Yes, sir."

"I don't understand that. I should say that only a clean-shaven man could have smoked this. Why, Watson, even your modest moustache would have been singed."

"A holder?" I suggested.

"No, no; the end is matted. I suppose there could not be two people in your rooms, Mrs. Warren?"

"No, sir. He eats so little that I often wonder it can keep life in one."

"Well, I think we must wait for a little more material. After all, you have nothing to complain of. You have received your rent, and he is not a troublesome lodger, though he is certainly an unusual one. He pays you well, and if he chooses to lie concealed it is no direct business of yours. We have no excuse for an intrusion upon his privacy until we have some reason to think that there is a guilty reason for it. I've taken up the matter, and I won't lose sight of it. Report to me if anything fresh occurs, and rely upon my assistance if it should be needed."

"There are certainly some points of interest in this case, Watson," he remarked, when the landlady had left us. "It may, of course, be trivial—individual eccentricity; or it may be very much deeper than appears on the surface. The first thing that strikes one is the obvious possibility that the person now in the rooms may be entirely different from the one who engaged them."

"Why should you think so?"

"Well, apart from this cigarette end, was it not suggestive that the only time the lodger went out was immediately after his taking the rooms? He came back—or someone came back—when all witnesses were out of the way. We have no proof that the person who came back was the person who went out. Then, again, the man who took the rooms spoke English well. This other, however, prints 'match' when it should have been 'matches.' I can imagine that the word was taken out of a dictionary, which would give the noun but not the plural. The laconic style may be to conceal the absence of knowledge of English. Yes, Watson, there are good reasons to suspect that there has been a substitution of lodgers."

"But for what possible end?"

"Ah! there lies our problem. There is one rather obvious line of investigation." He took down the great book in which, day by day, he filed the agony columns of the various London journals. "Dear me!" said he, turning over the pages, "what a chorus of groans, cries, and bleatings! What a ragbag of singular happenings! But surely the most valuable hunting ground that ever was given to a student of the unusual! This person is alone, and cannot be approached by letter without a breach of that absolute secrecy which is desired. How is any news or any message to reach him from without? Obviously by advertisement through a newspaper. There seems no other way, and fortunately we need concern ourselves with the one paper only. Here are the *Daily Gazette* extracts of the last fortnight. 'Lady with a black boa at Prince's Skating Club'—that we may pass. 'Surely Jimmy will not break his mother's heart'—that appears to be irrelevant. 'If the lady who fainted in the Brixton bus'—she does not interest me. 'Every day my heart longs'——Bleat, Watson—unmitigated bleat! Ah! this is a little more possible. Listen to this: 'Be patient. Will find some sure means of communication. Meanwhile, this column.—G' That is two days after Mrs. Warren's lodger arrived. It sounds plausible, does it not? The mysterious one could understand English, even if he could not print it. Let us see if we can pick up the trace again. Yes, here we are—three days later. 'Am making successful arrangements. Patience and prudence. The clouds will pass.—G' Nothing for a week after that. Then comes something more definite: 'The path is clearing. If I find chance signal message remember code agreed—one A, two B, and so on. You will hear soon.—G' That was in yesterday's paper, and there is nothing in today's. It's all very appropriate to Mrs. Warren's lodger. If we wait a little, Watson, I don't doubt that the affair will grow more intelligible."

So it proved; for in the morning I found my friend standing on the hearthrug with his back to the fire, and a smile of complete satisfaction upon his face.

"How's this, Watson?" he cried, picking up the paper from the table. " 'High red house with white stone facings. Third floor. Second window left. After dusk.—G' That is definite enough. I think after breakfast we must make a little reconnaissance of Mrs. Warren's neighbourhood. Ah, Mrs. Warren! what news do you bring us this morning?"

Our client had suddenly burst into the room with an explosive energy which told of some new and momentous development.

"It's a police matter, Mr. Holmes!" she cried. "I'll have no more of it! He shall pack out of that with his baggage. I would have gone straight up and told him so, only I thought it was but fair to you to take your opinion first. But I'm at the end of my patience, and when it comes to knocking my old man about—"

"Knocking Mr. Warren about?"

"Using him roughly, anyway!"

"But who used him roughly?"

"Ah! that's what we want to know! It was this morning, sir. Mr. Warren is a timekeeper at Morton & Waylight's, in Tottenham Court Road. He has to be out of the house before seven. Well, this morning he had not got ten paces down the road when two men came up behind him, threw a coat over his head, and bundled him into a cab that was beside the kerb. They drove him an hour, and then opened the door and shot him out. He lay in the roadway so shaken in his wits that he never saw what became of the cab. When he picked himself up he found he was on Hampstead Heath; so he took a bus home, and there he lies now on the sofa, while I came straight round to tell you what had happened."

"Most interesting," said Holmes. "Did he observe the appearance of these men—did he hear them talk?"

"No; he is clean dazed. He just knows that he was lifted up as if by magic and dropped as if by magic. Two at least were in it, and maybe three."

"And you connect this attack with your lodger?"

"Well, we've lived there fifteen years and no such happenings ever came before. I've had enough of him. Money's not everything. I'll have him out of my house before the day is done."

"Wait a bit, Mrs. Warren. Do nothing rash. I begin to think that this affair may be very much more important than appeared at first sight. It is clear now that some danger is threatening your lodger. It is equally clear that his enemies, lying in wait for him near your door, mistook your husband for him in the foggy morning light. On discovering their mistake they released him. What they would have done had it not been a mistake, we can only conjecture."

"Well, what am I to do, Mr. Holmes?"

"I have a great fancy to see this lodger of yours, Mrs. Warren."

"I don't see how that is to be managed, unless you break in the door. I always hear him unlock it as I go down the stair after I leave the tray."

"He has to take the tray in. Surely we could conceal ourselves and see him do it."

The landlady thought for a moment.

"Well, sir, there's the box room opposite. I could arrange a looking glass, maybe, and if you were behind the door——"

"Excellent!" said Holmes. "When does he lunch?"

"About one, sir."

"Then Dr. Watson and I will come round in time. For the present, Mrs. Warren, good-bye."

At half-past twelve we found ourselves upon the steps of Mrs. Warren's house—a high, thin, yellow-brick edifice in Great Orme Street, a narrow thoroughfare at the northeast side of the British Museum. Standing as it does near the corner of the street, it commands a view down Howe Street, with its more pretentious houses. Holmes pointed with a chuckle to one of these, a row of residential flats, which projected so that they could not fail to catch the eye.

"See, Watson!" said he. " 'High red house with stone facings.' There is the signal station all right. We know the place, and we know the code; so surely our task should be simple. There's a 'To Let' card in that window. It is evidently an empty flat to which the confederate has access. Well, Mrs. Warren, what now?"

"I have it all ready for you. If you will both come up and leave your boots below on the landing, I'll put you there now."

It was an excellent hiding place which she had arranged. The mirror was so placed that, seated in the dark, we could very plainly see the door opposite. We had hardly settled down in it, and Mrs. Warren left us, when a distant tinkle announced that our mysterious neighbour had rung. Presently the landlady appeared with the tray, laid it down upon a chair beside the closed door, and then, treading heavily, departed. Crouching together in the angle of the door, we kept our eyes fixed upon the mirror. Suddenly, as the landlady's footsteps died away, there was the creak of a turning key, the handle revolved, and two thin hands darted out and lifted the tray from the chair. An instant later it was hurriedly replaced, and I caught a glimpse of a dark, beautiful, horrified face glaring at the narrow opening of the box room. Then the door crashed to, the key turned once more, and all was silence. Holmes twitched my sleeve, and together we stole down the stair.

"I will call again in the evening," said he to the expectant landlady. "I think, Watson, we can discuss this business better in our own quarters."

"My surmise, as you saw, proved to be correct," said he, speaking from the depths of his easy chair. "There has been a substitution of lodgers. What I did not foresee is that we should find a woman, and no ordinary woman, Watson."

"She saw us."

"Well, she saw something to alarm her. That is certain. The general sequence of events is pretty clear, is it not? A couple seek refuge in London from a very terrible and instant danger. The measure of that danger is the rigour of their precautions. The man, who has some work which he must do, desires to leave the woman in absolute safety while he does it. It is not an easy problem, but he solved it in an original fashion, and so effectively that her presence was not even known to the landlady who supplies her with food. The printed messages, as is now evident, were to prevent her sex being discovered by her writing. The man cannot come near the woman, or he will guide their enemies to her. Since he cannot communicate with her direct, he has recourse to the agony column of a paper. So far all is clear."

"But what is at the root of it?"

"Ah, yes, Watson—severely practical, as usual! What is at the root of it all? Mrs. Warren's whimsical problem enlarges somewhat and assumes a more sinister aspect as we proceed. This much we can say: that it is no ordinary love escapade. You saw the woman's face at the sign of danger. We have heard, too, of the attack upon the landlord, which was undoubtedly meant for the lodger. These alarms, and the desperate need for secrecy, argue that the matter is one of life or death. The attack upon Mr. Warren further shows that the enemy, whoever they are, are themselves not aware of the substitution of the female lodger for the male. It is very curious and complex, Watson."

"Why should you go further in it? What have you to gain from it?"

"What, indeed? It is Art for Art's sake, Watson. I suppose when you doctored you found yourself studying cases without thought of a fee?"

"For my education, Holmes."

"Education never ends, Watson. It is a series of lessons, with the greatest for the last. This is an instructive case. There is neither money nor credit in it, and yet one would wish to tidy it up. When dusk comes we should find ourselves one stage advanced in our investigation."

When we returned to Mrs. Warren's rooms, the gloom of a London winter evening had thickened into one grey curtain, a dead monotone of colour, broken only by the sharp yellow squares of the windows and the blurred haloes of the gas lamps. As we peered from the darkened sitting room of the lodging house, one more dim light glimmered high up through the obscurity.

"Someone is moving in that room," said Holmes in a whisper, his gaunt and eager face thrust forward to the windowpane. "Yes, I can see his shadow. There he is again! He has a candle in his hand. Now he is peering across. He wants to be sure that she is on the lookout. Now he begins to flash. Take the message also, Watson, that we may check each other. A single flash—that is 'A,' surely. Now, then. How many did you make it? Twenty? So did I. That should mean 'T.' A T—that's intelligible enough! Another 'T.' Surely this is the beginning of a second word. Now, then—TENTA. Dead stop. That can't be all, Watson? 'ATTENTA' gives no sense. Nor is it any better as three words—'AT TEN TA,' unless 'T.A.' are a person's initials. There it goes again! What's that? ATTE—why, it is the same message over again. Curious, Watson, very curious! Now he is off once more! AT— why, he is repeating it for the third time. 'ATTENTA' three times! How often will he repeat it? No, that seems to be the finish. He has withdrawn from the window. What do you make of it, Watson?"

"A cipher message, Holmes."

My companion gave a sudden chuckle of comprehension. "And not a very obscure cipher, Watson," said he. "Why, of course, it is Italian! The 'A' means that it is addressed to a woman. 'Beware! Beware! Beware!' How's that, Watson?"

"I believe you have hit it."

"Not a doubt of it. It is a very urgent message, thrice repeated to make it more so. But beware of what? Wait a bit; he is coming to the window once more."

Again we saw the dim silhouette of a crouching man and the whisk of the small flame across the window, as the signals were renewed. They came more rapidly than before—so rapid that it was hard to follow them.

" 'PERICOLO'—*'Pericolo'*—Eh, what's that, Watson? Danger, isn't it? Yes, by Jove! it's a danger signal. There he goes again! 'PERI—' Halloa, what on earth——"

The light had suddenly gone out, the glimmering square of window had disappeared, and the third floor formed a dark band round the lofty building, with its tiers of shining casements. That last warning cry had been suddenly cut short. How, and by whom? The same thought occurred on the instant to us both. Holmes sprang up from where he crouched by the window.

"This is serious, Watson," he cried. "There is some devilry going forward! Why should such a message stop in such a way? I should put Scotland Yard in touch with this business—and yet, it is too pressing for us to leave."

"Shall I go for the police?"

"We must define the situation a little more clearly. It may bear some more innocent interpretation. Come, Watson, let us go across ourselves and see what we can make of it."

As WE WALKED rapidly down Howe Street I glanced back at the building which we had left. There, dimly outlined at the top window, I could see the shadow of a head, a woman's head, gazing tensely, rigidly, out into the night, waiting with breathless suspense for the renewal of that interrupted message. At the doorway of the Howe Street flats a man, muffled in a cravat and greatcoat, was leaning against the railing. He started as the hall light fell upon our faces.

"Holmes!" he cried.

"Why, Gregson!" said my companion, as he shook hands with the Scotland Yard detective. "Journeys end with lovers' meetings. What brings you here?"

"The same reasons that bring you, I expect," said Gregson. "How you got onto it I can't imagine."

"Different threads, but leading up to the same tangle. I've been taking the signals."

"Signals?"

"Yes, from that window. They broke off in the middle. We came over to see the reason. But since it is safe in your hands I see no object in continuing the business."

"Wait a bit!" cried Gregson, eagerly. "I'll do you this justice, Mr. Holmes, that I was never in a case yet that I didn't feel stronger for having you on my side. There's only the one exit to these flats, so we have him safe."

"Who is he?"

"Well, well, we score over you for once, Mr. Holmes. You must give us best this time." He struck his stick sharply upon the ground, on which a cabman, his whip in his hand, sauntered over from a four-wheeler which stood on the far side of the street. "May I introduce you to Mr. Sherlock Holmes?" he said to the cabman. "This is Mr. Leverton, of Pinkerton's American Agency."

"The hero of the Long Island cave mystery?" said Holmes. "Sir, I am pleased to meet you."

The American, a quiet, businesslike young man, with a clean-shaven, hatchet face, flushed up at the words of commendation. "I am on the trail of my life now, Mr. Holmes," said he. "If I can get Gorgiano——"

"What! Gorgiano of the Red Circle?"

"Oh, he has a European fame, has he? Well, we've learned all about him in America. We *know* he is at the bottom of fifty murders, and yet we have nothing positive we can take him on. I tracked him over from New York, and I've been close to him for a week in London, waiting some excuse to get my hand on his collar. Mr. Gregson and I ran him to ground in that big tenement house, and there's only the one door, so he can't slip us. There's three folk come out since he went in, but I'll swear he wasn't one of them."

"Mr. Holmes talks of signals," said Gregson. "I expect, as usual, he knows a good deal that we don't."

In a few clear words Holmes explained the situation as it had appeared to us. The American struck his hands together with vexation.

"He's onto us!" he cried.

"Why do you think so?"

"Well, it figures out that way, does it not? Here he is, sending out messages to an accomplice—there are several of his gang in London. Then suddenly, just as by your own account he was telling them that there was danger, he broke short off. What could it mean except that from the window he had suddenly either caught sight of us in the street, or in some way come to understand how close the danger was, and that he must act right away, if he was to avoid it? What do you suggest, Mr. Holmes?"

"That we go up at once and see for ourselves."

"But we have no warrant for his arrest."

"He is in unoccupied premises under suspicious circumstances," said Gregson. "That is good enough for the moment. When we have him by the heels we can see if New York can't help us to keep him. I'll take the responsibility of arresting him now."

Our official detectives may blunder in the matter of intelligence, but never in that of courage. Gregson climbed the stair to arrest this desperate murderer with the same absolutely quiet and businesslike bearing with which he would have ascended the official staircase of Scotland Yard. The Pinkerton man had tried to push past him, but Gregson had firmly elbowed him back. London dangers were the privilege of the London force.

The door of the left-hand flat upon the third landing was standing ajar. Gregson pushed it open. Within, all was absolute silence and darkness. I struck a match, and lit the detective's lantern. As I did so, and as the flicker steadied into a flame, we all gave a gasp of surprise. On the deal boards of the carpetless floor there was outlined a fresh track of blood. The red steps pointed towards us, and led away from an inner room, the door of which was closed. Gregson flung it open and held his light full blaze in front of him, whilst we all peered eagerly over his shoulders.

In the middle of the floor of the empty room was huddled the figure of an enormous man, his clean-shaven, swarthy face grotesquely horrible in its contortion, and his head encircled by a ghastly crimson halo of blood, lying in a broad wet circle upon the white woodwork. His knees were drawn up, his hands thrown out in agony, and from the centre of his broad, brown, upturned throat there projected the white haft of a knife driven blade-deep into his body. Giant as he was, the man must have gone down like a pole-axed ox before that terrific blow. Beside his right hand a most formidable horn-handled, two-edged dagger lay upon the floor, and near it a black kid glove.

"By George! it's Black Gorgiano himself!" cried the American detective. "Someone has got ahead of us this time."

"Here is the candle in the window, Mr. Holmes," said Gregson. "Why, whatever are you doing?"

Holmes had stepped across, had lit the candle, and was passing it backwards and forwards across the windowpanes. Then he peered into the darkness, blew the candle out, and threw it on the floor. "I rather think that will be helpful," said he. He came over and stood in deep thought while the two professionals were examining the body. "You say that three people came out from the flat while you were waiting downstairs," said he, at last. "Did you observe them closely?"

"Yes, I did."

"Was there a fellow about thirty, black-bearded, dark, of middle size?"

"Yes; he was the last to pass me."

"That is your man, I fancy. I can give you his description, and we have a very excellent outline of his footmark. That should be enough for you."

"Not much, Mr. Holmes, among the millions of London."

"Perhaps not. That is why I thought it best to summon this lady to your aid."

We all turned round at the words. There, framed in the doorway, was a tall and beautiful woman—the mysterious lodger of Blooms-bury. Slowly she advanced, her face pale and drawn with a frightful apprehension, her eyes fixed and staring, her terrified gaze riveted upon the dark figure on the floor.

"You have killed him!" she muttered. "Oh, *Dio mio*, you have killed him!" Then I heard a sudden sharp intake of her breath, and she sprang into the air with a cry of joy. Round and round the room she danced, her hands clapping, her dark eyes gleaming with delighted wonder, and a thousand pretty Italian exclamations pouring from her lips. It was terrible and amazing to see such a woman so convulsed with joy at such a sight. Suddenly she stopped and gazed at us all with a questioning stare.

"But you! You are police, are you not? You have killed Giuseppe Gorgiano. Is it not so?"

"We are police, madam."

She looked round into the shadows of the room.

"But where, then, is Gennaro?" she asked. "He is my husband, Gennaro Lucca. I am Emilia Lucca, and we are both from New York. Where is Gennaro? He called me this moment from this window, and I ran with all my speed."

"It was I who called," said Holmes.

"You! How could you call?"

"Your cipher was not difficult, madam. Your presence here was desirable. I know that I had only to flash '*Vieni*' and you would surely come."

The beautiful Italian looked with awe at my companion.

"I do not understand how you know these things," she said. "Giuseppe Gorgiano—how did he——" She paused, and then suddenly her face lit up with pride and delight. "Now I see it! My Gennaro! My splendid, beautiful Gennaro, who has guarded me safe from all harm, he did it, with his own strong hand he killed the monster! Oh, Gennaro, how wonderful you are! What woman could ever be worthy of such a man?"

"Well, Mrs. Lucca," said the prosaic Gregson, laying his hand upon the lady's sleeve with as little sentiment as if she were a Notting Hill hooligan, "I am not very clear yet who you are or what you are; but you've said enough to make it very clear that we shall want you at the Yard."

"You have killed him!" she muttered.
"Oh, Dio Mio, you have killed him!"

"One moment, Gregson," said Holmes. "I rather fancy that this lady may be as anxious to give us information as we can be to get it. You understand, madam, that your husband will be arrested and tried for the death of the man who lies before us? What you say may be used in evidence. But if you think that he has acted from motives which are not criminal, and which he would wish to have known, then you cannot serve him better than by telling us the whole story."

"Now that Gorgiano is dead we fear nothing," said the lady. "He was a devil and a monster, and there can be no judge in the world who would punish my husband for having killed him."

"In that case," said Holmes, "my suggestion is that we lock this door, leave things as we found them, go with this lady to her room, and form our opinion after we have heard what it is that she has to say to us."

Half an hour later we were seated, all four, in the small sitting room of Signora Lucca, listening to her remarkable narrative of those sinister events, the ending of which we had chanced to witness. She spoke in rapid and fluent but very unconventional English, which, for the sake of clearness, I will make grammatical.

"I was born in Posilippo, near Naples," said she, "and was the daughter of Augusto Barelli, who was the chief lawyer and once the deputy of that part. Gennaro was in my father's employment, and I came to love him, as any woman must. He had neither money nor position—nothing but his beauty and strength and energy—so my father forbade the match. We fled together, were married at Bari, and sold my jewels to gain the money which would take us to America. This was four years ago, and we have been in New York ever since.

"Fortune was very good to us at first. Gennaro was able to do a service to an Italian gentleman—he saved him from some ruffians in the place called the Bowery, and so made a powerful friend. His name was Tito Castalotte, and he was the senior partner of the great firm of Castalotte & Zamba, who are the chief fruit importers of New York. Signor Zamba is an invalid, and our new friend Castalotte has all power within the firm, which employs more than three hundred men. He took my husband into his employment, made him head of a department, and showed his good will towards him in every way. Signor Castalotte was a bachelor, and I believe that he felt as if Gennaro was his son, and both my husband and I loved him as if he were our father. We had taken and furnished a little house in Brooklyn, and our whole future seemed assured, when that black cloud appeared which was soon to overspread our sky.

"One night, when Gennaro returned from his work, he brought a fellow countryman back with him. His name was Gorgiano, and he had come also from Posilippo. He was a huge man, as you can testify, for you have looked upon his corpse. Not only was his body that of a giant, but everything about him was grotesque, gigantic, and terrifying. His voice was like thunder in our little house. There was scarce room for the whirl of his great arms as he talked. His thoughts, his emotions, his passions, all were exaggerated and monstrous. He talked, or rather roared, with such energy that others could but sit and listen, cowed with the mighty stream of words. His eyes blazed at you and held you at his mercy. He was a terrible and wonderful man. I thank God that he is dead!

"He came again and again. Yet I was aware that Gennaro was no more happy than I was in his presence. My poor husband would sit pale and listless, listening to the endless raving upon politics and upon social questions which made up our visitor's conversation. Gennaro said nothing, but I who knew him so well could read in his face some emotion which I had never seen there before. At first I thought that it was dislike. And then, gradually, I understood that it was more than dislike. It was fear—a deep, secret, shrinking fear. That night— the night that I read his terror—I put my arms round him and I implored him by his love for me and by all that he held dear to hold nothing from me, and to tell me why this huge man overshadowed him so.

"He told me, and my own heart grew cold as ice as I listened. My poor Gennaro, in his wild and fiery days, when all the world seemed against him and his mind was driven half mad by the injustices of life, had joined a Neapolitan society, the Red Circle, which was allied to the old Carbonari. The oaths and secrets of this brotherhood were frightful; but once within its rule no escape was possible. When we had fled to America Gennaro thought that he had cast it all off forever. What was his horror one evening to meet in the streets the very man who had initiated him in Naples, the giant Gorgiano, a man who had earned the name of 'Death' in the south of Italy, for he was red to the elbow in murder! He had come to New York to avoid the Italian police, and he had already planted a branch of this dreadful society in his new home. All this Gennaro told me, and showed me a summons which he had received that very day, a red circle drawn upon the head of it, telling him that a lodge would be held upon a certain date, and that his presence at it was required and ordered.

"That was bad enough, but worse was to come. I had noticed for some time that when Gorgiano came to us, as he constantly did, in the evening, he spoke much to me; and even when his words were to my husband those terrible, glaring, wild-beast eyes of his were always turned upon me. One night his secret came out. I had awakened what he called 'love' within him—the love of a brute—a savage. Gennaro had not yet returned when he came. He pushed his way in, seized me in his mighty arms, hugged me in his bear's embrace, covered me with kisses, and implored me to come away with him. I was struggling and screaming when Gennaro entered and attacked him. He struck Gennaro senseless and fled from the house which he was never more to enter. It was a deadly enemy that we made that night.

"A few days later came the meeting. Gennaro returned from it with a face which told me that something dreadful had occurred. It was worse than we could have imagined possible. The funds of the society were raised by blackmailing rich Italians and threatening them with violence should they refuse the money. It seems that Castalotte, our dear friend and benefactor, had been approached. He had refused to yield to threats, and he had handed the notices to the police. It was resolved now that such an example should be made of him as would prevent any other victim from rebelling. At the meeting it was arranged that he and his house should be blown up with dynamite. There was a drawing of lots as to who should carry out the deed. Gennaro saw our enemy's cruel face smiling at him as he dipped his hand in the bag. No doubt it had been prearranged in some fashion, for it was the fatal disc with the red circle upon it, the mandate for murder, which lay upon his palm. He was to kill his best friend, or he was to expose himself and me to the vengeance of his comrades. It was part of their fiendish system to punish those whom they feared or hated by injuring not only their own persons, but those whom they loved, and it was the knowledge of this which hung as a terror over my poor Gennaro's head and drove him nearly crazy with apprehension.

"All that night we sat together, our arms round each other, each strengthening each for the troubles that lay before us. The very next evening had been fixed for the attempt. By midday my husband and I were on our way to London, but not before he had given our benefactor full warning of his danger, and had also left such information for the police as would safeguard his life for the future.

"The rest, gentlemen, you know for yourselves. We were sure that our enemies would be behind us like our own shadows. Gorgiano had his private reasons for vengeance, but in any case we knew how ruthless, cunning, and untiring he could be. Both Italy and America are full of stories of his dreadful powers. If ever they were exerted it would be now. My darling made use of the few clear days which our start had given us in arranging for a refuge for me in such a fashion that no possible danger could reach me. For his own part, he wished to be free that he might communicate both with the American and with the Italian police. I do not myself know where he lived, or how. All that I learned was through the columns of a newspaper. But once, as I looked through my window, I saw two Italians watching the house, and I understood that in some way Gorgiano had found out our retreat. Finally Gennaro told me, through the paper, that he would signal to me from a certain window, but when the signals came they were nothing but warnings, which were suddenly interrupted. It is very clear to me now that he knew Gorgiano to be close upon him, and that, thank God! he was ready for him when he came. And now, gentlemen, I would ask you whether we have anything to fear from the law, or whether any judge upon earth would condemn my Gennaro for what he has done?"

"Well, Mr. Gregson," said the American, looking across at the official, "I don't know what your British point of view may be, but I guess that in New York this lady's husband will receive a pretty general vote of thanks."

"She will have to come with me and see the chief," Gregson answered. "If what she says is corroborated, I do not think she or her husband has much to fear. But what I can't make head or tail of, Mr. Holmes, is how on earth *you* got yourself mixed up in the matter."

"Education, Gregson, education. Still seeking knowledge at the old university. Well, Watson, you have one more specimen of the tragic and grotesque to add to your collection. By the way, it is not eight o'clock, and a Wagner night at Covent Garden! If we hurry, we might be in time for the second act."

V: The Disappearance of Lady Frances Carfax

"BUT WHY TURKISH?" asked Mr. Sherlock Holmes, gazing fixedly at my boots. I was reclining in a cane-backed chair at the moment, and my protruded feet had attracted his ever-active attention.

"English," I answered in some surprise. "I got them at Latimer's, in Oxford Street."

Holmes smiled with an expression of weary patience.

"The bath!" he said; "the bath! Why the relaxing and expensive Turkish rather than the invigorating homemade article?"

"Because for the last few days I have been feeling rheumatic and old. A Turkish bath is what we call an alternative in medicine—a fresh starting point, a cleanser of the system.

"By the way, Holmes," I added, "I have no doubt the connection between my boots and a Turkish bath is a perfectly self-evident one to a logical mind, and yet I should be obliged to you if you would indicate it."

"The train of reasoning is not very obscure, Watson," said Holmes with a mischievous twinkle. "It belongs to the same elementary class of deduction which I should illustrate if I were to ask you who shared your cab in your drive this morning."

"I don't admit that a fresh illustration is an explanation," said I, with some asperity.

"Bravo, Watson! A very dignified and logical remonstrance. Let me see, what were the points? Take the last one first—the cab. You observe that you have some splashes on the left sleeve and shoulder of your coat. Had you sat in the centre of a hansom you would probably have had no splashes, and if you had they would certainly have been symmetrical. Therefore it is clear that you sat at the side.

Therefore it is equally clear that you had a companion."

"That is very evident."

"Absurdly commonplace, is it not?"

"But the boots and the bath?"

"Equally childish. You are in the habit of doing up your boots in a certain way. I see them on this occasion fastened with an elaborate double bow, which is not your usual method of tying them. You have, therefore, had them off. Who has tied them? A bootmaker—or the boy at the bath. It is unlikely that it is the bootmaker, since your boots are nearly new. Well, what remains? The bath. Absurd, is it not? But, for all that, the Turkish bath has served a purpose."

"What is that?"

"You say that you have had it because you need a change. Let me suggest that you take one. How would Lausanne do, my dear Watson—first-class tickets and all expenses paid on a princely scale?"

"Splendid! But why?"

Holmes leaned back in his armchair and took his notebook from his pocket.

"One of the most dangerous classes in the world," said he, "is the drifting and friendless woman. She is the most harmless, and often the most useful of mortals, but she is the inevitable inciter of crime in others. She is helpless. She is migratory. She has sufficient means to take her from country to country and from hotel to hotel. She is lost, as often as not, in a maze of obscure *pensions* and boarding-houses. She is a stray chicken in a world of foxes. When she is gobbled up she is hardly missed. I much fear that some evil has come to the Lady Frances Carfax."

I was relieved at this sudden descent from the general to the particular. Holmes consulted his notes.

"Lady Frances," he continued, "is the sole survivor of the direct family of the late Earl of Rufton. The estates went, as you may remember, in the male line. She was left with limited means, but with some very remarkable old Spanish jewellery of silver and curiously cut diamonds to which she was fondly attached—too attached, for she refused to leave them with her banker and always carried them about with her. A rather pathetic figure, the Lady Frances, a beautiful woman, still in fresh middle age, and yet, by a strange chance, the last derelict of what only twenty years ago was a goodly fleet."

"What has happened to her, then?"

"Ah, what has happened to the Lady Frances? Is she alive or dead? There is our problem. She is a lady of precise habits, and for four years it has been her invariable custom to write every second week to Miss Dobney, her old governess, who has long retired, and lives in Camberwell. It is this Miss Dobney who has consulted me. Nearly five weeks have passed without a word. The last letter was from the Hôtel National at Lausanne. Lady Frances seems to have left there and given no address. The family are anxious, and, as they are exceedingly wealthy, no sum will be spared if we can clear the matter up."

"Is Miss Dobney the only source of information? Surely she had other correspondents?"

"There is one correspondent who is a sure draw, Watson. That is the bank. Single ladies must live, and their passbooks are compressed diaries. She banks at Silvester's. I have glanced over her account. The last cheque but one paid her bill at Lausanne, but it was a large one and probably left her with cash in hand. Only one cheque has been drawn since."

"To whom, and where?"

"To Miss Marie Devine. There is nothing to show where the cheque was drawn. It was cashed at the Crédit Lyonnais at Montpellier less than three weeks ago. The sum was fifty pounds."

"And who is Miss Marie Devine?"

"That also I have been able to discover. Miss Marie Devine was the maid of Lady Frances Carfax. Why she should have paid her this cheque we have not yet determined. I have no doubt, however, that your researches will soon clear the matter up."

"*My* researches!"

"Hence the health-giving expedition to Lausanne. You know that I cannot possibly leave London while old Abrahams is in such mortal terror of his life. Besides, on general principles it is best that I should not leave the country. Scotland Yard feels lonely without me, and it causes an unhealthy excitement among the criminal classes. Go, then, my dear Watson, and if my humble counsel can ever be valued at so extravagant a rate as twopence a word, it waits your disposal night and day at the end of the continental wire."

Two days later found me at the National Hotel at Lausanne, where

I received every courtesy at the hands of M. Moser, the well-known manager. Lady Frances, as he informed me, had stayed there for several weeks. She had been much liked by all who met her. Her age was not more than forty. She was still handsome, and bore every sign of having in her youth been a very lovely woman. M. Moser knew nothing of any valuable jewellery, but it had been remarked by the servants that the heavy trunk in the lady's bedroom was always scrupulously locked. Marie Devine, the maid, was as popular as her mistress. She was actually engaged to one of the headwaiters in the hotel, and there was no difficulty in getting her address. It was 11 Rue de Trajan, Montpellier. All this I jotted down, and felt that Holmes himself could not have been more adroit in collecting his facts.

Only one corner still remained in the shadow. No light which I possessed could clear up the cause for the lady's sudden departure. She was very happy at Lausanne. There was every reason to believe that she intended to remain for the season in her luxurious rooms overlooking the lake. And yet she had left at a single day's notice, which involved her in the useless payment of a week's rent. Only Jules Vibart, the lover of the maid, had any suggestion to offer. He connected the sudden departure with the visit to the hotel a day or two before of a tall, dark, bearded man. *"Un sauvage—un véritable sauvage!"* cried Jules Vibart. The man had rooms somewhere in the town. He had been seen talking earnestly to Madame on the promenade by the lake. Then he had called. She had refused to see him. He was English, but of his name there was no record. Madame had left the place immediately afterwards. Jules Vibart, and, what was of more importance, Jules Vibart's sweetheart, thought that this call and this departure were cause and effect. Only one thing Jules could not discuss. That was the reason why Marie had left her mistress. Of that he could or would say nothing. If I wished to know, I must go to Montpellier and ask her.

So ended the first chapter of my inquiry. The second was devoted to the place which Lady Frances Carfax had sought when she left Lausanne. Concerning this there had been some secrecy, which confirmed the idea that she had gone with the intention of throwing someone off her track. Otherwise why should not her luggage have been openly labelled for Baden? Both she and it reached the Rhenish spa by some circuitous route. This much I gathered from the manager of Cook's local office. So to Baden I went, after dispatching to Holmes an account of all my proceedings, and receiving in reply a telegram of half-humorous commendation.

At Baden the track was not difficult to follow. Lady Frances had stayed at the Englischer Hof for a fortnight. Whilst there she had made the acquaintance of a Dr. Shlessinger and his wife, a missionary from South America. Like most lonely ladies, Lady Frances found her comfort and occupation in religion. Dr. Shlessinger's remarkable personality, his wholehearted devotion, and the fact that he was recovering from a disease contracted in the exercise of his apostolic duties, affected her deeply. She had helped Mrs. Shlessinger in the nursing of the convalescent saint. He spent his day, as the manager described it to me, upon a lounge chair on the veranda, with an attendant lady upon either side of him. He was preparing a map of the Holy Land, with special reference to the kingdom of the Midianites, upon which he was writing a monograph. Finally, having improved much in health, he and his wife had returned to London, and Lady Frances had started thither in their company.

This was just three weeks before, and the manager had heard nothing since. As to the maid, Marie, she had gone off some days beforehand in floods of tears, after informing the other maids that she was leaving service forever. Dr. Shlessinger had paid the bill of the whole party before his departure.

"By the way," said the landlord, in conclusion, "you are not the only friend of Lady Frances Carfax who is inquiring after her just now. Only a week or so ago we had a man here upon the same errand."

"Did he give a name?" I asked.

"None; but he was an Englishman, though of an unusual type."

"A savage?" said I, linking my facts after the fashion of my illustrious friend.

"Exactly. That describes him very well. He is a bulky, bearded, sunburned fellow, who looks as if he would be more at home in a farmers' inn than in a fashionable hotel. A hard, fierce man, I should think, and one whom I should be sorry to offend."

Already the mystery began to define itself, as figures grow clearer with the lifting of a fog. Here was this good and pious lady pursued from place to place by a sinister and unrelenting figure. She feared him, or she would not have fled from Lausanne. He had still followed.

Sooner or later he would overtake her. Had he already overtaken her? Was *that* the secret of her continued silence? Could the good people who were her companions not screen her from his violence or his blackmail? What horrible purpose, what deep design, lay behind this long pursuit? There was the problem which I had to solve.

To Holmes I wrote showing how rapidly and surely I had got down to the roots of the matter. In reply I had a telegram asking for a description of Dr. Shlessinger's left ear. Holmes's ideas of humour are strange and occasionally offensive, so I took no notice of his ill-timed jest—indeed, I had already reached Montpellier in my pursuit of the maid, Marie, before his message came.

I had no difficulty in finding the ex-servant and in learning all that she could tell me. She was a devoted creature, who had only left her mistress because she was sure that she was in good hands, and because her own approaching marriage made a separation inevitable in any case. Her mistress had, as she confessed with distress, shown some irritability of temper towards her during their stay in Baden, and had even questioned her once as if she had suspicions of her honesty, and this had made the parting easier than it would otherwise have been. Lady Frances had given her fifty pounds as a wedding present. Like me, Marie viewed with deep distrust the stranger who had driven her mistress from Lausanne. With her own eyes she had seen him seize the lady's wrist with great violence on the public promenade by the lake. He was a fierce and terrible man. She believed that it was out of dread of him that Lady Frances had accepted the escort of the Shlessingers to London. She had never spoken to Marie about it, but many little signs had convinced the maid that her mistress lived in a state of continual nervous apprehension. So far she had got in her narrative, when suddenly she sprang from her chair and her face was convulsed with surprise and fear. "See!" she cried. "The miscreant follows still! There is the very man of whom I speak."

Through the open sitting room window I saw a huge, swarthy man with a bristling black beard walking slowly down the centre of the street and staring eagerly at the numbers of the houses. It was clear that, like myself, he was on the track of the maid. Acting upon the impulse of the moment, I rushed out and accosted him. "You are an Englishman," I said.

"What if I am?" he asked, with a most villainous scowl.

"May I ask what your name is?"

"No, you may not," said he, with decision.

The situation was awkward, but the most direct way is often the best. "Where is the Lady Frances Carfax?" I asked.

He stared at me in amazement.

"What have you done with her? Why have you pursued her? I insist upon an answer!" said I.

The fellow gave a bellow of anger and sprang upon me like a tiger. I have held my own in many a struggle, but the man had a grip of iron and the fury of a fiend. His hand was on my throat and my senses were nearly gone before an unshaven French *ouvrier*, in a blue blouse, darted out from a cabaret opposite, with a cudgel in his hand, and struck my assailant a sharp crack over the forearm, which made him leave go his hold. He stood for an instant fuming with rage and uncertain whether he should not renew his attack. Then, with a snarl of anger, he left me and entered the cottage from which I had just come. I turned to thank my preserver, who stood beside me in the roadway.

"Well, Watson," said he, "a very pretty hash you have made of it! I rather think you had better come back with me to London by the night express."

An hour afterwards Sherlock Holmes, in his usual garb and style, was seated in my private room at the hotel. His explanation of his sudden and opportune appearance was simplicity itself, for, finding that he could get away from London, he determined to head me off at the next obvious point of my travels. In the disguise of a working-man he had sat in the cabaret waiting for my appearance.

"And a singularly consistent investigation you have made, my dear Watson," said he. "I cannot at the moment recall any possible blunder which you have omitted. The total effect of your proceedings has been to give the alarm everywhere and yet to discover nothing."

"Perhaps you would have done no better," I answered bitterly.

"There is no 'perhaps' about it. I *have* done better. Here is the Hon. Philip Green, who is a fellow lodger with you in this hotel, and we may find in him the starting point for a more successful investigation."

A card had come up on a salver, and it was followed by the same bearded ruffian who had attacked me in the street. He started when he saw me.

"What is this, Mr. Holmes?" he asked. "I had your note and I have come. But what has this man to do with the matter?"

"This is my old friend and associate, Dr. Watson, who is helping us in this affair."

The stranger held out a huge, sunburned hand, with a few words of apology.

"I hope I didn't harm you. When you accused me of hurting her I lost my grip of myself. Indeed, I'm not responsible in these days. My nerves are like live wires. But this situation is beyond me. What I want to know, in the first place, Mr. Holmes, is how in the world you came to hear of my existence at all."

"I am in touch with Miss Dobney, Lady Frances's governess."

"Old Susan Dobney with the mob cap! I remember her well."

"And she remembers you. It was in the days before—before you found it better to go to South Africa."

"Ah, I see you know my whole story. I need hide nothing from you. I swear to you, Mr. Holmes, that there never was in this world a man who loved a woman with a more wholehearted love than I had for Frances. I was a wild youngster, I know—not worse than others of my class. But her mind was pure as snow. She could not bear a shadow of coarseness. So, when she came to hear of things that I had done, she would have no more to say to me. And yet she loved me—that is the wonder of it!—loved me well enough to remain single all her sainted days just for my sake alone. When the years had passed and I had made my money at Barberton I thought perhaps I could seek her out and soften her. I had heard that she was still unmarried. I found her at Lausanne, and tried all I knew. She weakened, I think, but her will was strong, and when next I called she had left the town. I traced her to Baden, and then after a time heard that her maid was here. I'm a rough fellow, fresh from a rough life, and when Dr. Watson spoke to me as he did I lost hold of myself for a moment. But for God's sake tell me what has become of the Lady Frances."

"That is for us to find out," said Sherlock Holmes, with peculiar gravity. "What is your London address, Mr. Green?"

"The Langham Hotel will find me."

"Then may I recommend that you return there and be on hand in case I should want you? I have no desire to encourage false hopes, but you may rest assured that all that can be done will be done for the safety of Lady Frances. I can say no more for the instant. I will leave you this card so that you may be able to keep in touch with us. Now, Watson, if you will pack your bag I will cable to Mrs. Hudson to make one of her best efforts for two hungry travellers at seven-thirty tomorrow."

A telegram was awaiting us when we reached our Baker Street rooms, which Holmes read with an exclamation of interest and threw across to me. "Jagged or torn," was the message, and the place of origin Baden.

"What is this?" I asked.

"It is everything," Holmes answered. "You may remember my seemingly irrelevant question as to this clerical gentleman's left ear. You did not answer it."

"I had left Baden, and could not inquire."

"Exactly. For this reason I sent a duplicate to the manager of the Englischer Hof, whose answer lies here."

"What does it show?"

"It shows, my dear Watson, that we are dealing with an exceptionally astute and dangerous man. The Rev. Dr. Shlessinger, missionary from South America, is none other than Holy Peters, one of the most unscrupulous rascals that Australia has ever evolved—and for a young country it has turned out some very finished types. His particular specialty is the beguiling of lonely ladies by playing upon their religious feelings, and his so-called wife, an Englishwoman named Fraser, is a worthy helpmate. The nature of his tactics suggested his identity to me, and this physical peculiarity—he was badly bitten in a saloon fight at Adelaide in '89—confirmed my suspicion. This poor lady is in the hands of a most infernal couple, who will stick at nothing, Watson. That she is already dead is a very likely supposition. If not, she is undoubtedly in some sort of confinement, and unable to write to Miss Dobney or her other friends. It is always possible that she never reached London, or that she has passed through it, but the former is improbable, as, with their system of registration, it is not easy for foreigners to play tricks with the continental police; and the latter is also unlikely, as these rogues could not hope to find any other place where it would be as easy to keep a person under restraint. All my instincts tell me that she is in London, but, as we have at present no possible means of telling where, we can only take the obvious steps, eat our dinner, and possess our souls in patience. Later in the evening I will stroll down and have a word with friend Lestrade at Scotland Yard."

But neither the official police nor Holmes's own small, but very efficient, organisation sufficed to clear away the mystery. Amid the crowded millions of London the three persons we sought were as completely obliterated as if they had never lived. Advertisements were tried, and failed. Clues were followed, and led to nothing. Every criminal resort which Shlessinger might frequent was drawn in vain. His old associates were watched, but they kept clear of him. And then suddenly, after a week of helpless suspense, there came a flash of light. A silver-and-brilliant pendant of old Spanish design had been pawned at Bevington's, in Westminster Road. The pawner was a large, clean-shaven man of clerical appearance. His name and address were demonstrably false. The ear had escaped notice, but the description was surely that of Shlessinger.

Three times had our bearded friend from the Langham called for news—the third time within an hour of this fresh development. His clothes were getting looser on his great body. He seemed to be wilting away in his anxiety. "If you will only give me something to do!" was his constant wail. At last Holmes could oblige him.

"He has begun to pawn the jewels. We should get him now."

"But does this mean that any harm has befallen the Lady Frances?"

Holmes shook his head very gravely. "Supposing that they have held her prisoner up to now, it is clear that they cannot let her loose without their own destruction. We must prepare for the worst."

"What can I do?"

"These people do not know you by sight?"

"No."

"It is possible that he will go to some other pawnbroker in the future. In that case, we must begin again. On the other hand, he has had a fair price and no questions asked, so if he is in need of ready money he will probably come back to Bevington's. I will give you a note to them, and they will let you wait in the shop. If the fellow comes you will follow him home. But no indiscretion, and, above all, no violence. I put you on your honour that you will take no step without my knowledge and consent."

For two days the Hon. Philip Green (he was, I may mention, the son of the famous admiral of that name who commanded the Sea of Azov fleet in the Crimean War) brought us no news. On the evening of the third he rushed into our sitting room, pale, trembling, with every muscle of his powerful frame quivering with excitement.

"We have him! We have him!" he cried.

He was incoherent in his agitation. Holmes soothed him with a few words, and thrust him into an armchair.

"Come, now, give us the order of events," said he.

"She came only an hour ago. It was the wife, this time, but the pendant she brought was the fellow of the other. She is a tall, pale woman, with ferret eyes."

"That is the lady," said Holmes.

"She left the office and I followed her. She walked up the Kennington Road, and I kept behind her. Presently she went into a shop. Mr. Holmes, it was an undertaker's."

My companion started. "Well?" he asked, in that vibrant voice which told of the fiery soul behind the cold grey face.

"She was talking to the woman behind the counter. I entered as well. 'It is late,' I heard her say, or words to that effect. The woman was excusing herself. 'It should be there before now,' she answered. 'It took longer, being out of the ordinary.' They both stopped and looked at me, so I asked some question and then left the shop."

"You did excellently well. What happened next?"

"The woman came out, but I had hid myself in a doorway. Her suspicions had been aroused, I think, for she looked round her. Then she called a cab and got in. I was lucky enough to get another and so to follow her. She got down at last at No. 36, Poultney Square, Brixton. I drove past, left my cab at the corner of the square, and watched the house."

"Did you see anyone?"

"The windows were all in darkness save one on the lower floor. The blind was down, and I could not see in. I was standing there, wondering what I should do next, when a covered van drove up with two men in it. They descended, took something out of the van, and carried it up the steps to the hall door. Mr. Holmes, it was a coffin."

"Ah!"

"For an instant I was on the point of rushing in. The door had been

"Mr. Holmes, it was a coffin."

opened to admit the men and their burden. It was the woman who had opened it. But as I stood there she caught a glimpse of me, and I think that she recognised me. I saw her start, and she hastily closed the door. I remembered my promise to you, and here I am."

"You have done excellent work," said Holmes, scribbling a few words upon a half-sheet of paper. "We can do nothing legal without a warrant, and you can serve the cause best by taking this note down to the authorities and getting one. There may be some difficulty, but I should think that the sale of the jewellery should be sufficient. Lestrade will see to all details."

"But they may murder her in the meanwhile. What could the coffin mean, and for whom could it be but for her?"

"We will do all that can be done, Mr. Green. Not a moment will be lost. Leave it in our hands. Now, Watson," he added, as our client hurried away, "he will set the regular forces on the move. We are, as usual, the irregulars, and we must take our own line of action. The situation strikes me as so desperate that the most extreme measures are justified. Not a moment is to be lost in getting to Poultney Square."

"Let us try to reconstruct the situation," said he, as we drove swiftly past the Houses of Parliament and over Westminster Bridge. "These villains have coaxed this unhappy lady to London, after first alienating her from her faithful maid. If she has written any letters they have been intercepted. Through some confederate they have engaged a furnished house. Once inside it, they have made her a prisoner, and they have become possessed of the valuable jewellery which has been their object from the first. Already they have begun to sell part of it, which seems safe enough to them, since they have no reason to think that anyone is interested in the lady's fate. When she is released she will, of course, denounce them. Therefore, she must not be released. But they cannot keep her under lock and key forever. So murder is their only solution."

"That seems very clear."

"Now we will take another line of reasoning. When you follow two separate chains of thought, Watson, you will find some point of intersection which should approximate to the truth. We will start now, not from the lady, but from the coffin, and argue backwards. That incident proves, I fear, beyond all doubt that the lady is dead. It points also to an orthodox burial with proper accompaniment of medical certificate and official sanction. Had the lady been obviously murdered, they would have buried her in a hole in the back garden. But here all is open and regular. What does that mean? Surely that they have done her to death in some way which has deceived the doctor, and simulated a natural end—poisoning, perhaps. And yet how strange that they should ever let a doctor approach her unless he were a confederate, which is hardly a creditable proposition."

"Could they have forged a medical certificate?"

"Dangerous, Watson, very dangerous. No, I hardly see them doing that. Pull up, cabby! This is evidently the undertaker's, for we have just passed the pawnbroker's. Would you go in, Watson? Your appearance inspires confidence. Ask what hour the Poultney Square funeral takes place tomorrow."

The woman in the shop answered me without hesitation that it was to be at eight o'clock in the morning.

"You see, Watson, no mystery; everything aboveboard! In some way the legal forms have undoubtedly been complied with, and they think that they have little to fear. Well, there's nothing for it now but a direct frontal attack. Are you armed?"

"My stick!"

"Well, well, we shall be strong enough. 'Thrice is he armed who hath his quarrel just.' We simply can't afford to wait for the police, or to keep within the four corners of the law. You can drive off, cabby. Now, Watson, we'll just take our luck together, as we have occasionally done in the past."

He had rung loudly at the door of a great dark house in the centre of Poultney Square. It was opened immediately, and the figure of a tall woman was outlined against the dim-lit hall.

"Well, what do you want?" she asked, sharply, peering at us through the darkness.

"I want to speak to Dr. Shlessinger," said Holmes.

"There is no such person here," she answered, and tried to close the door, but Holmes had jammed it with his foot.

"Well, I want to see the man who lives here, whatever he may call himself," said Holmes, firmly.

She hesitated. Then she threw open the door. "Well, come in!" said she. "My husband is not afraid to face any man in the world." She closed the door behind us, and showed us into a sitting room on the right side of the hall, turning up the gas as she left us. "Mr. Peters will be with you in an instant," she said.

Her words were literally true, for we had hardly time to look round the dusty and moth-eaten apartment in which we found ourselves before the door opened and a big, clean-shaven, bald-headed man stepped lightly into the room. He had a large red face, with pendulous cheeks, and a general air of superficial benevolence which was marred by a cruel, vicious mouth.

"There is surely some mistake here, gentlemen," he said, in an unctuous, make-everything-easy voice. "I fancy that you have been misdirected. Possibly if you tried farther down the street——"

"That will do; we have no time to waste," said my companion, firmly. "You are Henry Peters, of Adelaide, late the Rev. Dr. Shlessinger, of Baden and South America. I am as sure of that as that my own name is Sherlock Holmes."

Peters, as I will now call him, started and stared hard at his formidable pursuer. "I guess your name does not frighten me, Mr. Holmes," said he, coolly. "When a man's conscience is easy you can't rattle him. What is your business in my house?"

"I want to know what you have done with the Lady Frances Carfax, whom you brought away with you from Baden."

"I'd be very glad if you could tell me where that lady may be," Peters answered, coolly. "I've a bill against her for nearly a hundred pounds, and nothing to show for it but a couple of trumpery pendants that the dealer would hardly look at. She attached herself to Mrs. Peters and me at Baden (it is a fact that I was using another name at the time), and she stuck onto us until we came to London. I paid her bill and her ticket. Once in London, she gave us the slip, and, as I say, left these out-of-date jewels to pay her bills. You find her, Mr. Holmes, and I'm your debtor."

"I *mean* to find her," said Sherlock Holmes. "I'm going through this house till I do find her."

"Where is your warrant?"

Holmes half drew a revolver from his pocket. "This will have to serve till a better one comes."

"Why, you are a common burglar."

"So you might describe me," said Holmes, cheerfully. "My companion is also a dangerous ruffian. And together we are going through your house."

Our opponent opened the door. "Fetch a policeman, Annie!" said he. There was a whisk of feminine skirts down the passage, and the hall door was opened and shut.

"Our time is limited, Watson," said Holmes. "If you try to stop us, Peters, you will most certainly get hurt. Where is that coffin which was brought into your house?"

"What do you want with the coffin? It is in use. There is a body in it."

"I must see that body."

"Never with my consent."

"Then without it." With a quick movement Holmes pushed the fellow to one side and passed into the hall. A door half-open stood immediately before us. We entered. It was the dining room. On the table, under a half-lit chandelier, the coffin was lying. Holmes turned up the gas and raised the lid. Deep down in the recesses of the coffin lay an emaciated figure. The glare from the lights above beat down upon an aged and withered face. By no possible process of cruelty, starvation, or disease could this worn-out wreck be the still beautiful Lady Frances. Holmes's face showed his amazement, and also his relief.

"Thank God!" he muttered. "It's someone else."

"Ah, you've blundered badly for once, Mr. Sherlock Holmes," said Peters, who had followed us into the room.

"Who is this dead woman?"

"Well, if you really must know, she is an old nurse of my wife's, Rose Spender her name, whom we found in the Brixton Workhouse Infirmary. We brought her round here, called in Dr. Horsom, of 13, Firbank Villas—mind you take the address, Mr. Holmes—and had her carefully tended, as Christian folk should. On the third day she died— certificate says senile decay—but that's only the doctor's opinion, and, of course, you know better. We ordered her funeral to be carried out by Stimson & Co., of the Kennington Road, who will bury her at eight o'clock tomorrow morning. Can you pick any hole in that, Mr. Holmes? You've made a silly blunder, and you may as well own up to it. I'd give something for a photograph of your gaping, staring face when you pulled aside that lid expecting to see the Lady Frances Carfax, and only found a poor old woman of ninety."

Holmes's expression was as impassive as ever under the jeers of his antagonist, but his clenched hands betrayed his acute annoyance.

"I am going through your house," said he.

"Are you, though!" cried Peters, as a woman's voice and heavy steps sounded in the passage. "We'll soon see about that. This way, officers, if you please. These men have forced their way into my house, and I cannot get rid of them. Help me to put them out."

A sergeant and a constable stood in the doorway. Holmes drew his card from his case.

"This is my name and address. This is my friend, Dr. Watson."

"Bless you, sir, we know you very well," said the sergeant, "but you can't stay here without a warrant."

"Of course not. I quite understand that."

"Arrest him!" cried Peters.

"We know where to lay our hands on this gentleman if he is wanted," said the sergeant, majestically; "but you'll have to go, Mr. Holmes."

"Yes, Watson, we shall have to go."

A minute later we were in the street once more. Holmes was as cool as ever, but I was hot with anger and humiliation. The sergeant had followed us.

"Sorry, Mr. Holmes, but that's the law."

"Exactly, sergeant; you could not do otherwise."

"I expect there was good reason for your presence there. If there is anything I can do——"

"It's a missing lady, sergeant, and we think she is in that house. I expect a warrant presently."

"Then I'll keep my eye on the parties, Mr. Holmes. If anything comes along, I will surely let you know."

It was only nine o'clock, and we were off full cry upon the trail at once. First we drove to Brixton Workhouse Infirmary, where we found that it was indeed the truth that a charitable couple had called some days before, that they had claimed an imbecile old woman as a former servant, and that they had obtained permission to take her away with them. No surprise was expressed at the news that she had since died.

The doctor was our next goal. He had been called in, had found the woman dying of pure senility, had actually seen her pass away, and had signed the certificate in due form. "I assure you that everything was perfectly normal and there was no room for foul play in the matter," said he. Nothing in the house had struck him as suspicious, save that for people of their class it was remarkable that they should have no servant. So far and no farther went the doctor.

Finally, we found our way to Scotland Yard. There had been difficulties of procedure in regard to the warrant. Some delay was inevitable. The magistrate's signature might not be obtained until next morning. If Holmes would call about nine he could go down with Lestrade and see it acted upon. So ended the day, save that near midnight our friend, the sergeant, called to say that he had seen flickering lights here and there in the windows of the great dark house, but that no one had left it and none had entered. We could but pray for patience, and wait for the morrow.

Sherlock Holmes was too irritable for conversation and too restless for sleep. I left him smoking hard, with his heavy, dark brows knotted together, and his long, nervous fingers tapping upon the arms of his chair, as he turned over in his mind every possible solution of the mystery. Several times in the course of the night I heard him prowling about the house. Finally, just after I had been called in the morning, he rushed into my room. He was in his dressing gown, but his pale, hollow-eyed face told me that his night had been a sleepless one.

"What time was the funeral? Eight, was it not?" he asked, eagerly. "Well, it is seven-twenty now. Good heavens, Watson, what has become of any brains that God has given me? Quick, man, quick! It's life or death—a hundred chances on death to one on life. I'll never forgive myself, never, if we are too late!"

Five minutes had not passed before we were flying in a hansom down Baker Street. But even so it was twenty-five to eight as we passed Big Ben, and eight struck as we tore down the Brixton Road. But others were late as well as we. Ten minutes after the hour the hearse was still standing at the door of the house, and even as our foaming horse came to a halt the coffin, supported by three men, appeared on the threshold. Holmes darted forward and barred their way.

"Take it back!" he cried, laying his hand on the breast of the foremost. "Take it back this instant!"

"What the devil do you mean? Once again I ask you, where is your warrant?" shouted the furious Peters, his big red face glaring over the farther end of the coffin.

"The warrant is on its way. This coffin shall remain in the house until it comes."

The authority in Holmes's voice had its effect upon the bearers. Peters had suddenly vanished into the house, and they obeyed these new orders. "Quick, Watson, quick! Here is a screwdriver!" he shouted, as the coffin was replaced upon the table. "Here's one for you, my man: a sovereign if the lid comes off in a minute! Ask no questions—work away! That's good! Another! And another! Now pull all together! It's giving! It's giving! Ah, that does it at last!"

With a united effort we tore off the coffin lid. As we did so there came from the inside a stupefying and overpowering smell of chloroform. A body lay within, its head all wreathed in cotton wool, which had been soaked in the narcotic. Holmes plucked it off and disclosed the statuesque face of a handsome and spiritual woman of middle age. In an instant he had passed his arm round the figure and raised her to a sitting position.

"Is she gone, Watson? Is there a spark left? Surely we are not too late!"

For half an hour it seemed that we were. What with actual suffocation, and what with the poisonous fumes of the chloroform, the Lady Frances seemed to have passed the last point of recall. And then, at last, with artificial respiration, with injected ether, with every device that science could suggest, some flutter of life, some quiver of the eyelids, some dimming of a mirror, spoke of the slowly returning life. A cab had driven up, and Holmes, parting the blind, looked out at it. "Here is Lestrade with his warrant," said he. "He will find that his birds have flown. And there," he added, as a heavy step hurried along the passage, "is someone who has a better right to nurse this lady than we have. Good morning, Mr. Green; I think that the sooner we can move the Lady Frances the better. Meanwhile, the funeral may proceed, and the poor old woman who still lies in that coffin may go to her last resting place alone."

"Should you care to add the case to your annals, my dear Watson," said Holmes that evening, "it can only be as an example of that temporary eclipse to which even the best-balanced mind may be exposed.

Such slips are common to all mortals, and the greatest is he who can recognise and repair them. To this modified credit I may, perhaps, make some claim. My night was haunted by the thought that somewhere a clue, a strange sentence, a curious observation, had come under my notice and had been too easily dismissed. Then, suddenly, in the grey of the morning, the words came back to me. It was the remark of the undertaker's wife, as reported by Philip Green. She had said, 'It should be there before now. It took longer, being out of the ordinary.' It was the coffin of which she spoke. It had been out of the ordinary. That could only mean that it had been made to some special measurement. But why? Why? Then in an instant I remembered the deep sides, and the little wasted figure at the bottom. Why so large a coffin for so small a body? To leave room for another body. Both would be buried under the one certificate. It had all been so clear, if only my own sight had not been dimmed. At eight the Lady Frances would be buried. Our one chance was to stop the coffin before it left the house.

"It was a desperate chance that we might find her alive, but it *was* a chance, as the result showed. These people had never, to my knowledge, done a murder. They might shrink from actual violence at the last. They could bury her with no sign of how she met her end, and even if she were exhumed there was a chance for them. I hoped that such considerations might prevail with them. You can reconstruct the scene well enough. You saw the horrible den upstairs, where the poor lady had been kept so long. They rushed in and overpowered her with their chloroform, carried her down, poured more into the coffin to ensure against her waking, and then screwed down the lid. A clever device, Watson. It is new to me in the annals of crime. If our ex-missionary friends escape the clutches of Lestrade, I shall expect to hear of some brilliant incidents in their future career."

VI: The Adventure of the Dying Detective

Mrs. Hudson, the landlady of Sherlock Holmes, was a long-suffering woman. Not only was her first-floor flat invaded at all hours by throngs of singular and often undesirable characters, but her remarkable lodger showed an eccentricity and irregularity in his life which must have sorely tried her patience. His incredible untidiness, his addiction to music at strange hours, his occasional revolver practice within doors, his weird and often malodorous scientific experiments, and the atmosphere of violence and danger which hung around him made him the very worst tenant in London. On the other hand, his payments were princely. I have no doubt that the house might have been purchased at the price which Holmes paid for his rooms during the years that I was with him.

The landlady stood in the deepest awe of him, and never dared to interfere with him, however outrageous his proceedings might seem. She was fond of him, too, for he had a remarkable gentleness and courtesy in his dealings with women. He disliked and distrusted the sex, but he was always a chivalrous opponent. Knowing how genuine was her regard for him, I listened earnestly to her story when she came to my rooms in the second year of my married life and told me of the sad condition to which my poor friend was reduced.

"He's dying, Dr. Watson," said she. "For three days he has been sinking, and I doubt if he will last the day. He would not let me get a doctor. This morning when I saw his bones sticking out of his face and his great bright eyes looking at me I could stand no more of it. 'With your leave or without it, Mr. Holmes, I am going for a doctor this very hour,' said I. 'Let it be Watson, then,' said he. I wouldn't waste an hour in coming to him, sir, or you may not see him alive."

I was horrified, for I had heard nothing of his illness. I need not say that I rushed for my coat and my hat. As we drove back I asked for the details.

"There is little I can tell you, sir. He has been working at a case down at Rotherhithe, in an alley near the river, and he has brought this illness back with him. He took to his bed on Wednesday afternoon and has never moved since. For these three days neither food nor drink has passed his lips."

"Good God! Why did you not call in a doctor?"

"He wouldn't have it, sir. You know how masterful he is. I didn't dare to disobey him. But he's not long for this world, as you'll see for yourself the moment that you set eyes on him."

He was indeed a deplorable spectacle. In the dim light of a foggy November day the sickroom was a gloomy spot, but it was that gaunt, wasted face staring at me from the bed which sent a chill to my heart. His eyes had the brightness of fever, there was a hectic flush upon either cheek, and dark crusts clung to his lips; the thin hands upon the coverlet twitched incessantly, his voice was croaking and spasmodic. He lay listlessly as I entered the room, but the sight of me brought a gleam of recognition to his eyes.

"Well, Watson, we seem to have fallen upon evil days," said he, in a feeble voice, but with something of his old carelessness of manner.

"My dear fellow!" I cried, approaching him.

"Stand back! Stand right back!" said he, with the sharp imperiousness which I had associated only with moments of crisis. "If you approach me, Watson, I shall order you out of the house."

"But why?"

"Because it is my desire. Is that not enough?"

Yes, Mrs. Hudson was right. He was more masterful than ever. It was pitiful, however, to see his exhaustion.

"I only wished to help," I explained.

"Exactly! You will help best by doing what you are told."

"Certainly, Holmes."

He relaxed the austerity of his manner.

"You are not angry?" he asked, gasping for breath.

Poor devil, how could I be angry when I saw him lying in such a plight before me?

"It's for your own sake, Watson," he croaked.

"For *my* sake?"

"I know what is the matter with me. It is a coolie disease from Sumatra—a thing that the Dutch know more about than we, though they have made little of it up to date. One thing only is certain. It is infallibly deadly, and it is horribly contagious."

He spoke now with a feverish energy, the long hands twitching and jerking as he motioned me away.

"Contagious by touch, Watson—that's it, by touch. Keep your distance and all is well."

"Good heavens, Holmes! Do you suppose that such a consideration weighs with me for an instant? It would not affect me in the case of a stranger. Do you imagine it would prevent me from doing my duty to so old a friend?"

Again I advanced, but he repulsed me with a look of furious anger.

"If you will stand there I will talk. If you do not you must leave the room."

I have so deep a respect for the extraordinary qualities of Holmes that I have always deferred to his wishes, even when I least understood them. But now all my professional instincts were aroused. Let him be my master elsewhere, I at least was his in a sickroom.

"Holmes," said I, "you are not yourself. A sick man is but a child, and so I will treat you. Whether you like it or not, I will examine your symptoms and treat you for them."

He looked at me with venomous eyes.

"If I am to have a doctor whether I will or not, let me at least have someone in whom I have confidence," said he.

"Then you have none in me?"

"In your friendship, certainly. But facts are facts, Watson, and after all you are only a general practitioner with very limited experience and mediocre qualifications. It is painful to have to say these things, but you leave me no choice."

I was bitterly hurt.

"Such a remark is unworthy of you, Holmes. It shows me very clearly the state of your own nerves. But if you have no confidence in me I would not intrude my services. Let me bring Sir Jasper Meek or Penrose Fisher, or any of the best men in London. But someone you *must* have, and that is final. If you think that I am going to stand here and see you die without either helping you myself or bringing anyone else to help you, then you have mistaken your man."

"You mean well, Watson," said the sick man, with something between a sob and a groan. "Shall I demonstrate your own ignorance? What do you know, pray, of Tapanuli fever? What do you know of the black Formosa corruption?"

"I have never heard of either."

"There are many problems of disease, many strange pathological possibilities, in the East, Watson." He paused after each sentence to collect his failing strength. "I have learned so much during some recent researches which have a medico-criminal aspect. It was in the course of them that I contracted this complaint. You can do nothing."

"Possibly not. But I happen to know that Dr. Ainstree, the greatest living authority upon tropical disease, is now in London. All remonstrance is useless, Holmes. I am going this instant to fetch him."

I turned resolutely to the door.

Never have I had such a shock! In an instant, with a tiger spring, the dying man had intercepted me. I heard the sharp snap of a twisted key. The next moment he had staggered back to his bed, exhausted and panting after his one tremendous outflame of energy.

"You won't take the key from me by force, Watson. I've got you, my friend. Here you are, and here you will stay until I will otherwise. But I'll humour you." (All this in little gasps, with terrible struggles for breath between.) "You've only my own good at heart. Of course I know that very well. You shall have your way, but give me time to get my strength. Not now, Watson, not now. It's four o'clock. At six you can go."

"This is insanity, Holmes."

"Only two hours, Watson. I promise you will go at six. Are you content to wait?"

"I seem to have no choice."

"None in the world, Watson. Thank you, I need no help in arranging the clothes. You will please keep your distance. Now, Watson, there is one other condition that I would make. You will seek help, not from the man you mention, but from the one that I choose."

"By all means."

"The first three sensible words that you have uttered since you entered this room, Watson. You will find some books over there. I am somewhat exhausted; I wonder how a battery feels when it pours electricity into a non-conductor? At six, Watson, we resume our conversation."

But it was destined to be resumed long before that hour, and in circumstances which gave me a shock hardly second to that caused by his spring to the door. I had stood for some minutes looking at the silent figure in the bed. His face was almost covered by the clothes and he appeared to be asleep. Then, unable to settle down to reading, I walked slowly round the room, examining the pictures of celebrated criminals with which every wall was adorned. Finally, in my aimless perambulation, I came to the mantelpiece. A litter of pipes, tobacco pouches, syringes, penknives, revolver cartridges, and other débris was scattered over it. In the midst of these was a small black and white ivory box with a sliding lid. It was a neat little thing, and I had stretched out my hand to examine it more closely, when——

It was a dreadful cry that he gave—a yell which might have been heard down the street. My skin went cold and my hair bristled at that horrible scream. As I turned I caught a glimpse of a convulsed face and frantic eyes. I stood paralysed, with the little box in my hand.

"Put it down! Down, this instant, Watson—this instant, I say!"

His head sank back upon the pillow and he gave a deep sigh of relief as I replaced the box upon the mantelpiece. "I hate to have my things touched, Watson. You know that I hate it. You fidget me beyond endurance. You, a doctor—you are enough to drive a patient into an asylum. Sit down, man, and let me have my rest!"

The incident left a most unpleasant impression upon my mind. The violent and causeless excitement, followed by this brutality of speech, so far removed from his usual suavity, showed me how deep was the disorganisation of his mind. Of all ruins, that of a noble mind is the most deplorable. I sat in silent dejection until the stipulated time had passed. He seemed to have been watching the clock as well as I, for it was hardly six before he began to talk with the same feverish animation as before.

"Now, Watson," said he. "Have you any change in your pocket?"

"Yes."

"Any silver?"

"A good deal."

"How many half-crowns?"

"I have five."

"Ah, too few! Too few! How very unfortunate, Watson! However, such as they are you can put them in your watch pocket. And all the rest of your money in your left trouser pocket. Thank you. It will balance you so much better like that."

This was raving insanity. He shuddered, and again made a sound between a cough and a sob.

"You will now light the gas, Watson, but you will be very careful that not for one instant shall it be more than half on. I implore you to be careful, Watson. Thank you, that is excellent. No, you need not draw the blind. Now you will have the kindness to place some letters and papers upon this table within my reach. Thank you. Now some of that litter from the mantelpiece. Excellent, Watson! There is a sugar tongs there. Kindly raise that small ivory box with its assistance. Place it here among the papers. Good! You can now go and fetch Mr. Culverton Smith, of 13, Lower Burke Street."

To tell the truth, my desire to fetch a doctor had somewhat weakened, for poor Holmes was so obviously delirious that it seemed dangerous to leave him. However, he was as eager now to consult the person named as he had been obstinate in refusing.

"I never heard the name," said I.

"Possibly not, my good Watson. It may surprise you to know that the man upon earth who is best versed in this disease is not a medical man, but a planter. Mr. Culverton Smith is a well-known resident of Sumatra, now visiting London. An outbreak of the disease upon his plantation, which was distant from medical aid, caused him to study it himself, with some rather far-reaching consequences. He is a very methodical person, and I did not desire you to start before six because I was well aware that you would not find him in his study. If you could persuade him to come here and give us the benefit of his unique experience of this disease, the investigation of which has been his dearest hobby, I cannot doubt that he could help me."

I give Holmes's remarks as a consecutive whole, and will not attempt to indicate how they were interrupted by gaspings for breath and those clutchings of his hands which indicated the pain from which he was suffering. His appearance had changed for the worse during the few hours that I had been with him. Those hectic spots were more pronounced, the eyes shone more brightly out of darker hollows, and a cold sweat glimmered upon his brow. He still retained, however, the jaunty gallantry of his speech. To the last gasp he would always be the master.

"You will tell him exactly how you have left me," said he. "You will convey the very impression which is in your own mind—a dying man—a dying and delirious man. Indeed, I cannot think why the whole bed of the ocean is not one solid mass of oysters, so prolific the creatures seem. Ah, I am wandering! Strange how the brain controls the brain. What was I saying, Watson?"

"My directions for Mr. Culverton Smith."

"Ah, yes, I remember. My life depends upon it. Plead with him, Watson. There is no good feeling between us. His nephew, Watson—I had suspicions of foul play and I allowed him to see it. The boy died horribly. He has a grudge against me. You will soften him, Watson. Beg him, pray him, get him here by any means. He can save me—only he!"

"I will bring him in a cab, if I have to carry him down to it."

"You will do nothing of the sort. You will persuade him to come. And then you will return in front of him. Make any excuse so as not to come with him. Don't forget, Watson. You won't fail me. You never did fail me. No doubt there are natural enemies which limit the increase of the creatures. You and I, Watson, we have done our part. Shall the world, then, be overrun by oysters? No, no; horrible! You'll convey all that is in your mind."

I left him, full of the image of this magnificent intellect babbling like a foolish child. He had handed me the key, and with a happy thought I took it with me lest he should lock himself in. Mrs. Hudson was waiting, trembling and weeping, in the passage. Behind me as I passed from the flat I heard Holmes's high, thin voice in some delirious chant. Below, as I stood whistling for a cab, a man came on me through the fog.

"How is Mr. Holmes, sir?" he asked.

It was an old acquaintance, Inspector Morton, of Scotland Yard, dressed in unofficial tweeds.

"He is very ill," I answered.

He looked at me in a most singular fashion. Had it not been too fiendish, I could have imagined that the gleam of the fanlight showed exultation in his face.

"I heard some rumour of it," said he.

The cab had driven up, and I left him.

Lower Burke Street proved to be a line of fine houses lying in the vague borderland between Notting Hill and Kennington. The particular one at which my cabman pulled up had an air of smug and demure respectability in its old-fashioned iron railings, its massive folding door, and its shining brasswork. All was in keeping with a solemn butler who appeared framed in the pink radiance of a tinted electric light behind him.

"Yes, Mr. Culverton Smith is in. Dr. Watson! Very good, sir, I will take up your card."

My humble name and title did not appear to impress Mr. Culverton Smith. Through the half-open door I heard a high, petulant, penetrating voice.

"Who is this person? What does he want? Dear me, Staples, how often have I said that I am not to be disturbed in my hours of study?"

There came a gentle flow of soothing explanation from the butler.

"Well, I won't see him, Staples. I can't have my work interrupted like this. I am not at home. Say so. Tell him to come in the morning if he really must see me."

Again the gentle murmur.

"Well, well, give him that message. He can come in the morning, or he can stay away. My work must not be hindered."

I thought of Holmes tossing upon his bed of sickness, and counting the minutes, perhaps, until I could bring help to him. It was not a time to stand upon ceremony. His life depended upon my promptness. Before the apologetic butler had delivered his message I had pushed past him and was in the room.

With a shrill cry of anger a man rose from a reclining chair beside the fire. I saw a great yellow face, coarse-grained and greasy, with heavy double chin, and two sullen, menacing grey eyes which glared at me from under tufted and sandy brows. A high bald head had a small velvet smoking cap poised coquettishly upon one side of its pink curve. The skull was of enormous capacity, and yet, as I looked down I saw to my amazement that the figure of the man was small and frail, twisted in the shoulders and back like one who has suffered from rickets in his childhood.

"What's this?" he cried, in a high, screaming voice. "What is the meaning of this intrusion? Didn't I send you word that I would see you tomorrow morning?"

"What's this?" he cried . . .
"What is the meaning of this intrusion?"

"I am sorry," said I, "but the matter cannot be delayed. Mr. Sherlock Holmes——"

The mention of my friend's name had an extraordinary effect upon the little man. The look of anger passed in an instant from his face. His features became tense and alert.

"Have you come from Holmes?" he asked.

"I have just left him."

"What about Holmes? How is he?"

"He is desperately ill. That is why I have come."

The man motioned me to a chair, and turned to resume his own. As he did so I caught a glimpse of his face in the mirror over the mantelpiece. I could have sworn that it was set in a malicious and abominable smile. Yet I persuaded myself that it must have been some nervous contraction which I had surprised, for he turned to me an instant later with genuine concern upon his features.

"I am sorry to hear this," said he. "I only know Mr. Holmes through some business dealings which we have had, but I have every respect for his talents and his character. He is an amateur of crime, as I am of disease. For him the villain, for me the microbe. There are my prisons," he continued, pointing to a row of bottles and jars which stood upon a side table. "Among those gelatine cultivations some of the very worst offenders in the world are now doing time."

"It was on account of your special knowledge that Mr. Holmes desired to see you. He has a high opinion of you, and thought that you were the one man in London who could help him."

The little man started, and the jaunty smoking cap slid to the floor.

"Why?" he asked. "Why should Mr. Holmes think that I could help him in his trouble?"

"Because of your knowledge of Eastern diseases."

"But why should he think that this disease which he has contracted is Eastern?"

"Because, in some professional inquiry, he has been working among Chinese sailors down in the docks."

Mr. Culverton Smith smiled pleasantly and picked up his smoking cap.

"Oh, that's it—is it?" said he. "I trust the matter is not so grave as you suppose. How long has he been ill?"

"About three days."

"Is he delirious?"

"Occasionally."

"Tut, tut! This sounds serious. It would be inhuman not to answer his call. I very much resent any interruption to my work, Dr. Watson, but this case is certainly exceptional. I will come with you at once."

I remembered Holmes's injunction.

"I have another appointment," said I.

"Very good. I will go alone. I have a note of Mr. Holmes's address. You can rely upon my being there within half an hour at most."

It was with a sinking heart that I re-entered Holmes's bedroom. For all that I knew the worst might have happened in my absence. To my enormous relief, he had improved greatly in the interval. His appearance was as ghastly as ever, but all trace of delirium had left him and he spoke in a feeble voice, it is true, but with even more than his usual crispness and lucidity.

"Well, did you see him, Watson?"

"Yes; he is coming."

"Admirable, Watson! Admirable! You are the best of messengers."

"He wished to return with me."

"That would never do, Watson. That would be obviously impossible. Did he ask what ailed me?"

"I told him about the Chinese in the East End."

"Exactly! Well, Watson, you have done all that a good friend could. You can now disappear from the scene."

"I must wait and hear his opinion, Holmes."

"Of course you must. But I have reasons to suppose that this opinion would be very much more frank and valuable if he imagines that we are alone. There is just room behind the head of my bed, Watson."

"My dear Holmes!"

"I fear there is no alternative, Watson. The room does not lend itself to concealment, which is as well, as it is the less likely to arouse suspicion. But just there, Watson, I fancy that it could be done." Suddenly he sat up with a rigid intentness upon his haggard face. "There are the wheels, Watson. Quick, man, if you love me! And don't budge, whatever happens—whatever happens, do you hear? Don't speak! Don't move! Just listen with all your ears." Then in an instant his sudden access of strength departed, and his masterful, purposeful talk droned away into the low, vague murmurings of a semi-delirious man.

From the hiding place into which I had been so swiftly hustled I heard the footfalls upon the stair, with the opening and the closing of the bedroom door. Then, to my surprise, there came a long silence, broken only by the heavy breathings and gaspings of the sick man. I could imagine that our visitor was standing by the bedside and looking down at the sufferer. At last that strange hush was broken.

"Holmes!" he cried. "Holmes!" in the insistent tone of one who awakens a sleeper. "Can't you hear me, Holmes?" There was a rustling, as if he had shaken the sick man roughly by the shoulder.

"Is that you, Mr. Smith?" Holmes whispered. "I hardly dared hope that you would come."

The other laughed.

"I should imagine not," he said. "And yet, you see, I am here. Coals of fire, Holmes—coals of fire!"

"It is very good of you—very noble of you. I appreciate your special knowledge."

Our visitor sniggered.

"You do. You are, fortunately, the only man in London who does. Do you know what is the matter with you?"

"The same," said Holmes.

"Ah! You recognise the symptoms?"

"Only too well."

"Well, I shouldn't be surprised, Holmes. I shouldn't be surprised if it *were* the same. A bad lookout for you if it is. Poor Victor was a dead man on the fourth day—a strong, hearty young fellow. It was certainly, as you said, very surprising that he should have contracted an out-of-the-way Asiatic disease in the heart of London—a disease, too, of which I had made such a very special study. Singular coincidence, Holmes. Very smart of you to notice it, but rather uncharitable to suggest that it was cause and effect."

"I knew that you did it."

"Oh, you did, did you? Well, you couldn't prove it, anyhow. But what do you think of yourself spreading reports about me like that, and then crawling to me for help the moment you are in trouble? What sort of a game is that—eh?"

I heard the rasping, laboured breathing of the sick man. "Give me the water!" he gasped.

"You're precious near your end, my friend, but I don't want you to go till I have had a word with you. That's why I give you water. There, don't slop it about! That's right. Can you understand what I say?"

Holmes groaned.

"Do what you can for me. Let bygones be bygones," he whispered. "I'll put the words out of my head—I swear I will. Only cure me, and I'll forget it."

"Forget what?"

"Well, about Victor Savage's death. You as good as admitted just now that you had done it. I'll forget it."

"You can forget it or remember it, just as you like. I don't see you in the witness box. Quite another shaped box, my good Holmes, I assure you. It matters nothing to me that you should know how my nephew died. It's not him we are talking about. It's you."

"Yes, yes."

"The fellow who came for me—I've forgotten his name—said that you contracted it down in the East End among the sailors.

"I could only account for it so."

"You are proud of your brains, Holmes, are you not? Think yourself smart, don't you? You came across someone who was smarter this time. Now cast your mind back, Holmes. Can you think of no other way you could have got this thing?"

"I can't think. My mind is gone. For heaven's sake, help me!"

"Yes, I will help you. I'll help you to understand just where you are and how you got there. I'd like you to know before you die."

"Give me something to ease my pain."

"Painful, is it? Yes, the coolies used to do some squealing towards the end. Takes you as cramp, I fancy."

"Yes, yes; it is cramp."

"Well, you can hear what I say, anyhow. Listen now! Can you remember any unusual incident in your life just about the time your symptoms began?"

"No, no; nothing."

"Think again."

"I'm too ill to think."

"Well, then, I'll help you. Did anything come by post?"

"By post?"

"A box, by chance?"

"I'm fainting—I'm gone!"

"Listen, Holmes!" There was a sound as if he was shaking the dying man, and it was all that I could do to hold myself quiet in my hiding place. "You must hear me. You *shall* hear me. Do you remember a box—an ivory box? It came on Wednesday. You opened it—do you remember?"

"Yes, yes, I opened it. There was a sharp spring inside it. Some joke——"

"It was no joke, as you will find to your cost. You fool, you would have it and you have got it. Who asked you to cross my path? If you had left me alone I would not have hurt you."

"I remember," Holmes gasped. "The spring! It drew blood. This box—this on the table."

"The very one, by George! And it may as well leave the room in my pocket. There goes your last shred of evidence. But you have the truth now, Holmes, and you can die with the knowledge that I killed you. You knew too much of the fate of Victor Savage, so I have sent you to share it. You are very near your end, Holmes. I will sit here and I will watch you die."

Holmes's voice had sunk to an almost inaudible whisper.

"What is that?" said Smith. "Turn up the gas? Ah, the shadows begin to fall, do they? Yes, I will turn it up, that I may see you the better." He crossed the room and the light suddenly brightened. "Is there any other little service that I can do you, my friend?"

"A match and a cigarette."

I nearly called out in my joy and my amazement. He was speaking in his natural voice—a little weak, perhaps, but the very voice I knew. There was a long pause, and I felt that Culverton Smith was standing in silent amazement looking down at his companion.

"What's the meaning of this?" I heard him say at last, in a dry, rasping tone.

"The best way of successfully acting a part is to be it," said Holmes. "I give you my word that for three days I have tasted neither food nor drink until you were good enough to pour me out that glass of water. But it is the tobacco which I find most irksome. Ah, here *are* some cigarettes." I heard the striking of a match. "That is very much better. Halloa! Halloa! Do I hear the step of a friend?"

There were footfalls outside, the door opened, and Inspector Morton appeared.

"All is in order and this is your man," said Holmes.

The officer gave the usual cautions. "I arrest you on the charge of the murder of one Victor Savage," he concluded.

"And you might add the attempted murder of one Sherlock Holmes," remarked my friend with a chuckle. "To save an invalid trouble, Inspector, Mr. Culverton Smith was good enough to give our signal by turning up the gas. By the way, the prisoner has a small box in the right-hand pocket of his coat which it would be as well to remove. Thank you. I would handle it gingerly if I were you. Put it down here. It may play its part in the trial."

There was a sudden rush and a scuffle, followed by the clash of iron and a cry of pain.

"You'll only get yourself hurt," said the inspector. "Stand still, will you?" There was the click of the closing handcuffs.

"A nice trap!" cried the high, snarling voice. "It will bring *you* into the dock, Holmes, not me. He asked me to come here to cure him. I was sorry for him and I came. Now he will pretend, no doubt, that I have said anything which he may invent which will corroborate his insane suspicions. You can lie as you like, Holmes. My word is always as good as yours."

"Good heavens!" cried Holmes. "I had totally forgotten him. My dear Watson, I owe you a thousand apologies. To think that I should have overlooked you! I need not introduce you to Mr. Culverton Smith, since I understand that you met somewhat earlier in the evening. Have you the cab below? I will follow you when I am dressed, for I may be of some use at the station."

"I never needed it more," said Holmes, as he refreshed himself with a glass of claret and some biscuits in the intervals of his toilet. "However, as you know, my habits are irregular, and such a feat means less to me than to most men. It was very essential that I should impress Mrs. Hudson with the reality of my condition, since she was to convey it to you, and you in turn to him. You won't be offended, Watson? You will realise that among your many talents dissimulation finds no place, and that if you had shared my secret you would never have been able to impress Smith with the urgent necessity of his presence, which was the vital point of the whole scheme. Knowing his vindictive nature, I was perfectly certain that he would come to look upon his handiwork."

"But your appearance, Holmes—your ghastly face?"

"Three days of absolute fast does not improve one's beauty, Watson. For the rest, there is nothing which a sponge may not cure. With vaseline upon one's forehead, belladonna in one's eyes, rouge over the cheekbones, and crusts of beeswax round one's lips, a very satisfying effect can be produced. Malingering is a subject upon which I have sometimes thought of writing a monograph. A little occasional talk about half-crowns, oysters, or any other extraneous subject produces a pleasing effect of delirium."

"But why would you not let me near you, since there was in truth no infection?"

"Can you ask, my dear Watson? Do you imagine that I have no respect for your medical talents? Could I fancy that your astute judgment would pass a dying man who, however weak, had no rise of pulse or temperature? At four yards, I could deceive you. If I failed to do so, who would bring my Smith within my grasp? No, Watson, I would not touch that box. You can just see if you look at it sideways where the sharp spring like a viper's tooth emerges as you open it. I daresay it was by some such device that poor Savage, who stood between this monster and a reversion, was done to death. My correspondence, however, is, as you know, a varied one, and I am somewhat upon my guard against any packages which reach me. It was clear to me, however, that by pretending that he had really succeeded in his design I might surprise a confession. That pretence I have carried out with the thoroughness of the true artist. Thank you, Watson, you must help me on with my coat. When we have finished at the police station I think that something nutritious at Simpson's would not be out of place."

VII: His Last Bow

AN EPILOGUE OF SHERLOCK HOLMES

IT WAS NINE o'clock at night upon the second of August—the most terrible August in the history of the world. One might have thought already that God's curse hung heavy over a degenerate world, for there was an awesome hush and a feeling of vague expectancy in the sultry and stagnant air. The sun had long set, but one blood-red gash like an open wound lay low in the distant west. Above, the stars were shining brightly, and below, the lights of the shipping glimmered in the bay. The two famous Germans stood beside the stone parapet of the garden walk, with the long, low, heavily gabled house behind them, and they looked down upon the broad sweep of the beach at the foot of the great chalk cliffs on which Von Bork, like some wandering eagle, had perched himself four years before. They stood with their heads close together, talking in low, confidential tones. From below the two glowing ends of their cigars might have been the smouldering eyes of some malignant fiend looking down in the darkness.

A remarkable man this Von Bork—a man who could hardly be matched among all the devoted agents of the Kaiser. It was his talents which had first recommended him for the English mission, the most important mission of all, but since he had taken it over, those talents had become more and more manifest to the half-dozen people in the world who were really in touch with the truth. One of these was his present companion, Baron Von Herling, the chief secretary of the legation, whose huge 100-horsepower Benz car was blocking the country lane as it waited to waft its owner back to London.

"So far as I can judge the trend of events, you will probably be back in Berlin within the week," the secretary was saying. "When you get there, my dear Von Bork, I think you will be surprised at the welcome you will receive. I happen to know what is thought in the highest quarters of your work in this country." He was a huge man, the secretary; deep, broad, and tall, with a slow, heavy fashion of speech which had been his main asset in his political career.

Von Bork laughed.

"They are not very hard to deceive," he remarked. "A more docile, simple folk could not be imagined."

"I don't know about that," said the other thoughtfully. "They have strange limits and one must learn to observe them. It is that surface simplicity of theirs which makes a trap for the stranger. One's first impression is that they are entirely soft. Then one comes suddenly upon something very hard and you know that you have reached the limit, and must adapt yourself to the fact. They have, for example, their insular conventions which simply *must* be observed."

"Meaning 'good form' and that sort of thing?" Von Bork sighed, as one who had suffered much.

"Meaning British prejudice in all its queer manifestations. As an example I may quote one of my own worst blunders—I can afford to talk of my blunders, for you know my work well enough to be aware of my successes. It was on my first arrival. I was invited to a week-end gathering at the country house of a cabinet minister. The conversation was amazingly indiscreet."

Von Bork nodded. "I've been there," said he dryly.

"Exactly. Well, I naturally sent a résumé of the information to Berlin. Unfortunately our good chancellor is a little heavy-handed in these matters, and he transmitted a remark which showed that he was aware of what had been said. This, of course, took the trail straight up to me. You've no idea the harm it did me. There was nothing soft about our British hosts on that occasion, I can assure you. I was two years living it down. Now you, with this sporting pose of yours."

"No, no, don't call it a pose. A pose is an artificial thing. This is quite natural. I am a born sportsman. I enjoy it."

"Well, that makes it the more effective. You yacht against them, you hunt with them, you play polo, you match them in every game, your four-in-hand takes the prize at Olympia. I have even heard that you go the length of boxing with the young officers. What is the result? Nobody takes you seriously. You are a 'good old sport,' 'quite a decent fellow for a German,' a hard-drinking, night-club, knock-about-town, devil-may-care young fellow. And all the time this quiet country house of yours is the centre of half the mischief in England, and the sporting squire the most astute secret service man in Europe. Genius, my dear Von Bork—genius!"

"You flatter me, Baron. But certainly I may claim that my four years in this country have not been unproductive. I've never shown you my little store. Would you mind stepping in for a moment?"

The door of the study opened straight onto the terrace. Von Bork pushed it back, and, leading the way, he clicked the switch of the electric light. He then closed the door behind the bulky form which followed him, and carefully adjusted the heavy curtain over the latticed window. Only when all these precautions had been taken and tested did he turn his sunburned aquiline face to his guest.

"Some of my papers have gone," said he; "when my wife and the household left yesterday for Flushing they took the less important with them. I must, of course, claim the protection of the embassy for the others."

"Your name has already been filed as one of the personal suite. There will be no difficulties for you or your baggage. Of course, it is just possible that we may not have to go. England may leave France to her fate. We are sure that there is no binding treaty between them."

"And Belgium?"

"Yes, and Belgium, too."

Von Bork shook his head. "I don't see how that could be. There is a definite treaty there. She could never recover from such a humiliation."

"She would at least have peace for the moment."

"But her honour?"

"Tut, my dear sir, we live in a utilitarian age. Honour is a mediaeval conception. Besides, England is not ready. It is an inconceivable thing, but even our special war tax of fifty millions, which one would think made our purpose as clear as if we had advertised it on the front page of *The Times*, has not roused these people from their slumbers. Here and there one hears a question. It is my business to find an answer. Here and there also there is an irritation. It is my business to soothe it. But I can assure you that so far as the essentials go—the storage of munitions, the preparation for submarine attack, the arrangements for making high explosives—nothing is prepared. How then can England come in, especially when we have stirred her up such a devil's brew of Irish civil war, window-breaking Furies, and God knows what to keep her thoughts at home?"

"She must think of her future."

"Ah, that is another matter. I fancy that in the future, we have our own very definite plans about England, and that your information will be very vital to us. It is today or tomorrow with Mr. John Bull. If he prefers today we are perfectly ready. If it is tomorrow we shall be more ready still. I should think they would be wiser to fight with allies than without them, but that is their own affair. This week is their week of destiny. But you were speaking of your papers." He sat in the armchair with the light shining upon his broad bald head, while he puffed sedately at his cigar.

The large oak-panelled book-lined room had a curtain hung in the further corner. When this was drawn it disclosed a large brass-bound safe. Von Bork detached a small key from his watch chain, and after some considerable manipulation of the lock he swung open the heavy door.

"Look!" said he, standing clear, with a wave of his hand.

The light shone vividly into the opened safe, and the secretary of the embassy gazed with an absorbed interest at the rows of stuffed pigeonholes with which it was furnished. Each pigeonhole had its label, and his eyes as he glanced along them read a long series of such titles as "Fords," "Harbour defences," "Aeroplanes," "Ireland," "Egypt," "Portsmouth forts," "The Channel," "Rosyth," and a score of others. Each compartment was bristling with papers and plans.

"Colossal!" said the secretary. Putting down his cigar he softly clapped his fat hands.

"And all in four years, Baron. Not such a bad show for the hard-drinking, hard-riding country squire. But the gem of my collection is coming and there is the setting all ready for it." He pointed to a space over which "Naval Signals" was printed.

"But you have a good dossier there already."

"Out of date and wastepaper. The Admiralty in some way got the alarm and every code has been changed. It was a blow, Baron—the worst setback in my whole campaign. But thanks to my chequebook and the good Altamont all will be well tonight."

The Baron looked at his watch, and gave a guttural exclamation of disappointment.

"Well, I really can wait no longer. You can imagine that things are moving at present in Carlton Terrace and that we have all to be at our posts. I had hoped to be able to bring news of your great coup. Did Altamont name no hour?"

Von Bork pushed over a telegram:

Will come without fail tonight and bring new sparking plugs.
ALTAMONT

"Sparking plugs, eh?"

"You see, he poses as a motor expert and I keep a full garage. In our code everything likely to come up is named after some spare part. If he talks of a radiator it is a battleship, of an oil pump a cruiser, and so on. Sparking plugs are naval signals."

"From Portsmouth at midday," said the secretary, examining the superscription. "By the way, what do you give him?"

"Five hundred pounds for this particular job. Of course he has a salary as well."

"The greedy rogue. They are useful, these traitors, but I grudge them their blood money."

"I grudge Altamont nothing. He is a wonderful worker. If I pay him well, at least he delivers the goods, to use his own phrase. Besides he is not a traitor. I assure you that our most pan-Germanic Junker is a sucking dove in his feelings towards England as compared with a real bitter Irish-American."

"Oh, an Irish-American?"

"If you heard him talk you would not doubt it. Sometimes I assure you I can hardly understand him. He seems to have declared war on the King's English as well as on the English King. Must you really go? He may be here any moment."

"No. I'm sorry, but I have already overstayed my time. We shall expect you early tomorrow, and when you get that signal book through the little door on the Duke of York's steps you can put a triumphant Finis to your record in England. What! Tokay!" He indicated a heavily sealed dust-covered bottle which stood with two high glasses upon a salver.

"May I offer you a glass before your journey?"

"No, thanks. But it looks like revelry."

"Altamont has a nice taste in wines, and he took a fancy to my Tokay. He is a touchy fellow, and needs humouring in small things. I have to study him, I assure you." They had strolled out onto the terrace again, and along it to the further end where at a touch from the Baron's chauffeur the great car shivered and chuckled.

"Those are the lights of Harwich, I suppose," said the secretary, pulling on his dust coat. "How still and peaceful it all seems. There may be other lights within the week, and the English coast a less tranquil place! The heavens, too, may not be quite so peaceful if all that the good Zeppelin promises us comes true. By the way, who is that?"

Only one window showed a light behind them; in it there stood a lamp, and beside it, seated at a table, was a dear old ruddy-faced woman in a country cap. She was bending over her knitting and stopping occasionally to stroke a large black cat upon a stool beside her.

"That is Martha, the only servant I have left."

The secretary chuckled.

"She might almost personify Britannia," said he, "with her complete self-absorption and general air of comfortable somnolence. Well, au revoir, Von Bork!" With a final wave of his hand he sprang into the car, and a moment later the two golden cones from the headlights shot forward through the darkness. The secretary lay back in the cushions of the luxurious limousine, with his thoughts so full of the impending European tragedy that he hardly observed that as his car swung round the village street it nearly passed over a little Ford coming in the opposite direction.

Von Bork walked slowly back to the study when the last gleams of the motor lamps had faded into the distance. As he passed he observed that his old housekeeper had put out her lamp and retired. It was a new experience to him, the silence and darkness of his widespread house, for his family and household had been a large one. It was a relief to him, however, to think that they were all in safety and that, but for that one old woman who had lingered in the kitchen, he had the whole place to himself. There was a good deal of tidying up to do inside his study and he set himself to do it, until his keen, handsome face was flushed with the heat of the burning papers. A leather valise stood beside his table, and into this he began to pack very neatly and systematically the precious contents of his safe. He had hardly got started with the work, however, when his quick ears caught the sound of a distant car. Instantly he gave an exclamation of satisfaction, strapped up the valise, shut the safe, locked it, and hurried out on to the terrace. He was just in time to see the lights of a small car come to a halt at the gate. A passenger sprang out and advanced swiftly towards him, while the chauffeur, a heavily built, elderly man, with a grey moustache, settled down, like one who resigns himself to a long vigil.

"Well?" asked Von Bork eagerly, running forward to meet his visitor.

For answer the man waved a small brown-paper parcel triumphantly above his head.

"You can give me the glad hand tonight, mister," he cried. "I'm bringing home the bacon at last."

"The signals?"

"Same as I said in my cable. Every last one of them, semaphore, lamp code, Marconi—a copy, mind you, not the original. That was too dangerous. But it's the real goods, and you can lay to that." He slapped the German upon the shoulder with a rough familiarity from which the other winced.

"Come in," he said. "I'm all alone in the house. I was only waiting for this. Of course a copy is better than the original. If an original were missing they would change the whole thing. You think it's all safe about the copy?"

The Irish-American had entered the study and stretched his long limbs from the armchair. He was a tall, gaunt man of sixty, with clear-cut features and a small goatee beard which gave him a general resemblance to the caricatures of Uncle Sam. A half-smoked, sodden cigar hung from the corner of his mouth, and as he sat down he struck a match and relit it. "Making ready for a move?" he remarked as he looked round him. "Say, mister," he added, as his eyes fell upon the safe from which the curtain was now removed, "you don't tell me you keep your papers in that?"

"Why not?"

"Gosh, in a wide-open contraption like that! And they reckon you to be some spy. Why a Yankee crook would be into that with a can opener. If I'd known that any letter of mine was goin' to lie loose in a thing like that I'd have been a mug to write to you at all."

"It would puzzle any crook to force that safe," Von Bork answered. "You won't cut that metal with any tool."

"But the lock?"

"No, it's a double combination lock. You know what that is?"

"Search me," said the American.

"Well, you need a word as well as a set of figures before you can get the lock to work." He rose and showed a double-radiating disc round the keyhole. "This outer one is for the letters, the inner one for the figures."

"Well, well, that's fine."

"So it's not quite as simple as you thought. It was four years ago that I had it made, and what do you think I chose for the word and figures?"

"It's beyond me."

"Well, I chose August for the word, and 1914 for the figures, and here we are."

The American's face showed his surprise and admiration.

"My, but that was smart! You had it down to a fine thing."

"Yes, a few of us even then could have guessed the date. Here it is, and I'm shutting down tomorrow morning."

"Well, I guess you'll have to fix me up also. I'm not staying in this gol-darned country all on my lonesome. In a week or less from what I see, John Bull will be on his hind legs and fair ramping. I'd rather watch him from over the water."

"But you're an American citizen?"

"Well, so was Jack James an American citizen, but he's doing time in Portland all the same. It cuts no ice with a British copper to tell him you're an American citizen. 'It's British law and order over here,' says he. By the way, mister, talking of Jack James, it seems to me you don't do much to cover your men."

"What do you mean?" Von Bork asked sharply.

"Well, you are their employer, ain't you? It's up to you to see that they don't fall down. But they do fall down, and when did you ever pick them up? There's James——"

"It was James's own fault. You know that yourself. He was too self-willed for the job."

"James was a bonehead—I give you that. Then there was Hollis."

"The man was mad."

"Well, he went a bit woozy towards the end. It's enough to make a man bughouse when he has to play a part from morning to night with a hundred guys all ready to set the coppers wise to him. But now there is Steiner——"

Von Bork started violently, and his ruddy face turned a shade paler. "What about Steiner?"

"Well, they've got him, that's all. They raided his store last night, and he and his papers are all in Portsmouth gaol. You'll go off and he, poor devil, will have to stand the racket, and lucky if he gets off with his life. That's why I want to get over the water as soon as you do."

Von Bork was a strong, self-contained man, but it was easy to see that the news had shaken him.

"How could they have got onto Steiner?" he muttered. "That's the worst blow yet."

"Well, you nearly had a worse one, for I believe they are not far off me."

"You don't mean that!"

"Sure thing. My landlady down Fratton way had some inquiries, and when I heard of it I guessed it was time for me to hustle. But what I want to know, mister, is how the coppers know these things? Steiner is the fifth man you've lost since I signed on with you, and I know the name of the sixth if I don't get a move on. How do you explain it, and ain't you ashamed to see your men go down like this?"

Von Bork flushed crimson.

"How dare you speak in such a way!"

"If I didn't dare things, mister, I wouldn't be in your service. But I'll tell you straight what is in my mind. I've heard that with you German politicians when an agent has done his work you are not sorry to see him put away."

Von Bork sprang to his feet.

"Do you dare to suggest that I have given away my own agents!"

"I don't stand for that, mister, but there's a stool pigeon or a cross somewhere, and it's up to you to find out where it is. Anyhow I am taking no more chances. It's me for little Holland, and the sooner the better."

Von Bork had mastered his anger.

"We have been allies too long to quarrel now at the very hour of victory," he said. "You've done splendid work and taken risks and I can't forget it. By all means go to Holland, and you can get a boat from Rotterdam to New York. No other line will be safe a week from now. I'll take that book and pack it with the rest."

The American held the small parcel in his hand, but made no motion to give it up.

"What about the dough?" he asked.

"The what?"

"The boodle. The reward. The £500. The gunner turned damned nasty at the last, and I had to square him with an extra hundred dollars or it would have been nitsky for you and me. 'Nothin' doin'!' says he, and he meant it too, but the last hundred did it. It's cost me two hundred pound from first to last, so it isn't likely I'd give it up without gettin' my wad."

Von Bork smiled with some bitterness. "You don't seem to have a very high opinion of my honour," said he, "you want the money before you give up the book."

"Well, mister, it is a business proposition."

"All right. Have your way." He sat down at the table and scribbled a cheque, which he tore from the book, but he refrained from handing it to his companion. "After all, since we are to be on such terms, Mr. Altamont," said he, "I don't see why I should trust you any more than you trust me. Do you understand?" he added, looking back over his shoulder at the American. "There's the cheque upon the table. I claim the right to examine that parcel before you pick the money up."

The American passed it over without a word. Von Bork undid a winding of string and two wrappers of paper. Then he sat gazing for a moment in silent amazement at a small blue book which lay before him. Across the cover was printed in golden letters *Practical Handbook of Bee Culture*. Only for one instant did the master spy glare at this strangely irrelevant inscription.

The next he was gripped at the back of his neck by a grasp of iron, and a chloroformed sponge was held in front of his writhing face.

"Another glass, Watson!" said Mr. Sherlock Holmes, as he extended the bottle of Imperial Tokay.

The thick-set chauffeur, who had seated himself by the table, pushed forward his glass with some eagerness.

"It is a good wine, Holmes."

"A remarkable wine, Watson. Our friend upon the sofa has assured me that it is from Franz Joseph's special cellar at the Schoenbrunn

Palace. Might I trouble you to open the window, for chloroform vapour does not help the palate."

The safe was ajar, and Holmes standing in front of it was removing dossier after dossier, swiftly examining each, and then packing it neatly in Von Bork's valise. The German lay upon the sofa sleeping stertorously with a strap round his upper arms and another round his legs.

"We need not hurry ourselves, Watson. We are safe from interruption. Would you mind touching the bell. There is no one in the house except old Martha, who has played her part to admiration. I got her the situation here when first I took the matter up. Ah, Martha, you will be glad to hear that all is well."

The pleasant old lady had appeared in the doorway. She curtseyed with a smile to Mr. Holmes, but glanced with some apprehension at the figure upon the sofa.

"It is all right, Martha. He has not been hurt at all."

"I am glad of that, Mr. Holmes. According to his lights he has been a kind master. He wanted me to go with his wife to Germany yesterday, but that would hardly have suited your plans, would it, sir?"

"No, indeed, Martha. So long as you were here I was easy in my mind. We waited some time for your signal tonight."

"It was the secretary, sir."

"I know. His car passed ours."

"I thought he would never go. I knew that it would not suit your plans, sir, to find him here."

"No, indeed. Well, it only meant that we waited half an hour or so until I saw your lamp go out and knew that the coast was clear. You can report to me tomorrow in London, Martha, at Claridge's Hotel."

"Very good, sir."

"I suppose you have everything ready to leave?"

"Yes, sir. He posted seven letters today. I have the addresses as usual."

"Very good, Martha. I will look into them tomorrow. Good night. These papers," he continued, as the old lady vanished, "are not of very great importance, for, of course, the information which they represent has been sent off long ago to the German government. These are the originals which could not safely be got out of the country."

"Then they are of no use."

"I should not go so far as to say that, Watson. They will at least show our people what is known and what is not. I may say that a good many of these papers have come through me, and I need not add are thoroughly untrustworthy. It would brighten my declining years to see a German cruiser navigating the Solent according to the minefield plans which I have furnished. But you, Watson," he stopped his work and took his old friend by the shoulders; "I've hardly seen you in the light yet. How have the years used you? You look the same blithe boy as ever."

"I feel twenty years younger, Holmes. I have seldom felt so happy as when I got your wire asking me to meet you at Harwich with the car. But you, Holmes—you have changed very little—save for that horrible goatee."

"These are the sacrifices one makes for one's country, Watson," said Holmes, pulling at his little tuft. "Tomorrow it will be but a dreadful memory. With my hair cut and a few other superficial changes I shall no doubt reappear at Claridge's tomorrow as I was before this American stunt—I beg your pardon, Watson, my well of English seems to be permanently defiled—before this American job came my way."

"But you had retired, Holmes. We heard of you as living the life of a hermit among your bees and your books in a small farm upon the South Downs."

"Exactly, Watson. Here is the fruit of my leisured ease, the *magnum opus* of my latter years!" He picked up the volume from the table and read out the whole title, *Practical Handbook of Bee Culture, with some Observations upon the Segregation of the Queen.* Alone I did it. Behold the fruit of pensive nights and laborious days, when I watched the little working gangs as once I watched the criminal world of London."

"But how did you get to work again?"

"Ah, I have often marvelled at it myself. The foreign minister alone I could have withstood, but when the premier also deigned to visit my humble room——! The fact is, Watson, that this gentleman upon the sofa was a bit too good for our people. He was in a class by himself. Things were going wrong, and no one could understand why they were going wrong. Agents were suspected or even caught, but there was evidence of some strong and secret central force. It was absolutely necessary to expose it. Strong pressure was brought upon me to look into the matter. It has cost me two years, Watson, but they have not been devoid of excitement. When I say that I started my pilgrimage at Chicago, graduated in an Irish secret society at Buffalo, gave serious trouble to the constabulary at Skibbareen and so eventually caught the eye of a subordinate agent of Von Bork, who recommended me as a likely man, you will realise that the matter was complex. Since then I have been honoured by his confidence, which has not prevented most of his plans going subtly wrong and five of his best agents being in prison. I watched them, Watson, and I picked them as they ripened. Well, sir, I hope that you are none the worse!"

The last remark was addressed to Von Bork himself, who after much gasping and blinking had lain quietly listening to Holmes's statement. He broke out now into a furious stream of German invective, his face convulsed with passion. Holmes continued his swift investigation of documents while his prisoner cursed and swore.

"Though unmusical, German is the most expressive of all languages," he observed, when Von Bork had stopped from pure exhaustion. "Hullo! Hullo!" he added, as he looked hard at the corner of a tracing before putting it in the box. "This should put another bird in the cage. I had no idea that the paymaster was such a rascal, though I have long had an eye upon him. Mister Von Bork, you have a great deal to answer for."

The prisoner had raised himself with some difficulty upon the sofa and was staring with a strange mixture of amazement and hatred at his captor.

"I shall get level with you, Altamont," he said, speaking with slow deliberation, "if it takes me all my life I shall get level with you!"

"The old sweet song," said Holmes. "How often have I heard it in days gone by. It was a favourite ditty of the late lamented Professor Moriarty. Colonel Sebastian Moran has also been known to warble it. And yet I live and keep bees upon the South Downs."

"Curse you, you double traitor!" cried the German, straining against his bonds and glaring murder from his furious eyes.

"No, no, it is not so bad as that," said Holmes, smiling. "As my speech surely shows you, Mr. Altamont of Chicago had no existence in fact. I used him and he is gone."

"Then who are you?"

"It is really immaterial who I am, but since the matter seems to interest you, Mr. Von Bork, I may say that this is not my first acquaintance with the members of your family. I have done a good deal of business in Germany in the past, and my name is probably familiar to you."

"I would wish to know it," said the Prussian grimly.

"It was I who brought about the separation between Irene Adler and the late King of Bohemia when your cousin Heinrich was the imperial envoy. It was I also who saved from murder, by the Nihilist Klopman, Count Von und Zu Grafenstein, who was your mother's elder brother. It was I——"

Von Bork sat up in amazement.

"There is only one man," he cried.

"Exactly," said Holmes.

Von Bork groaned and sank back on the sofa. "And most of that information came through you," he cried. "What is it worth? What have I done? It is my ruin forever!"

"It is certainly a little untrustworthy," said Holmes. "It will require some checking, and you have little time to check it. Your admiral may find the new guns rather larger than he expects, and the cruisers perhaps a trifle faster."

Von Bork clutched at his own throat in despair.

"There are a good many other points of detail which will, no doubt, come to light in good time. But you have one quality which is very rare in a German, Mr. Von Bork, you are a sportsman and you will bear me no ill will when you realise that you, who have outwitted so many other people, have at last been outwitted yourself. After all, you have done your best for your country, and I have done my best for mine, and what could be more natural? Besides," he added, not unkindly, as he laid his hand upon the shoulder of the prostrate man, "it is better than to fall before some more ignoble foe. These papers are now ready, Watson. If you will help me with our prisoner, I think that we may get started for London at once."

It was no easy task to move Von Bork, for he was a strong and a desperate man. Finally, holding either arm, the two friends walked him very slowly down the garden walk which he had trod with such proud confidence when he received the congratulations of the famous diplomatist only a few hours before. After a short, final struggle he was hoisted, still bound hand and foot, into the spare seat of the little car. His precious valise was wedged in beside him.

"There's an east wind coming, Watson."

"I trust that you are as comfortable as circumstances permit," said Holmes, when the final arrangements were made. "Should I be guilty of a liberty if I lit a cigar and placed it between your lips?"

But all amenities were wasted upon the angry German.

"I suppose you realise, Mr. Sherlock Holmes," said he, "that if your government bears you out in this treatment it becomes an act of war."

"What about your government and all this treatment?" said Holmes, tapping the valise.

"You are a private individual. You have no warrant for my arrest. The whole proceeding is absolutely illegal and outrageous."

"Absolutely," said Holmes.

"Kidnapping a German subject."

"And stealing his private papers."

"Well, you realise your position, you and your accomplice here. If I were to shout for help as we pass through the village——"

"My dear sir, if you did anything so foolish you would probably enlarge the two limited titles of our village inns by giving us 'The Dangling Prussian' as a signpost. The Englishman is a patient creature, but at present his temper is a little inflamed and it would be as well not to try him too far. No, Mr. Von Bork, you will go with us in a quiet, sensible fashion to Scotland Yard, whence you can send for your friend Baron Von Herling and see if even now you may not fill that place which he has reserved for you in the ambassadorial suite. As to you, Watson, you are joining up with your old service, as I understand, so London won't be out of your way. Stand with me here upon the terrace, for it may be the last quiet talk that we shall ever have."

The two friends chatted in intimate converse for a few minutes, recalling once again the days of the past whilst their prisoner vainly wriggled to undo the bonds that held him. As they turned to the car, Holmes pointed back to the moonlit sea, and shook a thoughtful head.

"There's an east wind coming, Watson."

"I think not, Holmes. It is very warm."

"Good old Watson! You are the one fixed point in a changing age. There's an east wind coming all the same, such a wind as never blew on England yet. It will be cold and bitter, Watson, and a good many of us may wither before its blast. But it's God's own wind nonetheless, and a cleaner, better, stronger land will lie in the sunshine when the storm has cleared. Start her up, Watson, for it's time that we were on our way. I have a cheque for five hundred pounds which should be cashed early, for the drawer is quite capable of stopping it, if he can."

VIII: The Story of the Man with the Watches

THERE ARE many who will still bear in mind the singular circumstances which, under the heading of the Rugby Mystery, filled many columns of the daily press in the spring of the year 1892. Coming as it did at a period of exceptional dulness, it attracted perhaps rather more attention than it deserved, but it offered to the public that mixture of the whimsical and the tragic which is most stimulating to the popular imagination. Interest drooped, however, when, after weeks of fruitless investigation, it was found that no final explanation of the facts was forthcoming, and the tragedy seemed from that time to the present to have finally taken its place in the dark catalogue of inexplicable and unexpiated crimes. A recent communication (the authenticity of which appears to be above question) has, however, thrown some new and clear light upon the matter. Before laying it before the public it would be as well, perhaps, that I should refresh their memories as to the singular facts upon which this commentary is founded. These facts were briefly as follows:

At five o'clock upon the evening of the 18th of March in the year already mentioned a train left Euston Station for Manchester. It was a rainy, squally day, which grew wilder as it progressed, so it was by no means the weather in which anyone would travel who was not driven to do so by necessity. The train, however, is a favourite one among Manchester businessmen who are returning from town, for it does the journey in four hours and twenty minutes, with only three stoppages upon the way. In spite of the inclement evening it was, therefore, fairly well filled upon the occasion of which I speak. The guard of the train was a tried servant of the company—a man who had worked for twenty-two years without blemish or complaint. His name was John Palmer.

The station clock was upon the stroke of five, and the guard was about to give the customary signal to the engine driver, when he observed two belated passengers hurrying down the platform. The one was an exceptionally tall man, dressed in a long black overcoat with an astrakhan collar and cuffs. I have already said that the evening was an inclement one, and the tall traveller had the high, warm collar turned up to protect his throat against the bitter March wind. He appeared, as far as the guard could judge by so hurried an inspection, to be a man between fifty and sixty years of age, who had retained a good deal of the vigour and activity of his youth. In one hand he carried a brown leather Gladstone bag. His companion was a lady, tall and erect, walking with a vigorous step which outpaced the gentleman beside her. She wore a long, fawn-coloured dust cloak, a black, close-fitting toque, and a dark veil which concealed the greater part of her face. The two might very well have passed as father and daughter. They walked swiftly down the line of carriages, glancing in at the windows, until the guard, John Palmer, overtook them.

"Now, then, sir, look sharp, the train is going," said he.

"First-class," the man answered.

The guard turned the handle of the nearest door. In the carriage which he had opened there sat a small man with a cigar in his mouth. His appearance seems to have impressed itself upon the guard's memory, for he was prepared afterwards to describe or to identify him. He was a man of thirty-four or thirty-five years of age, dressed in some grey material, sharp-nosed, alert, with a ruddy, weather-beaten face, and a small, closely cropped black beard. He glanced up as the door was opened. The tall man paused with his foot upon the step.

"This is a smoking compartment. The lady dislikes smoke," said he, looking round at the guard.

"All right! Here you are, sir!" said John Palmer. He slammed the door of the smoking carriage, opened that of the next one, which was empty, and thrust the two travellers in. At the same moment he sounded his whistle, and the wheels of the train began to move. The man with the cigar was at the window of his carriage, and said something to the guard as he rolled past him, but the words were lost in the bustle of the departure. Palmer stepped into the guard's van as it came up to him, and thought no more of the incident.

Twelve minutes after its departure the train reached Willesden

Junction, where it stopped for a very short interval. An examination of the tickets has made it certain that no one either joined or left it at this time, and no passenger was seen to alight upon the platform. At 5:14 the journey to Manchester was resumed, and Rugby was reached at 6:50, the express being five minutes late.

At Rugby the attention of the station officials was drawn to the fact that the door of one of the first-class carriages was open. An examination of that compartment, and of its neighbour, disclosed a remarkable state of affairs.

The smoking carriage in which the short, red-faced man with the black beard had been seen was now empty. Save for a half-smoked cigar, there was no trace whatever of its recent occupant. The door of this carriage was fastened. In the next compartment, to which attention had been originally drawn, there was no sign either of the gentleman with the astrakhan collar or of the young lady who accompanied him. All three passengers had disappeared. On the other hand, there was found upon the floor of this carriage—the one in which the tall traveller and the lady had been—a young man, fashionably dressed and of elegant appearance. He lay with his knees drawn up, and his head resting against the further door, an elbow upon either seat. A bullet had penetrated his heart, and his death must have been instantaneous. No one had seen such a man enter the train, and no railway ticket was found in his pocket, nor were there any markings upon his linen, nor papers or personal property which might help to identify him. Who he was, whence he had come, and how he had met his end were each as great a mystery as what had occurred to the three people who had started an hour and a half before from Willesden in those two compartments.

I have said that there was no personal property which might help to identify him, but it is true that there was one peculiarity about this unknown young man which was much commented upon at the time. In his pockets were found no fewer than six valuable gold watches, three in the various pockets of his waistcoat, one in his ticket pocket, one in his breast pocket, and one small one set in a leather strap and fastened round his left wrist. The obvious explanation that the man was a pickpocket, and that this was his plunder, was discounted by the fact that all six were of American make, and of a type which is rare in England. Three of them bore the mark of the Rochester Watch-making Company; one was by Mason, of Elmira; one was unmarked; and the small one, which was highly jewelled and ornamented, was from Tiffany, of New York. The other contents of his pocket consisted of an ivory knife with a corkscrew by Rodgers, of Sheffield; a small circular mirror, one inch in diameter; a readmission slip to the Lyceum Theatre; a silver box full of vesta matches, and a brown leather cigar case containing two cheroots—also two pounds fourteen shillings in money. It was clear then that whatever motives may have led to his death, robbery was not among them. As already mentioned, there were no markings upon the man's linen, which appeared to be new, and no tailor's name upon his coat. In appearance he was young, short, smooth-cheeked, and delicately featured. One of his front teeth was conspicuously stopped with gold.

On the discovery of the tragedy an examination was instantly made of the tickets of all passengers, and the number of the passengers themselves was counted. It was found that only three tickets were unaccounted for, corresponding to the three travellers who were missing. The express was then allowed to proceed, but a new guard was sent with it, and John Palmer was detained as a witness at Rugby. The carriage which included the two compartments in question was uncoupled and sidetracked. Then, on the arrival of Inspector Vane, of Scotland Yard, and of Mr. Henderson, a detective in the service of the railway company, an exhaustive inquiry was made into all the circumstances.

That crime had been committed was certain. The bullet, which appeared to have come from a small pistol or revolver, had been fired from some little distance, as there was no scorching of the clothes. No weapon was found in the compartment (which finally disposed of the theory of suicide), nor was there any sign of the brown leather bag which the guard had seen in the hand of the tall gentleman. A lady's parasol was found upon the rack, but no other trace was to be seen of the travellers in either of the sections. Apart from the crime, the question of how or why three passengers (one of them a lady) could get out of the train, and one other get in during the unbroken run between Willesden and Rugby, was one which excited the utmost curiosity among the general public, and gave rise to much speculation in the London press.

John Palmer, the guard, was able at the inquest to give some evidence which threw a little light upon the matter. There was a spot between Tring and Cheddington, according to his statement, where, on account of some repairs to the line, the train had for a few minutes slowed down to a pace not exceeding eight or ten miles an hour. At that place it might be possible for a man, or even for an exceptionally active woman, to have left the train without serious injury. It was true that a gang of plate-layers was there, and that they had seen nothing, but it was their custom to stand in the middle between the metals, and the open carriage door was upon the far side, so that it was conceivable that someone might have alighted unseen, as the darkness would by that time be drawing in. A steep embankment would instantly screen anyone who sprang out from the observation of the navvies.

The guard also deposed that there was a good deal of movement upon the platform at Willesden Junction, and that though it was certain that no one had either joined or left the train there, it was still quite possible that some of the passengers might have changed unseen from one compartment to another. It was by no means uncommon for a gentleman to finish his cigar in a smoking carriage and then to change to a clearer atmosphere. Supposing that the man with the black beard had done so at Willesden (and the half-smoked cigar upon the floor seemed to favour the supposition), he would naturally go into the nearest section, which would bring him into the company of the two other actors in this drama. Thus the first stage of the affair might be surmised without any great breach of probability. But what the second stage had been, or how the final one had been arrived at, neither the guard nor the experienced detective officers could suggest.

A careful examination of the line between Willesden and Rugby resulted in one discovery which might or might not have a bearing upon the tragedy. Near Tring, at the very place where the train slowed down, there was found at the bottom of the embankment a small pocket Testament, very shabby and worn. It was printed by the Bible Society of London, and bore an inscription: "From John to Alice. Jan. 13th, 1856," upon the flyleaf. Underneath was written: "James. July 4th, 1859," and beneath that again: "Edward. Nov. 1st, 1869," all the entries being in the same handwriting. This was the only clue, if it could be called a clue, which the police obtained, and the coroner's verdict of, "Murder by a person or persons unknown" was the unsatisfactory ending of a singular case. Advertisement, rewards, and inquiries proved equally fruitless, and nothing could be found which was solid enough to form the basis for a profitable investigation.

It would be a mistake, however, to suppose that no theories were formed to account for the facts. On the contrary, the press, both in England and in America, teemed with suggestions and suppositions, most of which were obviously absurd. The fact that the watches were of American make, and some peculiarities in connection with the gold stopping of his front tooth, appeared to indicate that the deceased was a citizen of the United States, though his linen, clothes, and boots were undoubtedly of British manufacture. It was surmised, by some, that he was concealed under the seat, and that, being discovered, he was for some reason, possibly because he had overheard their guilty secrets, put to death by his fellow passengers. When coupled with generalities as to the ferocity and cunning of anarchical and other secret societies, this theory sounded as plausible as any.

The fact that he should be without a ticket would be consistent with the idea of concealment, and it was well known that women played a prominent part in the Nihilistic propaganda. On the other hand, it was clear, from the guard's statement, that the man must have been hidden there *before* the others arrived, and how unlikely the coincidence that conspirators should stray exactly into the very compartment in which a spy was already concealed! Besides, this explanation ignored the man in the smoking carriage, and gave no reason at all for his simultaneous disappearance. The police had little difficulty in showing that such a theory would not cover the facts, but they were unprepared in the absence of evidence to advance any alternative explanation.

There was a letter in the *Daily Gazette*, over the signature of a well-known criminal investigator, which gave rise to considerable discussion at the time. He had formed a hypothesis which had at least ingenuity to recommend it, and I cannot do better than append it in his own words.

"Whatever may be the truth," said he, "it must depend upon some bizarre and rare combination of events, so we need have no hesitation in postulating such events in our explanation. In the absence of data we must abandon the analytic or scientific method of investigation, and must approach it in the synthetic fashion. In a word, instead of taking known events and deducing from them what has occurred, we must build up a fanciful explanation if it will only be consistent with known events. We can then test this explanation by any fresh facts which may arise. If they all fit into their places, the probability is that we are upon the right track, and with each fresh fact this probability increases in a geometrical progression until the evidence becomes final and convincing.

"Now, there is one most remarkable and suggestive fact which has not met with the attention which it deserves. There is a local train running through Harrow and King's Langley, which is timed in such a way that the express must have overtaken it at or about the period when it eased down its speed to eight miles an hour on account of the repairs of the line. The two trains would at that time be travelling in the same direction at a similar rate of speed and upon parallel lines. It is within everyone's experience how, under such circumstances, the occupant of each carriage can see very plainly the passengers in the other carriages opposite to him. The lamps of the express had been lit at Willesden, so that each compartment was brightly illuminated, and most visible to an observer from outside.

"Now, the sequence of events as I reconstruct them would be after this fashion. This young man with the abnormal number of watches was alone in the carriage of the slow train. His ticket, with his papers and gloves and other things, was, we will suppose, on the seat beside him. He was probably an American, and also probably a man of weak intellect. The excessive wearing of jewellery is an early symptom in some forms of mania.

"As he sat watching the carriages of the express which were (on account of the state of the line) going at the same pace as himself, he suddenly saw some people in it whom he knew. We will suppose for the sake of our theory that these people were a woman whom he loved and a man whom he hated—and who in return hated him. The young man was excitable and impulsive. He opened the door of his carriage, stepped from the footboard of the local train to the footboard of the express, opened the other door, and made his way into the presence of these two people. The feat (on the supposition that the trains were going at the same pace) is by no means so perilous as it might appear.

"Having now got our young man without his ticket into the carriage in which the elder man and the young woman are travelling, it is not difficult to imagine that a violent scene ensued. It is possible that the pair were also Americans, which is the more probable as the man carried a weapon—an unusual thing in England. If our supposition of incipient mania is correct, the young man is likely to have assaulted the other. As the upshot of the quarrel the elder man shot the intruder, and then made his escape from the carriage, taking the young lady with him. We will suppose that all this happened very rapidly, and that the train was still going at so slow a pace that it was not difficult for them to leave it. A woman might leave a train going at eight miles an hour. As a matter of fact, we know that this woman *did* do so.

"And now we have to fit in the man in the smoking carriage. Presuming that we have, up to this point, reconstructed the tragedy correctly, we shall find nothing in this other man to cause us to reconsider our conclusions. According to my theory, this man saw the young fellow cross from one train to the other, saw him open the door, heard the pistol shot, saw the two fugitives spring out onto the line, realised that murder had been done, and sprang out himself in pursuit. Why he has never been heard of since—whether he met his own death in the pursuit, or whether, as is more likely, he was made to realise that it was not a case for his interference—is a detail which we have at present no means of explaining. I acknowledge that there are some difficulties in the way. At first sight, it might seem improbable that at such a moment a murderer would burden himself in his flight with a brown leather bag. My answer is that he was well aware that if the bag were found his identity would be established. It was absolutely necessary for him to take it with him. My theory stands or falls upon one point, and I call upon the railway company to make strict inquiry as to whether a ticket was found unclaimed in the local train through Harrow and King's Langley upon the 18th of March. If such a ticket were found my case is proved. If not, my theory may still be the correct one, for it is conceivable either that he travelled without a ticket or that his ticket was lost."

To this elaborate and plausible hypothesis the answer of the police and of the company was, first, that no such ticket was found; secondly, that the slow train would never run parallel to the express; and, thirdly, that the local train had been stationary in King's Langley Station when the express, going at fifty miles an hour, had flashed past it. So perished the only satisfying explanation, and five years have elapsed without supplying a new one. Now, at last, there comes a statement which covers all the facts, and which must be regarded as authentic. It took the shape of a letter dated from New York, and addressed to the same criminal investigator whose theory I have quoted. It is given here in extenso, with the exception of the two opening paragraphs, which are personal in their nature:

"You'll excuse me if I am not very free with names. There's less reason now than there was five years ago when Mother was still living. But for all that, I had rather cover up our tracks all I can. But I owe you an explanation, for if your idea of it was wrong, it was a mighty ingenious one all the same. I'll have to go back a little so as you may understand all about it.

"My people came from Bucks, England, and emigrated to the States in the early fifties. They settled in Rochester, in the state of New York, where my father ran a large dry goods store. There were only two sons: myself, James, and my brother, Edward. I was ten years older than my brother, and after my father died I sort of took the place of a father to him, as an elder brother would. He was a bright, spirited boy, and just one of the most beautiful creatures that ever lived. But there was always a soft spot in him, and it was like mold in cheese, for it spread and spread, and nothing that you could do would stop it. Mother saw it just as clearly as I did, but she went on spoiling him all the same, for he had such a way with him that you could refuse him nothing. I did all I could to hold him in, and he hated me for my pains.

"At last he fairly got his head, and nothing that we could do would stop him. He got off into New York, and went rapidly from bad to worse. At first he was only fast, and then he was criminal; and then, at the end of a year or two, he was one of the most notorious young crooks in the city. He had formed a friendship with Sparrow MacCoy, who was at the head of his profession as a bunco-steerer, green-goodsman, and general rascal. They took to cardsharping, and frequented some of the best hotels in New York. My brother was an excellent actor (he might have made an honest name for himself if he had chosen), and he would take the parts of a young Englishman of title, of a simple lad from the West, or of a college undergraduate, whichever suited Sparrow MacCoy's purpose. And then one day he dressed himself as a girl, and he carried it off so well, and made himself such a valuable decoy, that it was their favourite game afterwards. They had made it right with Tammany and with the police, so it seemed as if nothing could ever stop them, for those were in the days before the Lexow Commission, and if you only had a pull, you could do pretty nearly anything you wanted.

"And nothing would have stopped them if they had only stuck to cards and New York, but they must needs come up Rochester way, and forge a name upon a cheque. It was my brother that did it, though everyone knew that it was under the influence of Sparrow MacCoy. I bought up that cheque, and a pretty sum it cost me. Then I went to my brother, laid it before him on the table, and swore to him that I would prosecute if he did not clear out of the country. At first he simply laughed. I could not prosecute, he said, without breaking our mother's heart, and he knew that I would not do that. I made him understand, however, that our mother's heart was being broken in any case, and that I had set firm on the point that I would rather see him in a Rochester gaol than in a New York hotel. So at last he gave in, and he made me a solemn promise that he would see Sparrow MacCoy no more, that he would go to Europe, and that he would turn his hand to any honest trade that I helped him to get. I took him down right away to an old family friend, Joe Willson, who is an exporter of American watches and clocks, and I got him to give Edward an agency in London, with a small salary and a 5 percent commission on all business. His manner and appearance were so good that he won the old man over at once, and within a week he was sent off to London with a case full of samples.

"It seemed to me that this business of the cheque had really given my brother a fright, and that there was some chance of his settling down into an honest line of life. My mother had spoken with him, and what she said had touched him, for she had always been the best of mothers to him, and he had been the great sorrow of her life. But I knew that this man Sparrow MacCoy had a great influence over Edward, and my chance of keeping the lad straight lay in breaking the connection between them. I had a friend in the New York detective force, and through him I kept a watch upon MacCoy. When within a fortnight of my brother's sailing I heard that MacCoy had taken a berth in the *Etruria*, I was as certain as if he had told me that he was going over to England for the purpose of coaxing Edward back again into the ways that he had left. In an instant I had resolved to go also, and to put my influence against MacCoy's. I knew was a losing fight, but I thought, and my mother thought, that it was my duty. We passed the last night together in prayer for my success, and she gave me her own Testament that my father had given her on the day of their marriage in the old country, so that I might always wear it next my heart.

"I was a fellow traveller on the steamship with Sparrow MacCoy, and at least I had the satisfaction of spoiling his little game for the voyage. The very first night I went into the smoking room, and found him at the head of a card table, with half a dozen young fellows who were carrying their full purses and their empty skulls over to Europe. He was settling down for his harvest, and a rich one it would have been. But I soon changed all that.

" 'Gentlemen,' said I, 'are you aware whom you are playing with?'

" 'What's that to you? You mind your own business!' said he, with an oath.

" 'Who is it, anyway?' asked one of the dudes.

" 'He's Sparrow MacCoy, the most notorious cardsharper in the States.'

"Up he jumped with a bottle in his hand, but he remembered that he was under the flag of the effete old country, where law and order run, and Tammany has no pull. Gaol and the gallows wait for violence and murder, and there's no slipping out by the back door on board an ocean liner.

" 'Prove your words, you—!' said he.

" 'I will!' said I. 'If you will turn up your right shirtsleeve to the shoulder, I will either prove my words or I will eat them.'

"He turned white and said not a word. You see, I knew something of his ways, and I was aware that part of the mechanism which he and all such sharpers use consists of an elastic down the arm with a clip just above the wrist. It is by means of this clip that they withdraw from their hands the cards which they do not want, while they substitute other cards from another hiding place. I reckoned on it being there, and it was. He cursed me, slunk out of the saloon, and was hardly seen again during the voyage. For once, at any rate, I got level with Mister Sparrow MacCoy.

"But he soon had his revenge upon me, for when it came to influencing my brother he outweighed me every time. Edward had kept himself straight in London for the first few weeks, and he had done some business with his American watches, until this villain came across his path once more. I did my best, but the best was little enough. The next thing I heard there had been a scandal at one of the Northumberland Avenue hotels: a traveller had been fleeced of a large sum by two confederate cardsharpers, and the matter was in the hands of Scotland Yard. The first I learned of it was in the evening paper, and I was at once certain that my brother and MacCoy were back at their old games. I hurried at once to Edward's lodgings. They told me that he and a tall gentleman (whom I recognised as MacCoy) had gone off together, and that he had left the lodgings and taken his things with him. The landlady had heard them give several directions to the cabman, ending with Euston Station, and she had accidentally overheard the tall gentleman saying something about Manchester. She believed that that was their destination.

"A glance at the timetable showed me that the most likely train was at five, though there was another at 4:35 which they might have caught. I had only time to get the later one, but found no sign of them either at the depôt or in the train. They must have gone on by the earlier one, so I determined to follow them to Manchester and search for them in the hotels there. One last appeal to my brother by all that he owed to my mother might even now be the salvation of him. My nerves were overstrung, and I lit a cigar to steady them. At that moment, just as the train was moving off, the door of my compartment was flung open, and there were MacCoy and my brother on the platform.

"They were both disguised, and with good reason, for they knew that the London police were after them. MacCoy had a great astrakhan collar drawn up, so that only his eyes and nose were showing. My brother was dressed like a woman, with a black veil half down his face, but of course it did not deceive me for an instant, nor would it have done so even if I had not known that he had often used such a dress before. I started up, and as I did so MacCoy recognised me. He said something, the conductor slammed the door, and they were

". . . just as the train was moving off,
the door of my compartment was flung open . . ."

shown into the next compartment. I tried to stop the train so as to follow them, but the wheels were already moving, and it was too late.

"When we stopped at Willesden, I instantly changed my carriage. It appears that I was not seen to do so, which is not surprising, as the station was crowded with people. MacCoy, of course, was expecting me, and he had spent the time between Euston and Willesden in saying all he could to harden my brother's heart and set him against me. That is what I fancy, for I had never found him so impossible to soften or to move. I tried this way and I tried that; I pictured his future in an English gaol; I described the sorrow of his mother when I came back with the news; I said everything to touch his heart, but all to no purpose. He sat there with a fixed sneer upon his handsome face, while every now and then Sparrow MacCoy would throw in a taunt at me, or some word of encouragement to hold my brother to his resolutions.

" 'Why don't you run a Sunday school?' he would say to me, and then, in the same breath: 'He thinks you have no will of your own. He thinks you are just the baby brother and that he can lead you where he likes. He's only just finding out that you are a man as well as he.'

"It was those words of his which set me talking bitterly. We had left Willesden, you understand, for all this took some time. My temper got the better of me, and for the first time in my life I let my brother see the rough side of me. Perhaps it would have been better had I done so earlier and more often.

" 'A man!' said I. 'Well, I'm glad to have your friend's assurance of it, for no one would suspect it to see you like a boarding-school missy. I don't suppose in all this country there is a more contemptible-looking creature than you are as you sit there with that Dolly pinafore upon you.' He coloured up at that, for he was a vain man, and he winced from ridicule.

" 'It's only a dust cloak,' said he, and he slipped it off. 'One has to throw the coppers off one's scent, and I had no other way to do it.' He took his toque off with the veil attached, and he put both it and the cloak into his brown bag. 'Anyway, I don't need to wear it until the conductor comes round,' said he.

" 'Nor then, either,' said I, and taking the bag I slung it with all my force out of the window. 'Now,' said I, 'you'll never make a Mary Jane

of yourself while I can help it. If nothing but that disguise stands between you and a gaol, then to gaol you shall go.'

"That was the way to manage him. I felt my advantage at once. His
supple nature was one which yielded to roughness far more readily
than to entreaty. He flushed with shame, and his eyes filled with tears.
But MacCoy saw my advantage also, and was determined that I should
not pursue it.

" 'He's my pard, and you shall not bully him,' he cried.

" 'He's my brother, and you shall not ruin him,' said I. 'I believe a
spell of prison is the very best way of keeping you apart, and you
shall have it, or it will be no fault of mine.'

" 'Oh, you would squeal, would you?' he cried, and in an instant
he whipped out his revolver. I sprang for his hand, but saw that I was
too late, and jumped aside. At the same instant he fired, and the bullet which would have struck me passed through the heart of my unfortunate brother.

"He dropped without a groan upon the floor of the compartment,
and MacCoy and I, equally horrified, knelt at each side of him, trying to bring back some signs of life. MacCoy still held the loaded revolver in his hand, but his anger against me and my resentment towards
him had both for that moment been swallowed up in this sudden
tragedy. It was he who first realised the situation. The train was for
some reason going very slowly at the moment, and he saw his opportunity for escape. In an instant he had the door open, but I was
as quick as he, and jumping upon him the two of us fell off the footboard and rolled in each other's arms down a steep embankment. At
the bottom I struck my head against a stone, and I remembered nothing more. When I came to myself I was lying among some low bushes,
not far from the railroad track, and somebody was bathing my head
with a wet handkerchief. It was Sparrow MacCoy.

" 'I guess I couldn't leave you,' said he. 'I didn't want to have the
blood of two of you on my hands in one day. You loved your brother,
I've no doubt; but you didn't love him a cent more than I loved him,
though you'll say that I took a queer way to show it. Anyhow, it seems
a mighty empty world now that he is gone, and I don't care a continental whether you give me over to the hangman or not.'

"He had turned his ankle in the fall, and there we sat, he with his
useless foot, and I with my throbbing head, and we talked and talked

until gradually my bitterness began to soften and to turn into something like sympathy. What was the use of revenging his death upon a man who was as much stricken by that death as I was? And then, as my wits gradually returned, I began to realise also that I could do nothing against MacCoy which would not recoil upon my mother and myself. How could we convict him without a full account of my brother's career being made public—the very thing which of all others we had to avoid? It was really as much our interest as his to cover the matter up, and from being an avenger of crime I found myself changed to a conspirator against justice. The place in which we found ourselves was one of those pheasant preserves which are so common in the old country, and as we groped our way through it I found myself consulting the slayer of my brother as to how far it would be possible to hush it up.

"I soon realised from what he said that unless there were some papers of which we knew nothing in my brother's pockets, there was really no possible means by which the police could identify him or learn how he had got there. His ticket was in MacCoy's pocket and so was the ticket for some baggage which they had left at the depôt. Like most Americans, he had found it cheaper and easier to buy an outfit in London than to bring one from New York, so that all his linen and clothes were new and unmarked. The bag, containing the dust cloak, which I had thrown out of the window, may have fallen among some bramble patch where it is still concealed, or may have been carried off by some tramp, or may have come into the possession of the police, who kept the incident to themselves. Anyhow, I have seen nothing about it in the London papers. As to the watches, they were a selection from those which had been intrusted to him for business purposes. It may have been for the same business purposes that he was taking them to Manchester, but—well, it's too late to enter into that.

"I don't blame the police for being at fault. I don't see how it could have been otherwise. There was just one little clew that they might have followed up, but it was a small one. I mean that small circular mirror which was found in my brother's pocket. It isn't a very common thing for a young man to carry about with him, is it? But a gambler might have told you what such a mirror may mean to a cardsharper. If you sit back a little from the table, and lay the mirror, face upwards, upon your lap, you can see, as you deal, every card that you give to your adversary. It is not hard to say whether you see a man or raise him when you know his cards as well as your own. It was as much a part of a sharper's outfit as the elastic clip upon Sparrow MacCoy's arm. Taking that, in connection with the recent frauds at the hotels, the police might have got hold of one end of the string.

"I don't think there is much more for me to explain. We got to a village called Amersham that night in the character of two gentlemen upon a walking tour, and afterwards we made our way quietly to London, whence MacCoy went on to Cairo and I returned to New York. My mother died six months afterwards, and I am glad to say that to the day of her death she never knew what had happened. She was always under the delusion that Edward was earning an honest living in London, and I never had the heart to tell her the truth. He never wrote; but then, he never did write at any time, so that made no difference. His name was the last upon her lips.

"There's just one other thing that I have to ask you, sir, and I should take it as a kind return for all this explanation, if you could do it for me. You remember that Testament that was picked up. I always carried it in my inside pocket, and it must have come out in my fall. I value it very highly, for it was the family book with my birth and my brother's marked by my father in the beginning of it. I wish you would apply at the proper place and have it sent to me. It can be of no possible value to anyone else. If you address it to X, Bassano's Library, Broadway, New York, it is sure to come to hand."

IX: The Story of the Lost Special

THE CONFESSION of Herbert de Lernac, now lying under sentence of death at Marseilles, has thrown a light upon one of the most inexplicable crimes of the century—an incident which is, I believe, absolutely unprecedented in the criminal annals of any country. Although there is a reluctance to discuss the matter in official circles, and little information has been given to the press, there are still indications that the statement of this archcriminal is corroborated by the facts, and that we have at last found a solution for a most astounding business. As the matter is eight years old, and as its importance was somewhat obscured by a political crisis which was engaging the public attention at the time, it may be as well to state the facts as far as we have been able to ascertain them. They are collated from the Liverpool papers of that date, from the proceedings at the inquest upon John Slater, the engine driver, and from the records of the London and West Coast Railway Company, which have been courteously put at my disposal. Briefly, they are as follows.

On the 3rd of June, 1980, a gentleman, who gave his name as Monsieur Louis Caratal, desired an interview with Mr. James Bland, the superintendent of the Central London and West Coast Station in Liverpool. He was a small man, middle-aged and dark, with a stoop which was so marked that it suggested some deformity of the spine. He was accompanied by a friend, a man of imposing physique, whose deferential manner and constant attention suggested that his position was one of dependence. This friend or companion, whose name did not transpire, was certainly a foreigner, and probably, from his swarthy complexion, either a Spaniard or a South American. One peculiarity was observed in him. He carried in his left hand a small black leather dispatch box, and it was noticed by a sharp-eyed clerk in the

189

Central office that this box was fastened to his wrist by a strap. No importance was attached to the fact at the time, but subsequent events endowed it with some significance. Monsieur Caratal was shown up to Mr. Bland's office, while his companion remained outside.

Monsieur Caratal's business was quickly dispatched. He had arrived that afternoon from Central America. Affairs of the utmost importance demanded that he should be in Paris without the loss of an unnecessary hour. He had missed the London express. A special must be provided. Money was of no importance. Time was everything. If the company would speed him on his way, they might make their own terms.

Mr. Bland struck the electric bell, summoned Mr. Potter Hood, the traffic manager, and had the matter arranged in five minutes. The train would start in three-quarters of an hour. It would take that time to insure that the line should be clear. The powerful engine called Rochdale (No. 247 on the company's register) was attached to two carriages, with a guard's van behind. The first carriage was solely for the purpose of decreasing the inconvenience arising from the oscillation. The second was divided, as usual, into four compartments, a first-class, a first-class smoking, a second-class, and a second-class smoking. The first compartment, which was the nearest to the engine, was the one allotted to the travellers. The other three were empty. The guard of the special train was James McPherson, who had been some years in the service of the company. The stoker, William Smith, was a new hand.

Monsieur Caratal, upon leaving the superintendent's office, rejoined his companion, and both of them manifested extreme impatience to be off. Having paid the money asked, which amounted to fifty pounds five shillings, at the usual special rate of five shillings a mile, they demanded to be shown the carriage, and at once took their seats in it, although they were assured that the better part of an hour must elapse before the line could be cleared. In the meantime a singular coincidence had occurred in the office which Monsieur Caratal had just quitted.

A request for a special is not a very uncommon circumstance in a rich commercial centre, but that two should be required upon the same afternoon was most unusual. It so happened, however, that Mr. Bland had hardly dismissed the first traveller before a second entered with a similar request. This was a Mr. Horace Moore, a gentlemanly man of military appearance, who alleged that the sudden serious illness of his wife in London made it absolutely imperative that he should not lose an instant in starting upon the journey. His distress and anxiety were so evident that Mr. Bland did all that was possible to meet his wishes. A second special was out of the question, as the ordinary local service was already somewhat deranged by the first. There was the alternative, however, that Mr. Moore should share the expense of Monsieur Caratal's train, and should travel in the other empty first-class compartment, if Monsieur Caratal objected to having him in the one which he occupied. It was difficult to see any objection to such an arrangement, and yet Monsieur Caratal, upon the suggestion being made to him by Mr. Potter Hood, absolutely refused to consider it for an instant. The train was his, he said, and he would insist upon the exclusive use of it. All argument failed to overcome his ungracious objections, and finally the plan had to be abandoned. Mr. Horace Moore left the station in great distress, after learning that his only course was to take the ordinary slow train which leaves Liverpool at six o'clock. At four thirty-one exactly by the station clock the special train, containing the crippled Monsieur Caratal and his gigantic companion, steamed out of the Liverpool station. The line was at that time clear, and there should have been no stoppage before Manchester.

The trains of the London and West Coast Railway run over the lines of another company as far as this town, which should have been reached by the special rather before six o'clock. At a quarter after six considerable surprise and some consternation were caused amongst the officials at Liverpool by the receipt of a telegram from Manchester to say that it had not yet arrived. An inquiry directed to St. Helens, which is a third of the way between the two cities, elicited the following reply:

TO JAMES BLAND, SUPERINTENDENT, CENTRAL L. & W.C., LIVERPOOL—SPECIAL PASSED HERE AT 4:52, WELL UP TO TIME—DOWSER, ST. HELENS

This telegram was received at 6:40. At 6:50 a second message was received from Manchester:

NO SIGN OF SPECIAL AS ADVISED BY YOU.

And then ten minutes later a third, more bewildering:

PRESUME SOME MISTAKE AS TO PROPOSED RUNNING OF SPECIAL.
LOCAL TRAIN FROM ST. HELENS TIMED TO FOLLOW IT HAS JUST
ARRIVED AND HAS SEEN NOTHING OF IT. KINDLY WIRE ADVICES.
MANCHESTER

The matter was assuming a most amazing aspect, although in some respects the last telegram was a relief to the authorities at Liverpool. If an accident had occurred to the special, it seemed hardly possible that the local train could have passed down the same line without observing it. And yet, what was the alternative? Where could the train be? Had it possibly been sidetracked for some reason in order to allow the slower train to go past? Such an explanation was possible if some small repair had to be effected. A telegram was dispatched to each of the stations between St. Helens and Manchester, and the superintendent and traffic manager waited in the utmost suspense at the instrument for the series of replies which would enable them to say for certain what had become of the missing train. The answers came back in the order of questions, which was the order of the stations beginning at the St. Helens end:

SPECIAL PASSED HERE FIVE O'CLOCK. COLLINS GREEN
SPECIAL PASSED HERE SIX PAST FIVE. EARLESTOWN
SPECIAL PASSED HERE 5:10. NEWTON
SPECIAL PASSED HERE 5:20. KENYON JUNCTION
NO SPECIAL TRAIN HAS PASSED HERE. BARTON MOSS

The two officials stared at each other in amazement.

"This is unique in my thirty years of experience," said Mr. Bland.

"Absolutely unprecedented and inexplicable, sir. The special has gone wrong between Kenyon Junction and Barton Moss."

"And yet there is no siding, as far as my memory serves me, between the two stations. The special must have run off the metals."

"But how could the four-fifty parliamentary pass over the same line without observing it?"

"There's no alternative, Mr. Hood. It *must* be so. Possibly the local train may have observed something which may throw some light upon the matter. We will wire to Manchester for more information, and to Kenyon Junction with instructions that the line be examined instantly as far as Barton Moss."

The answer from Manchester came within a few minutes:

NO NEWS OF MISSING SPECIAL. DRIVER AND GUARD OF SLOW TRAIN POSITIVE THAT NO ACCIDENT BETWEEN KENYON JUNCTION AND BARTON MOSS. LINE QUITE CLEAR, AND NO SIGN OF ANY-THING UNUSUAL. MANCHESTER

"That driver and guard will have to go," said Mr. Bland, grimly. "There has been a wreck and they have missed it. The special has obviously run off the metals without disturbing the line—how it could have done so passes my comprehension—but so it must be, and we shall have a wire from Kenyon or Barton Moss presently to say that they have found her at the bottom of an embankment."

But Mr. Bland's prophecy was not destined to be fulfilled. A half-hour passed, and then there arrived the following message from the stationmaster of Kenyon Junction:

THERE ARE NO TRACES OF THE MISSING SPECIAL. IT IS QUITE CERTAIN THAT SHE PASSED HERE, AND THAT SHE DID NOT ARRIVE AT BARTON MOSS. WE HAVE DETACHED ENGINE FROM GOODS TRAIN, AND I HAVE MYSELF RIDDEN DOWN THE LINE, BUT ALL IS CLEAR, AND THERE IS NO SIGN OF ANY ACCIDENT.

Mr. Bland tore his hair in his perplexity.

"This is rank lunacy, Hood!" he cried. "Does a train vanish into thin air in England in broad daylight? The thing is preposterous. An engine, a tender, two carriages, a van, five human beings—and all lost on a straight line of railway! Unless we get something positive within the next hour I'll take Inspector Collins, and go down myself."

And then at last something positive did occur. It took the shape of another telegram from Kenyon Junction.

"Regret to report that the dead body of John Slater, driver of the special train, has just been found among the gorse bushes at a point two and a quarter miles from the Junction. Had fallen from his engine, pitched down the embankment, and rolled among bushes. Injuries to his head, from the fall, appear to be cause of death. Ground has now been carefully examined, and there is no trace of the missing train."

The country was, as has already been stated, in the throes of a political crisis, and the attention of the public was further distracted by the important and sensational developments in Paris, where a huge scandal threatened to destroy the government and to wreck the reputations of many of the leading men in France. The papers were full of these events, and the singular disappearance of the special train attracted less attention than would have been the case in more peaceful times. The grotesque nature of the event helped to detract from its importance, for the papers were disinclined to believe the facts as reported to them. More than one of the London journals treated the matter as an ingenious hoax, until the coroner's inquest upon the unfortunate driver (an inquest which elicited nothing of importance) convinced them of the tragedy of the incident.

Mr. Bland, accompanied by Inspector Collins, the senior detective officer in the service of the company, went down to Kenyon Junction the same evening, and their research lasted throughout the following day, but was attended with purely negative results. Not only was no trace found of the missing train, but no conjecture could be put forward which could possibly explain the facts. At the same time, Inspector Collins's official report (which lies before me as I write) served to show that the possibilities were more numerous than might have been expected.

"In the stretch of railway between these two points," said he, "the country is dotted with ironworks and collieries. Of these, some are being worked and some have been abandoned. There are no fewer than twelve which have small gauge lines which run trolly cars down to the main line. These can, of course, be disregarded. Besides these, however, there are seven which have or have had proper lines running down and connecting with points to the main line, so as to convey their produce from the mouth of the mine to the great centres of distribution. In every case these lines are only a few miles in length. Out of the seven, four belong to collieries which are worked out, or at least to shafts which are no longer used. These are the Redgauntlet, Hero, Slough of Despond, and Heartsease mines, the latter having ten years ago been one of the principal mines in Lancashire. These four side lines may be eliminated from our inquiry, for, to prevent possible accidents, the rails nearest to the main line have been taken up, and there is no longer any connection. There remain three other side lines leading (*a*) to the Carnstock Iron Works; (*b*) to the Big Ben Colliery; (*c*) to the Perseverance Colliery.

"Of these the Big Ben line is not more than a quarter of a mile long, and ends at a dead wall of coal waiting removal from the mouth of the mine. Nothing had been seen or heard there of any special. The Carnstock Iron Works line was blocked all day upon the 3rd of June by sixteen truckloads of hematite. It is a single line, and nothing could have passed. As to the Perseverance line, it is a large double line, which does a considerable traffic, for the output of the mine is very large. On the 3rd of June this traffic proceeded as usual; hundreds of men, including a gang of railway plate-layers, were working along the two miles and a quarter which constitute the total length of the line, and it is inconceivable that an unexpected train could have come down there without attracting universal attention. It may be remarked in conclusion that this branch line is nearer to St. Helens than the point at which the engine driver was discovered, so that we have every reason to believe that the train was past that point before misfortune overtook her.

"As to John Slater, there is no clue to be gathered from his appearance or injuries. We can only say that, as far as we can see, he met his end by falling off his engine, though why he fell, or what became of the engine after his fall, is a question upon which I do not feel qualified to offer an opinion." In conclusion, the inspector offered his resignation to the Board, being much nettled by an accusation of incompetence in the London papers.

A month elapsed, during which both the police and the company prosecuted their inquiries without the slightest success. A reward was offered and a pardon promised in case of crime, but they were both unclaimed. Every day the public opened their papers with the conviction that so grotesque a mystery would at last be solved, but week after week passed by, and a solution remained as far off as ever. In broad daylight, upon a June afternoon in the most thickly inhabited portion of England, a train with its occupants had disappeared as completely as if some master of subtle chemistry had volatilised it into gas. Indeed, among the various conjectures which were put forward in the public press there were some which seriously asserted that supernatural, or, at least, preternatural, agencies had been at work, and that the deformed Monsieur Caratal was probably a person who was better known under a less polite name. Others fixed upon his swarthy companion as being the author of the mischief, but what it was exactly which he had done could never be clearly formulated in words.

Amongst the many suggestions put forward by various newspapers or private individuals, there were one or two which were feasible enough to attract the attention of the public. One which appeared in the *Times*, over the signature of an amateur reasoner of some celebrity at that date, attempted to deal with the matter in a critical and semi-scientific manner. An extract must suffice, although the curious can see the whole letter in the issue of the 3rd of July.

> It is one of the elementary principles of practical reasoning (he remarked) that when the impossible has been eliminated the residuum, *however improbable*, must contain the truth. It is certain that the train left Kenyon Junction. It is certain that it did not reach Barton Moss. It is in the highest degree unlikely, but still possible, that it may have taken one of the seven available side lines. It is obviously impossible for a train to run where there are no rails, and, therefore, we may reduce our improbables to the three open lines, namely, the Carnstock Iron Works, the Big Ben and the Perseverance. Is there a secret society of colliers, an English camorra, which is capable of destroying both train and passengers? It is improbable, but it is not impossible. I confess that I am unable to suggest any other solution. I should certainly advise the company to direct all their energies towards the observation of those three lines, and of the workmen at the end of them. A careful supervision of the pawnbrokers' shops of the district might possibly bring some suggestive facts to light.

The suggestion coming from a recognised authority upon such matters created considerable interest, and a fierce opposition from those who considered such a statement to be a preposterous libel upon an honest and deserving set of men. The only answer to this criticism was a challenge to the objectors to lay any more feasible explanation before the public. In reply to this two others were forthcoming (*Times*, July 7th and 9th). The first suggested that the train might have run off the metals and be lying submerged in the Lancashire and Staffordshire Canal, which runs parallel to the railway for some hundreds of yards. This suggestion was thrown out of court by the published depth of the canal, which was entirely insufficient to conceal so large an object. The second correspondent wrote calling attention to the bag which appeared to be the sole luggage which the travellers had brought with them, and suggesting that some novel explosive of immense and pulverising power might have been concealed in it. The obvious absurdity, however, of supposing that the whole train might be blown to dust while the metals remained uninjured reduced any such explanation to a farce. The investigation had drifted into this hopeless position when a new and most unexpected incident occurred, which raised hopes never destined to be fulfilled.

This was nothing less than the receipt by Mrs. McPherson of a letter from her husband, James McPherson, who had been the guard of the missing train. The letter, which was dated July 5th, 1890, was dispatched from New York, and came to hand upon July 14th. Some doubts were expressed as to its genuine character, but Mrs. McPherson was positive as to the writing, and the fact that it contained a remittance of a hundred dollars in five-dollar notes was enough in itself to discount the idea of a hoax. No address was given in the letter, which ran in this way:

MY DEAR WIFE—I have been thinking a great deal, and I find it very hard to give you up. The same with Lizzie. I try to fight against it, but it will always come back to me. I send you some money which will change into twenty English pounds. This should be enough to bring both Lizzie and you across the Atlantic, and you will find the Hamburg boats which stop at Southampton very good boats, and cheaper than Liverpool. If you could come here and stop at the Johnston House I would try and send you word how to meet, but things are very difficult with me at present, and I am not very happy, finding it hard to give you both up. So no more at present, from your loving husband,

JAMES MCPHERSON

For a time it was confidently anticipated that this letter would lead to the clearing up of the whole matter, the more so as it was ascertained that a passenger who bore a close resemblance to the missing guard had travelled from Southampton under the name of Summers in the Hamburg and New York liner *Vistula*, which started upon the 7th of June. Mrs. McPherson and her sister Lizzie Dolton went across to New York as directed, and stayed for three weeks at the Johnston House, without hearing anything from the missing man. It is probable that some injudicious comments in the press may have warned him that the police were using them as a bait. However this may be, it is certain that he neither wrote nor came, and the women were eventually compelled to return to Liverpool.

And so the matter stood, and has continued to stand up to the present year of 1898. Incredible as it may seem, nothing has transpired during these eight years which has shed the least light upon the extraordinary disappearance of the special train which contained Monsieur Caratal and his companion. Careful inquiries into the antecedents of the two travellers have only established the fact that Monsieur Caratal was well known as a financier and political agent in Central America, and that during his voyage to Europe he had betrayed extraordinary anxiety to reach Paris. His companion, whose name was entered upon the passenger lists as Eduardo Gomez, was a man whose record was a violent one, and whose reputation was that of a bravo and a bully. There was evidence to show, however, that he was honestly devoted to the interests of Monsieur Caratal, and that the latter, being a man of puny physique, employed the other as a guard and protector. It may be added that no information came from Paris as to what the objects of Monsieur Caratal's hurried journey may have been. This comprises all the facts of the case up to the publication in the Marseilles papers of the recent confession of Herbert de Lernac, now under sentence of death for the murder of a merchant named Bonvalot. This statement may be literally translated as follows:

"It is not out of mere pride or boasting that I give this information, for, if that were my object, I could tell a dozen actions of mine which are quite as splendid; but I do it in order that certain gentlemen in Paris may understand that I, who am able here to tell about the fate of Monsieur Caratal, can also tell in whose interest and at whose request the deed was done, unless the reprieve which I am awaiting comes to me very quickly. Take warning, messieurs, before it is too late! You know Herbert de Lernac, and you are aware that his deeds are as ready as his words. Hasten then, or you are lost!

"At present I shall mention no names—if you only heard the names, what would you not think!—but I shall merely tell you how cleverly I did it. I was true to my employers then, and no doubt they will be true to me now. I hope so, and until I am convinced that they have betrayed me, these names, which would convulse Europe, shall not be divulged. But on that day . . . well, I say no more!

"In a word, then, there was a famous trial in Paris, in the year 1890, in connection with a monstrous scandal in politics and finance. How monstrous that scandal was can never be known save by such confidential agents as myself. The honour and careers of many of the chief men in France were at stake. You have seen a group of ninepins standing, all so rigid, and prim, and unbending. Then there comes the ball from far away and pop, pop, pop—there are your ninepins on the floor. Well, imagine some of the greatest men in France as these ninepins, and then this Monsieur Caratal as the ball which could be seen coming from far away. If he arrived, then it was pop, pop, pop for all of them. It was determined that he should not arrive.

"I do not accuse them all of being conscious of what was to happen. There were, as I have said, great financial as well as political interests at stake, and a syndicate was formed to manage the business. Some subscribed to the syndicate who hardly understood what were its objects. But others understood very well, and they can rely upon it that I have not forgotten their names. They had ample warning that Monsieur Caratal was coming long before he left South America, and they knew that the evidence which he held would certainly mean ruin to all of them. The syndicate had the command of an unlimited amount of money—absolutely unlimited, you understand. They looked round for an agent who was capable of wielding this gigantic power. The man chosen must be inventive, resolute, adaptive—a man in a million. They chose Herbert de Lernac, and I admit that they were right.

"My duties were to choose my subordinates, to use freely the power which money gives, and to make certain that Monsieur Caratal should never arrive in Paris. With characteristic energy I set about my commission within an hour of receiving my instructions, and the steps which I took were the very best for the purpose which could possibly be devised.

"A man whom I could trust was dispatched instantly to South America to travel home with Monsieur Caratal. Had he arrived in time the ship would never have reached Liverpool; but, alas, it had already started before my agent could reach it. I fitted out a small armed brig to intercept it, but again I was unfortunate. Like all great organisers I was, however, prepared for failure, and had a series of alternatives prepared, one or the other of which must succeed. You must not underrate the difficulties of my undertaking, or imagine that a mere commonplace assassination would meet the case. We must destroy not only Monsieur Caratal, but Monsieur Caratal's documents, and Monsieur Caratal's companions also, if we had reason to believe that he had communicated his secrets to them. And you must remember that they were on the alert, and keenly suspicious of any such attempt. It was a task which was in every way worthy of me, for I am always most masterful where another would be appalled.

"I was all ready for Monsieur Caratal's reception in Liverpool, and I was the more eager because I had reason to believe that he had made arrangements by which he would have a considerable guard from the moment that he arrived in London. Anything which was to be done must be done between the moment of his setting foot upon the Liverpool quay and that of his arrival at the London and West Coast terminus in London. We prepared six plans, each more elaborate than the last; which plan would be used would depend upon his own movements. Do what he would, we were ready for him. If he had stayed in Liverpool, we were ready. If he took an ordinary train, an express, or a special, all was ready. Everything had been foreseen and provided for.

"You may imagine that I could not do all this myself. What could I know of the English railway lines? But money can procure willing agents all the world over, and I soon had one of the acutest brains in England to assist me. I will mention no names, but it would be unjust to claim all the credit for myself. My English ally was worthy of such an alliance. He knew the London and West Coast line thoroughly, and he had the command of a band of workers who were trustworthy and intelligent. The idea was his, and my own judgment was only required in the details. We bought over several officials, amongst whom the most important was James McPherson, whom we had ascertained to be the guard most likely to be employed upon a special train. Smith, the stoker, was also in our employ. John Slater, the engine driver, had been approached, but had been found to be obstinate and dangerous, so we desisted. We had no certainty that Monsieur Caratal would take a special, but we thought it very probable, for it was of the utmost importance to him that he should reach Paris without delay. It was for this contingency, therefore, that we made special preparations—preparations which were complete down to the last detail long before his steamer had sighted the shores of England. You will be amused to learn that there was one of my agents in the pilot boat which brought that steamer to its moorings.

"The moment that Caratal arrived in Liverpool we knew that he suspected danger and was on his guard. He had brought with him as an escort a dangerous fellow, named Gomez, a man who carried weapons, and was prepared to use them. This fellow carried Caratal's confidential papers for him, and was ready to protect either them or his master. The probability was that Caratal had taken him into his counsels, and that to remove Caratal without removing Gomez would be a mere waste of energy. It was necessary that they should be involved in a common fate, and our plans to that end were much facilitated by their request for a special train. On that special train you will understand that two out of the three servants of the company were really in our employ, at a price which would make them independent for a lifetime. I do not go so far as to say that the English are more honest than any other nation, but I have found them more expensive to buy.

"I have already spoken of my English agent—who is a man with a considerable future before him, unless some complaint of the throat carries him off before his time. He had charge of all arrangements at Liverpool, whilst I was stationed at the inn at Kenyon, where I awaited a cipher signal to act. When the special was arranged for, my agent instantly telegraphed to me and warned me how soon I should have everything ready. He himself under the name of Horace

Moore applied immediately for a special also, in the hope that he would be sent down with Monsieur Caratal, which might under certain circumstances have been helpful to us. If, for example, our great coup had failed, it would then have become the duty of my agent to have shot them both and destroyed their papers. Caratal was on his guard, however, and refused to admit any other traveller. My agent then left the station, returned by another entrance, entered the guard's van on the side farthest from the platform, and travelled down with McPherson, the guard.

"In the meantime you will be interested to know what my own movements were. Everything had been prepared for days before, and only the finishing touches were needed. The side line which we had chosen had once joined the main line, but it had been disconnected. We had only to replace a few rails to connect it once more. These rails had been laid down as far as could be done without danger of attracting attention, and now it was merely a case of completing a juncture with the line, and arranging the points as they had been before. The sleepers had never been removed, and the rails, fishplates, and rivets were all ready, for we had taken them from a siding on the abandoned portion of the line. With my small but competent band of workers, we had everything ready long before the special arrived. When it did arrive, it ran off upon the small side line so easily that the jolting of the points appears to have been entirely unnoticed by the two travellers.

"Our plan had been that Smith the stoker should chloroform John Slater the driver, and so that he should vanish with the others. In this respect, and in this respect only, our plans miscarried—I except the criminal folly of McPherson in writing home to his wife. Our stoker did his business so clumsily that Slater in his struggles fell off the engine, and though fortune was with us so far that he broke his neck in the fall, still he remained as a blot upon that which would otherwise have been one of those complete masterpieces which are only to be contemplated in silent admiration. The criminal expert will find in John Slater the one flaw in all our admirable combinations. A man who has had as many triumphs as I can afford to be frank, and I therefore lay my finger upon John Slater, and I proclaim him to be a flaw.

"But now I have got our special train upon the small line two kilometers, or rather more than one mile in length, which leads, or rather used to lead, to the abandoned Heartsease mine, once one of the largest coal mines in England. You will ask how it is that no one saw the train upon this unused line. I answer that along its entire length it runs through a deep cutting, and that, unless someone had been on the edge of that cutting, he could not have seen it. There *was* someone on the edge of that cutting. I was there. And now I will tell you what I saw.

"My assistant had remained at the points in order that he might superintend the switching off of the train. He had four armed men with him, so that if the train ran off the line—we thought it probable, because the points were very rusty—we might still have resources to fall back upon. Having once seen it safely on the side line, he handed over the responsibility to me. I was waiting at a point which overlooks the mouth of the mine, and I was also armed, as were my two companions. Come what might, you see, I was always ready.

"The moment that the train was fairly on the side line, Smith, the stoker, slowed down the engine, and then, having turned it on to the fullest speed again, he and McPherson, with my English lieutenant, sprang off before it was too late. It may be that it was this slowing down which first attracted the attention of the travellers, but the train was running at full speed again before their heads appeared at the open window. It makes me smile to think how bewildered they must have been. Picture to yourself your own feelings if, on looking out of your luxurious carriage, you suddenly perceived that the lines upon which you ran were rusted and corroded, red and yellow with disuse and decay! What a catch must have come in their breaths as in a second it flashed upon them that it was not Manchester but Death which was waiting for them at the end of that sinister line. But the train was running with frantic speed, rolling and rocking over the rotten line, while the wheels made a frightful screaming sound upon the rusted surface. I was close to them, and could see their faces. Caratal was praying, I think—there was something like a rosary dangling out of his hand. The other roared like a bull who smells the blood of the slaughterhouse. He saw us standing on the bank, and he beckoned to us like a madman. Then he tore at his wrist and threw his dispatch box out of the window in our direction. Of course, his meaning was obvious. Here was the evidence, and they would promise to be silent if their lives were spared. It would have been very agreeable if we

"But the train was running with frantic speed, rolling and rocking, while the wheels made a frightful screaming sound . . ."

could have done so, but business is business. Besides, the train was now as much beyond our control as theirs.

"He ceased howling when the train rattled round the curve and they saw the black mouth of the mine yawning before them. We had removed the boards which had covered it, and we had cleared the square entrance. The rails had formerly run very close to the shaft for the convenience of loading the coal, and we had only to add two or three lengths of rail in order to lead to the very brink of the shaft. In fact, as the lengths would not quite fit, our line projected about three feet over the edge. We saw the two heads at the window: Caratal below, Gomez above; but they had both been struck silent by what they saw. And yet they could not withdraw their heads. The sight seemed to have paralysed them.

"I had wondered how the train running at a great speed would take the pit into which I had guided it, and I was much interested in watching it. One of my colleagues thought that it would actually jump it, and indeed it was not very far from doing so. Fortunately, however, it fell short, and the buffers of the engine struck the other lip of the shaft with a tremendous crash. The funnel flew off into the air. The tender, carriages, and van were all mashed into one jumble, which, with the remains of the engine, choked for a minute or so the mouth of the pit. Then something gave way in the middle, and the whole mass of green iron, smoking coals, brass fittings, wheels, woodwork, and cushions all crumpled together and crashed down into the mine. We heard the rattle, rattle, rattle, as the débris struck against the walls, and then quite a long time afterwards there came a deep roar as the remains of the train struck the bottom. The boiler may have burst, for a sharp crash came after the roar, and then a dense cloud of steam and smoke swirled up out of the black depths, falling in a spray as thick as rain all round us. Then the vapour shredded off into thin wisps, which floated away in the summer sunshine, and all was quiet again in the Heartsease mine.

"And now, having carried out our plans so successfully, it only remained to leave no trace behind us. Our little band of workers at the other end had already ripped up the rails and disconnected the side line, replacing everything as it had been before. We were equally busy at the mine. The funnel and other fragments were thrown in, the shaft was planked over as it used to be, and the lines which led to it were torn up and taken away. Then, without flurry, but without delay, we all made our way out of the country, most of us to Paris, my English colleague to Manchester, and McPherson to Southampton, whence he emigrated to America. Let the English papers of that date tell how thoroughly we had done our work, and how completely we had thrown the cleverest of their detectives off our track.

"You will remember that Gomez threw his bag of papers out of the window, and I need not say that I secured that bag and brought them to my employers. It may interest my employers now, however, to learn that out of that bag I took one or two little papers as a souvenir of the occasion. I have no wish to publish these papers; but, still, it is every man for himself in this world, and what else can I do if my friends will not come to my aid when I want them? Messieurs, you may believe that Herbert de Lernac is quite as formidable when he is against you as when he is with you, and that he is not a man to go to the guillotine until he has seen that every one of you is en route for New Caledonia. For your own sake, if not for mine, make haste, Monsieur de—, and General—, and Baron—(you can fill up the blanks for yourselves as you read this). I promise you that in the next edition there will be no blanks to fill.

"P.S. As I look over my statement there is only one omission which I can see. It concerns the unfortunate man McPherson, who was foolish enough to write to his wife and to make an appointment with her in New York. It can be imagined that when interests like ours were at stake, we could not leave them to the chance of whether a man in that class of life would or would not give away his secrets to a woman. Having once broken his oath by writing to his wife, we could not trust him anymore. We took steps therefore to insure that he should not see his wife. I have sometimes thought that it would be a kindness to write to her and to assure her that there is no impediment to her marrying again."

X: The Field Bazaar

"I SHOULD certainly do it," said Sherlock Holmes.

I started at the interruption, for my companion had been eating his breakfast with his attention entirely centred upon the paper which was propped up by the coffeepot. Now I looked across at him to find his eyes fastened upon me with the half-amused, half-questioning expression which he usually assumed when he felt that he had made an intellectual point.

"Do what?" I asked.

He smiled as he took his slipper from the mantelpiece and drew from it enough shag tobacco to fill the old clay pipe with which he invariably rounded off his breakfast.

"A most characteristic question of yours, Watson," said he. "You will not, I am sure, be offended if I say that any reputation for sharpness which I may possess has been entirely gained by the admirable foil which you have made for me. Have I not heard of debutantes who have insisted upon plainness in their chaperones? There is a certain analogy."

Our long companionship in the Baker Street rooms had left us on those easy terms of intimacy when much may be said without offence. And yet I acknowledge that I was nettled at his remark.

"I may be very obtuse," said I, "but I confess that I am unable to see how you have managed to know that I was . . . I was . . ."

"Asked to help in the Edinburgh University Bazaar."

"Precisely. The letter has only just come to hand, and I have not spoken to you since."

"In spite of that," said Holmes, leaning back in his chair and putting his fingertips together, "I would even venture to suggest that the object of the bazaar is to enlarge the university cricket field."

I looked at him in such bewilderment that he vibrated with silent laughter.

"The fact is, my dear Watson, that you are an excellent subject," said he. "You are never blasé. You respond instantly to any external stimulus. Your mental processes may be slow but they are never obscure, and I found during breakfast that you were easier reading than the leader in the *Times* in front of me."

"I should be glad to know how you arrived at your conclusions," said I.

"I fear that my good nature in giving explanations has seriously compromised my reputation," said Holmes. "But in this case the train of reasoning is based upon such obvious facts that no credit can be claimed for it. You entered the room with a thoughtful expression, the expression of a man who is debating some point in his mind. In your hand you held a solitary letter. Now last night you retired in the best of spirits, so it was clear that it was this letter in your hand which had caused the change in you."

"This is obvious."

"It is all obvious when it is explained to you. I naturally asked myself what the letter could contain which might have this effect upon you. As you walked you held the flap side of the envelope towards me, and I saw upon it the same shield-shaped device which I have observed upon your old college cricket cap. It was clear, then, that the request came from Edinburgh University—or from some club connected with the university. When you reached the table you laid down the letter beside your plate with the address uppermost, and you walked over to look at the framed photograph upon the left of the mantelpiece."

It amazed me to see the accuracy with which he had observed my movements. "What next?" I asked.

"I began by glancing at the address, and I could tell, even at the distance of six feet, that it was an unofficial communication. This I gathered from the use of the word 'Doctor' upon the address, to which, as a Bachelor of Medicine, you have no legal claim. I knew that university officials are pedantic in their correct use of titles, and I was thus enabled to say with certainty that your letter was unofficial. When on your return to the table you turned over your letter and allowed me to perceive that the enclosure was a printed one, the idea of a bazaar first occurred to me. I had already weighed the possibility of its being a political communication, but this seemed improbable in the present stagnant conditions of politics.

"When you returned to the table your face still retained its expression and it was evident that your examination of the photograph had not changed the current of your thoughts. In that case it must itself bear upon the subject in question. I turned my attention to the photograph, therefore, and saw at once that it consisted of yourself as a member of the Edinburgh University Eleven, with the pavilion and cricket field in the background. My small experience of cricket clubs has taught me that next to churches and cavalry ensigns they are the most debt-laden things upon earth. When upon your return to the table I saw you take out your pencil and draw lines upon the envelope, I was convinced that you were endeavouring to realise some projected improvement which was to be brought about by a bazaar. Your face still showed some indecision, so that I was able to break in upon you with my advice that you should assist in so good an object."

I could not help smiling at the extreme simplicity of his explanation.

"Of course, it was as easy as possible," said I.

My remark appeared to nettle him.

"I may add," said he, "that the particular help which you have been asked to give was that you should write in their album, and that you have already made up your mind that the present incident will be the subject of your article."

"But how—!" I cried.

"It is as easy as possible," said he, "and I leave its solution to your own ingenuity. In the meantime," he added, raising his paper, "you will excuse me if I return to this very interesting article upon the trees of Cremona, and the exact reasons for their pre-eminence in the manufacture of violins. It is one of those small outlying problems to which I am sometimes tempted to direct my attention."

XI: How Watson
Learned the Trick

Watson had been watching his companion intently ever since he had sat down to the breakfast table. Holmes happened to look up and catch his eye.

"Well, Watson, what are you thinking about?" he asked.

"About you."

"Me?"

"Yes, Holmes, I was thinking how superficial are these tricks of yours, and how wonderful it is that the public should continue to show interest in them."

"I quite agree," said Holmes. "In fact, I have a recollection that I have myself made a similar remark."

"Your methods," said Watson severely, "are really easily acquired."

"No doubt," Holmes answered with a smile. "Perhaps you will yourself give an example of this method of reasoning."

"With pleasure," said Watson. "I am able to say that you were greatly preoccupied when you got up this morning."

"Excellent!" said Holmes. "How could you possibly know that?"

"Because you are usually a very tidy man and yet you have forgotten to shave."

"Dear me! How very clever!" said Holmes. "I had no idea, Watson, that you were so apt a pupil. Has your eagle eye detected anything more?"

"Yes, Holmes. You have a client named Barlow, and you have not been successful in his case."

"Dear me, how could you know that?"

"I saw the name outside his envelope. When you opened it you gave a groan and thrust it into your pocket with a frown on your face."

"Admirable! You are indeed observant. Any other points?"

"I fear, Holmes, that you have taken to financial speculation."

"How *could* you tell that, Watson?"

"You opened the paper, turned to the financial page, and gave a loud exclamation of interest."

"Well, that is very clever of you, Watson. Any more?"

"Yes, Holmes, you have put on your black coat, instead of your dressing gown, which proves that you are expecting some important visitor at once."

"Anything more?"

"I have no doubt that I could find other points, Holmes, but I only give you these few, in order to show you that there are other people in the world who can be as clever as you."

"And some not so clever," said Holmes. "I admit that they are few, but I am afraid, my dear Watson, that I must count you among them."

"What do you mean, Holmes?"

"Well, my dear fellow, I fear your deductions have not been so happy as I should have wished."

"You mean that I was mistaken."

"Just a little that way, I fear. Let us take the points in their order: I did not shave because I have sent my razor to be sharpened. I put on my coat because I have, worse luck, an early meeting with my dentist. His name is Barlow, and the letter was to confirm the appointment. The cricket page is beside the financial one, and I turned to it to find if Surrey was holding its own against Kent. But go on, Watson, go on! It's a very superficial trick, and no doubt you will soon acquire it."

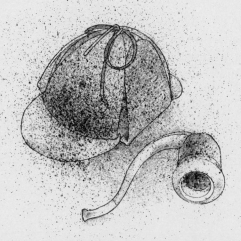

Afterword

The author of this afterword, Philip A. Shreffler, is a long-time member of the famous Sherlock Holmes society known as The Baker Street Irregulars. From 1985 through 1992 he served as editor of the Irregulars' publication, The Baker Street Journal, *an Irregular Quarterly of Sherlockiana, and he holds the prestigious Two-Shilling Award, the BSI's highest honor. He is the author of numerous books and articles on Sherlock Holmes and other topics.*

In December of 1893 Arthur Conan Doyle murdered Sherlock Holmes—deliberately, premeditatedly and in cold blood. That was the month in which the *Strand* magazine published the Holmes adventure entitled "The Final Problem," the tale that had Holmes and his nemesis, the evil genius Professor Moriarty, plummeting together in a death struggle over Switzerland's Reichenbach Falls. By that time Doyle had written two dozen Holmes stories, had made a substantial sum of money on them and had become so closely identified with his detective creation that his reading public—always clamoring for more Holmes—was ignoring the writer's other work. "I think of slaying Holmes," Doyle wrote in a letter to his mother in 1891. "He takes my mind from better things." The "better things," in Doyle's estimation anyway, were works of historical fiction. And in a diary entry just after he'd completed "The Final Problem," he wrote, with brutal simplicity: "Killed Holmes."

But Sherlock Holmes' loyal devotees were not to be denied. Doyle actually managed to resist the public's demands for more Holmes stories for almost a decade. Then, in 1901, he caved in—due as much to offers of lucrative publishing contracts as anything else—and gave the world *The Hound of the Baskervilles,* serialized in the *Strand* during that and the following year. However, *The Hound* did not bring Holmes back from his Alpine tomb; it was merely a flashback to an earlier portion of his career.

Still, the moment of Holmes' genuine return was imminent, and it occurred at last in October of 1903 with "The Adventure of the Empty House." In that story Dr. Watson explained to his jubilant readers that Holmes indeed had *not* perished "in that dreadful cauldron of swirling water and seething foam," but had escaped and hidden out for two years while he laid plans for a final assault on the remnants of Professor Moriarty's sinister criminal organization. What mattered—what really mattered—was that Sherlock Holmes was back among the living, back in action again, as wise, penetratingly perceptive and devastatingly logical as ever before.

The stories collected here in *The Further Adventures of Sherlock Holmes* belong to the later group of Doyle compositions—the majority of them published between 1908 and 1917. And they are indeed Sherlock Holmes at his best—even in "His Last Bow," in which a sixty-year-old Holmes at the very end of his professional career outwits a wily and cocky German spy.

It should be noted that four of the stories in this collection are a bit unusual. Indeed, they are felicitous additions to the sixty stories that are normally published together as the complete Holmes saga. Two of them—"The Story of the Man with the Watches" and "The Story of the Lost Special"—are Holmes mysteries that do not name Sherlock Holmes as the detective, and they were written during that ten-year period when Doyle had supposedly finished with Sherlock Holmes forever. The other two—"The Field Bazaar" (1896) and "How Watson Learned the Trick" (1924)—are fond, good-natured parodies in which Holmes' famous deception of seeming to "read minds" is demonstrated by the detective successfully, and by Watson quite unsuccessfully. In all four of the stories the creator of Sherlock Holmes and Dr. Watson was having a bit of sport with his own literary offspring, and in doing so, he gave the world a quartette of Sherlockian amusements of which the general reading public even today is largely unaware.

In fact, in both "The Man with the Watches" and "The Lost Special," solutions to the mysteries are offered by "an amateur reasoner of some celebrity," a "well-known criminal investigator"—who is certainly Sherlock Holmes—and in both cases, Holmes' solutions are wrong! The plots of these stories are inventive—especially in "The Lost Special," where Doyle manages to make an entire passenger train disappear from the face of the earth, a literary conjuring trick worthy of the best stage magician. That Holmes fails to solve these cases was Doyle's way of poking gentle fun at his detective, who—in the sixty mainstream adventures—virtually never makes an error and is almost a logical superman. In a way it's comforting to know that Holmes is human, that even the loftiest of brains can have an off day.

What's more, "The Lost Special" and "The Man with the Watches" link Sherlock Holmes even more closely to Doyle than many of the other adventures. In his long career, Doyle himself often enjoyed playing detective. Like Holmes in these two stories, he occasionally wrote letters to the newspapers suggesting solutions to popular real-life mysteries of the day. Sometimes Doyle's theories proved to be correct; sometimes, like Holmes here, he was totally off the mark. If the creator could make mistakes, why not the creation?

But it is, of course, the adventures in which Sherlock Holmes triumphs in serious criminal investigations that are the most satisfying to us as readers. And the eight that are included in this book represent a fascinating look at the Holmes-Watson relationship in a wide range of cases, some of them rather gruesome: political intrigue, kidnapping, poisoning, murder and dismemberment, and even a fiendishly clever attempt on Holmes' life.

The opening of "The Adventure of the Bruce-Partington Plans," is among the most atmospheric of any of the stories: "In the third week of November, in the year 1895, a dense yellow fog settled down upon London. From the Monday to the Thursday I doubt whether it was ever possible from our windows in Baker Street to see the loom of the opposite houses." What is perhaps a little surprising to many readers is that, though we think of Holmes' London as draped in fog most of the time, there are actually only nine of the sixty stories that mention fog! But here in "The Bruce-Partington Plans" is all the fog-shrouded romance that we hunger for in Sherlock Holmes. And as the story develops, we learn—to Watson's and our amazement—the fact that Holmes' brother Mycroft (first introduced much earlier, in "The Adventure of the Greek Interpreter") is so highly placed in his job with the British government that sometimes he *is* the government. So it is that Mycroft involves Sherlock and Watson in a chase through the London fog after a master spy who is about to make off with a set of secret submarine plans, the loss of which would positively cripple the British navy. And the plot, with its brilliant use of the railway-coach red herring, is as ingenious as any that Doyle ever concocted for a Holmes story.

There are some pretty hair-raising adventures here too, grisly in a way that might have been inappropriate when Doyle first began writing about Holmes in 1887. Most of the stories in *The Further Adventures*, remember, were published in the early twentieth century. And while there are some fairly grim descriptions of murder victims in the nineteenth-century Holmes tales, there's really nothing to compare with a cardboard box containing two severed human ears or the claustrophobic horror of almost being buried alive—in the same coffin with another corpse, no less—which is the fate of the unfortunate Lady Frances Carfax. Nor is there anything like Watson's description of the freezing terror that he and Holmes experience when they are under the influence of the devil's-foot drug, which killed one person outright and drove two others stark, staring mad.

"The Adventure of the Devil's Foot," incidentally, is an important case not just because of its terrifying plot but also because it gives us a rare glimpse into how very much Dr. Watson matters to his friend Sherlock Holmes. Contrary to some film versions of Watson, the doctor is no bumbling idiot, but is an intelligent and sensitive companion for his detective compatriot. In earlier adventures Watson complains that Holmes is "a little too scientific for my tastes—it approaches cold-bloodedness" (*A Study in Scarlet*) and that "You are really an automaton—a calculating machine . . . there is something positively inhuman in you at times" (*The Sign of the Four*). But in "The Devil's Foot," after Holmes subjects not only himself but Dr. Watson to the life-threatening effects of the *radix pedis diaboli* drug and they both barely survive, the detective cries, "Upon my word, Watson! . . . I owe you both my thanks and an apology. It was an unjustifiable experiment even for oneself, and doubly so for a friend. I am really very sorry." And Dr. Watson, overcome with emotion, tells us that he "had never seen so much of Holmes's heart before." After the many years of their association, this is a kind of turning point in their relationship. Holmes is revealed as far more than just the heartless "calculating machine" that he so often appears to be.

And that dramatic moment permits us to go back and reread the earlier adventures in a completely different light. Though Watson has long known that Holmes cares deeply for him, this seems to be the first time that Doyle allows Holmes to show it so openly. As the effects of the drug subside, Watson adds humbly and with the great loyalty for which he is famous, "You know . . . that it is my greatest joy and privilege to help you."

And help Holmes he does. In "The Adventure of Wisteria Lodge" he helps him to deal with a Latin American dictator and his thugs; in "The Adventure of the Red Circle," to solve a murder associated with a secret Italian political organization; and in "The Adventure of the Dying Detective," to act as both witness and Holmes' protector when the thoroughly detestable Culverton Smith makes an attempt on Holmes' life.

Watson is even there at the end of Holmes' remarkable career as the world's first consulting detective. The case entitled "His Last Bow" is indeed Holmes' final case. Of course Doyle wrote more Sherlock Holmes stories after "His Last Bow," but it is clear that they were meant to take place earlier. The action of the story occurs on August 2, 1914—the very day before Germany declared war on France, starting World War I. In that "most terrible August in the history of the world," Holmes—in his disguise as the American "Altamont"—is acting as a double agent on behalf of the British government, supposedly in cahoots with the German spy Von Bork, but actually exposing the dangerous Prussian. It is a case that Holmes has been working on undercover for two years. At its climax, who should we find coming to the detective's aid but the devoted Watson, who hasn't seen his friend for at least the two years of Holmes' investigation—and driving his "little Ford," the first time, by the by, that motor cars are introduced into the otherwise horse-drawn world of Sherlock Holmes.

In "His Last Bow," then, there is a double poignancy and a message about what the Sherlock Holmes stories had come to mean. Even before Doyle was half finished writing all of the Holmes adventures, the century had turned, and his readers found themselves in a world of horseless carriages and even of airplanes. Since most of the stories are set in the late 1800s, the London of Sherlock Holmes was already being looked at nostalgically by twentieth-century readers—as the good old days of gas lamps and double-decked buses pulled by horses. Even though the first telephone system had been installed in London in 1878, Holmes rarely uses it and prefers instead to rely on telegrams for rapid communication. His favored mode of transportation is the horse-drawn hansom cab, and the electric lights that were steadily replacing gas are seldom mentioned.

In short, the Holmes stories take place on the very cusp of a new century and a new world, a world in which, frankly, Holmes must feel fairly ill at ease. We learn in "His Last Bow" that Holmes is a man of sixty, and though that is hardly an ancient age, it is certainly late in life to change established habits. Somehow, envisioning Sherlock Holmes driving around in big black sedans and fighting World War II Nazis, as he did in some of the Basil Rathbone-Nigel Bruce movies made in the late 30's and 40's, is very wrong. It was World War I— with its introduction into warfare of the tank, the airplane, the machine gun and poison gas—that ended forever the slower-paced nineteenth-century life which had surrounded Holmes in the majority of his adventures. And so it seems more than appropriate that the day before the German guns began to fire in Europe should be the day on which Holmes brings his life as a detective to a close. Sherlock Holmes was never meant for the twentieth century; that belonged to hard-boiled detectives like Sam Spade and Philip Marlowe.

But there is one further way in which "His Last Bow" touches an emotional chord in us. If this represents the close of Holmes' career, it is also the end of the Holmes-Watson partnership—certainly the closest partnership in all of literature. While the German agent Von Bork lies struggling, bound hand and foot, in the back seat of Watson's car, the two old friends take a private moment to amble together, "recalling once again the days of the past." And we recall that past with them: their first meeting more than thirty years earlier in the chemical laboratory of St. Bartholomew's Hospital, the frenzied clients bursting into their Baker Street flat, and the devious windings through the streets of London or the chases on foot across rural moors in search of an imperiling villain. With perhaps even greater affection we recall those intimate moments in front of a blazing fire in their sitting room as Watson enjoys reading one of Clark Russell's sea stories, and Holmes pastes newspaper clippings about evildoers into his comprehensive index books of criminals while the wind sobs in the chimney. And now as we walk with the pair of them along that path overlooking the English Channel, we realize that—as Holmes himself says—"this may be the last quiet talk that we shall ever have."

Holmes is aware that the world he and Watson knew is about to be shattered. "There's an east wind coming, Watson," says Holmes, speaking of the impending war and the new epoch that it portends. "I think not, Holmes," replies Watson, missing Holmes' chilling meaning altogether and supposing that the detective is merely discussing the weather. "It is very warm."

"Good old Watson!" says Holmes, quite likely with easy humor and profound respect for his friend in his voice. "You are the one fixed point in a changing age."

A changing age. A fixed point. These are concepts fundamental to what we love in Sherlock Holmes. For Dr. Watson is not the only fixed point in the Holmes stories. The stories themselves are fixed points in our own changing world. And what *we* know is that no matter what our future may hold, there is always the fixed point of Arthur Conan Doyle's Sherlockian adventures, the desperate client's step upon the stair, the dark mystery of the seemingly unsolvable case, the hawk-faced detective and his inseparable companion. And it is our great good fortune that we shall never find ourselves having a "last quiet talk" with Holmes and Watson, that no one will ever be able to murder them for us—as long as there are books like this one to be read again and again, as long as our hearts draw us ever back to the stones of Baker Street where, if our ears are carefully attuned, we may hear the clip-clop of horses' hoofs and the sonorous notes from Holmes' violin drifting along with the fog.

Philip A. Shreffler
St. Louis, Missouri
1993

THE LOST ART OF LISTENING

The Lost Art
of Listening

❖

MICHAEL P. NICHOLS

THE GUILFORD PRESS
New York   London

©1995 Michael P. Nichols
The Guilford Press
A Division of Guilford Publications, Inc.
72 Spring Street, New York, NY 10012

Printed in the United States of America

This book is printed on acid-free paper.

Last digit is print number: 9 8 7 6 5 4 3 2 1

Library of Congress Cataloging-in-Publication Data

Nichols, Michael P.
    The lost art of listening / Michael P. Nichols.
       p. cm.
    Includes bibliographical references and index.
    ISBN 0-89862-267-0
    1. Listening. 2. Interpersonal relations. 3. Interpersonal
communication. I. Title. II. Series.
BF323.L5N53 1994
153.6'8—dc20   94-38111
                                                        CIP

To Salvador Minuchin,
a man of compassion
who isn't afraid to tell the truth

Contents

PART THREE

❖

GETTING THROUGH TO EACH OTHER

PART FOUR

❖

LISTENING IN CONTEXT

THE LOST ART OF LISTENING

Introduction

Nothing hurts more than the sense that people close to us aren't really listening to what we have to say. We never outgrow the need to communicate what it feels like to live in our separate, private worlds of experience. That's why a sympathetic ear is such a powerful force in human relationships—and why the failure to be heard and understood is so painful.

My ideas about listening have been sharpened by twenty years of work as a psychoanalyst and family therapist. Refereeing arguments between intimate partners, coaching parents to communicate with their children, and struggling myself to sustain empathy as my patients faced their demons ultimately has led me to the conclusion that much of the conflict in our lives can be explained by one simple but unhappy fact: we don't really listen to each other.

Jumping in to say what's on our minds—before we've even acknowledged what the other person said—short-circuits the possibility of mutual understanding. Speaking without listening, hearing without understanding is like snipping an electrical cord in two, then plugging it in anyway, hoping somehow that something will light up. Most of the time, of course, we don't deliberately set out to break the connection. In fact, we're often baffled and dismayed by a feeling of being left sitting around in the dark.

Modern culture has developed conceptions of individualism that picture us as finding our own bearings within, declaring independence from the webs of interlocution that formed us, or at least neutralizing them. It is as though when we become finished persons we outgrow

our need for attention, like training wheels. All this is not to say that we can't be autonomous, in the sense of self-directing, or even original, able to think and act on our own. But we cannot leap out of the human condition and become self-sustaining, secure, and satisfied without need for conversation—conversation in a broad sense, that is some kind of interchange with others.

We think of ourselves as individuals, but we are embedded in networks of relationship that define us and sustain us. Even as the most independent adults, we have moments when we cannot clarify what we feel until we talk about it with someone who knows us, who cares about what we think, or at least is willing to listen.

Contemporary pressures have, regrettably, shrunk our attention spans and impoverished the quality of listening in our lives. We live in hurried times, when dinner is something we zap in the microwave and keeping up with the latest books and movies means reading the reviews. That's all we've got time for. Running to and from our many obligations, we close ourselves off from the world around us with headphones, exercising strict control over what we allow in.

In the limited time we still preserve for family and friends, conversation is often preempted by soothing and passive distractions. Too tired to talk and listen, we settle instead for the lulling charms of electronic devices that project pictures, make music, or bleep across display screens. Is it this way of life that's made us forget how to listen? Perhaps. But maybe the modern approach to life is the effect rather than the cause. Maybe we lead this kind of life because we're seeking some sort of solace, something to counteract the dimming of the spirit we feel when no one is listening.

How we lost the art of listening is certainly a matter for debate. What is not debatable, my experience tells me, is that the loss leaves us with an ever-widening hole in our lives. It might begin as a vague sense of discontent, sadness, or deprivation. We miss the irreplaceable sustenance of lending an attentive ear and of receiving the same in return, but we don't know what's wrong or how to fix it. Over time this lack of listening invades our most prized relationships. Within couples and families we unnecessarily hurt each other by failing to acknowledge what each other says. Whatever the arena, our hearts experience the failure to be heard as an absence of concern.

Conflict doesn't necessarily disappear when we acknowledge each other's point of view, but it's almost certain to get worse if we don't. So why don't we take time to hear each other out?

Because the simple art of listening isn't always so simple. Often it's a burden. Not, perhaps, the perfunctory attention we grant automatically as part of the give-and-take of everyday life. But the sustained attention of careful listening—that may take heroic and unselfish restraint. To listen well we must forget ourselves and submit to the other person's need for attention.

While it's true that some people are easier to listen to than others, conversations take place between two people, both of whom contribute to the outcome. Unfortunately, when we fail to get through to each other, we have a tendency to fall back on blaming. It's his fault: he's selfish or insensitive. Or it's my fault: I'm too dependent or don't express myself well.

The fact that we experience life (and its famous complications) from inside our own skin makes it hard for us to see the circular patterns of stimulus and response between us and our conversation partners. It takes reflection to step back from the frustrations of misunderstanding and recognize the extent to which we all participate in the problems that plague us. But this is the problem of living in this world with other people: we create our own relationships and must, in turn, sustain and be sustained by them.

Most failures of understanding are *not* due to self-absorption or bad faith, but to defensive reactions that crowd out understanding and concern. Each of us has characteristic ways of reacting emotionally in key relationships. We don't hear what's said because something in the speaker's message triggers hurt, anger, or fear.

Unfortunately, all the advice in the world about "active listening" can't overcome the maddening tendency to react to each other this way. To become better listeners, and use empathy to transform our relationships, we must identify and harness the emotional triggers that generate anxiety and cause misunderstanding and conflict. We *can* understand each other, once we learn to recognize our own defensive reactions and take charge of our responses.

If this seems too formidable a task, remember that most of us are more capable than we give ourselves credit for. We concentrate pretty hard at work, and most of us still enjoy hours of earnest, open conversation with a few friends. In fact, talk with friends is a model of what conversation can be: free enough to talk about what matters; sufficiently concerned (and sufficiently unthreatened) to listen, understand, and acknowledge; honest enough to tell the truth; and tactful enough to know when not to. More relationships can be like this.

In the process of writing this book, I've tried to become a better listener, in my personal as well as professional life, to listen a little harder to my wife's complaints without getting defensive and to hear my children's opinions before giving them my own. However, several times I've had painful conversations that left me bruised and feeling defeated. My wife would speak sharply to me about not helping out more around the house (or not listening to her) and I'd feel attacked; or I'd call my editor one too many times to complain about the burdens of writing and she'd make *me* feel like a burden for calling; or my friend Rich would call me the part of your anatomy you sit on for acting like I was entitled to some special consideration. Not only didn't I listen at these times—hear and acknowledge what the other person was saying, and then give my side—but I got all knotted up inside, hurt and angry, and completely unwilling to talk to that person, ever again as long as I live.

I'm sure you know how painful such encounters with misunderstanding can be. When my wife "yelled at me," my editor was "mean to me," and my friend "picked on me," I got hurt and withdrew. But what made these incidents so especially painful was that just when I thought I was learning to listen better, these setbacks set me all the way back. Instead of just thinking that things hadn't gone well and needed repair, I felt defeated and inadequate. How could I, who couldn't even get along with the people in my own life, have the temerity to write a book about listening? How could I teach anyone anything about listening if I couldn't listen to hard things without getting blown away?

I think you know how that feels. When we try to change something in our lives, whether it's our diet or work habits or listening skills, and we experience a setback, we have a tendency to feel hopeless and give up. Suddenly all the progress we thought we were making seems like an illusion. Maybe if I were reading a book about listening and experienced these setbacks, I would have given up. But, fortunately or unfortunately, I had a commitment to finish writing this book, and so after a while of brooding in hurt silence I'd go back and try to talk to the person I'd quarreled with—only this time with a firm resolve to listen to his or her side before telling mine. In the process, I learned to see how my relationships go through cycles of closeness and distance and, even more important, how I could influence those cycles by the quality of my own listening.

This book is an invitation to think about the ways we talk and listen to each other: why listening is such a powerful force in our lives; how

to listen deeply, with sustained immersion in another's experience; and how to prevent good listening from being spoiled by bad habits.

Among the secrets of successful communication we will consider are:

- The difference between real dialogue and just taking turns talking
- Setting aside your own agenda while someone else is speaking
- Hearing what people mean, not just what they say
- How to get through to someone who never seems to listen
- How to deal with people who get defensive when you try to tell them something
- How to ask for support without getting unwanted advice
- How to get an uncommunicative person to open up
- What makes some people react so violently to criticism
- How to share a difference of opinion without making the other person feel criticized
- How to make sure both sides get heard in heated discussions
- How speakers undermine their own messages
- Responding to a speaker's feelings instead of imposing your own
- Cutting down on criticism and nagging
- Establishing credibility so that people listen to you
- Understanding how the nature of a relationship affects listening
- Facing rather than avoiding conflict

The Lost Art of Listening is divided into four sections. Part I explains why listening is so important in our lives—far more important than we usually realize—and how, for many of us, it's a lack of sympathetic attention more than stress or overwork that accounts for the loss of enthusiasm and optimism in our lives. Part II explores the hidden assumptions, unconscious needs, and emotional defensiveness that are the real reasons people don't listen. We'll see what makes listeners too defensive to hear what we're saying and how people who vent emotion rather than expressing it may not get heard, even though they have something important to say.

After exploring the major roadblocks to listening, we'll examine in Part III how people can understand and control emotional reactions to become better listeners. And I'll explain how you can make yourself heard, even in the most difficult situations, by developing a sensitivity to the reactions of your listeners and by toning down your own emotionality. Finally, in Part IV, we'll see how listening breaks down in particular types of relationship, including intimate partnerships, family relationships, between friends, and at work. I'll explain how listen-

ing is complicated by the specific dynamics of each of these various relationships and how to use that knowledge to break through to each other.

Regardless of how much we take it for granted, the importance of listening cannot be overestimated. The gift of our attention and understanding makes other people feel validated and valued. Our ability to listen, and listen well, creates goodwill that comes back to us. But effective listening is also the best way to enjoy others, to learn from them, and to make them interesting to be with. I hope this book can help take us a step in the direction of showing more of the concern we feel for each other.

PART ONE

THE YEARNING
TO BE UNDERSTOOD

CHAPTER ONE

"Did You Hear What I Said?"

WHY LISTENING IS SO IMPORTANT

Sometimes it seems that nobody listens anymore.

"He expects me to listen to his problems, but he's never interested in mine."

"She's always complaining."

"He never talks to me. The only time I find out what's going on in his life is when I overhear him telling someone else. Why doesn't he ever tell *me* these things?"

"I can't talk to her because she's so critical."

Wives complain that their husbands take them for granted. Husbands complain that their wives nag and ramble on, taking forever to get to the point.

She feels a violation of their connection. He doesn't trust the connection.

Few motives in human experience are as powerful as the yearning to be understood. Being listened to means that we are taken seriously, that our ideas and feelings are known and, ultimately, that what we have to say matters.

The yearning to be listened to and understood is a yearning to escape our separateness and bridge the space that divides us. We reach
out and try to overcome that separateness by revealing what's on our
minds and in our hearts, hoping for understanding. Getting that understanding should be simple, but it isn't.

The essence of good listening is empathy, which can be achieved
only by suspending our preoccupation with ourselves and entering into
the experience of the other person. Part intuition and part effort, it's
the stuff of human connection.

A listener's empathy—understanding what we're trying to say *and*
showing it—builds a bond of understanding, linking us to someone who
understands and cares and thus confirming that our feelings are recognizable and legitimate. The power of empathic listening is the power
to transform relationships. When deeply felt but unexpressed feelings
take shape in words that are shared and come back clarified, the result
is a reassuring sense of being understood and a grateful feeling of shared
humanness with the one who understands.

If listening strengthens our relationships by cementing our connection with one another, it also fortifies our sense of self. In the presence
of a receptive listener, we're able to clarify what we think and discover
what we feel. Thus, in giving an account of our experience to someone
who listens, we are better able to listen to ourselves. Our lives are
coauthored in dialogue.

IT HURTS NOT TO BE LISTENED TO

The need to be taken seriously and responded to is frustrated every day,
and not just by that one special person from whom we expect so
much.Parents complain that their children don't listen. Children complain that their parents are too busy arguing or lecturing to hear their
side of things. Even friends, usually a reliable source of shared understanding, are often too busy to listen to one another these days. And
if we sometimes feel cut off from sympathy and understanding in the
private sphere, we've grown not even to expect courtesy and attention
in public settings.

Our right to be heard is often violated in small ways that we don't
necessarily remember, by others who don't necessarily realize. That
doesn't make it hurt any less.

When I told a psychiatrist friend that I was collecting experiences
on the theme "It hurts not to be listened to," he sent me this example:

"I called a friend and colleague and left a message asking if we could meet at a particular time. He didn't answer, and I felt a little anxious and confused. Should I call again to remind him? After all, I know he's busy. Should I wait another day or two and hope he'll answer? Should I not have asked him in the first place? All this leaves me uneasy."

The first thing that struck me about this example was how even a little thing like an unanswered phone message can leave someone feeling unresponded to—and troubled. Then I was really struck—like a slap in the face—by the realization that my friend was talking about *me.* Suddenly I was embarrassed, and then defensive. The reason I hadn't returned his call—doesn't matter. (We always have reasons for not responding.) What matters is how my failure to respond confused and hurt my friend and that I never had any inkling of it.

If an oversight like that can hurt, how much more painful is it when the subject is of real importance to the speaker?

––––––◆––––––

Listening is so basic that we take it for granted. Unfortunately, most of us think of ourselves as better listeners than we really are.

––––––◆––––––

When you come home from a business trip, eager to tell your partner how it went, and he listens but after a minute or two something in his eyes goes to sleep, you feel hurt, betrayed. When you call your parents to share a triumph and they don't seem really interested, you feel deflated and slightly foolish for having allowed yourself to feel excited and to hope for appreciation.

Just as it hurts not to be listened to when you're excited about something special, it's painful not to feel listened to by some*one* special, someone you expect to be especially attuned to you.

Derek's best friend in college was Roger. They were both political science majors and shared a passion for politics. Together they followed every detail of the Watergate investigation, relishing each new revelation as though they were a series of deliciously wicked Charles Addams cartoons. But much as they took cynical delight in the exposure of corruption in the Nixon White House, their friendship went well beyond politics.

Derek remembered the wonderful feeling of talking to Roger for hours, impelled by the momentum of some deep and inexplicable sym-

pathy. There was the pleasure of being able to say anything he wanted and the pleasure of hearing Roger say everything he'd always thought but never expressed. Unlike most of Derek's other friends, Roger wasn't a competitive conversationalist. He really listened.

When they went on to graduate schools in different cities, they kept up their friendship. Derek would visit Roger or Roger would visit Derek at least once a month. They'd play pool or see a movie and go out for Chinese food; and then afterward, no matter how late it got, they'd stay up talking.

Then Derek got married, and things changed. Roger didn't become distant the way some friends do after one marries, nor did Derek's wife dislike Roger. The distance that Roger felt was a small thing, but it made a big difference. "It's difficult to describe exactly, but I often end up feeling awkward and disappointed when I speak with Derek. He listens, but somehow he doesn't seem really interested anymore. He doesn't ask questions. He used to be involved rather than just accepting. It makes me sad. I still feel excited about the things going on in my life, but telling Derek just makes me feel unconnected and alone with them."

Roger's lament says something important about listening. It isn't just not being interrupted that we want. Sometimes people appear to be listening but aren't really hearing. A lot of people are good at being silent when we talk. Sometimes they betray their lack of real attention by glancing around and shifting their weight back and forth. At other times, however, listeners show no sign of inattention, but still we know they aren't really hearing what we have to say. It feels like they don't care.

Derek's passive interest was especially painful to Roger because of the closeness they'd shared. But the friends had reached an impasse; Roger couldn't open himself to his friend the way he'd done in the past, and Derek was mystified about the dynamics that were separating them.

Friendship is voluntary, and so talking about it is optional. Roger didn't want to criticize Derek or make demands. Besides, how does one friend tell another that he feels no longer cared about? And so Roger never did talk to Derek about feeling estranged. Too bad, because when a relationship goes sour, talking about it may be the only way to make things right again.

———◆———

It's especially hurtful not to be listened to in those relationships you count on for understanding.

———◆———

After a while most of us learn to do a pretty good imitation of being grownups and shrug off a lot of slights and misunderstandings. If, in the process, we become a little calloused, well maybe that's just the price we pay for living in this world. But sometimes not being responded to leaves us feeling so wounded and bitter that it can make us retreat from relationships, even for years.

When a woman discovered that her husband was having an affair, she felt as if someone had kicked her in the guts. In her shock and grief and anger, she turned to the person she was closest to—her mother-in-law. The mother-in-law tried to be understanding and supportive, but it was, after all, very difficult to listen to the bitter things her daughter-in-law was saying about her own son. Still, she tried. Apparently, however, the support she offered wasn't enough. Eventually the marital crisis passed and the couple reconciled, but the daughter-in-law, feeling that her mother-in-law hadn't been there when she needed her most, never spoke to her again.

The mother-in-law in this sad story was baffled and hurt by her daughter-in-law's stubborn silence. Other people's hurt and consequent hurtful behavior often seem unreasonable to us. What makes it reasonable to them is their feeling wounded by lack of responsiveness.

To listen is to pay attention, take an interest, care about, take to heart, validate, acknowledge, be moved . . . appreciate. Listening is in fact so central to human existence as to often escape notice; or, rather, it appears in so many guises that it is seldom grasped as the overarching need that it is. Sometimes, as Roger, the estranged daughter-in-law, and so many others have discovered, we don't realize how important being listened to is until we feel we've been cheated out of it.

Once in a while, however, we become aware of how much it means to be listened to. You can't decide whether or not to take a new job, and so you call an old friend to talk it over. She doesn't tell you what to do, but the fact that she listens, really listens, helps you see things more clearly. Another time you're just getting to know someone but you like him so much that, after a wonderful dinner in a restaurant, you take a risk and ask him over to your place for coffee. When he says, "No thanks, I've got to get up early," you feel rejected. Convinced that he doesn't really like you and not wanting to be hurt further, you start avoiding him. After a few days, however, he asks, in a very sincere way, what's wrong, and once again you take a risk and tell him that your feelings were hurt. To your great relief, instead of arguing, he listens and accepts what you have to say.

Why can't it always be that way? I speak; you listen. It's that simple. Isn't it? Unfortunately, it isn't. Talking and listening is a unique
relationship in which speaker and listener are constantly switching roles,
both jockeying for position, one's needs competing with the other's.
If you doubt it, try telling someone about a problem you're having and
see how long it takes before he interrupts to tell you about a problem
of his own, to describe a similar experience of his own, or to offer
advice—advice that may suit him more than it does you (and is more
responsive to his own anxiety than to what you're trying to say).

A man in therapy was exploring his relationship with his loving
but distant father when he suddenly remembered the happy times they'd
spent together playing with his electric trains. It was a Lionel set that
had been his father's and his grandfather's before him. Caught up in
the memory, the man grew increasingly excited as he recalled the joy
and pride and sense of belonging he had felt sharing this family tradi-
tion with his father. As the man's enthusiasm mounted, the therapist
launched into a long narrative about *his* train set and how he had gotten the other kids in the neighborhood to bring over their tracks and
train cars to build a huge neighborhood setup in his basement. After
the therapist had gone on at some length, the patient could no longer
contain his anger about being cut off. "Why are you telling me about
your trains?!" he demanded. The therapist hesitated, then, with that
level, impersonal voice we reserve for confiding something intimate,
he said lamely, "I was just trying to be friendly."

The therapist had made an all-too-common mistake (actually he'd
made several, but this is Be Kind to Therapists Week). He'd assumed
that establishing some common ground between him and his patient
was a sign of listening, that sharing his own experience was the equiva-
lent of empathy. In fact, though, he had switched the focus to himself,
making his patient feel discounted, misunderstood, unappreciated. That's
what hurt.

As is the way with words that become familiar, *empathy* may not
adequately convey the elusive and immensely powerful process of
genuinely appreciating the inner experience of another person. Empathic
listening is like the close reading of a poem; it takes in the words and
gets to what's behind them. The difference is that while empathy is
actively imaginative, it is fundamentally receptive rather than creative.
When we attend to a work of art, our idiosyncratic response has its

own validity, but when we attend to someone who's trying to tell us something, it's accurate empathy, not creativity, that counts.

THE IMPORTANCE OF BEARING WITNESS

Listening has not one but two purposes: taking in information and bearing witness to another's expression. By momentarily stepping out of his or her own frame of reference and into ours, the person who listens well acknowledges and affirms us. That affirmation, that validation is absolutely essential for sustaining the self-affirmation known as self-respect. Without being listened to, we are shut up in the solitude of our own hearts.

A thirty-six-year-old woman was so unnerved by a "minor incident" that she wondered if she needed psychotherapy. Marnie, who was executive vice president of a public policy institute, had arranged a meeting with the lieutenant governor to present a proposal she'd developed involving the regulation of a large state industry. Of necessity she'd invited her boss to the meeting, although she would have been able to make a more effective presentation of her proposal without him. The boss, in turn, had invited the institute's chief lobbyist, who would later have to convince legislators of the need for the proposed regulation. The meeting began, as Marnie expected, with her boss rambling on in a loose philosophical discussion that circled but never quite got to the point. When he finished, he turned not to Marnie but to the lobbyist to present the proposal. Marnie was stunned. The lobbyist began to speak, and fifteen minutes later the meeting ended, without Marnie's ever having gotten to say a word—about *her* proposal.

Marnie couldn't wait to tell her husband what had happened. Unfortunately he was out of town on business and wouldn't be back for three days. She was used to her husband's business trips; what she wasn't used to was how cut off she felt. She really needed to talk to him. As the evening wore on, Marnie's disappointment grew and then changed character. Instead of simply feeling frustrated, she began to feel inadequate. Why was she so dependent on her husband? Why couldn't she handle her own emotions?

Marnie decided that her problem was insecurity. If she were more secure, she wouldn't need anyone so much. She wouldn't be so vulnerable or so easily hurt; she'd be self-sufficient.

Marnie's complaint—the unexpected urgency to be heard—and her conclusion, that if she'd developed more self-esteem growing up, she wouldn't need to depend so much on other people's responsiveness, is a common one. Needing someone to respond to us makes us feel insecure and dependent and tempts us to believe that if we were stronger we wouldn't need other people. That way they wouldn't be able to disappoint us so much.

Being listened to helps us grow up feeling secure; but, contrary to what some people would like to believe, we never become whole and complete, finished products, like a statue or a monument. On the contrary, like any living thing, human beings require nourishment not only to grow up strong but also to maintain their strength and vitality. Listening nourishes our sense of worth.

The more insecure you are, the more reassurance you need. But all of us, no matter how secure and well adjusted, need attention to sustain us. In case this isn't immediately evident, all you need to do is note how we all have our own preferred ways of announcing our news. If my wife has news, for example, she's likely to call me at work or tell me as soon as we both get home. If she has something to say, she says it. Not me. If I have good news, I hoard it, save it up to announce with a fanfare—dying to be made a fuss over.

I once worked for months trying to land a book contract. My wife knew I was working on the book, but I didn't let her know that a contract was imminent. Waiting and hoping, and trying not to let myself hope for too much, I had extravagant fantasies about getting good news—no, about sharing it. Telling my wife would be the payoff. What I absolutely didn't want to do was simply tell her; I wanted—I needed—my announcement to be a big deal. The day the contract finally arrived I was ecstatic. But the most important part was looking forward to telling my wife. So I called her at work and told her I had a surprise for her: I was taking her out for a fancy dinner. She said fine and didn't ask any questions. (She's only known me for thirty years.)

By the time I got home, my wife had changed into a silk dress and was ready to go out. She could tell I was excited, but she waited patiently to find out why. At the restaurant, I ordered a bottle of champagne, and when it came she asked, still patient, "Do you have something to tell me?" I pulled out my contract and presented it with all the savoir-faire of a ten-year-old showing off his report card. She saw at once what it was, and her face lit up with a huge beaming grin. That look—her

love and pride—was indescribably sweet. My own smile was wet with tears.

What elaborate lengths we go to for such moments! Those of us who feel the need to arrange special occasions for our announcements share a good deal with those who don't need to calculate so. The period of time during which we're waiting to tell our news is charged with anxious anticipation. We can feel the tension building. The tension has to do with an aroused impulse—to confess or confront or show off or propose—to make an impact on another person and be responded to. The excitement comes from hope for a positive response; the anxiety comes from fear of rejection or indifference.

Whom you choose to tell what says something about your relationship to yourself—and to the other people in your life. Your presentation of self involves pride and shame—and whom you choose to share them with. With whom do you feel safe to cry? To rage? To brag? To confess something truly shameful?

———◆———

A good listener is a witness, not a filter for your experience.

———◆———

As soon as you're able to say what's on your mind—and be heard and acknowledged—you are unburdened. It's like having an ache or an itch suddenly relieved. If this completion comes quickly, as it often does in day-to-day conversations, you may hardly be aware of your need for understanding. But the disappointment you feel when you're not heard and the tension you feel waiting and hoping to be heard are signs of how important being listened to is. There are times when all that can be thought must be spoken and heard, communicated and shared, when ignorance and silence are pain, and to speak is to try to alleviate that pain.

BEING HEARD MEANS BEING TAKEN SERIOUSLY

The need to be heard, which is something we ordinarily take for granted, turns out to be one of the most powerful motive forces in human nature. Being listened to is the medium through which we discover ourselves as understandable and acceptable—or not. We care about the people who listen to us. We may even love them. But, for a time at least, we use them.

When we're activated by the need for appreciation, we relate to others as *selfobjects*, psychoanalyst Heinz Kohut's telling expression for a responsive other, someone we relate to not as an independent person with his or her own agenda but as someone-there-for-us.[1]

Perhaps the idea of using listeners as selfobjects reminds you of those bores who are always talking about themselves and don't seem to care about what you have to say. When they do listen, their hearts aren't in it; they're only waiting to change the subject back to themselves, their problems, their accomplishments.

This lack of appreciation can be especially painful when it occurs between us and our parents. It's maddening when they can't seem to let us be people in our own right, individuals with legitimate ideas and aspirations. Watching our parents listening to other people right in front of us can be especially aggravating. Why don't they show *us* a little of that attention? Here's the writer Harold Brodkey in *The Runaway Soul* dramatizing this irritating experience through the conversation of a young woman and her boyfriend. The boyfriend speaks first:

"Does your dad ever listen, or does he just do monologues?"

"He just does monologues. Doesn't he let you talk?"

"Only if I insist on it. Then we do alternate monologues."

"Well, that's it, then. He talks to you more than he does to me now."

Of course the woman's father talks to her boyfriend more than he does to her. The boyfriend is a fresh audience, new blood.

The people who hurt us the most are invariably the ones with whom we think we do have a special relationship, who make us feel that our attention and understanding are particularly important to them—until we see how easily they shift their interest to someone else. Right in the middle of confiding in us, they'll catch someone else's eye and break off to talk to *that* person. We discover that what we thought was an understanding shared only with us is something they've told a dozen other people. So much for our unique qualities as confidants! What's so hurtful about these promiscuous "intimates" isn't that they use us but that they rob us of the feeling that we're important to them, that we're special.

Although none of us likes to see (especially in ourselves) the kind of blatant narcissism that disregards the feelings of others, the truth

[1]Heinz Kohut, *The Analysis of the Self* (New York: International Universities Press, 1971).

is, much of the time we're all hopelessly absorbed with ourselves. The subject of narcissism turns out to be crucial in exploring the role of listening in the psychological birth of self-esteem. I introduce it here only to note that one aspect of our need for other people is entirely selfish. Being listened to maintains our narcissistic equilibrium—or, to put it more simply, it helps us feel whole.

When Roxanne and her parents finished unloading the station wagon, she felt a sinking sensation and was conscious for the first time of all the things she didn't have. Anxiously she watched as the other students and their families trooped into the dormitory, loaded down with beautiful pillows and quilts, ten-speed bicycles, stereo sets and cartons of records and cassettes, curling irons, personal computers, tennis rackets, and lacrosse sticks. Roxanne had never even seen a lacrosse stick. By the time her parents drove off, leaving her standing in front of South Hall, her excitement about starting college had given way to dread.

She never did get over her sense of isolation that first year. Everyone else seemed to make friends so easily. Not her. She called home a lot and tried to tell her parents how awful it was. But they said things like "Don't worry, honey; everybody's a little lonesome at first," and "You should make more friends," and "Maybe you just have to study a little harder." If only it were that easy!

Reassuring someone isn't the same as listening.

By the first of December Roxanne was skipping classes, missing meals, and crying herself to sleep. When she felt she couldn't stand it anymore, she made an appointment at the student counseling center.

Roxanne was surprised when the therapist said to call her Noreen. She wasn't used to that kind of openness in adults. Noreen turned out to be the most sympathetic and caring person Roxanne had ever met. She didn't tell Roxanne what to do or analyze her feelings; she just listened. For Roxanne, it was a new experience.

With Noreen's help, Roxanne was able to get through that first year and the three years that followed. Noreen helped her discover that her feelings of insecurity stemmed from never feeling really loved by her parents. Roxanne had always thought they were pretty good parents, but she could see now that they never actually knew her very well.

Her father was always busy, and her mother never really took her seriously as a person.

Eventually Noreen convinced Roxanne that she would never be free of her anger—and vulnerability to depression—until she worked things out with her parents. When Roxanne agreed, Noreen suggested that she get in touch with me for a few family therapy sessions; both of them knew that Roxanne's parents mistrusted Noreen because they believed she'd turned their daughter against them.

Roxanne and her parents arrived separately for our first meeting, and although they were all smiles and affability, the three of them seemed as wary as cats circling a snake. I had suggested to Roxanne over the phone that we go slow in this first meeting, that she try not to unload the full weight of her anger but rather search for some common ground with her parents. But that wasn't the truth about what she was feeling, and the truth was precisely what she was after. She started in on her father. When she was little, she'd loved him, she said, but as she got older she increasingly saw him as ridiculous and irrelevant. (He worked hard, had a crew cut, voted Republican, and was a patriot. Almost nothing in his life caused him second thoughts.) After listening to his daughter's ungenerous assessment, Roxanne's father said, "So that's how you see me?" and then retreated into silence, his own brand of armor.

Then Roxanne turned to her mother. She called her "shallow," "phony," and—the cruelest thing a child can say to a mother—"interested only in yourself." Roxanne's mother tried to listen but couldn't. "That's not true!" she protested. "Why do you have to exaggerate everything?" This only infuriated Roxanne more, and the two of them lashed back and forth at each other with increasingly shrill voices.

I tried to calm them down but wasn't very successful. Roxanne was hell-bent on *communicating*—not talking, that old-fashioned process of give-and-take, but *communicating*—that fashionable development where one insistent family member imparts some critical information to the others, "confronting" them with "the truth" whether they want to hear it or not. Eventually Roxanne's mother left the session in tears.

The following week I met with Roxanne alone. She was sorry the meeting hadn't gone differently but glad to have gotten her feelings out. She thought her mother had shown herself to be the unaccepting person Roxanne knew her to be. They weren't on speaking terms, and that was just fine with her, Roxanne said.

Six months later, much to my surprise, Roxanne called to say that

she and her parents wanted to come for another meeting. This time the conversation was friendly but superficial. Roxanne complimented her mother on her shoes and asked about her younger sister. Her mother asked how Roxanne was doing. Had she gotten over all that bitterness? Roxanne, feeling once again patronized and dismissed, tried to avoid reacting but couldn't. Furiously, she accused her mother of not really being interested in how she was feeling and caring only about polite formalities. My heart sank. But this time Roxanne's mother didn't react angrily or cut her daughter off. She didn't say much, but she didn't interrupt to defend herself either. What enabled her to listen to her daughter's angry accusations this time, I don't know. But she did.

One of a mother's heaviest burdens is being the primary target of her children's primitive swings between need and rage. The rage is directed at the hand that rocks the cradle no matter how loving its care. It's part of breaking away. Roxanne's mother seemed to sense this, seemed to remember that her little girl was still a little girl in some ways.

Roxanne seemed to expect retaliation from her mother. But when it wasn't forthcoming, she calmed down considerably. She had wanted, it seemed, only to be heard.

After that, Roxanne's relationship with her family changed dramatically. Previously limited to monologues or muteness, they entered into dialogue. Roxanne phoned and wrote. She shared confidences with her mother. Not always, of course, and not always successfully, but Roxanne had become much more open to her mother as a person, rather than perceiving her simply as a mother, who was somehow supposed to make everything right. She, in turn, became less a child and more a young woman, ready for life on her own.

Roxanne's unfulfilled need to be listened to had cut her off from other people and filled her with resentment. Unburdening herself was like breaking down a wall that had for a long time kept her from feeling connected to other people her own age. That her feelings were somewhat infantile says only that they were a long time unspoken. Talking to Noreen, who didn't have a stake in defending herself, helped Roxanne find her voice.

That second meeting with Roxanne and her parents had produced one of those moments that happen once in a while in families, when someone says something and everything shifts. Only it wasn't what Roxanne said that caused the shift; she'd said it all before. It was that her mother put aside her own claims to being right and just listened.

When we learn to hear the unspoken feelings that lie beneath another's anger or impatience, we discover the power to release the bitterness that keeps people apart. With a little effort, we can learn to hear the hurt behind expressions of hostility, the resentment behind avoidance, and the vulnerability that makes people afraid to speak and afraid to truly listen. When we understand the healing power of listening, we can even begin to listen to things that make us uneasy.

Being heard means being taken seriously. It satisfies our need for self-expression and our need to feel connected to others. The receptive listener allows us to express what we think and feel. Hearing and acknowledging us helps us clarify both the thoughts and the feelings, in the process firming our sense of ourselves. By affirming that we are understandable, the listener helps confirm our common humanity. Not being listened to makes us feel ignored and unappreciated, cut off and alone. The need to be known, to have our experience understood and accepted by someone who really listens, is meat and drink to the human heart.

Without a sufficient amount of sympathetic understanding in our lives we're haunted by an amorphous unease that leaves us anxious and lonely. Such feelings are hard to tolerate, and so we seek solace in passive escapism; we snap on the TV, treat ourselves to Ben and Jerry's, or escape into popular fiction about people whose lives are exciting. There is, of course, nothing wrong with relaxing. But why do we turn on the TV even when there's nothing to watch? And why do we feel uneasy without the car radio playing, even when it's just noise?

We usually associate passive escapism with release from stress. While it's true that many of us feel stressed out at the end of the day, it may not be overwork that wears us down, but a lack of understanding in our lives. Chief among the missing elements is the attention and appreciation of responsive selfobjects, people who care and listen to us with interest.

When the quality of our relationships isn't sufficient to maintain our equilibrium and enthusiasm—or when we're not up to making them so—we seek escape from morbid self-consciousness. We seek excitement, enthusiasm, responsiveness, gratification—the same kinds of feelings that can be had from a long heart-to-heart talk with someone we care about. But without the ballast of someone to talk to, some of us will continue to drown out the silence, as though without some kind of electronic entertainment to distract us, we may hear the low rumblings of despair.

CHAPTER TWO

"Thanks for Listening"

HOW LISTENING SHAPES US
AND CONNECTS US
TO EACH OTHER

We define and sustain ourselves in conversation with others. Recognition—being listened to—is the response from another person that makes our feelings, actions, and intentions meaningful. It allows us to realize our own agency and authorship in a tangible way. But, as we saw in Chapter 1, the expression and recognition so fundamental to our well-being is a mutual, reciprocal process. Our lives are coauthored in dialogue. So, if being recognized through listening is to define and sustain us, it must come from someone whom we in turn recognize. Striking a balance between expression (talking) and recognition (listening) is what allows us and the people we care about to interact as sovereign equals.

If your life, or even a key relationship in it, is unbalanced—if it doesn't allow you sufficient self-expression or mutual recognition—you will be the poorer for it. This chapter will show how listening is critical to the formation of a strong and healthy self *and* to the formation of strong and healthy relationships.

What makes listening such a force in shaping character is the power of words to match and share experience—or contradict and falsify it. What is understood and accepted—"Yes, isn't that wonderful!"—

becomes part of your social self, the self you own and share. Some of what is not appreciated—"You shouldn't be feeling that way in the first place"—becomes part of your private self, known but not shared, split off, sometimes kept secret even from yourself. Ominously, much of what fails to find acceptance becomes part of your disavowed self, what interpersonal psychiatrist Harry Stack Sullivan called the "not me."[1] Some parents may be too anxious to tolerate a child's anger; others may be too embarrassed to tolerate their children's sexual feelings. Each of us grows up with some experiences of self so poisoned with anxiety that they aren't assimilated into the rest of our personality. Listening shapes us; lack of listening twists us.

A young mother wearing denim was berating her little girl for wanting to have a Barbie doll. It was a "stupid" thing to want; the child should be "ashamed" of herself; she should "have more self-respect." It was painful to hear. The sad irony of a mother hammering away at a little girl's pride to teach her self-respect was hard to escape. Should the mother let her daughter have a Barbie, like all the other kids? That's up to her, but she should respect her daughter's right to have opinions of her own.

Gradually, with cooperation between parent and child, a self is formed, organized by language and listening, based in part on the child's natural experience, in part on the values imposed by the parents. The listened-to child grows up relatively secure and whole. The unlistened-to child lacks the understanding that firms self-acceptance and is "bent out of shape" by the wishes and anxieties of others. This is what the famous psychotherapist Carl Rogers meant when he said that the child's innate tendency toward self-actualization is subverted by the need to please.[2]

What never gets heard affects more than a difference between the sociably shareable and the private; it drives a split between the true self and a false self.

The seeds of listening are sown in childhood, in the quality of the relationship between parent and child. Parents who listen make their

---

[1] Harry Stack Sullivan, *The Interpersonal Theory of Psychiatry* (New York: Norton, 1953).

[2] Carl Rogers, *Client-Centered Therapy* (Boston: Houghton Mifflin, 1951).

children feel worthwhile and appreciated. Being listened to helps build a strong, secure self, endowing the child with sufficient self-respect to develop his or her own unique talents and ideals and to approach relationships with confidence and tolerance.

That understanding builds self-assurance is hardly news. Most of us can picture a mother with smiling eyes listening enthusiastically to a child eagerly describing some triumph or comforting a sad-faced child crying over some minor tragedy. And we all know how bad it feels to watch a father reduce a child to tears of rage and frustration for making a mistake. Of course such scenes, repeated over and over, have an impact on a child. What may not be so obvious is how early or how profoundly the quality of listening begins to shape character.

HOW LISTENING SHAPES SELF-RESPECT

To begin with, the self is not a given, like having red hair or being tall, but a perspective on awareness, and an interpersonal one at that. The self is how we personify what we are, as shaped by our experience of being responded to by others. Character is formed in relationships, and the quality of self depends on the nature of that response, the quality of listening we receive.

Among recent findings with the most profound implications for understanding the importance of listening is the work of infant researcher Daniel Stern.[3] Stern's most radical discovery is that the infant is never totally undifferentiated (symbiotic) from the mother.

Margaret Mahler's influential psychoanalytic theory of separation and individuation was based on the implicit assumption that we grow up and out of relationships, rather than becoming more active and sovereign *within* them. But once we accept the idea that infants don't begin life as part of an undifferentiated unity, the question is not only how we separate from our parents, but also how we learn to connect. The issue isn't how we become free of people, but how we actively make ourselves heard and understood in relationship to them.

This view of the self as having a fundamental need for expression and recognition emerged not only from the observation of infants but also in consulting rooms, where psychotherapists began to hear the infant cry in the adult voice. The desperate anguish of those who feel

[3]Daniel Stern, *The Interpersonal World of the Infant* (New York: Basic Books, 1985).

empty and alone, unable to connect to themselves or to others, leads to the question "What does it take to make us feel whole?" A large part of the answer is listening.

In charting the development of children, Stern identified four progressively more complex senses of self, each defining a different domain of self-experience and social relatedness. It turns out that second only to the need for food and shelter is the need for understanding. Even infants need listening to thrive. "Listening" to an infant may sound somewhat grand, but it is precisely that—the quality of parental understanding and acknowledgment—that plays such a decisive role in making us what we are.

Let's look now at the unfolding of these four senses of self to see how listening shapes character.

"Here I Am":
The Sense of an Emergent Self (Birth to 2 Months)

The infant's need for listening is simple but imperative. With the sudden pressure of physical need, life goes from lovely to all wrong. Hunger breaks over the body like an angry storm. It starts slowly; the baby has a sense of something going awry. Then fussing turns to full-throated crying as the baby tries to hurl the pain sensations out and away. This crying serves as a distress signal, like a siren, to alert the parents and demand a response from them.

Being a parent at this stage is simple. As I recall, my wife and I, our empathic sensitivities honed to razor sharpness by months of sleep deprivation, were flung into action by the slightest peep. Blessed with a disposition as placid as a howler monkey, our first little darling would ever so gently summon us for her nightly lactose intolerance test. I, never the insensitive father, was usually first to respond. "Honey," I'd coo, grinding my teeth to keep them warm, "do something!" At which my mate, ever appreciative of my support, would hasten to the little one's side to administer whatever first aid was required. Ah, parenthood.

Babies are little and cute and helpless, but their smiling, gazing, fretting, and crying are commanding messages; they must be listened to. At this stage parents, thinking primarily about satisfying the baby's needs, may not recognize the extent of the social interaction involved in the process. But even before the baby achieves self-consciousness, parents invest it with their expectations and aspirations. From day one, they relate to the baby as both an actual and a potential self.

Our impulse toward understanding is irresistible. Developmental

psychologist Aidan Macfarlane's observations of new mothers talking to their infants brought to them for the first time after delivery show that the mothers attribute meaning to each sign and sound.[4] "What's that frown for? The world's a little scary, huh?" Mothers don't really believe the infant understands, but they assign meaning to what their infants are doing and respond accordingly. In time, they create little formats of interaction, jointly constructed little worlds. This is the child's first culture.

Parents immediately ascribe to their infants intentions ("Oh, you want that"), motives ("You're doing that so Mommy will hurry up and feed you"), and authorship of action ("You did that on purpose, didn't you?"). In doing this, parents are responding to and helping create an emergent self. Such motives and intentions make human behavior understandable, and parents invariably treat their infants as understandable beings—that is, as the people they are to become (just so long as they become the people their parents want them to become).

------◆------

Who we are and what we say triggers other people's response to us. That response and our connection to others remain vital to our psychological well-being.

------◆------

When babies are too young to talk, it's important for their parents to understand what they feel but cannot say. When a baby cries, the parents must figure out what's wrong. Does he want to be fed? Does she need a diaper change? Does he want to be held? (Imagine the baby's feelings. What a chasm separates her from these two giant, nervous creatures nature has assigned as her waitpersons. Would they ever catch on?) When the baby grows up and learns to talk, she becomes better at putting her needs and feelings into words. Better, but not perfect. Sometimes we all need a little help in making ourselves understood.

Infants are helplessly dependent on their parents. When the parents are absent, angry, or otherwise unresponsive, the child is alone and terrified; he feels the bottom dropping out of the whole world. This primal connection to others begins as a matter of life and death, over which we have little control when we're infants. Gradually we become aware of our own half of the equation (some people more gradually than other).

[4] Aiden Macfarlane, *The Psychology of Childbirth* (Cambridge, MA: Harvard University Press, 1977).

"Hey, Look At Me!":
The Sense of a Core Self (2 to 7 Months)

Between eight and twelve weeks, infants become truly gregarious. The social smile emerges; they begin to vocalize and make eye-to-eye contact. When the baby looks up and smiles and coos, or splashes in the bath, or giggles with delight, how could you *not* love her? Surely, we would like to think, all parents respond intuitively to such communications. Unfortunately, this isn't so. Some parents are so preoccupied, depressed, or otherwise distracted that they ignore their babies. And, perhaps more common, many parents respond to their babies not as little people with their own rhythms and moods but as foils for the parents' own needs.

Every infant has an optimal level of excitement. Activity beyond that level constitutes overstimulation, and the experience becomes upsetting; below that level, stimulation is, well, unstimulating, boring. Parents must learn to read their babies. By taking their children seriously as persons, responding to the children's feelings rather than imposing their own, parents convey understanding and acceptance that children take in and transform into self-respect.

The next time you see an adult interacting with a baby, notice the difference between responding in tune with the child's level of excitement and imposing the adult's emotions on the child. If you see a parent with blunted emotions ignoring a bright-eyed baby, you're witnessing the beginning of a long, sad process by which unresponsive parents wither the enthusiasm of their children like unwatered flowers.

Having quite enough unwatered flowers at the office, thank you, I wasn't about to have any around my house. I remember tiptoeing into the baby's room at eventide, right about the time she was dozing—or pretending to. What my fiendish masculine intuition told me she really wanted was not rest but to be hurled violently up to the ceiling and then come crashing toward the floor—like a skydiver without a parachute—only to be plucked from the jaws of death by Daddy. Whee!

Too choked with joy to speak, the little mite showed her pleasure by widening her eyes like saucers while her face turned a lovely shade of blue.

Excessive enthusiasm may be less depressing, but it isn't necessarily more responsive. We've all seen grown-ups at it—"baby love"—the

fulsome tone of voice, the honeyed words, the endless marveling and exclaiming. When babies are little, it's almost automatic; babies are so animated themselves that they drive up the intensity of our response. But when this adult enthusiasm regularly exceeds the baby's own, the result is a jarring discontinuity. Loving parents share the moods of their children and show it.

———◆———

It isn't exuberance or any other emotion that conveys loving appreciation; it's being noticed, understood, and taken seriously.

———◆———

The baby whose parents tickle and poke and jiggle and shake her when she's not in the mood is as alone with her real self as the baby whose parents ignore her. This imposition of the parents' agenda is, in what psychiatrist R. D. Laing so tellingly called the "politics of experience," the mystification in which the child's reality gets lost.[5] Not being understood and taken seriously as a person in your own right—even at this early age—is the root of aloneness and insecurity. In the words of psychoanalyst Ernest Wolf, "Solitude, psychological solitude, is the mother of anxiety."[6]

"Honey, I'm Cold. Don't You Want a Sweater?": The Sense of a Subjective Self (7 to 15 Months)

By about one year of age the baby realizes that he has an inner, private mental world, with intentions, desires, feelings, thoughts, and memories, which are invisible to others unless he makes an attempt to reveal them. The possibility of sharing these invisible contents of the mind is the source of the greatest human happiness and frustration.

Imagine for a moment that you're a baby who hasn't yet learned to talk, and you want a cookie. What do you do if you see the cookie but it's out of reach? Simple. You get your mother to read your mind.

Mind reading may sound extravagant, but isn't that what communication boils down to? The baby must gain Mother's attention, express what's on his mind, and do so in a way that Mother receives and

[5] R. D. Laing, *The Politics of Experience* (New York: Pantheon, 1967).
[6] Ernest Wolf, "Developmental Line of Self-Object Relations," in Arnold Goldberg, ed., *Advances in Self Psychology* (New York: International Universities Press, 1980).

understands the message. "I want a cookie" is a simple message, easily sent and easily received, even without words. When it comes to more complicated messages, babies (like you and me) have to work harder to express themselves—and hope their listeners will work hard enough to understand.

The possibility of sharing experience creates the possibility for confirmation of the self as understandable and acceptable; it also creates the possibility of intimacy, the desire to know and be known. What's at stake is nothing less than discovering what part of the private world of inner experience is shareable and what part falls outside the pale of commonly recognized and accepted human experience.

Being listened to spells the difference between feeling accepted and feeling isolated.

The possibility of sharing mental states between people also raises the possibility of misunderstanding. For example, babies are remarkably eager explorers. Sitting on Mommy's or Daddy's lap, a baby may probe a finger into the parent's mouth or nose or tug at a strand of hair to see if it will come loose. The parent who takes this exploration as an act of aggression may get annoyed and attribute hostility to the baby. If so, the parent may follow up this feeling with a rebuke, a slap, or some rejection of the baby, who had only been doing what comes naturally at this age.

The misunderstood baby is confused by the parent's lack of understanding, upset and frightened by the rebuke and rejection. *Maybe it was a mistake*, the baby thinks. Then if the baby repeats the exploration, to clarify the confusion or to evoke a different response this time or even to retaliate, the baby may now do so with a more energetic assertiveness. Now the parent will assume that his or her original misunderstanding was confirmed: the baby *is* being aggressive.

If this situation is repeated, the parent's false interpretation may become the infant's (and later the child's) official and accepted one: exploration is aggression, and it's bad. The baby may come to see himself as aggressive, even hostile. Someone else's reality has become his. Misunderstanding undermines not only our trust in others, but also our trust in our own perceptions.

The word for sharing experience is *intersubjectivity*. The reason for this fancy term where an ordinary word like *communication* might do

is to keep us from forgetting that understanding is a joint achievement: one person trying to express what's on his or her mind, the other trying to read it. Reading a child's mind begins with *attunement*.

Attunement, a parent's ability to share the child's affective state, is a pervasive feature of parent–child interactions with profound consequences. It's the forerunner of empathy and the essence of human understanding. Attunement begins with the intuitive parental response of sharing the baby's mood and showing it. The baby reaches out excitedly and grabs a toy. When the toy is in her grasp, she lets out an exuberant "aah!" and looks at her mother. Mother responds in kind, sharing the baby's exhilaration and showing it by smiling and nodding and saying "Yes!" The mother has understood and shared the child's mood. That's attunement.

One demonstration of the baby's need for an attuned response is the *still-face procedure*. If a mother (or father) goes still-faced—impassive and expressionless—in the middle of an interaction, the baby will become upset and withdraw. Infants after about two-and-a-half months of age react strongly to this still face. They look about. Their smiles die away and they frown. They make repeated attempts to reignite the mother by smiling and gesturing and calling her. If they don't succeed, they finally turn away, looking unhappy and confused.[7] It hurts to reach out to someone who doesn't respond.

"No, I Don't Want a Nap! I Want to Play": The Sense of a Verbal Self (15 to 18 Months)

Learning to speak creates a new type of connection between adult and child. The acquisition of language has traditionally been seen as a major step in the achievement of a separate identity apart from the parent, next only to locomotion. But the opposite is also true: the acquisition of language is a potent force for union and intimacy.

The developmental psychologists Arnold Sameroff and Robert Emde summarize an extensive literature that shows that emotional unresponsiveness produces an infant with "a restricted range of emotional expressiveness; less clear signaling; and a predominance of disengagement, distress, or avoidance in interactions. Under these conditions, clinicians may also see a 'turning off' of affective interactions and, in extreme cases, sustained sadness or depression."[8] In other words, the

[7]Daniel Stern, *Diary of a Baby* (New York: Basic Books, 1990).

[8]Arnold Sameroff and Rober Emde, eds., *Relationship Disturbances in Early Childhood* (New York: Basic Books, 1989), 47.

child whose communications aren't appreciated and responded to eventually gives up and turns inward.

---◆---

When we see sadness or depression in someone, we tend to assume that something's wrong, that something has happened. Maybe that something is that nobody's listening.

---◆---

THE LISTENED-TO CHILD IS A CONFIDENT CHILD

By the time children get to be four or five, empathy or its absence has molded their personalities in recognizable ways. The securely understood child grows up to expect others to be available and receptive. This is demonstrated by a tendency to draw effectively on preschool teachers as resources. The listened-to child who becomes ill or injured at school will confidently turn to teachers for support. In contrast, it's particularly at such times that insecure children fail to seek contact. "A boy is disappointed and folds his arms and sulks. A girl bumps her head under a table and crawls off to be by herself. A child is upset on the last day of school; she sits frozen and expressionless on a couch."[9] Such reactions are typical—and don't change much as the unlistened-to child gets older.

At the same time, preschoolers with a history of empathic listening are more engaged and more at ease with their peers. They expect interactions to be positive and thus are more eager for them. They are able to make more friends and are happier. They are also good listeners. Already by four or five, empathic failure—not abuse or cruelty, but simple, everyday lack of understanding—results in a self that is isolated and insecure, vulnerable to rejection and therefore fearful of new people and experience.

Imagine five-year-old Tammy, weaned on understanding, telling her playmate next door about a bully in kindergarten. "And then he pushed me and hogged all the crayons!"

A tiny cloud momentarily overshadowed her friend Ryan's even tinier face. Bullies were not his favorite people. But listening sympathet-

---

[9]Alan Sroufe, "Relationships, Self, and Individual Adaptation," in Arnold Sameroff and Robert Emde, eds., *Relationship Disturbances in Early Childhood* (New York: Basic Books, 1989), 88–89.

ically, he knew, was for sissies. Confident that if his own ire were suffi-ciently aroused, he could demolish a grape with a single blow of his fist, Ryan counseled war. "You should put paint in his hair and spank him with your ruler when he does that."

Here were two kindred spirits, meeting at last on a plane of perfect understanding. "Thanks," said Tammy gratefully, "but I think I hear my mother calling. Nice talking to you."

The need for listening is based partly on the need to sustain our sense of significance. The listener's understanding presence serves as a selfobject to satisfy our need for attention and appreciation. But the idea that listening is something one person *gives* to the other is only partly true. Another vital aspect of listening is mutuality.

LISTENING BRIDGES THE SPACE BETWEEN US

Mutuality is a sense not merely of being understood and valued but of sharing—of being-with another person. Here it isn't just *I* but *we* that is important. Our experience is made fuller by sharing it with another person.

When I want to "share" a thought or feeling that means a lot to me, what I really want is to be understood, taken seriously and appreciat-ed. (Calling this "sharing" is an unctuous euphemism; what we really want is to express ourselves and be heard.) It is *I* who wants to be vali-dated. But if I see an especially funny cartoon in *The New Yorker*, I immediately think of someone to share *it* with. (Here, "sharing" is ap-propriate, because the experience sought is mutual, communal.) In this instance I don't want to be admired or valued; I just want to share the laughter.

As psychologist Ruthellen Josselson says in *The Space Between Us*,[10] mutuality is a powerful but neglected aspect of human ex-perience. When we're young and alive, before life blunts our naked nerve endings, the yearning for mutuality takes its most intense form in the hungering for a soul mate. We find and invent that special someone with whom we can share light moments and deep thoughts.

Mutuality is the stuff of everyday human exchange. We swap know-ing comments about the president's latest gaffe, complain about the

[10]Ruthellen Josselson, *The Space Between Us: Exploring the Dimensions of Human Relationships* (San Francisco: Jossey-Bass, 1992).

weather, and chat idly about the day's schedule. Nothing important is happening, just life and shared humanity. One woman said, "That's why when I'm away on business I call my husband at the end of the day—to tell him that the meeting went OK or it's raining or I forgot to pack my good shoes." This woman doesn't *need* anything; she calls just to share the everyday observations and opinions and complaints that otherwise back up and burden us in isolation.

Most theories of human relationship emphasize one or another aspect of connection, whether it's mutuality, the selfobject function, holding, attachment, or caring. All these many modes of relatedness are ways of reaching through the space that separates us. Underlying all our agendas, however, is the fact that speech is the primary mode of relating and being listened to is the primary means of being understood and appreciated. By "appreciated" I don't necessarily mean admired, but rather perceived and accepted as we feel ourselves to be. When we talk about being down in the dumps, it doesn't help to be told how wonderful we are; we want our discontent recognized. We want to be known.

As we're reminded from time to time when we're misjudged or hurt more than anyone realizes, however, no one can really see our selves. They see what they can and are willing to see, and they know what we tell them. The rest is private, mystery.

The way we become known is through empathic responsiveness, what Heinz Kohut called "mirroring."[11] The good listener (or "mirroring selfobject") appreciates us as we are, accepting the feelings and ideas that we express as they are. In the process, we feel understood, acknowledged, and accepted.

Empathy—the human echo—is the indispensable stuff of emotional well-being. What is adequately mirrored becomes, in time, part of the true and lived self. The child who is heard and appreciated has a better chance to grow up whole. The adult who is heard and appreciated is more likely to continue to feel that way.

Unshared Thoughts Diminish Us

Some people are good at getting appreciated, but they work too hard at it. They aren't open to all of themselves, and so what gets appreciat-

[11]Kohut's two great (though unfortunately dense) works are: Heinz Kohut, *The Analysis of the Self* (New York: International Universities Press, 1971); and Heinz Kohut, *The Restoration of the Self* (New York: International Universities Press, 1977).

ed is only the face they show to the world. Reassurance isn't very reassuring to the person with too many secrets.

Why, then, do some people say so little about themselves?

The answer is, life teaches them to hold back. The innocent eagerness for appreciation we bring to our earliest relationships exposes us to consequences. Some people are lucky. They get the attention they need and thereafter approach life with confidence and openness. Others aren't so lucky. They don't get listened to, and as a consequence they avoid opening up. What might appear to be modesty in some such cases may have more to do with the reluctance to reexpose old wounds. Many people learn instead to channel their need for appreciation into personal ambition or doing things for other people.

Not being listened to is hard on the heart; and so to varying degrees we cover our need for understanding with mechanisms of defense.

Some people become experts at avoidance and cultivate the capacity to be alone. The charm of solitude, recently elaborated by British psychiatrist Anthony Storr,[12] is that it provides space for repose and reflection, time for looking within the self, time for creative endeavor. Solitude offers rest and respite from the noisy claims of everyday social living. But some of the penchant for being alone is defensive—an accommodation to being hurt by not being heard. The defenses that form the solitary person's character support a grand illusion: the illusion of self-reliance. If we could only examine the contemplation of one's own feelings that passes for introspection, we'd discover that the silence of the solitary is often filled with imagined conversations.

Unshared thoughts diminish us not only by making us less authentic and less whole, as we've discussed, but also by eating at us relentlessly. Repression is not like putting something away on the closet shelf and forgetting about it; repression takes a constant expenditure of energy that slowly wears us slowly down.

The feeling of not being understood is one of the most painful in human experience. Not being appreciated and responded to depletes

---

[12]Anthony Storr, *Solitude: A Return to the Self* (New York: The Free Press, 1988).

our vitality and makes us feel less alive. When we're with someone who doesn't listen, we shut down. When we're with someone who's interested and responsive—a good listener—we perk up and come alive. Being listened to is as vital to our enthusiasm for life as love and work. So is listening. Understanding the dynamics of listening enables us to deepen and enrich our relationships. It involves learning how to suspend our own emotional agenda and then realizing the rewards of genuine empathy. When our own listening becomes blocked by the emotions that the speaker arouses in us, we conspire to produce our own isolation. It doesn't have to be that way.

CHAPTER THREE

"Why Don't People Listen?"

HOW COMMUNICATION
BREAKS DOWN

Ellen was finding it more difficult than she'd imagined to stay home all day with two small children. She had planned to go back to work soon after the children were born but then decided that it was more important to be at home with them until they started school. What she missed most about not working was having people to talk with. Listening to who wanted a cookie and who had to go to the potty and what Big Bird was up to got pretty tedious by the end of the day. Greg, Ellen's husband, was surprisingly unsympathetic. He helped put the kids to bed and spent time with them on weekends, but when he came home after work he didn't even pretend to be interested in Ellen's account of her day. She was hurt, and she was angry.

"I know Greg works hard and wants to rest. But I work hard too. All I want is a few minutes of adult conversation. But if I dare to interrupt his precious six o'clock news to try to talk to him, he just gets mad. It isn't worth it, and I've had just about all I can take." Her eyes were full of tears.

"DID YOU HEAR WHAT I SAID?"

Why don't people listen? There's no shortage of easy answers to this question. Most focus on the listener. (Husbands are notoriously unsym-

37

pathetic listeners.) Ellen's explanation for Greg's unavailability wasn't entirely critical—"I know he needs time to unwind"—but it was, after all, focused entirely on him. His lack of listening was *his* doing.

In fact, listening (or the lack of it) is a two-person process. According to Greg, it was frustrating to talk with Ellen about the kids. "She's always complaining. She says they won't leave her alone, even when she goes to the bathroom. But she encourages it! She smothers them. She won't let them alone to play by themselves, and she refuses to take any time for herself. And the thing that really bothers me is the way she always sides with the younger one. Everything Terri does is cute; everything Charles does is wrong. If I try to say anything, even very nicely, she starts crying and says I'm always picking on her. So I've learned to keep my mouth shut."

Ellen felt neglected because Greg wouldn't talk to her, but her contribution to the problem was not being open to his point of view. The fact that Greg's position differs from hers, and may even be critical, makes it hard to hear. Unfortunately, when two people are in conflict about something important, unless each is able to at least acknowledge the other's point of view, the result is likely to be an emotional cutoff.

Greg felt discounted because Ellen complained about a problem of her own making (as he saw it) and wouldn't listen to his opinion. And yet Greg manages neither to listen nor to get his point of view across. If he could separate listening from advising, perhaps Ellen would get some sympathy for her feelings, and then he might be able to communicate his perspective more effectively. Of course it's difficult for him to set aside his own feelings long enough to listen to his wife's, especially on a subject that he feels so strongly about. But maybe that's not a good enough excuse for a husband and father's retreat.

When people don't listen to us, we can't help feeling it's their fault: they're selfish or inconsiderate. (When *we* don't listen, it's because we're bored or tired or don't like being talked down to.) The truth is, listening is a complex process. Even though failures of listening all end in the same painful experience of not being heard, there are many reasons people don't listen.

Several years ago a young couple came to me complaining of difficulties in communicating. When I asked what the problem was, the husband said, "It's my wife; she's boring." (Who says men are reticent with their feelings?) Restraining my urge to react to this nasty crack, I asked him to explain. The man was a lawyer, working as a campaign adviser

in a gubernatorial election campaign. His days were filled with strategy sessions, speechwriting conferences, meetings with the candidate, television interviews, arranging appearances across the state, defending attacks from the opposition, and planning counterattacks. When he came home at night, his head spinning from the excitement and frustration of the crusade, he mumbled a greeting to his wife and collapsed onto the couch with a drink and the newspaper.

When I asked why he wasn't more eager to talk over the events of the day, he said his wife wasn't interested. She was a graphic design artist and not at all, he contended, concerned about politics.

She protested that although she might not know a lot about politics, she *was* interested in him and what he was doing. He wasn't convinced.

I asked him to think of someone that he *knew* was interested in the campaign, someone with whom he could talk enthusiastically. Imagine, I told him, how different you are with that person. He allowed as that might be true. Then I asked him—just for an experiment—to come home for one week and pretend that his wife was that interested person, the person he found it so exciting to talk to. He agreed to try it.

The next week they returned beaming. "Guess what?" he said. "She's not boring anymore."

This young lawyer's uncommunicativeness could have been taken as just another example of men's silences. Are men emotionally illiterate? Trapped in doing—working, playing, achieving—do they have no language of feeling? Such stereotyping ignores the interactive nature of communication and the powerful role of expectations. When people don't say much, it's less likely that they have nothing on their minds than that they don't trust the other person to be interested or tolerant enough to hear it. My suggestion to this man—that he pretend his wife *was* interested—encouraged him to break his silence. But it was his approaching her with enthusiasm, taking interest in talking to her, that broke the pattern of avoidance. The truth is that we become more interesting ourselves when we assume interest on the part of our listeners.

WHY SOMEONE DOSEN'T HEAR WHAT YOU THINK YOU SAID

Sometimes people don't hear us because they've had a bad day. They may be preoccupied with the angry things someone said or with all the

extra work they have to do and thus not be able to listen to anything at all. Or they may be turned off to us by any number of things—they assume that we're talking to them only because we want something or that we're going to give them a lecture or that we don't really care about them. Listeners often don't hear because they have a preconceived notion of what we're going to say. Or they can't hear us because they can't suspend their own needs or because what we say makes them anxious. In short, although hurt feelings may tempt us to blame failures of listening on other people's recalcitrance, the reasons for not listening are many and complex.

When the communicative process breaks down, we—who are doing our best—tend to assume that the other person didn't say what he meant or didn't hear what we were saying. Usually, both parties to misunderstanding feel that way. But it may be helpful to realize that between speaker and listener are two filters to meaning.[1]

The speaker, who has an *intention* of what he or she wants to communicate, sends a *message,* and that message has an *impact* on the listener.

Good communication means having the impact you meant to have, that is *intent* equals *impact.* But every message must pass first through the filter of the speaker's clarity of expression and second through the listener's ability to hear what was said. Unfortunately, there are many times when intent doesn't equal impact and many reasons why this is the case.

Some of the reasons for misunderstanding are simple and can be improved, like learning a skill. For example, by learning to give feedback, listeners tell speakers about the impact of their messages and give them a chance to clarify their intentions. But many more reasons for misunderstanding are less straightforward and not amenable to simple formulas for improvement. Our young lawyer's assumption that his wife wasn't interested in his work is just one example of the psychological complications of listening.

Transference and Countertransference

This dynamic, the speaker's tendency to impose certain expectations on the listener, is what, in the psychoanalytic situation, is called *transference.* For simplicity's sake, the idea of transference is often reduced

[1]John Gottman, Cliff Notarius, Jonni Gonso, and Howard Markman, *A Couples Guide to Communication* (Chicago: Research Press, 1976).

to the notion that the patient assumes that the silent analyst is a car-
bon copy of one of his or her parents—judging her harshly just like her
father did or enthralled with his accomplishments like his mother was.
In fact transference refers to *all* the ways in which a person's experience
of a relationship becomes organized according to the configurations of
self-image and expectations of others that unconsciously structure his
or her subjective universe. Transference isn't limited to the therapeutic
situation—and it isn't only distortion.

Countertransference, the psychoanalytic term for the complexity introduced by the listener, refers to how the listener's subjectivity shapes
his or her experience of the conversation. Like transference, countertransference isn't simply distortion, because our expectations and reactions to each other actually shape and reshape our relationships. The
woman who expects men to talk only about themselves may inquire
more than she discloses, thereby confirming her expectations. The man
who expects to find his wife's accounts of the day uninteresting may fail
to ask the kinds of questions that might make it interesting to him; as a
result, he gets out of the conversation pretty much what he puts into it.

We'll explore the speaker's contributions to misunderstanding later,
though as you'll discover it's never entirely possible to separate speaker
and listener.

The principal forces contributing to the listener's filter are the
listener's own agenda, preconceived notions and expectations, and defensive emotional reactions.

The Listener's Own Agenda

In the summer of 1992 Ariel Dorfman's play *Death and the Maiden*, star-
ring Glenn Close, Richard Dreyfuss, and Gene Hackman, drew large
audiences on Broadway. This play of ideas in the guise of a political
thriller takes place in a country that might be Chile in the immediate
aftermath of a corrupt dictatorship. The setting is a beach house on
the night that the lawyer, Gerardo (Richard Dreyfuss), is asked to investigate certain crimes of the recent past; his wife, Paulina (Glenn
Close), was one such victim. And when Roberto Miranda (Gene Hackman) gives her husband a lift after his tire blows out, she recognizes
his voice as that of the doctor who raped her. Paulina gets a gun and
ties the doctor to a chair. But her husband doesn't believe her. How
could she recognize the man who raped and tortured her from just his
voice? He can't believe that the good Samaritan who stopped to help

him on the road could actually be the evil man who did such terrible things to his wife. She assures him that there is no mistake: she could never forget that voice. Still her husband can't believe her. The play turns on the wife's desperation and the husband's incredulity. The ending is ambiguous.

I first heard about *Death and the Maiden* from a patient who took it as an allegory of a husband's failure to listen to his wife, despite the urgency of her appeal. She knew how the woman felt. I replied that as a metaphor for misunderstanding the story was one-sided, stressing as it did only the husband's failure to listen, rather than also dealing with the wife's failure to make herself understood. I wasn't familiar with the play, but I wanted my patient to quit blaming her husband for their problems and begin to see their communication as a process that took place between them. It wasn't until later that I realized that I was recreating a similar story: a woman was trying to tell a man something—in this case that the play was profoundly affecting and that it reminded her of not being listened to by her husband—and the man was not listening.

When I finally got around to reading the play, I responded the same way my patient did. It's a powerful story about a woman desperate for understanding and desperately not understood.

I didn't listen to my patient with the best of intentions. Oh, I heard what she said all right, but I was too eager to teach her a lesson about listening to really understand what she was saying—that the play was upsetting and reminded her of her own situation. My response, "Yes, but . . . ," had the effect of making her wrong and me right. Failures of listening often take that form.

To listen well, it's necessary to let go of what's on your mind long enough to hear what's on the other person's. Feigned attentiveness doesn't work.

Remember Roger, whose friend Derek grew distant from him after he got married? Roger might have been able to talk to Derek if he'd concentrated on saying how he felt, without blaming Derek or forcing him to explain himself. If you can express your feelings without trying to compel anything from the other person, you're more likely to get heard—and more likely to hear what the other person is feeling.

Preconceived Notions

By the time we emerge from adolescence most of us have become self-protective. We know where our naked nerve endings are and don't often

expose them. We open ourselves selectively and, like any creature with a soft underbelly, retreat from unfriendly encounters. Sometimes, however, it's too late to pull back inside our shells. When the pressure of upset makes us open ourselves to someone we think we can trust, failed understanding can be as bruising as a mugging.

When his son told him he was dropping out of college, Seth tried hard to be understanding. He didn't want to burden Jamie with his own expectations, and so he did his best to hide his disappointment. Still, he was deeply disappointed and needed someone to talk to. Hoping that his brother would understand how he felt, Seth gave him a call. It wasn't easy for Seth to talk about his feelings, so he started out making small talk. After a few minutes Seth warmed to the conversation and, taking a deep breath, told his brother that Jamie had dropped out of school and that he was very upset about it. There was a pause, and then his brother went on to talk about something else. Seth was stunned—not just hurt, but amazed that his brother could act so unfeelingly. With great effort, he confronted his brother, saying "Didn't you hear what I said?" His brother replied that he had never thought of Seth as someone who needed emotional support. Both brothers were on the brink of addressing the past and present they shared; if they could only open up and listen to one another, they had an opportunity to clarify and strengthen their relationship. But it didn't happen.

The expectations with which we approach each other are, as we shall see, just one of many ways we create the listening we get. Nor can the process be reduced to the behavior of the participants—the words—and therefore always be improved by "skills training" or pretending to take an interest or other calculated strategies. (Conversation can, of course, be reduced to a behavioral analysis, but only by trivializing the thoughts and feelings, yearnings and defensiveness of the people involved.) Dialogue takes place between two people with not just ears and tongues but hearts and minds—and all the famous complications therein.

———◆———

An understanding attitude doesn't presume to know a person's thoughts and feelings. Instead, it is an openness to listen and discover.

———◆———

Emotional Reactivity

As I mentioned in the Introduction, we all have certain ways of reacting emotionally within particular relationships. The closer the relationship, the more vulnerable we are to hearing something said as hurtful, frightening, threatening, or infuriating even when it wasn't meant that way. Because of the dynamics of the relationship, our expectations of the other person, or what we've become accustomed to in previous relationships, we get defensive, which makes it impossible to listen to and understand what the speaker meant to say.

A simple "Have you taken the garbage out yet?" might be taken as a rebuke by one whose parents never expected him to do anything right. His response might be an overreactive "Can't you leave me alone for one second?!"

It's not always the listener's defensiveness, of course, that gives rise to heated emotional reactions. Sometimes it's the speaker's provocation.

"Why do I always have to ask you three times before you do anything?" when it really means "Have you taken the garbage out yet?" will almost inevitably trigger a defensive reaction. For that matter, even "Haven't you taken the garbage out *yet?*" could provoke an emotional response. If you don't watch how you say things as well as what you say, it's easy to provoke those you love.

Then there are those touchy subjects that can almost be counted on to set off an explosion. As I explain later, in Chapters 6 and 9, topics likely to be toxic among couples are things like money, the children, and sex. To have a really fruitful discussion about any of these, where both people really listen, requires special effort. You might have to watch not only what you say and how you say it but also where, when, and why.

This is not to imply that we need to spend our lives tiptoeing around each other. What it does mean is that all of us need to step back and calm down, being aware of what sets us off and what sets off those we want to communicate with, if we are to get through to each other.

When we don't, many exchanges degenerate to such clever repartee as "You're such a bitch!" and "Oh, grow up!" before falling apart altogether as one or both people storm out of the room.

UNDERSTANDING THE RULES OF THE LISTENING GAME: BEYOND LINEAR THINKING

We don't usually stop to examine patterns of misunderstanding in our lives because we're stuck in our own point of view. Misunderstanding hurts, and when we're hurt we tend to look outside ourselves for explanations. But the problem isn't just that when something goes wrong we look for someone to blame. The problem is linear thinking. We reduce human interactions to a matter of personalities. "He doesn't listen because he's too preoccupied with himself." "She's hard to listen to because she goes on and on about everything." Some people blame themselves ("Maybe I'm not that interesting"), but it's almost always easier to appreciate the other person's contribution.

Attributing other people's lack of understanding to character is armor for our ignorance and passivity. That some people repeat their annoying ways with most others they come in contact with doesn't prove that lack of responsiveness is fixed in character; it only proves that these individuals trigger many people to play out the reciprocal role in their dramas of two-part disharmony.

The fixed-character position assumes that it's extremely difficult for people to change. But you don't change relationships by changing other people. You change patterns of relating by changing yourself in relation to them. Personality is dynamic, not fixed. The dynamic personality position posits that it *is* possible for people to change; all we have to do is change our response to each other. We are not victims—we are participants, in a real way, and the consequences of our participation are profound.

To participate effectively, we must know something about the rules of the game.

I remember how confused I was the first time I saw a lacrosse game. From where I sat it looked as if some kids were just standing around while the rest raced up and down the field, using their sticks to pass the ball back and forth, club each other, or both. I got the gist of it—it was like soccer played by Road Warriors—but a lot of it was hard to follow. Why, for instance, did the team that lost the ball out of bounds sometimes get it back and sometimes not? And why, sometimes when one kid whacked another with his stick, did everybody cheer, while at other times the referee called a foul? The problem was, of course, that I couldn't see the whole field and didn't know the rules of the game.

The same disadvantages—not seeing the whole field and not knowing the rules of the game—keep us from understanding our successes and failures at communicating with one another.

Earlier I said that listening is a two-person process, but even that is oversimplified. Actually, even an uncomplicated communication has several components: the listener, the speaker, the message, various implicit messages, the context, and, because the process doesn't flow one-way from speaker to listener, the listener's response. Even a brief consideration of these elements in the listening process reveals more reasons for misunderstanding than simply bad faith on the part of the listener.

"What Are You Trying to Say?"

The message is the content of what a speaker says. But the message sent isn't always the one intended.

A family of four is invited to spend Sunday afternoon at the lake house of friends of the father. When the teenage daughter asks if she can bring along one of her friends, her father says, "I don't think we should bring extra guests when we're invited to dinner." The daughter looks hurt, and the man's wife says, "You're being silly; they never mind extra company." The man gets angry and withdraws, brooding over his feeling that his wife always takes the children's side and never listens to him.

The problem here is a common one: the message sent wasn't the one intended. One of the unfortunate things we learn along with being "polite" and not being "selfish" is not to say directly what we want. Instead of saying "I want . . . " we say "We should . . . " or "Do you want . . . ?" When we're taking a trip in the car and we get hungry, we say "Isn't it getting late?" (When I was growing up I learned that guests weren't supposed to put people to any trouble. If you went to someone's house and wanted a glass of water, you didn't ask; you looked thirsty. If they did offer you something, you politely declined. Only if they insisted was it OK to accept. A really good boy waited until a glass of water was offered at least twice before accepting.)

Because this convention of indirectness is so universal, it doesn't usually cause problems. If the other person in the room says "Are you cold?" you usually know he means "I'm cold. Can we turn up the heat?" But indirection can cause problems when stronger feelings are involved. The father in our example didn't want his daughter to bring a friend.

Perhaps his wife was right; the people who invited them wouldn't mind. But somehow *he* minded. Maybe he wanted his daughter to remain more a part of the family and less an independent person with friends of her own. Or maybe he wanted her to be part of the grown-ups' conversation, instead of off with her friend, because he found it easier to talk about the children's doings than his own. That's the trouble with indirection: there are always a lot of *maybes*.

When we're conflicted over certain of our own needs, we may infer (rightly or wrongly) that others would object even to hearing our wishes, much less acceding to them. Because indirection leads to so much misunderstanding and so many arguments that are beside the point, it does more harm than good. Two people can't have an honest disagreement about whether or not they want to move to another city as long as they engage in diversionary arguments about whether going or staying would be better for the children.[2]

One reason others argue with us in a way that seems to negate our feelings is that we blur the distinction between our feelings and the facts. Instead of saying "I don't want her to bring a friend," the father tries to cloud his motives and bolster his argument by appealing to *shoulds*. When his wife argues with what he says instead of what he means, he feels rejected. Like every listener, he measured the intentions of other speakers by what they said—or what he heard—and asked that they measure him by what he intended to say.

As speakers we want to be heard—but not merely to be heard; we want to be understood, heard for what we think we're saying, for what we know we meant. Similar impasses occur when we insist we said one thing and our listener heard another. Instead of saying "What I meant to say was . . . ," we go on insisting what we *did* say.

"Why Don't You Say What You Mean?"

Implicit messages tell us more than what's being said; they tell us how we're meant to receive what's being said. Depending on the situation, inflection, and motives of the speaker, "Let's have lunch" could mean "I'm hungry," "I'd like to see you again," or "Please leave now; I'm busy." The statements "I love you" and "I'm sorry" are of course notorious for

---

[2]There are times, however, when the most effective statement of what you want is less then completely candid. For people who have trouble saying no, rather than trying to explain why they don't want to do something, it may be easier to say "I'd love to, but I can't."

having multiple meanings. Knowing the other person makes it easier to decode implicit messages; suspecting his or her motives can make it harder.

According to Gregory Bateson, one of the founders of family therapy, all communications have two levels of meaning: *report* and *command*.[3] The report (or message) is the information conveyed by the words. The second or command level (which Bateson also called *metacommunication*) conveys information on how the report is to be taken and a statement of the nature of the relationship.

If a wife scolds her husband for running the dishwasher when it's only half full and he says OK but turns around and does exactly the same thing two days later, she may be annoyed that he doesn't listen to her. She means the message. But maybe he didn't like the metamessage. Maybe he doesn't like her telling him what to do as though she were his mother.

In attempting to define the nature of our relationships we qualify our messages by posture, facial expression, and tone of voice. For example, a rising inflection on the last two words turns "You did that on purpose" from an accusation to a question. The whole impact of a statement may change depending on which words are emphasized. Consider the difference between "Are *you* telling me it isn't true?" and "Are you telling me it *isn't* true?" Pauses, gestures, and gaze also tell us how to interpret what is being said. Although we may not need the ponderous· term *metacommunication*, misunderstandings about what is implied and how messages are to be taken are major reasons for problems in listening.

One winter when I was working hard and feeling sorry for myself, I wrote to a sympathetic friend, and in the letter I said jokingly that I was running away to spend two weeks on the white beaches of a deserted Caribbean island. The only trouble was that I didn't *say* it, I *wrote* it, and she missed the irony I intended. The medium didn't carry my tone of voice or the facial expression that modified the message. Instead of getting the sympathy I was (indirectly) asking for, I got back a rather testy note to the effect that it's nice to know that some people have the time and money to indulge themselves.

We know what we mean; problems arise when we expect others

---

[3]Jurgen Ruesch and Gregory Bateson, *Communication: The Social Matrix of Psychiatry* (New York: Norton, 1951).

to. How is our communication to be taken? Is it chat? A confession? An outpouring of emotion? When our listeners fail to grasp that we're upset and need to have our feelings listened to, who's to blame?

A woman told her husband that something her boss said made her afraid that she might be in for trouble at work. The husband responded by saying no, he didn't think so; it didn't sound that way. When she replied that he didn't listen to her, both of them got upset. She was annoyed because he didn't listen to her feelings. He was hurt because he *was* listening. He had responded sincerely. He just didn't realize how upset she was.

Perhaps to some people this woman's upset would have been apparent. Maybe a friend would have realized that she needed to have her feelings acknowledged, not disagreed with. But she wasn't married to that friend. She was married to a man who didn't automatically understand how she wanted to be listened to. (Some people try to make that clear: "I'm worried about something, and I need to talk about it." "I need your advice." "I just need you to listen.")

Occasionally—but not as often as most people think—the implicit message in a communication is a request for the speaker to do something. The teenage boy who says "I'm hungry" isn't just making small talk. (A teenage boy's appetite is not an idle thing.) Usually, however, *the* most important implicit message in what people say is the feeling behind the content.

When we're little, before we learn to act grown-up by masking our feelings, our communications are full of ill-disguised emotion. You don't have to be a neurolingustics expert to figure out what children are feeling when they say "There's monsters under my bed" or "Nobody wants to play with me." The same emotions may be implicit, if less obviously implied, when an adult says "I've got that big meeting coming up tomorrow" or "I called to see if Fred and Teddy wanted to go to the movies, but they weren't home." One of the most effective ways to improve understanding is to listen for both content and implicit feelings in what people say.

Much of communication is implicit and—when people are on the same wavelength—decoded automatically. Often, however, what is implicit—what we take for granted—is not obvious to everyone. Much misunderstanding could be cleared up if we learned to do two things: appreciate the other person's perspective and, at times, clarify what usually remains implicit.

"Is This a Good Time?"

The context of communication is the setting: the time, the place, who else is present, and, because communication cannot be reduced to the obvious, people's expectations. We ordinarily accommodate our talking and listening to the context of an exchange without even thinking about it. We don't spring bad news on people the minute they walk in the door, we don't talk loudly in public, and we don't argue in front of the kids. (As you can't see by the twinkle in my eye, I'm being ironic.)

No matter how much certain people care about us, there are times when they don't have the energy and patience to listen. If a husband calls his wife at work and starts to talk at length about something that doesn't seem terribly important, she may get impatient sooner than she would if the same conversation occurred at home. By contrast, even though her husband usually retreats behind the paper at the end of the day, a wife may succeed in getting his full attention by signaling her need for it. "Honey, I need to talk to you about something important."

Unfortunately, in many relationships spouses have different preferred times to talk. He likes to talk when he comes home at the end of the day. She's busy then and prefers to talk later, when they're watching TV or getting ready for bed. Fishing for understanding at the wrong time is like trying to catch a trout in the noonday sun.

———◆———

When to talk: not when your partner needs some space or time to be alone.

———◆———

The idea that timing affects the listening we get may be painfully obvious; unfortunately, when needs collide, the resulting failures of understanding are obviously painful. The end of the day can be especially difficult. Partners may be frazzled and frustrated. Worn out from running around all day, trying to make other people happy, attending mind-deadening meetings, fighting traffic, or chasing after children and answering endless questions, they have little energy left over for hearing each other.

The unhappy irony is that the domestic conversation people are too tired to engage in might provide emotional refueling: talking and listening reinvigorate us. If we take listening for granted, we may assume that the people we care about will listen to us whenever we feel

like talking. But if we realize that good listening doesn't happen automatically, we'll learn to give a little more thought to finding the right time to approach people.

Setting has an obvious physical effect on listening—in terms of privacy and noise level, for example—and an equally powerful effect in terms of conditioned cues. Familiar settings, like a therapist's office or a friend's kitchen, can be reassuring places in which to open up. Other familiar settings, like your own kitchen or bedroom, can be anything but conducive to conversation. Memories of misunderstanding and distraction cling to some rooms like the smell of wet dog.

Conversation in many settings is governed by unwritten rules, some of which are obvious (to most people). At cocktail parties, for example, where conversational subgroups constantly shift in size and membership, conversations may be warm, candid, even intimate, but they are also generally brief (which may explain the warmth and candor). Anyone who tries to talk too long in a such a setting may strain a listener's sense of decorum.

Rules of decorum are based on a shared sense of what's appropriate and probably originally derive from practical considerations, like noninterference with others and respect for special places. Thus, talking loudly in a cathedral, on a train, or at the movies is frowned on.[4] Because rules of decorum are implicit and widely shared, we tend to take them for granted, not realizing that we have done so until we or someone else breaks them.

In addition to general rules of propriety, most of us have personal preferences for settings in which we're comfortable talking. Some people like to talk on the telephone, for example. (Why, I have no idea.) Some people like to talk when they go for a ride in the car; others prefer to read or look out the window. And, of course, we may be in the mood for conversation in a particular setting at one time and not another. Often the best way to get someone's attention is to invite her away from familiar surroundings—by taking a walk, say, or going out to a restaurant. Many of these preferences are sufficiently obvious that we adjust to them automatically. We know not to call certain people at home in the evening, and we learn the most promising times and places to get the listening we need. When we don't, feelings get hurt. We

---

[4]People who get annoyed at those who talk in the movies forget that the advent of videotape rentals has blurred the distinction between movie theater and living room. They also fail to consider situational priorities that might make theater conversation understandable. Yes, even people who talk to the movies deserve consideration, and so they should be shot as painlessly as possible.

blame others for not hearing us, and, alternately, we feel put upon by their lack of consideration in imposing on us at the wrong time.

Whenever conversation takes place in the presence of others, some aspects of listening are expressively accentuated while others are suppressed. If a couple goes out to dinner and the man talks about problems at work, the woman will probably listen more intently than she does at home because the setting suggests intimacy. If they bring along the children, however, she's liable to be less attentive to him and also less likely to talk about her own concerns. Sometimes that's *why* people bring the children. Togetherness is a hedge against intimacy as well as loneliness.

Most of us have had the disconcerting experience of talking to someone who seems to be interested until someone else appears. In some situations this is unavoidable. If two people are having lunch and a third person joins them, it's not reasonable to expect to continue a private conversation. But in other instances the person talking about something important might expect the listener not to accept and encourage an interruption, to say, for example, to a telephone caller, "Sorry, I can't talk now; I'm busy." Or if two people are having a confidential conversation in a public place, one might expect the other to greet a casual acquaintance who happens by, but not to break off the conversation or signal the third person that he or she is welcome to join in. Third parties are to intimate conversation what rain is to picnics.

Sometimes the effect of third parties works the other way. An adult may show more animated and sustained interest in a child's conversation when other adults are watching. Similarly a man who often interrupts his wife at home may show more respect and forbearance when they're out with another couple.

I remember once when I was being interviewed on a morning television show how the host, a dynamic and attractive woman in her early forties, was fascinated and intrigued by the book I'd written. She sat very close, kept her eyes on mine, and asked all the right questions. Here was this radiant woman, totally engrossed in what I had to say. It was very flattering. Then a commercial break came up, and the light in her face went out like the red light on the camera. I ceased to exist. After the break the interview resumed, and so did my interviewer's intense show of interest. Her pretense, in the face of a whole audience of third parties (and my susceptibility), was disconcerting, but after all, it was her job to show interest.

There's a big difference between showing interest and really taking interest.

WHY SOME PEOPLE ARE SO HARD TO LISTEN TO

Even when you play by the rules, some people are hard to listen to. In some cases that's because their accounts run on to Homeric length. They're generous with details. You ask about their vacation and they tell you about packing the car, getting lost on the way, and all the various wrong turns. They tell you about the weather and who said what and where they ate lunch and what they had for dinner, and they keep telling you until something other than tact stops them. Others may not talk at all about what they did but instead go on at great windy length about what everyone else did, all those objectionable others who are such problems in their lives.

It's also hard to listen to people who talk incessantly about their preoccupations—a mother with a difficult child who talks of little else, a careerist who wants to talk only about his work, a man with allergies who's always complaining about his sinus trouble. One person's headache can become another's if she has to hear about it all the time. It isn't just the repetition that we tire of; it's being cast in the helpless role of one who is importuned about a problem with no solution, or at least no solution the complainer wants to consider. (If the complainer doesn't expect a solution, a simple acknowledgment of his feelings—"Gee, that's too bad"—may give a satisfactory punctuation to the exchange.)

Some people who talk too much are like that with everybody, but often, whether we appreciate it or not, some of them talk at such length with us because they talk so little with anyone else. Who other than his wife does the husband with no friends talk to? Who other than the friend who seems to have her life together and talks so little about herself does the overburdened wife talk to? Some people need our attention, but if the conversation is consistently one-sided, maybe part of the reason is that we respond too passively.

Sometimes speakers are hard to listen to because they're unaware of what they've said—or of its infuriating implications. When the listener reacts to what *wasn't* said, the speaker responds with righteous indigna-

tion, wounded by the listener's "overreaction." If a mother says to her teenage daughter "Is *that* what you're wearing to school?" and the daughter bursts into tears and says "You're always criticizing me!" the mother might protest that the daughter is reacting unreasonably. "All I said was 'Is that what you're wearing to school?' How come you get so upset about a simple question?" Such questions are as simple as parents are free of judgmentalness and children are free of sensitivity to it.

My father has a way of packing what feels like a whole lot of disconfirmation into one little innocent statement that drives me crazy. If I tell him that something is so, even when it's not something particularly unusual or controversial, he'll often say "It could be." Arghh!! I think he does this because he can't tolerate overt conflict. So if somebody tells him something that he didn't know or isn't completely convinced is the case, he says "It could be." To me, this feels much worse than an argument. An argument, you can argue with. "It could be" makes you feel discounted. One consequence of these interchanges is that I become stubborn in my opinions. Having had my fill of being doubted, I can't stand not to be believed when I'm stating a fact. Like the fact that Lake Champlain is one of the five Great Lakes.

In case you think I've slid from talking about speakers to complaining about listeners, you're right. While it's possible to separate speakers and listeners conceptually, in practice they are inextricably intertwined. Listening is codetermined.

Some people are hard to listen to because they say so little, or at least little of a personal nature. If the urge to voice true feelings to sympathetic ears is such a driving desire, why are so many people numb and silent? Because life happens to them—slights, hurts, cruelty, mockery, and shame. These things are hard on the heart.

We come to relationships wounded. Longing for attention, we don't always get it. Expecting to be taken seriously, we get argued with or ignored or treated as cute but inconsequential. Needing to share our feelings, we run into disapproval or mockery. Opening up and getting no response or, worse, humiliation, is like walking into a wall in the dark. If this happens often enough, we shut down and erect our own walls.

Although a speaker's reticence may be seen as a fixed trait of personality, such traits are really nothing more than habits based on expectations formed from past relationships. People who don't talk to us are people who don't expect us to listen.

Therapists who encounter resistance to speaking freely engage in what is called *defense analysis*—pointing out to the patient *that* he is holding back, *how* he is holding back (perhaps by talking about trivia), and speculating about *what* might be on his mind and *why* he might hesitate to bring it up. Therapists have license that the average person lacks to ask such probing questions, but it's not against the law to inquire if a friend is finding it difficult to open up for some reason or to point out gently that she doesn't seem to talk much about herself. We shape our relationships by our response.

Does the person who isn't very forthcoming with you have reason to believe that you're interested in what he thinks and feels? That you'll listen without interrupting? That you can tolerate disagreement? Anger? Openness is a product of interaction.

MEN ARE FROM MARS?

As we head further into the nineties, the social construction of gender—men do this, women do that—polarizes relations between men and women as never before. As the old complementarity gives way to a new symmetry, conflict seems to be the price for equality.

Several books in recent years have gained enormous popularity by telling us that men and women communicate differently and then explaining what those differences are. Among the most popular was John Gray's *Men Are From Mars, Women Are From Venus*, in which the author argues that men need space while women crave company. If we learn to respect the inevitable differences that crop up between two people who live together by attributing such differences to gender rather than to stubbornness or ill will, maybe that's a good thing. And if we learn not to react unsympathetically to what our partners say, that's certainly a good thing. But perhaps the most important thing is not so much to learn *how* to react to these other, alien creatures, but to learn not to *overreact* and learn instead to listen. Perhaps the best response to Freud's famous question "What do women want?" might have been "Why don't you ask—and then listen?"

Once, differences between men and women were thought to be bred in the bone, and this biological determinism was used to justify all manner of inequity. After years of effort to break down these separate but unequal categories, a new wave of feminist scholars has reasserted what they once fought: gender differences. Jean Baker Miller has emphasized

responsiveness and mutuality as especially important to women in relationships,[5] and Carol Gilligan has argued that for women the qualities of care and connection are fundamental to selfhood, organizers of identity, and moral development.[6] According to Gilligan, men build towers and women build webs.

Thus far the greatest impact of the new work by feminist psychologists has been a reaffirmation of gender differences—but this time with a positive construction of the psychology of women. In her 1978 book, *The Reproduction of Mothering*, Nancy Chodorow pointed out that because boys and girls are parented primarily by mothers, they grow up with different orientations to attachment and independence.[7] Boys must separate themselves from their mothers to claim their masculinity, which is why boys of a certain age start shrinking from their mothers' hugs and why "sissy" and "mamma's boy" are still such powerful invectives. Girls, on the other hand, do not have to renounce their mothers' caring and connection to become women; they learn to become themselves *through* connection.

In the wake of Nancy Chodorow and Carol Gilligan, the idea of inherent gender differences has come to define the discourse on men and women to such an extent that many writers now take for granted that women are *fundamentally* different from men in ways that make them better at listening. For people who accept this premise, life is simple: all the complexities of relationship can be dispensed with in favor of one all-purpose explanation. Men do this; women do that. End of discussion.

This new wave of sexual typecasting is reflected in the popular reception of books that reduce every nuance, every polarity of conversation between men and women to one gender distinction: men seek power; women seek relationship. Sadly, a lot of people now take this for granted.

Perhaps the best way to begin making a difference in the quality of listening between men and women is to *unmake* a difference. My point isn't that there aren't conversational differences between men and women but that perhaps it's time to stop exaggerating, stereotyping, and glorifying them.

Why are so many women and men so willing to assume that we're

---

[5]Jean Baker Miller, *Toward a New Psychology of Women* (Boston: Beacon Press, 1976).

[6]Carol Gilligan, *In a Different Voice* (Cambridge, MA: Harvard University Press, 1982).

[7]Nancy Chodorow, *The Reproduction of Mothering: Psychoanalysis and the Sociology of Gender* (Berkeley: University of California Press, 1978).

separated by a vast gender gap, that we speak different languages, and that our destinies take us in different directions? Is it really a woman's nature to be caring and seek connection? Is it really a man's nature to be independent and seek power? Or do these polarities reflect the ways our culture has—thus far—shaped the universal yearning to be appreciated?

Sometimes social and political factors provide the underlying explanation for so-called gender distinctions. Might caring, for example, which has been represented as a gender difference, be more adequately understood as a way of negotiating from a position of low power? Perhaps some women (and some men) are caring because of a need to please, which stems from a lack of a sense of personal power. Thus the same woman who appeals to the need for caring in debates with her husband may emphasize rules in arguments with her children. The same social embeddedness that promotes caring may sometimes make it difficult for women to recognize their own self-interest. Perhaps rather than our apologizing for or celebrating gender differences, it might be more useful for us to talk *with* each other, instead of about each other, and to move toward partnership, not polarization.

Perhaps if we started listening to one another we could move toward greater balance, in ourselves and our relationships. Perhaps women raised to believe that happiness is to be found in selfless service to others could learn more respect for their own strivings and capacity for independent achievement. Perhaps men who seek identity only in achievement could learn greater respect for the neglected dimensions of caring and concern. In the process of relaxing rigid definitions of what it means to be a man or a woman, perhaps fathers might learn to loosen the tight boundaries they draw around themselves and reduce the gulf across which they relate to others and guard their "masculinity." Perhaps mothers, in learning more respect for their own self-interest, would learn more respect for the boundary separating themselves and their children and allow the children greater room and freedom to become themselves.

If we can avoid thinking of gender difference as fixed and given, perhaps we might begin to entertain the possibility that boys can and should identify with their mothers' nurturance and care to become more fully realized men and better fathers. Similarly, we might begin to see that girls can identify with their fathers as well as their mothers to feel entitled to be independent persons with their own wishes. Maybe God invented the idea of two parents so that children could draw on the best of both of them.

Comforting as it may be to blame lack of understanding on other people's stubbornness or insensitivity or gender, the reasons we don't listen to each other turn out to be more complex. It isn't selfishness, but complications of character and relationship that keep us from listening and being listened to.

A fuller appreciation of the dynamics of listening makes it a little easier for us to begin hearing each other. Is it necessary to dissect every misunderstanding and analyze it according to message, subtext, context, speaker, listener, and response? Of course not. The simple, heroic act of stepping back from our own injured feelings and considering the other person's point of view is quite enough of an accomplishment.

So why are we so sensitive to misunderstanding that we have trouble seeing the other person's side of things? To answer that question and continue to move toward hearing each other, let's look more closely at the emotional factors that complicate listening.

THE REAL REASONS
PEOPLE DON'T LISTEN

CHAPTER FOUR

"When Is It My Turn?"

THE HEART OF LISTENING: THE STRUGGLE TO SUSPEND OUR OWN NEEDS

Twenty-five years ago I took my first course in how to be a good listener. I was in graduate school, and the course was called Elementary Clinical Methods. We learned about making eye contact and asking open-ended questions and how to avoid talking about ourselves (by parrying personal questions with the therapist's famous evasion, "Why do you ask?"). We practiced on each other during role-play sessions, and I learned a lot of interesting things about my classmates. Then we went to the state hospital to practice on patients, and I learned that maybe I wasn't cut out for this work.

It was the first time I'd ever been in a mental hospital, and I was filled with fascination and horror. Maybe I expected to see an axe murderer or perhaps a scene out of *The Snake Pit*. Actually, in those days before the widespread use of tranquilizers, some of the back wards *were* like snake pits. But in the ward for new admissions, where they sent us, the patients were mostly just very unhappy people.

My first real patient was a young mother who'd become depressed after coming home from the hospital with her second baby. She looked

disheveled and lonely and empty, and I felt terribly sorry for her. I asked her why she'd come to the hospital and why she felt so hopeless and where she grew up and other things like that. She answered my questions, but the interview never really went anywhere. Every time I'd ask another question, she'd respond, but only briefly, and then wait for me to say something. Since I didn't have anything to say, it was an awkward wait.

It was my first interview, and I was sorely disappointed that it didn't go well. Eventually I learned not to ask so many questions and, if someone didn't seem to have much to say, to comment on that reticence, inviting the person to explain it rather than trying to fight it with questions. But the real problem in that first interview didn't have to do with technique. I wasn't truly interested in that woman; I was more interested in being a therapist.

This troubling experience illustrates the most vital and difficult requirement for listening. When it's genuine, listening demands taking an interest in the speaker and what he or she has to say.

Taking an interest can easily be sentimentalized by equating it with sincerity or caring. Sincerity and caring are certainly fine characteristics, but listening isn't a matter of character, nor is it something that good people do automatically. To take an interest in someone else, we must suspend the interests of the self.

Listening is the art by which we use empathy to reach across the space between us. Passive attention doesn't work.

Not only is listening an active process; it often takes a deliberate effort to suspend our own needs and reactions—as Roxanne's mother so bravely demonstrated by holding her own feelings in check long enough to listen to her daughter's fierce resentment. To listen well, you must hold back what you have to say and control the urge to interrupt or argue.

The act of listening requires a submersion of the self and immersion in the other. This isn't always easy. We may be interested but too concerned with controlling or instructing or reforming the other person to be truly open to his point of view. Parents have trouble hearing their children as long as they can't suspend their urgent need to set them straight. And, as I'm afraid I've demonstrated, even therapists,

presumably exemplars of understanding, are often too busy trying to change people to really listen to them. (Unfortunately, most people aren't eager to be changed by someone who doesn't take the time to understand them.) That failures of understanding occur in psychotherapy, just as everywhere else, is a fact often missed as long as therapists remain too wrapped up in their own theories and intentions to give themselves over to sustained immersion in the other person.

Although therapists may be less likely than the average person to interrupt to disagree, some are so anxious to be perceived as sympathetic that they offer sentimentality instead of compassion. "Oh yes," they say with their eyes, "*I understand how you feel.*" Sympathetic or not, condescending kindness from a patronizing person isn't the same thing as listening. The superficially sensitive therapist doesn't have to listen because he already knows what he wants to say: "*Oh yes, I understand.*" Listening is a strenuous but silent activity.

Suspending the self does not of course mean *losing* the self—though that seems to be precisely what some people are afraid of. Otherwise, why do they insist on relentlessly repeating their own arguments, when a simple acknowledgment of what the other person is trying to say would be the first step toward mutual understanding? It's as though saying "I understand what you're trying to say" meant "You're right and I'm wrong." Or that to give someone who's angry at you a fair hearing and then say "I see why you're upset with me" meant "I surrender." Ironically, when the fear of never getting your turn is so strong that you don't hear the other person out, it becomes a self-fulfilling prophecy.

I'll have some practical suggestions for breaking this pattern in Chapter 7, but first it's important to understand more about the difficulty involved in the simple art of listening.

Genuine listening involves a brief suspension of self. You won't always notice this because it's reflexive and taken for granted and because in most conversations we take turns. But you might catch yourself rehearsing what you're going to say next when the other person is talking. Simply holding your tongue while the other person speaks isn't the same thing as listening. To really listen you have to suspend your own agenda, forget about what you might say next, and concentrate on being a receptive vehicle for the other person.

The listener's responsiveness is experienced subjectively by the speaker as—at least temporarily—vital to a sense of being understood, of being taken seriously. Listeners feel that pressure.

THE BURDEN OF LISTENING

Listening puts a burden on the listener. Not only do we have to suspend the needs of the self; we also feel the weight of the other person's need to be heard. Attention must be paid.

But, some people might object, isn't empathy an active expression of the self? Isn't listening something we extend to each other as a natural part of being human? Yes and no. Empathy is an active form of engagement—but it is engagement with the other. At times we're interested in and curious about what the other person is saying, and listening is effortless. But there almost inevitably comes a moment when we cease to be engrossed. We lose interest or feel the urge to interrupt. It is at this moment that listening takes self-control.

---◆---

Genuine listening means suspending memory, desire, and judgment—and, for a few moments at least, existing for the other person.

---◆---

Suppressing your own urge to talk can be harder than it sounds. After all, you have things on your mind too. To listen well, you may have to restrain yourself from disagreeing or giving advice or talking about your own experience. Temporarily, at least, listening is a one-sided relationship.

In everyday give-and-take conversations, you may not notice that burden. But you can feel the pressure to be attentive whenever another person needs to talk for more than a few moments. Even if you care about the person and are interested in what she has to say, still you're caught.

You need to be silent. You need to be selfless.

Doreen asked her father out to lunch so the two of them could have a chance to talk a little more personally than they did when her mother was around. But when they sat down at the restaurant, he started in on his usual diatribe against the bureaucracy. His bosses were "morons," and none of his co-workers cared about anything but "putting in their time until retirement."

Doreen had heard it all before a million times. She nodded and looked interested and thought about her upcoming sales conference. Once or twice she started to interrupt, but something about the way her father spoke with more feeling than usual made her heart move.

She stopped thinking about the sales conference and started listening to what he was saying. As she did, she began to hear the hurt and disappointment underneath his carping. Suddenly she was filled with intense sadness at her father's life and his isolation. The sadness had less to do with his frustrations at work than that his constant complaining about it had made other people in the family stop listening to him. Doreen's annoyance gave way to a powerful sense of sympathy and connection with her father. For the first time, she understood how lonely he felt. Later, when she said so, her father's eyes filled with tears and he thanked her for caring.

Sometimes we're so touched by what people say that listening just happens. Other times we don't realize the effort required to be a good listener because the circumstances make it seem effortless. The other person's need for our listening is obvious, and so we make ourselves available. When your child bursts into the house after school and says "Guess what happened!" you don't have work at listening.

My son was home sick yesterday, and when I called at lunchtime to ask him how he was feeling, I didn't have to make any effort to suspend my interests to tune in to his. Nor would anyone else have had to in my place. I was interested in his feelings, I intended to listen to him, and I did. We all do this dozens of times each day, at least for a few minutes.

Often, however, it's not that easy. Much of the time listening takes work.

When I came home after work, my son was lying on the couch watching MTV. Again I asked him how he was feeling, but this time it wasn't quite as easy for me to listen. As usual, he wasn't wearing a shirt or socks, and I had to suppress the urge to nag him about that. He was watching two brainless but arrogant cartoon teenagers rating videos in which everything was either "cool" or "it sucks," and I had to make an effort to ignore that. I had things on my mind that I wanted to talk about, and I wanted to go out on the back porch and read the mail before it was time for dinner. None of these considerations was terribly pressing or unusual. It took only a little effort to suppress them long enough to listen to my son for a little while. Had he needed to talk for more than a few minutes, however, I would have had to make a more active effort to suspend these other agendas—or I would not have been able to listen.

Of course suspending our needs so as to listen means more than

just allowing the other person time to talk. It doesn't mean just being willing to let a certain amount of time elapse while that person has his say, only to leap in with your own agenda when he's finished.

We're not fooled by the feigned attentiveness of the restless narcissist, who may allow us a few minutes of airtime but is waiting only to take over the stage. On the other hand, when we open up to someone we do expect to be interested and that person listens but then instead of responding changes the subject to himself, we feel betrayed. It's like a slap in the face; we feel as though he didn't hear a word we said.

David's friend Elena was telling him that she was worried about going back to school to get her master's degree after being out of school for six years. She'd been wanting to do this for a long time, and David, who had his master's degree, had encouraged her warmly. When she told him that she'd been accepted but was concerned about doing the work, David was so enthusiastic about her finally having taken the big step that he jumped in to say how great it was that she was doing this for herself and that she'd gotten into such a good program. Elena got quiet and changed the subject. David later learned that his encouragement hadn't been very encouraging. Elena was trying to tell him that she was worried, and his telling her how great it all was made her feel unresponded to. Ironically, David's expression of confidence in Elena felt like pressure, one more thing to live up to.

Like David, most people think they're better listeners than they really are. At best they allow the other person to state his case, and then they make their own private interpretation of what the other person said. At worst they're preparing their own argument while the other person is still talking.

Unfortunately, most people are more likely to react with their own interpretations of another's point of view than to listen carefully enough to make certain that they understand. David thought he was listening but wasn't able to suspend his need to have Elena not worry or for himself to be seen as supportive long enough to hear her out. A lot of us have difficulty listening when it means having to sit still and share someone's uneasiness or uncertainty. We have to say something quick to make the anxiety go away.

To listen well, we have to read the needs of the speaker and respond to the context. For example, when parents ask, "What did you do in school today?" children often answer, "Nothing." What follows is fre-

quently a battle of questions and monosyllabic answers. The parent wants to hear what happened in school but doesn't listen to what the child is saying. The child is saying something like "Nothing interesting enough for me to want to talk about right now. I just want to be left alone." A child at school is exposed and vulnerable all day. Other kids look at you and pass judgment on what you're wearing, whom you're with, what you say, how your hair is fixed, and just about anything you might do that's visible. Teachers watch to see if you did your homework and if you're paying attention and to be certain you're not making noise in the halls or generally having any fun. After being the subject of such scrutiny all day, most children want nothing more than to be left alone. Their "nothing" isn't coy or withholding; it's self-protective.

The parents' side of this conversation isn't hard to understand either. They're curious about what goes on in their children's lives. They want to know if everything is OK. They want to know if their children are doing what they should be doing. They don't want to be shut out. Besides, sometimes kids say "nothing" but really *do* have something to say. Maybe you have to show them that you're really interested to convince them to open up. Asking them about their day and really being prepared to listen shows interest. Honoring their right to respond the way they want shows respect as well as interest— interest in them and respect for their feelings. Children who sense that their parents are interested in hearing what they have to say—as opposed to anxiously interrogating or prying or living vicariously—will open up when they're ready.

If it's difficult to suspend the self with our children, imagine how much more difficult it is with another adult, whom we don't expect to have to "indulge" in any way—especially when we have our own problems.

Sometimes we fall into the habit of listening without effort because we put so much effort into other things. When we work until we're spent, we become preoccupied with our own sense of being unappreciated and careless of concern for others. It's especially hard to listen when we feel that *we* haven't gotten the attention we need. Here's an example:

A woman who's having a bad day at the office wishes she could be at home with her five-year-old. She's vexed about work and envious of her college professor husband who, because it's summer, is at home all day with the boy. When she gets home, instead of complaining about her day, she asks her husband how his day went. He complains about the burden of having to amuse a five-year-old and the difficulty of figuring

out what to do with all that unstructured time. She listens impatiently for a minute or two and then says, "Why are you complaining? You're lucky to have all this time off. Think of all the things you could do!" Her husband is hurt—first she asks him how his day went, then she criticizes him for telling her—and the woman herself is resentful. The woman in this example wasn't able to listen to her husband because she wasn't able to suspend her own feelings long enough to be receptive to his. After talking about this episode, the woman concluded that she needed to try harder to overcome or contain the stress of her work. (Perhaps it would be more reasonable for her to realize that when she comes home after a bad day she may need to talk about it before she's ready to listen.)

"But I Am Listening"

The selflessness of genuine listening is hard to sustain, and so in a number of ways we fool ourselves into thinking we're listening when in fact we aren't.

"That Reminds Me of the Time . . . "
(Translation: "I can top that.")

When friends sit around having a casual conversation, they'll get on a particular subject and take turns telling their own stories. Maybe Carol will describe how her dachshund won't do his business outside in the winter because the minute he feels the icy snow on his paws he clickety-clicks over to the door and whines to be let back in. Then Murray will tell about the time his Russsian wolfhound lay at death's door for two days, until they found a small burr in his long silky fur, and when they removed it, Sasha suddenly made a miraculous recovery. Then maybe I'll tell something fascinating (to me, at least) about my cat Ralphie's latest adventure.

In this kind of friendly exchange it's OK just to take turns. The person telling a casual anecdote doesn't really need an elaborate response. However, there are times when someone has something important to say and doesn't want to hear your story until she's had a chance to tell what happened to her and how she felt—and get some acknowledgment. She needs a little time and attention. The woman who's just had her car towed away doesn't want to be interrupted to hear about the time that happened to you three years ago.

Interrupting someone to tell a similar story is a common example of how listeners don't restrain themselves. Sometimes this is annoyingly obvious, as when people call attention to themselves boorishly and blatantly by cutting in to say, "That reminds me of when. . . ." Most of us don't do that. If someone needs to talk, we listen. At times, however, the speaker's need for attention isn't obvious, and instead of devoting ourselves to receptive listening we respond from our own needs. A friend starts to tell us about an accident and, in an attempt to show empathy, we interrupt to tell her about ours—which, after all, was more upsetting to us, even though it happened six months ago.

Why do people do that? Why do we interrupt to tell our own stories? Most conversation is interactive. We're engaged, and much of what people say to us triggers something in our own experience. If I tell you something annoying that my father does, you're likely to think of something annoying that your father does. Or if I tell you about the time I fell in love for the first time, you're likely to remember your first love. But listening to people means hearing them out. Giving them sufficient time to say what's on their mind and taking sufficient interest to follow and acknowledge their experience.

"Oh, How Awful!"
(Translation: "You poor, helpless thing.
Here's another fine mess you got yourself into.")

Another example of listeners failing to restrain themselves is responding with excessive sympathy, a gift that usually means more to the giver than the receiver. Exaggerated concern may seem less selfish than turning the conversation around to yourself, but acting distressed isn't the same thing as really listening. Listening means taking in, not taking over.

Real listening requires attunement—reading and acknowledging the speaker's experience, not the kind of cranked-up sentiment that may fool small children but usually comes across to adults as patronizing and false. Expressions of concern from the person who always makes a big fuss over what you say become as meaningless as Muzak.

Once again, the problem is failing to suspend the self. Instead of holding himself back long enough to listen and to hear what you're saying, the excessive responder jumps in with an expression of sympathetic concern—as if to say, "Oh, I understand . . . (don't bother going on)."

When listening is genuine, the emphasis is on the speaker, not the listener.

When something goes wrong, Christine no longer calls her mother to get a little sympathy. She's learned that if she has the flu or one of the kids breaks a finger, not telling her mother is the only way to avoid an exaggerated show of concern. These things may not be very consequential, but she would like to share them. She doesn't, because when her mother says "Oh, that's awful" and makes too big a deal out of everything, she feels not understood, but that *her mother* is worried—as though *she's* the one with the problem.

———◆———

An empathic response is restrained, largely silent; following, not leading, it encourages the speaker to go deeper into his or her experience.

———◆———

Part of the problem is confusing empathy with sympathy. Sympathy is more limited and limiting; it means to feel the same as rather than to be understanding. Nor does empathy mean, as many people seem to think, worrying about, praising, cheering up, effusive gushing, consoling, or even encouraging. It means understanding.

"Well, If I Were You . . . "
(Translation: "Stop bothering me with your whining and *do* something about it.")

According to some experts, men show interest by giving advice while women show interest by sharing similar experiences.[1] Unasked-for advice is annoying. It feels like being told what to do, being told that our feelings aren't valid because we wouldn't have to have them if we'd only do what the oh-so-helpful person we're talking to suggests. (Responding with a similar story, as just discussed, can be equally unwelcome, especially if the person interrupts your story before you're finished or otherwise goes on without acknowledging what you've said.) When I'm telling someone about an experience or a problem and he or she responds with unwelcome advice, I say, "Thanks, but I don't need any advice; I just need to be listened to." (At least that's what I'd *like* to say.) Do men give more unasked-for advice than women? Maybe. Not in my experience. Perhaps in yours.

A few years ago I did something uncharacteristic for me and joined a men's group. I guess I was looking for friends. It turned out to be a

[1]Deborah Tannen, *You Just Don't Understand* (New York: William Morrow, 1990).

wonderful experience, largely because the other men in the group were all unusually thoughtful and sensitive people. One day we were talking about how we respond when a friend tells us about a problem, and I was surprised to hear most of the others say that they usually try to offer advice. I thought friends didn't do that, but just listened and tried to be understanding. I guess advice giving was trained out of me.

It's true, of course, that sometimes people *want* advice. Some individuals want advice all the time. They think that other people should have an answer for their distress and should try to alleviate it. This emotional need stirs our expectations that advice is wanted. Even if it doesn't work (or get followed), giving advice may suggest that the listener cares and takes the speaker's problems seriously.

The real issue in listening isn't whether we do or don't give advice but whether or not our response is focused on reading and responding to the other person's feelings or is simply a way of dealing with our own. Telling the person with a problem to "do something constructive" reflects a listener's inability to tolerate his or her own anxiety. So too may be pushing others to "Express your feelings" or using imperatives such as "You have to confront him about it." The difference between listening well and not is the difference between being receptive and responsive on the one hand and being reactive or introducing one's own agenda on the other. Failure to suspend the self in favor of the other reflects a lack of autonomy and a blurring of boundaries.

"Have You Heard the One About . . . ?
(Translation: "Never mind what you were saying;
your concerns are boring.")

Another familiar failure to restrain the self is the jokester, who's always quipping, allaying his own anxiety and calling attention to himself instead of tuning in to the speaker. There are times when your fast-quipping friend is funny and you don't mind his making a joke out of something. But there are other times when you're trying to talk and his wisecracking is annoying. What the jokester offers is the thin, unreliable rhetoric of distraction in place of authentic emotional engagement. This feeling of being distracted happens a lot when you're already having a conversation with someone and the jokester joins in. Only he doesn't join in. He doesn't tune in to you and what you're saying; he just uses something you say as a trigger to make a joke.

People who joke all the time are more or less annoying, depending

on how funny they are. We can understand their constant joking by realizing that they have a lot of nervous energy and may have learned to make jokes as a defense against boredom. But, like other failures to restrain the self, someone who always interrupts our conversation with gags can be insensitive and annoying.

"Don't Feel That Way"
(Translation: "Don't upset me with your upset.")

Do you remember the last time someone did you a really big favor and you were so grateful that you looked forward to saying thanks in a special way? Maybe you sent fresh flowers or gave the person a nice bottle of wine to show your appreciation. Or maybe you put your gratitude into words. Did the person accept your thanks or say something like "Oh, it was nothing, don't mention it?" You can understand someone's feeling embarrassed about being thanked profusely, but it leaves you feeling slightly dismissed (as if you've been told it was presumptuous for you to assume that the person would go to any real trouble for the likes of you). Wouldn't it be nice to be able to look someone in the eye and say "Thank you" and have him meet your eyes and say "You're welcome"?

You get a similar but perhaps stronger feeling of being dismissed when you tell someone about being angry or scared about something and she reassures you that there's no need to feel that way.

A lot of failed listening takes the form of telling other people not to feel the way they do. It's frustrating when people tell us we shouldn't worry or feel guilty or be so scared. The intention may be generous, but the effect is to cheat us out of having our feelings acknowledged. Most attempts to talk people out of their troubles are correctly understood as rejection—namely, "Don't upset me with your upset."

When someone is worried or upset enough to talk about it, listening to what the person's saying and acknowledging those feelings is responsive to that person. Reassuring the person that there's nothing to worry about is *not* responsive to him; it's responsive to the listener's own uneasiness.

If someone tells you that she is worried about the future, and you can control it, then by all means do so. Otherwise, hear the person out. Even if you *know* (or think you do) that things will turn out OK (in the future), saying so (predicting the future) doesn't erase the worry (in the present). Reassuring someone instead of hearing him out may ease his mind slightly, but the disconcerting effect of not being taken seriously is usually the stronger reaction. Telling someone not to worry

doesn't convince her to stop worrying; it may convince her that she shouldn't feel the way she does—or that she should give up trying to talk about her feelings to you.

The best way to keep this section simple would be to say that telling people not to feel the way they do is not listening to them and leave it at that. However, there are times when it feels OK to be reassured. You're not too happy with your new haircut, and a friend says, "No, it looks great," or you're feeling bad about not having accomplished much, and someone reminds you of all that you have accomplished and you feel better. The line between wanting to be reassured and wanting to be heard may not always be easy to discern. The more the speaker expresses self-doubt or worry or concern in a questioning or tentative way, the more likely he is to want reassurance. The stronger the feelings, the more likely he is to appreciate being heard and acknowledged. When in doubt, listen.

Do Women Listen Differently from Men?

My assertion that the genuine listener must suspend the self runs counter to popular linguist Deborah Tannen's idea that "Many women, when they talk among themselves in situations that are casual, friendly, and focused on rapport, use cooperative overlapping: Listeners talk along with speakers to show participation and support."[2]

Yes, there are times when mutuality and the pleasures of connection are more important than the need to be heard out by a self-reflecting other. But Tannen stereotypes the sexes by claiming that women engage in "rapport-talk," while men specialize in "report-talk." Men, according to Tannen, engage in self-display, while, "For most women, the language of conversation is primarily the language of rapport: a way of establishing connections and negotiating relationships."[3] "For most men, talk is primarily a means to preserve independence and maintain status in a hierarchical social order."[4]

Tannen gives as an example of the clashing between the sexes (which a lot of people like to think of as inevitable) a man telling a story about having to make up a shortfall in his cash register from his own pocket. The women listening to him "kept overlapping his story

[2]Tannen, 208.

[3]Tannen, 77.

[4]Tannen, 77.

with comments and expressions of sympathy, elaborating on how un-fair it was. . . . "[5] This, according to Tannen, is "rapport-talk." But the woman (or man) who interrupts with expressions of sympathy may not really be receptive; her frequent expressions of sympathy and elabora-tions may be an effort to assert herself—not as a competitive self, but as a sympathetic and appreciative person. Many "supportive" people are like that. They don't say "Look at me, I'm terrific"; they say "Look at me, I'm supportive."

When the people I know talk about feelings—what's really on their minds, what they're excited about, what's troubling them—they want to be listened to and acknowledged, not interrupted with advice or told that someone else had a similar experience. They want listeners who will take the time to listen and acknowledge what they're saying, not immediately turn the focus to themselves.

The inability to set aside one's own needs for long enough to listen is a function of personality, current state of mind, and relationship to the speaker. Some people always turn the conversation around to them-selves. Narcissism or hypochondriasis or just plain immaturity leaves them with limited ability to consider anything but themselves. There are certain people who rarely talk about themselves but can't listen without imposing their own opinions on everything. These people may not be self-centered (concerned only for themselves), but they are egocen-tric (stuck in their own point of view) and certainly no fun to talk to.

Being listened to through the screen of a loved one's bias or anxie-ty leaves us feeling isolated and lonely, as though our feelings weren't valid, as though we didn't count. Children unlucky enough to grow up with biased listening become alienated from their experience. Their view of themselves is shaped by a distorted mirror. Adults subject to egocentric listeners who aren't open to hearing their experience from their perspective feel shut down, angry or deflated, and alienated from those relationships.

Those listeners who are more or less always in an unreceptive state find themselves shut out and shunned, often with no real idea why. They never connect because they never cross the space between them-selves and others. In Chapter 7 we'll see how listeners can learn to take in and acknowledge what people say without permeating their responses with "me" messages.

[5]Tannen, 201.

CHAPTER FIVE

"You Hear Only What You Want to Hear?"

HOW HIDDEN ASSUMPTIONS PREJUDICE LISTENING

Listening, as we've seen, takes effort. But sometimes that effort is prejudiced: our own internal sensitivities filter what we hear and what we say. Those sensitivities take the form of preconceived expectations and defensive emotional reactions. I'll explain how what we expect to hear filters what we do hear in this chapter and then get to emotional reactivity in the next. Understand, though, that just as it isn't always easy to separate the speaker's and listener's contributions to misunderstanding, it isn't always possible to separate expectations from emotions that interfere with listening.

HOW OUR ATTITUDE ABOUT THE SPEAKER BIASES WHAT WE HEAR

One way to learn something about the forces that influence listening is to hear the same story from two different sides.

Lucy was a special-education teacher who had a humiliating encounter with the principal of her school. When the principal wanted to find space for a new reading instructor, she sent Lucy a memo saying

that she would have to move to a small room in the basement, previously used for storage. Lucy prided herself on being flexible, but being told to move to the basement made her feel devalued and that the principal had little respect for the special needs of her children.

When Lucy called to discuss this unsatisfactory arrangement, the principal made an appointment to see her that afternoon. But when Lucy showed up at four o'clock, the principal had gone to another meeting and left a note suggesting they get together later. Ten days went by before the principal finally made time to talk to her. By that point Lucy had to make an extra effort to control her anger to make the case, as calmly as possible, that moving to the basement just wasn't acceptable. Instead of listening, the principal, who'd obviously made up her mind, got irritated and defensive. At one point, when Lucy protested that the specially equipped classroom in which the children now met had always been her room, the principal said archly, "Oh, did you bring it from home?" Lucy left the meeting in tears.

As soon as she got home, Lucy called her sister Katrine, who since their mother's recent death was the only living member of her family. But when Lucy tried to explain what had happened, Katrine kept interrupting her with questions. "What exactly did you say that made that woman so defensive? You must have said something to set her off like that." Lucy couldn't believe it. Instead of being supportive, her sister was blaming *her* for the incident. It felt like a slap in the face. "Just listen, Katrine, will you!" she pleaded. That shut Katrine up for the moment, but Lucy could tell that her sister wasn't at all sympathetic and wasn't really listening, so she said good-bye and hung up.

When Lucy told me about this incident two days later, she said that her sister just hadn't been there for her when she'd needed her most. It certainly sounded that way. But by one of those strange twists of fate that sometimes happen, I got to hear Katrine's version of the same event the following week.

According to Katrine, she's had lifelong problems talking with her sister. "Lucy has always dominated our conversations. She loves to talk about herself, but she hardly ever listens to anything I have to say. If I pause for a minute, she immediately jumps in with some comment or criticism." But the thing that bothered Katrine most was that Lucy was always complaining. "She's always telling me about hassles with somebody—other teachers, neighbors, supermarket clerks, even the nice old man in the Chinese take-out place. And it's always the other person's fault. I used to try to listen—after all, she is my sister. But as I've

gotten older, I just don't have time for her negativism." According to Katrine, Lucy was hard to listen to because she'd used up her credit.

It's common for speakers not to be heard because their credibility is low. A father's credibility, for example, may be determined by whether his wife and children think he's tuned in to what's going on in the family or too preoccupied with himself and his work to have any idea about what's happening around the house. If he's had an affair or drinks too much—even though he espouses rule-keeping to the children—they may not respect him enough to hear what he has to say. A parent's external world status also affects his or her credibility. A father who is laid off and out of work may lose credibility. This may not be because his family is judgmental, but because people who have lost self-respect in their own eyes often express themselves with a bitter or defensive edge that makes them hard to listen to. Listening is always codetermined.

The minute you pick up the phone and hear some people's voices, you're wary. They're asking you how things are going, acting interested, but you're waiting for the pitch. They call only when they want something. Even if you like them, even if you want to be friends, the one-sided nature of these relationships wears thin after a while. When you answer the phone and they say hello, they can probably hear the enthusiasm drop out of your voice. Do they have any idea why? Do you dare tell them?

Credibility is also influenced by whether you're viewed as being in an appropriate position with a particular setting. A colleague who's seen as not really caring much about what goes on at work may not be listened to even when he has something worthwhile to say. A mother who talks to her adolescent children as though they were still little kids may be experienced as out of touch and therefore incapable of having legitimate concerns and feelings.

A lot of grandparents don't get heard when they give advice about bringing up baby. Their mistake is not necessarily being pushy or intrusive but rather being out of touch with their children's anxious insecurity about being parents. The grandparents are not heard because their children perceive their advice as undermining their own shaky authority. In this case, the grandparents' mistake may be treating their children as though they were *more* grown-up, in charge and confident, than they feel.

A speaker's credibility is also affected by whether or not his or her messages are clear and pertinent. If your father-in-law muddles his mes-

sages with malapropisms and obscure metaphors, you may work at trying to understand him as part of building a relationship with your spouse's family. But if you have to work too hard at it, after a while you may give up. If your father always changes the subject to talk about himself, you will come to expect this and may get out of the habit of listening. People who abuse the privilege of listening by going on and on or by flitting from one subject to another whenever they have the floor may create the expectation that listening to them is too much work, so why bother?

When the speaker has lost credibility but the relationship has a good track record, the listener may pay attention even though he or she may not really hear. You might give the aunt who's always been nice to you the courtesy of your attention even though you don't respect her enough to really listen to what she's trying to say. But if there is relentless repetition of a message—any message—you're likely to withdraw even the courtesy of attention, replacing it with conflict or distance.

HOW OUR EXPECTATIONS MAKE US HYPERSENSITIVE: THE DISCOVERIES OF OBJECT RELATIONS THEORY

Our relationship to each other and to the world around us depends on a unique capacity to transcend immediate experience by making a reproduction of it inside the mind, where we can then manipulate the possibilities. One of the simplest examples of this is a baby learning to tolerate his mother's absence by remembering her presence and relying on her return. This mental structuralization of experience can be the source of creative alteration of circumstances or of deadening inflexibility that sets some people so at odds with the world around them.

From the start, our lives revolve around relations with others. The residue of these relationships leaves internal images of self, other, and self-in-relation-to-others. As adults we react not only to the actual other but also to an internal other. Object relations theory focuses on this internal other—the mental images we have of other people, built up from experience and expectation. (*Object relations* may seem a cold-blooded term for human intercourse, but *objects* refers to mental images of other people that are the object of our actions, not to the people themselves.)

The details of object relations theory are rich with particulars for explaining our preconceived assumptions and emotional sensitivities,

but the essence is quite simple: we relate to people in the present part-ly on the basis of the expectations formed by our early experience. (A man who emerges from puppyhood with a clear picture of his father lording it over his mother may vow always to be kind and considerate to his own wife—at all times unstinting in his criticism and counsel.)

Contemporary relationships and earlier ones (encoded in the in-ner world of objects) interact in circular fashion. Life circumstances main-tain internal expectations and are chosen because of them and interpreted in light of them. The past is alive in memory—and it runs our lives more than we know.

To understand the depth of some people's hypersensitivity to mak-ing mistakes, we might turn to Melanie Klein's notion of the *depressive position,* namely the painful discovery that love and hurt can go together.[1] To understand other people's rage at criticism, we might consider Ronald Fairbairn's idea that the neurotic's ego is split into an *exciting ego* (leaving him longing for total love) and a *rejecting ego* (lead-ing him to expect rejection), so that his relationships take on an "all good" or "all bad" quality and shift dramatically from one to the other.[2] To explain why some people attack and others withdraw when they get hurt, we might look to the dynamic variations in how their respec-tive families shaped their narcissistic need for attention. Some people get attention for being good; in their families anger and assertiveness may be beyond the pale. For others, who get attention for achievement, vulnerability and weakness may be intolerable.

What's common to these and other object-relations formulations is the idea that the neurotic person encounters others not as an equal but as a fearful child, intimidated not so much by the reality of other people as by imagined extreme expectations. In this respect, we're all a little neurotic.

HOW WE LEARN TO OVERREACT

Some of the expectations we bring to our conversations are built up from the history of our relationships with those specific individuals. But some of what we expect to hear is part of the deep structure of our per-

---

[1]Melanie Klein, "Notes on some schizoid mechanisms," *International Journal of Psycho-Analysis,* 1946, 27, 99–110.

[2]Ronald Fairbairn, *An Object-Relations Theory of the Personality* (New York: Basic Books, 1952).

sonalities, the residue of our earliest relationships. To understand listening and the dynamics of relationship it's necessary to consider not only what goes on between people but also what goes on inside them.

———◆———

More than we like to realize, we continue to live in the shadow of the families we grew up in.

———◆———

The sometimes vast difference between words spoken and thoughts intended is nothing compared to the often vaster gulf between what is said and what is heard. Whenever someone, speaker or listener, seems to be responding to a private interpretation, it might be useful to ask: What *would* make that response understandable? Once you start thinking this way—namely, that people act the way they do for a reason—you'll know something about the way they were treated by their parents.

One reason we carry oversensitivities from home around with us rather than having resolved them is that most of us leave home somewhere in the transition from adolescent to mature adult responsiveness. In the busy time of our twenties, when we're making a start on love and work, we react to the expectation that we can't really talk to our parents by distancing ourselves from them. But then, often somewhere in our thirties, we decide to close the gap and rebuild our relationship with our parents, this time on a firmer, more mature footing.

People who do decide to work on their relationship with their parents often go at it with certain unfortunate expectations. They imagine themselves settling old scores and righting ancient wrongs, like avenging angels, or suddenly waking sleeping intimacy, as though family ties, cherished, strained, or severed, could be refashioned overnight. The truth is, when you go home, you're more like one of nature's humbler creatures, and you have to keep your wits about you to avoid getting stuck on the family's emotional flypaper.

Peggy and her parents agreed on many things—the value of hard work, the need to build something for the future, the importance of family. But agreement is something children and parents can always overcome, and Peggy and her parents managed to get into a shouting match on just about every visit. Most visits would start off well. Love and news would carry them through the first couple of days, but the inevitable blowup was like a ticking time bomb, set for three days and waiting to go off.

Like most people, Peggy couldn't stop wishing her parents were different. She loved them, and they loved her; she just wished they would grow up. Her mother was loud and abrasive, always eager for company but always complaining and never with a kind word to say about anybody. Her father was altogether a quieter soul, self-possessed, cool, some would say aloof. He showed his love by offering advice, whether you asked for it or not, and by repairing things around the house, whether they needed it or not. Peggy found him impossible to talk to. When she tried to tell him what was going on in her life, he never really listened.

Unlike most people, who acknowledge the turmoil they feel on family visits but don't recognize their own contribution, Peggy *was* willing to look at her part in the cycles of conflict with her parents. First she figured out what it was that her parents did that made her reactive. Her mother assumed the right to criticize anything and anyone, but her meanest comments were reserved for family members who did anything assertively independent. When Peggy's brother's wife decided to start her own business, Peggy's mother wanted to know, "Who does she think she is!" She was totally unsupportive when Peggy's cousin got a divorce, even though it had been a disastrous marriage from the start. And when another cousin decided to move out of her parents' house (she wasn't getting married), Peggy's mother said, "There's only one reason a twenty-year-old woman gets her own apartment, and *I* don't happen to approve of that."

Next Peggy learned to see how her mother's negativism and intrusiveness triggered anxiety and rage in her. The fact that she'd learned to expect it made her hypersensitive. The minute her mother started in on someone, Peggy got upset, anxious and angry at the same time. She felt she was being pressured to join her mother in anger and criticalness, and if she resisted she felt as though she herself were under attack. She usually held her tongue, but the effort to repress protest only put her anger under pressure, which after a while led to an eruption. The longer she held back, the more her feelings of neglect and rage would build. When she finally did blow up, her mother would get hurt and withdraw, leaving Peggy feeling helpless and despicable at the same time.

Peggy also began to see that although she rebelled against her mother's criticalness, she had learned from her mother and had incorporated the habit of assuming responsibility for other people's feelings and reactions. Whereas her mother was hostile and controlling, Peggy

was benignly controlling—worrying excessively about her own children, always doing things for other people. The expectation of merging with those you love was the same for mother and daughter—only their way of showing it was different. The "nicer" and more "helpful" Peggy was, the more she expected there to be no walls between herself and those she cared for. She felt guilty for not doing enough and repressed her anger for not getting enough. Eventually, when her children or her friends or her husband did something that made her feel shut out, she'd erupt in angry criticism, just as she'd done with her mother. These scenes never changed anything. As you've no doubt noticed, venting anger is not the same as voicing feelings in a way that makes them heard.

When she first consulted me about the relationship with her mother, Peggy said that she had tried everything. Her "everything" ran the gamut from A to C, appeasement to confrontation. The alternative, calmly stating her own point of view, never occurred to her, because by the time she finally responded to her mother's criticism she was so angry that she lost control.

The word for impetuous lack of control and unrestrained emotionalism is *childish*. The place where we learn (or don't learn) restraint is in our families. But it isn't in childhood that we overcome childishness; that isn't in the cards. As young children, we looked up to our parents. (But then we were short and looked up to everything.) Later, if they said something to incite or provoke us, we either absorbed it or cried. It was as teenagers that we began to see through our parents; we stopped putting up with the exasperating things they said and started fighting back.

Most teenagers become so hypersensitive to their parents that they flare up at the least hint of indignity, like dry grass struck by lightning. (If you have a teenager in captivity, you know what I mean.) If adolescence is a time for becoming your own person, late adolescence is a time for transforming your relationship with your parents from a childish basis to an adult one. Unfortunately, most of us leave home in the midst of that transformation. Distance and infrequent contact afford us the illusion that we're grown up, but for most of us who left home at eighteen or so, our relationships with our parents remain frozen in adolescent patterns.

Only one thing robs Superman of his mature powers: kryptonite, a piece of his home planet. A surprising number of adult men and women are similarly rendered helpless by even a brief visit with their parents.

Superman becomes mortal in contact with kryptonite; mortals become teenagers in contact with their parents. We revert to childish roles when we get anxious because we never fully learn to resist parental provocation.

Our parents may be the most important unfinished business of our lives.

OUR DIVIDED SELVES

We don't easily face our own shortcomings, and it's particularly painful to confront our inability to listen. When we do, it's natural to become critical and get discouraged: "I'm a lousy listener," "I'm selfish," "I'm too controlling." Instead of thinking of ourselves in such global, negative terms, it's possible to realize that only a particular part of ourselves is having trouble listening. Using a little imagination to personify our parts as subpersonalities (residues of early object relations) may lead us to their source.[3]

Take, for example, a husband who regularly finds himself shutting his ears when his wife tries to tell him that she needs more from him. With a little introspection, he might discover a part of himself that feels like a little boy who expects to be reprimanded by his mother. The little boy doesn't want to hear it; his mother's criticism makes him feel disapproved of and controlled; he wants to be left alone. The husband can calm down his "little boy part" by realizing—really getting it— that his wife isn't his mother. She's not trying to control him. Even if she sounds critical, what she's really trying to express is her loneliness and her need for him. It's not we who are afraid to listen; it's those

[3]According to Henry A. Murray, "A personality is a full congress of orators and pressure groups, of children, demagogues, Macchiavellis . . . Caesars and Christs. . . . " "What Should Psychologists Do About Psychoanalysis?" *Journal of Abnormal and Social Psychology 35*, (1940): 160–61.

Eric Berne's transactional analysis personified Freud's superego, ego, and id as parent, adult, and child. *Transactional Analysis in Psychotherapy* (New York: Grove Press, 1967).

In literature we find Pirandello's *Six Characters in Search of an Author* and Stevenson's tortured Dr. Jekyll and Mr. Hyde.

Although many people have used the metaphor of subpersonalities, I have found the "internal family systems" model of Richard Schwartz particularly useful. "Our Multiple Selves." *Family Therapy Networker 11*, (1987): 25–31; 80–83. Richard Schwartz, Know thy selves. *Family Therapy Networker 12*, (1988): 21–29.

fearful parts of us that, once triggered, reduce us to childish insecurity and the anxiety that accompanies it.

Some of our subpersonalities manifest themselves in warring inner voices that fuel those painful and tedious arguments we have with ourselves. The rival voices are normally apparent only when we're in conflict—facing a difficult decision or torn between two choices. This is when it's wise to remember that calm fosters unity; conflict sunders it. The next time you find yourself caught up in internal debate, consider the possibility that the thoughts and feelings on either side of the argument aren't just transient and situational. Maybe those competing voices have a lot to say. Maybe they've been saying similar things to you all your life, and maybe they've been fighting those same other voices that they're fighting now. We usually listen to one part, the one that represents the overdeveloped parts of our personalities. Here's an example:

Once or twice a year David Berlow takes time off from teaching at the university to spend a week by himself at a friend's house on Cape Cod. He likes to get away to spend some concentrated time writing and unwinding. But each time he goes he gets into a debate with himself about whether to spend most of his time working or relaxing. One voice says that he should really concentrate on working because that's the most important thing. The other voice counters that he's always working and that this is his only chance to really relax by himself. Each time the debate is the same, and always quite frustrating. He really wants to do both, get a lot of work done and spend a few whole days swimming and fishing. But even though the debate is always hard fought, the voice that tells him to work always wins.

The people who know us can usually predict our choices, even if we still agonize over them. In David Berlow's case, the voice that says work always wins over the one that says play. His wife could tell you that. And she's learned, after much trial and error, that the only way for her and the children to get the attention of the part of David that likes to play is to reassure the part that worries about getting enough work done. She knows, for example, that he won't be able to relax on the family vacation unless he brings along some work to do in the morning. And if she tries to get him to visit her parents for the weekend, she always helps him find a little time to get some work done. She's not just thoughtful; she's smart.

A good opportunity to learn more about the opposing voices inside you is the next time you find it necessary to ask someone's advice. The need to ask is a sign that the contending voices have nearly equal claim on your attention. But beyond the specifics of the situation, what is the nature of those voices? Does the question of whether or not to go to a meaningless staff meeting symbolize a debate between the dutiful child and the independent one? And if you ask someone's advice, aren't you aware of what he or she will say? And do you sometimes seek out the right person to give you the answer that part of you really wants to hear?

What does all this have to do with listening? Whenever someone asks your advice or shrinks from you or gets impatient with you, it's worthwhile to think about what parts of the person might be at war with each other. It may be useful to remember these conflicting voices when you're tempted to give obvious advice—telling people to stop drinking so much, start exercising more, do their homework, or quit smoking—rather than listening for what they really want from you. Can you tell these people anything they don't already know? If not, how about trying appreciate where they're at instead of pushing them to where you think they ought to go?

Giving predictable advice to adolescents—urging them to stop doing things that aren't good for them—is a classic mistake made by adults. The voice of "no" is one that teenagers are already well aware of. A more effective way to get through to them (or anyone else with self-destructive habits) is to adopt a more neutral attitude and simply ask them about the effects of whatever they're doing. Unfortunately, when this question comes from a person who is in fact anxious to make the child change, it won't be heard. Teenagers can smell control a mile away.

The compulsion to pursue self-destructive behavior can be pretty strong, not easy to countermand with platitudinous advice. Not only do smoking and drinking and overeating feel good, but they're also supported by inner voices that whisper, "Go on, you deserve it. To hell with all those killjoys." Sometimes our inner voices work as a team in a control and release cycle. The voice of guilty self-reproach heaps on the punishment that produces the control that eventually leads to another rebellious release.

Psychologists call the interface between the voice that says "do it" and the one that says "no" the *vertical split*.[4] Unlike the horizontal split

---

[4]Heinz Kohut, *The Analysis of the Self* (New York: International Universities Press, 1971).

(repression), the vertical split doesn't keep wishes out of consciousness, only on the back burner. In the case of a woman who spends too much money on clothes or drinks too much, the voice on the "do it" side of the vertical split is the one that usually doesn't get heard—no one says to her, "You're special; you deserve to be treated that way"—and that's why she acts out its dictates. It takes empathy to bring out and reassure the shy voice that says to her, *Go ahead, you need this; you deserve it.*

Thinking in terms of subpersonalities can be especially helpful in heated and reactive discussions. Instead of thinking of being at odds with someone, sometimes it's more useful to think of parts of one of you trying to change parts of the other. In a typical situation provoked by a teenager's coming home late, his father gets mad and demands to know what happened. His accusatory tone makes the boy feel judged and demeaned, and he counters angrily, which drives up the father's rage to the point where his wife tells him to calm down and stop shouting. This infuriates the father, and he leaves the house. If you were the father, you would probably think of the boy as disrespectful and the mother as interfering. If you were the boy, you'd view the father as controlling. Instead, think of the conflict as being waged among parts of them. A rebellious part of the boy activates a controlling part of the father, which in turn mobilizes a protective part of the mother to shield the boy from his father's temper. If you were any one of these people and you began to think this way, how difficult would it be to control your part? How might the problem be affected if each of you could stay calm and avoid letting your reactive parts take over?

Take another example. Does the question of whether or not to confront your partner with something that's bothering you represent the competing voices of a compliant child, who believes that she shouldn't complain or people will get mad at her; a hurt part; and an angry part? Of the last two, which one is more scared to speak up? Why? If you can identify those parts that have trouble speaking up, can you find any way to reassure them? Would it help to tell the person you have trouble speaking up to about the scared part of you? Would he (or she) be more understanding if you asked for his (or her) help to express this part of you?

Let's take a look at a familiar interaction between intimate partners, using the notion of subpersonalities. A woman has trouble listening to her husband because he often expresses himself with anger and intense frustration. Is this the sensitive and vulnerable man she mar-

ried that she hears, or is it an echo of mounting anxiety and danger from long ago? And who is the "she" who's doing the hearing? The part of her who's strong and cares deeply about her husband or a little girl part who trembled to hear her parents quarreling about her father's explosive temper and her mother's shame about it in front of others?

Finding the "parts" (obstacles or constraints) that get in the way of our receptivity and then releasing these constraints is a very different way of thinking from accusing ourselves of being immature or selfish or inadequate. It isn't that we're bad listeners; it's our hidden emotional agenda that crowds out understanding and concern. When we clear away automatic emotional reactions—criticism, fear, hurt— we get to compassion, curiosity, and tenderness. Instead of condemning ourselves for being "bad listeners," we can learn to identify and relax those parts of ourselves that interfere. In so doing, we release ourselves for effective listening.

CHAPTER SIX

"Why Do You Always Overreact?!"

HOW EMOTIONALITY MAKES US DEFENSIVE

One of the major reasons people don't listen is that they become emotionally reactive. Something in the speaker's message triggers hurt, anger, or fear, which activates defensiveness and blocks understanding. Emotional reactivity is like throwing a switch and having the electricity come on, only instead of music you get static. The static is anxiety.

"What's Really Bothering You?"

Perhaps the hardest messages for us to listen to without reacting emotionally are those that involve criticism. Most of us like to think that we can accept constructive criticism, and, on the other hand, most of us know people who can't.

Once a month the Outpatient Psychiatry staff at Briarcliff Medical Center reviews a sample of patient charts to assess the treatment being provided in the clinic. This may sound like a good idea, but the review has become progressively more tedious as the need to monitor bureaucratic forms has crowded out time for considering the quality of care patients are receiving. At the last meeting the staff discovered that a few of the charts selected for review had already been examined at the previ-

ous month's meeting. When the director mentioned this to the secretary, she said, "Then get them yourself—I can't do everything!" and stormed out of the room.

If you believed that this kind of reaction was common from this woman, you'd have no trouble recognizing her as one of those hypersensitive people who can't take criticism. If, on the other hand, you knew her to be one of the most even-tempered people around, you'd assume she was having a bad day. You'd be right. Her assistant had been out sick, and she'd had to stay three hours late the night before and come to work two hours early to get the charts ready. Of course she was on edge.

When people overreact uncharacteristically, we usually assume that something's bothering them. If our relationship with them has a history of goodwill, we give the person the benefit of the doubt and often try to find out what the real problem is. But what about those people who regularly respond inappropriately? Are they having a bad life?

Corinne was a very intelligent woman who couldn't allow herself to make mistakes. She kept up with *Forbes, Barrons,* and the *Wall Street Journal,* but she also watched ESPN and read *The Sporting News.* She especially loved baseball and took pleasure in writing a newsletter about her favorite team, the Atlanta Braves, and circulating it at the office. When one of the team's star pitchers injured his shoulder, Corinne wrote that this might turn out to be a blessing in disguise if it allowed a certain relief pitcher to prove that he was as good a starter as some insiders suspected. When Corinne read a draft of the piece over the phone to her cousin Drew, she said it was great, except for one thing: the pitcher was injured playing against Pittsburgh, not Philadelphia, as Corinne had written. Glad to get the facts straight, Corinne corrected her error. When the newsletter came out, a senior staff member told Corinne that he loved her article, but it was Philadelphia, not Pittsburgh, where the fateful injury took place.

Corinne was so humiliated by this minor mistake that she was thrown into a tailspin. She cried and felt like a fool and couldn't bring herself to go to work the next day.

She was a shy person who preferred to express herself in writing rather than conversation; to her, being listened to meant having what she wrote appreciated. Being wrong meant feeling the opposite of appreciated. Instead of getting angry at her cousin for giving her the wrong information, she was ashamed of herself for not getting the story straight.

Nobody likes to make mistakes, but clearly Corinne's reaction was excessive.

Another example of reacting inappropriately may be more familiar, in form if not intensity. Lenny was a devoted husband and father as well as a good provider. He worked hard and spent the rest of his time with the family. He did his share of household chores and was emotionally involved in the life of the family. His wife's one complaint was that he was too critical.

The only thing that struck me as unusual about this situation was the degree to which Sheila absorbed all of Lenny's complaints without objecting or answering with any complaints of her own. He was the lord and master, and it was her job to cater to him. When Lenny said, "You should clean all the snow off the car before you start to drive," Sheila protested feebly, "I was in a hurry to get to the cleaners." When Lenny countered, "You're always in too much of a hurry," Sheila capitulated, "I guess you're right."

Experience has taught me to listen not only to what people say but also for what they're not saying and to wonder why. I soon found out why Sheila hesitated to protest. Once she said, "Don't you think you're being a little unfair?" and Lenny flew into a rage. He started shouting at her. "You *never* listen to anything I say! You have *no* respect for me. You say you love me, but it's a *goddamned* lie!" It was awful. I don't really remember all of what he said because, frankly, I was too upset. What's more, the same thing happened every time Sheila said anything critical to Lenny. His reaction was so angry and intense that it was impossible to hear what he was feeling or to modulate what he was saying.

Having read these two accounts, you can probably guess something of what both Corinne and Lenny felt. But clearly the intensity of their reactions was inappropriate to the situation. Let me also tell you that these are two instances when it's a lot easier to read about something than to witness it firsthand. Corinne's abject remorse and Lenny's rage made listening to them almost impossible. What makes people respond so inappropriately? Long memories.

From these brief descriptions, some people might say that Corinne was insecure and oversensitive and Lenny suffered from unresolved aggression. Others might say that Corinne's turning her anger inward and Lenny's lashing out were typical of their genders. In fact these inferences are so general and judgmental as to constitute virtually meaning-

less clichés. For a more subtle appreciation of a person's overreaction we need to know its trigger.

————◆————

A listener's emotional reaction seems inappropriate only as long as you can't see his or her memory.

————◆————

As a therapist, when I see someone responding "inappropriately," I ask myself what circumstances would make the response appropriate. (In my own relationships I just get upset like everyone else.) What circumstances would make it reasonable for a woman to feel hopelessly worthless for having made a mistake? (Hint: Most of us manage to survive childhood, but not all of us outgrow it.)

Corinne was the last in line of five children in a talented and ambitious family. She had an older sister "who was jealous and competitive" and three brothers "who never loved me." Her father was cerebral and distant; her mother was depressed, an underachiever who drank too much. Corinne was the baby, but rather than being doted on she was ignored. Early on, she decided that the only possibility of ever being loved was to be the perfect child, "docile and mediocre"—docile so as not to burden her parents, mediocre so as not to challenge her siblings. They tolerated her as long as she played the good little sister, but they couldn't acknowledge any signs of accomplishment from her. Deprived of acceptance themselves, they belittled their little sister's achievements and mocked her mistakes. They called her "lardass," "Miss Piggy," "stupid," and "retard." Even the smallest slip-up could trigger their scornful laughter. Years later Corinne was still so hypersensitive to humiliation that she sank into despair whenever she made the slightest error. The man who pointed out her mistake did not say "retard," but that's what she heard.

What made Lenny so critical of others and so unable to tolerate criticism in return? Not the kind of cruel treatment you might expect. Lenny's parents were decent and loving people. But their relative lack of involvement outside the family led them to expect a lot from each other and from their children. When they didn't get what they wanted, they criticized and complained. This alone might not have made Lenny so unable to tolerate criticism. But his parents, for all their basic goodness, never gave him the consistent empathy that would have solidified his sense of worth. Without a store of loving memories, without a sense of being taken seriously and appreciated just for himself, and

without expectations of more understanding to come, Lenny was filled with deep and ugly fears of worthlessness. Hard work and family devotion kept these repressed feelings at bay, until, that is, someone said anything remotely resembling what Lenny himself feared in his heart of hearts—that he was no good.

I once had a gray and white cat named Tina who was perfectly friendly, except that once in a while she'd lash out violently with her claws. These attacks were unexpected and unprovoked. One minute Tina would be purring to have her head stroked; the next thing you knew you'd have a bloody claw mark on the back of your hand. Eventually we took her to the vet and learned that she had a wound in her hip—possibly from a car accident when she was a kitten—so that what seemed to us like a harmless touch could actually be very painful.

Shame and insecurity are the wounds that make people react violently to criticism. Some people retreat from hurt feelings, while others attack. The most shame-sensitive individuals flare up at the slightest sign of criticism. Such people are hard to live with. But reacting to criticism with hurt and anger is something we all do. What varies is only the threshold of response.

The universal human vulnerability to criticism is related to the universal yearning for love and approval. What we really want to hear is that we're terrific (sometimes "OK" will do).

Our sensitivity to criticism varies with the situation. We're hurt most by criticism of something that feels like an important part of ourselves—our motives, for example, or the products of our creativity, or, during adolescence (and sometimes slightly beyond), our appearance. We're especially sensitive to criticism from someone whose opinion we care about. The right person saying the wrong thing can puncture the ego like a pin bursting a balloon.

What Makes Us Intolerant?

When you're trying to figure out why you or anyone else overreacts, keep in mind one of the great ironies of understanding: we're likely to be as accepting of others as we are of ourselves. That's why those lucky enough to be raised with self-respect make better listeners. Still, we needn't be stuck where we find ourselves. If we learn to respect and appreciate other people's feelings, we will learn to treat our own feelings more kindly in the process.

What we can't tolerate in others is what we can't tolerate in ourselves.

We can't listen well to other people as long as we project the mistaken idea that parts of us aren't good enough to be loved, respected, and treated fairly. A wider respect for human dignity flows from and enhances respect for ourselves. Tolerance and appreciation of our own and other people's feelings helps us hear and understand the hurt that inevitably lies behind anger and resentment. When our feelings aren't heard, our spirits are suppressed and distorted.

WHAT TURNS CONVERSATIONS INTO ARGUMENTS?

Reacting emotionally to what another person says is the number-one reason conversations turn into arguments.

If you're not sure what emotional reactivity is, take inventory of your feelings the next time you rush out of the bathroom to catch the phone on the last ring—and it turns out to be somebody selling you something. That agitation, that anxious upset that makes you want to slam down the phone, is emotional reactivity. Is it wrong or unjustified? No, of course not. But it's that feeling, in relationships that do count, that makes it hard to listen, hard to think straight, and hard to say what you want to say.

Reactivity is like a child interrupting an adult conversation—it isn't bad; it's inopportune. Our intrusive emotions may need to be hushed, but they may also need to be listened to later. Why are we reactive? What are the reactive parts of ourselves, and what are they reacting to? Disruptive feelings are messages from our inner spirit about something we need to change or pay attention to in our lives. Our reactivity can lead us to parts of ourselves that we haven't yet befriended—mute and helpless parts, frightened and lonely parts.

If Corinne were to tell a friend how stupid she felt for screwing up the newsletter, the friend might try to reassure her by telling her not to worry. After all, everyone makes mistakes, right? Yes, but when Corinne made a mistake, she could hear the savage brothers sneering at her: "Lardass! retard!" And she'd feel again what she'd been spending her whole adult life running away from: that she was ugly and stupid and helpless, and nobody loved her, and nobody would ever love her.

Lenny's always dishing out but never being able to take criticism might seem more reasonable if you realized that deep down he, too, felt worthless and inconsequential. Inside him were dark and ugly voices he anxiously shut his ears to lest he get in touch with the part of him that still felt like a little boy who was never good enough for his parents.

What turns conversations into arguments for some people (not infrequently mothers) is not so much something inside of them as the fact that they can't face, can't listen to, can't tolerate certain things in people close to them.

One of my patients doesn't want to hear what's going on in her daughter's life. It's too upsetting. The daughter was arrested for prostitution at age fifteen. Despite her mother's heroic efforts to be understanding and firm, the daughter continued to get into trouble, using drugs, hanging around with a motorcycle gang, coming home drunk night after night. Finally, when the daughter was eighteen, her parents insisted that she get her own apartment. They supported her for a while, then gradually tapered off. The daughter now works as a cocktail waitress, when she works, but her parents are reasonably sure that she's heavily involved with drugs and that she probably still prostitutes herself from time to time. They know she occasionally gets arrested for drunk and disorderly behavior, because they've had to go to the jail in the middle of the night and bail her out. Her mother still loves her of course, but finds it necessary to cushion their relationship by visiting infrequently and avoiding the details of the daughter's activities, which she finds too upsetting to listen to.

This mother's avoidance is based on a correct assessment of her own vulnerability. It isn't just worry that she's avoiding; she can't listen to her daughter's troubles without feeling the need to rescue and reform her. The temptation to tell her daughter to stop taking drugs and hanging around dangerous characters (as though these were novel ideas) interferes with listening; giving in to that temptation triggers shouting matches.

The worst thing about reactivity is that it's contagious. When anxiety jumps the gap from speaker to listener, it escalates through a series of actions and reactions, which may eventually lead to an emotional cutoff. The cutoff may be as simple—and simply frustrating—as one person walking out of the room or as sad as one person walking out of the other person's life.

The next time you have the misfortune to witness two people arguing without hearing each other, notice what each of them does to

keep the argument going. (If you're one of the parties to the argument, notice only what the other person does; the alternative is too demanding.) Notice, too, how the argument could end if either one of them would let go. In the runaway logic of reactive quarreling, both parties feel compelled to get in the last word.

The ability to listen rests on how successfully we resist the impulse to react emotionally to the position of the other. The more actions we feel compelled to take to reduce or avoid our anxiety, the less flexible we are in relationships.

Let me give you an example from the wide perspective of a public situation—before focusing on the more anxiety-arousing settings of personal exchange. The next time you attend a lecture or observe a news conference, notice the hostile questions. You'll note that many "questions" aren't really questions at all, but rhetorical attempts to prove that the speaker is wrong and the listener is right. Observe how the speaker handles these questions. Some speakers try to remain calm by finding something to agree with; others get defensive and counterattack.

A speaker is likely to get defensive if she feels that a questioner is trying to make her wrong and himself right. "Excuse me, but haven't you overlooked . . . [you dummy]?" Few such "listeners" really want answers to their questions; they just want to be right. The speaker who gets defensive and tries to counter (put down, really) the questioner often hopes to "win" the exchange by saying "No, actually . . . [I *am* right; *you're* wrong]." In rare instances a clever speaker can succeed in putting down a hostile questioner with superior intellect or knowledge of the subject. More often the questioner, who maybe wanted to make a point, feels dismissed, cheated out of the opportunity to have his voice heard.

When neither party to an exchange is willing to break the spiral of reactivity, both of them are likely to end up feeling angry and misunderstood.

Listening with a Clenched Mind

Listeners intent on avoiding conflict may not listen because they're too busy protecting themselves to be open to what the other is trying to say. Listeners intent on talking speakers out of unhappy feelings or independent inclinations won't hear what the speaker thinks because it

might be threatening. Even speakers who have something worthwhile to say may not get heard if they make the other person feel criticized or misunderstood; the potential listener is likely to become defensive or angry and counterattack or withdraw, making listening the last thing on his or her emotional agenda. Misunderstanding is further occluded when each one broods over the awful things the other one does and one or both of them eventually finds someone else to complain to.

Subjects Too Hot to Handle

Married couples famously have trouble talking about children, sex, and money. The immediate problem with these subjects isn't differences in points of view but the emotional reaction that the expression of those differences elicits. Even though both partners are equally reactive, they may show it in different ways. One may press for more surface calm, while the other may feel unresponded to and press for more emotional involvement. Each becomes highly attuned to slights, hurts, and criticism. Some people's radar is so good that they pick up these signals even before they're sent.

After he and Shirley have a blowup, Don becomes distant and sulky. (Sound familiar?) After a while, though, he calms down and tries to make amends. He says he's sorry for overreacting or for snapping at her for not doing something. But she never apologizes. She either just accepts Don's apology or, if she's really mad, takes it as permission to say more about how what he did upset her. Don's least favorite version of this is "You *always* do that, and I hate it!"

Finally Don told Shirley that he truly was sorry when they argued and often really could see his part in it, but it really bothered him that she never apologized. "It's like everything is my fault, like you don't have any part in our problems. It's not fair."

Shirley blew up. "What am I supposed to say, 'It's *my* fault you're so grouchy'? 'I'm sorry *you* don't like my driving'? 'I'm sorry the baby was sick'?" At this Don threw up his hands and walked out of the room.

What makes it so hard for some people to apologize? Guilty consciences. In her heart of hearts, Shirley blamed herself for everything that went wrong in her relationships. She blamed herself for Don's moods (if she was *really* a good wife, he'd be happy all the time); she blamed herself for not enjoying sex with him more (she must be inhibited); she even blamed herself when the baby got sick (if she were a better mother, nothing bad would ever happen to her child). She came from a family

that specialized in blaming. The result was extreme sensitivity to anything anyone might say that triggered her own inner self-blame. That's the nature of reactivity.

———◆———

We're most reactive to the things we secretly accuse ourselves of.

———◆———

"HOW COME YOU LISTEN TO EVERYBODY BUT ME?"

Husbands and wives often complain that their spouses never listen to what they say but come home and announce that they just heard something very interesting—and that "something" is precisely what the spouse has already told them. Recently, for example, when Marilyn told her husband that she'd decided to see a friend's chiropractor about her back, he hit the ceiling. "I've been telling you to see a chiropractor for years! Now all of a sudden when your precious friend Mary Elizabeth tells you, you listen. How come you never listen to me?"

Marilyn was so taken aback by her husband's outburst that she was unable to answer. But even if she had known what to say, her husband didn't stick around to hear it. He stormed out and slammed the door. Later, she did answer him at length, in her head, where most of us make our best comebacks.

True, he *had* told her to see a chiropractor. But she hadn't asked his advice. When she complained to him about her back, she wanted sympathy, not advice. He was always telling her what to do! Why couldn't he just listen?

When Marilyn told me about this episode, I thought her assertion that she wanted sympathy from her husband, not advice, was true as far as it went, but that it was missing something. It turned out that when her husband gave advice, it was usually in an intense, pressured way, his response to the anxiety her complaints generated in him. She usually ignored his advice, not just because she wasn't in the market for advice but because it was delivered with an emotional pressure that pushed her away.

This is typical of how messages get deflected. It isn't the content that makes people deaf; it's the emotionality behind it. A speaker's eagerness or annoyance or anxiety or tension is often felt by listeners as pressure to make them wrong or to change their way of thinking. As if it

weren't hard enough to tone down one's own emotionality, doing so is often made even more difficult by the condition of the relationship.

HOW SOME SPEAKERS MAKE US HARD OF HEARING

Even if we don't always know what to do about it, we've all had plenty of experience with listeners whose emotional reactivity makes them defensive or argumentative instead of hearing what we're trying to say. An equally important but less commonly recognized barrier to understanding is the speaker's emotionality. A speaker who expresses himself or herself in a highly emotional way makes listeners anxious and therefore hard of hearing.

————◆————

Some people have no idea how pressured and provoking their tone of voice is, but they come at you like a bad dentist.

————◆————

The hardest people to listen to are those who treat us with neglect and dictatorial disregard of our feelings. The pressured speaker may not know how he comes across, but his urgent, anxious manner of speaking, emphatic hand gestures, or conclusion of every other statement with "Right?" (apparently demanding agreement) makes us feel backed into a corner.

A Charged Atmosphere

The emotional state between speaker and listener has a lot to do with the quality of understanding that can pass between them. If the atmosphere is calm, especially if it has a history of being calm, the listener can usually hear what the speaker is trying to get across. But if there's anxiety in the air—or even just intense feeling—the listener may be too tense to take in what's said. The listener may be anxious about not wanting to be blamed, or pressured to change, or being proven wrong. Speakers who trigger such feelings, venting emotion in a way that makes listeners feel backed against the wall, may not get heard, even though they have something important to say. It's the way hard things get said that determines whether or not they get heard.

The emotional state of a relationship depends not only on the way individuals express themselves but also on the extent to which the people remain differentiated as individuals.

A differentiated individual is a mature and autonomous person who knows where his or her skin ends and other people's begin. In emotionally undifferentiated relationships anxiety becomes increasingly infectious and the partners intensely reactive to each other, especially on "hot" subjects. Among some couples money is such a charged issue that you can see the sparks begin to fly at the first mention of the word. A mother who is poorly differentiated from her small daughter may be so threatened by the familiar childish retort "I don't love you!" that she either rescinds her rules or gets into a pointless discussion that begins with "But *I* love you." A more well-differentiated parent doesn't feel so tied to and threatened by her daughter's protests. Such a parent has enough distance to realize that "I don't love you!" just means "I'm angry that you won't let me have my way." Differentiation is achieved by learning to separate what you think from what you feel—and by learning to be yourself while respecting other people's right to be themselves.

When boundaries between people are blurred and individuals become emotionally fused, almost any emotion from the speaker will make a listener reactive. As differentiation decreases, individuality is less well defined, and emotional reactivity becomes more intense. Poorly differentiated and highly reactive people may come across as emotionally demanding or avoidant.

An "independent" husband may be aware of his "dependent" wife's emotional reactivity but blind to his own. He sees her attachment because she shows it directly. When he gets mad at her for objecting to his wanting to go off by himself, he says, "You're so dependent! Why don't you develop some interests of your own and quit hanging on me?" She cries and accuses him of being selfish. As far as he's concerned, she's emotionally immature. She's so dependent that he can't even complain without her getting hysterical. What he *doesn't* see is how vulnerable and dependent *he* is on her feeling positively toward him, so much so that he's completely unable to hear her complaints as an expression of her feelings. He hears what she says only as a judgment and threat to himself and a constraint on what he wants to do. And so he goes off and broods in self-righteous hurt and anger about his wife's inability to respond to him without reacting emotionally.

Gail just had to talk to Leon about needing some help around the house. She knew it was a sore subject because they'd both grown up with the expectation that cooking and washing dishes and doing the laundry was something wives did. But, damn it, with both of them working and the kids to look after, this family couldn't afford the luxury

of a wife. For three months since starting her new job, Gail had put off asking Leon for help because she didn't want to start a fight. But she was finding it impossible to get dinner on the table before the kids started getting cranky, and so she just had to talk to him.

So that night after dinner Gail told Leon how unfair it was for her to have to do all the cooking and cleaning now that she was working. As she spoke, the anger and frustration she'd been sitting on for three months came pouring out.

Leon, who knew he wasn't doing his share, listened as Gail talked about how hurt she was that he hadn't even offered to help. But as she went on about all she had to do and how little he did, Gail started talking faster and more pressured, waving her hands about as though her words couldn't keep pace with her feelings. Leon listened with growing upset.

What started out sounding like a legitimate request turned into a tirade. Instead of listening and feeling like cooperating, he started feeling attacked and got defensive. "Why do you have to go *on and on* about everything? And why do you have to exaggerate so: You do *everything*, and I do *nothing*. Who earns the real money in this family?"

That did it. Gail burst out crying, and Leon, who couldn't take it anymore, stormed out of the room and slammed the door. Gail was left alone crying in the living room, feeling how unfair it was that Leon was too selfish to care about her.

Sometimes the speaker's emotion stirs emotions in the listener, making it particularly difficult for the listener to be the receptive vehicle that the speaker requires. When it comes to telling your side, particularly in a relationship with a history of tension, the best way to be heard is to tone down your emotionality. Even if you don't make the mistake of blaming the other person, he or she may feel attacked if you express yourself in an anxious or pressured manner. The trouble is, sometimes it's hard not to.

The reason we don't recognize the impact of our tone of voice is that we hear what we feel like, not what we sound like.

Elise gets annoyed because Jay takes the other side of almost every issue she brings up. This is a common complaint. Most subjects are complex enough to have two sides; when someone close to us points to

one side, we have a natural tendency to think of the other. The trouble is, it doesn't feel good to say the cup is half empty only to be told "No, it's half full." Jay's tendency always to take the opposite position made Elise feel not just disagreed with but also negated.

Once she commented that the neighbor's porch railing looked as if it was in bad shape and might break; someone might get hurt. Jay looked at the railing—which was in halfway good shape—and said, "I don't think so; it looks OK to me." When Elise tried to tell him what she was feeling—"I hate it when you disagree with everything I say"— Jay felt attacked and controlled. "Must I agree with everything you say?" he wanted to know. Like many reasonable married people, they discussed the issue without raising their voices or hearing each other.

Elise could understand Jay's feeling that it wasn't fair for him to have to agree with everything she said; but that wasn't what she wanted. She just wanted him to acknowledge her feelings. He heard that, sort of, but didn't know what he was supposed to do. "If you say the porch railing looks like it's going to break, and I don't think it is, how am I supposed to know that you're just expressing your feelings and that I'm only supposed to acknowledge them? How do I know what you want if you don't tell me?"

One reason Jay had trouble hearing Elise was that she often expressed herself with very strong emotion. Even clear, meaningful messages were so charged with intense feeling that Jay reacted to her anxiety rather than to her statement. Instead of getting through to him, she became something to brace against.

Elise gets excitable and raises her voice because she's been holding things in and is eager to get them out. But when she gets anxious, Jay gets tight, and he's more aware of the knot in his stomach than of what Elise is trying to tell him. When she told him how much it bothered her that he always disagreed with her, it was the upset she conveyed that made him defensive, not the message.

Even though they tried, Elise and Jay were never able to hear each other in heated discussions. Only when I interrupted and talked to them one at a time were they able to listen without a defensive response. It turned out that Elise had grown up with a father who demanded rigid adherence to his rules and had argued with and invalidated his children's every opinion. Both Jay and Elise recalled her brother and his habit of responding to even the most insignificant disagreement as though it were a declaration of war: "Either you're with me, or you're against me."

Jay and Elise aren't very different from many intimate partners who sometimes despair of ever really being heard by the other. If you want to be listened to and heard, consider how much emotionality and anxiety you have—or how much gets churned up when you speak to certain people about certain things. Listeners react to that emotion. If you can reduce your own emotional intensity, you may get heard, even when the subject is a difficult one. Remember: it isn't so much what you say as how you say it that determines whether or not you get heard. That's one reason people are often more open to what they read than to what someone says to them. (At least I hope so.)

Let's take another look at the interaction between Jay and Elise. Jay had trouble hearing his wife because she often expressed herself with anxious emotion, her sentences flapping at him like flags in a high wind. When her voice rankled and he shrank back into himself, he didn't hear the sweet, eager girl he fell in love with but an echo of harshness from long ago. The "he" who was doing the hearing wasn't the part of him who was strong and loved his wife but a little boy part, the one who could never stand to hear that harsh and powerful voice telling him that he couldn't go out to play, that he had to stay trapped in the house all afternoon, buried alive in chores.

Is it men that Medusa turns to stone, or is it the little boys inside them?

HURT FEELINGS AND BROKEN CONNECTIONS

As a family therapist, I'm often consulted about longstanding impasses in relationships. Wives complain that their husbands don't care how they feel; husbands complain that their wives nag and are more emotional than reasonable; parents complain that their children avoid them; people who feel they are treated unjustly in the family complain that they're singled out unfairly; and adult children complain that they can't get close to their parents. Many of these individuals come to therapy by themselves because the people they're concerned about refuse even to talk about the problem.

Michael's sister Susan moved to the West Coast after a bitter and acrimonious divorce. When she called from Los Angeles to talk to him, her ex-husband, who just happened to have stopped by, answered the phone. Susan was mortified, then furious. She felt betrayed and stopped

speaking to her brother. When Susan didn't return Michael's phone calls, he got so upset that he took a plane to California the next day to straighten things out. But when he got there, Susan left town for the weekend because she still wasn't ready to talk to him. Michael was livid. He could understand that she was upset, but *he* hadn't done anything wrong. And to refuse to see him after he had gone all the way to California—that he could not forgive.

The first step to healing a ruptured relationship is to understand the other person's point of view. Try to figure out what that person might be feeling and then say it in a way that invites him to elaborate. Until you acknowledge the other person's position, he's unlikely to be open to yours. He may listen, but he won't hear.

Michael tried to apologize to his sister, but his heart wasn't in it. After all, he hadn't done anything wrong. So although he was willing to say he was sorry she was upset, he just had to add that he hadn't done anything to be blamed for. Unfortunately, when someone feels wounded and aggrieved, any attempt to justify your own behavior, no matter how innocent or well meaning it was, may cancel your acknowledgment of her feelings. Michael was infuriated when his sister refused to see him, but she rightly intuited that his attempt to make up carried a lot of pressure for her to forgive him. If Susan had been less emotionally reactive or less upset, Michael's attempts to heal the breach might have worked. But when someone is really hurt and bitter, the only thing he or she wants to hear is an apology, not an apology loaded with self-justification. The greatest lesson in humility may be learning to say "I'm sorry I hurt you" without having to protest your innocence.

I saw Michael a total of three times over several months. In our first meeting I made exactly the same mistake I am here preaching against. Instead of acknowledging his hurt and anger, I advised him to reach out to his sister. Since he felt that he'd already done so and been spurned, he rejected my advice.

Our second meeting occurred five months later. He'd been getting on with his life and had calmed down about what happened between him and his sister. Time and distance had softened his anger, and he was ready for suggestions about how to patch up the break with Susan. I advised him to write her a letter acknowledging the hurt and betrayal she felt and saying that he was sorry. I cautioned him that the letter

must be absolutely devoid of two elements that would render it ineffective: any hint of self-justification, expressed or implied, and any pressure or suggestion, expressed or implied, that his sister needed to do something about his apology. It had to be an honest apology—"I'm sorry I hurt you"—nothing more and nothing less. I also warned him that his sister's first response might be an angry one—something that can be hard to take after you apologize. He understood that and said he could accept it.

Four days after Michael wrote to his sister, he received a letter from her saying how betrayed she felt when her ex-husband answered the phone at her own brother's house. How could Michael have been so insensitive? After that Susan's letter lightened. She wrote about her job in California and a new friendship and asked Michael what he was up to. They've been on good terms ever since.

"HE NEVER TALKS TO ME"

How can you listen well when certain important people in your life seem to withhold themselves from you and resist all your efforts at intimacy?

People cultivate protective reticence in emotional relations because they don't want to get hurt. The introvert moves through life in a protective bubble of psychological distance not because his need for attention has ceased but because he's ceased to allow himself to feel it. Inside the prison of his defenses he preoccupies himself with other things. He keeps busy, he reads, he thinks, and he has long conversations in his head, where no one else can mess them up. Like many prisoners, he can be comfortable in his limited and protected routines, but the idea of parole into the wide world of other people and emotions terrifies him.

Although the emotional reticence of someone you care about can be powerfully frustrating, the reticent don't feel powerful. They feel vulnerable. People who withhold themselves from us are trying to insulate themselves from their own exquisite sensitivity to emotionality. It isn't all them, either. In the process of trying to get closer to someone who doesn't say much, we often set up a pursuer–distancer dynamic.

Pursuers and Distancers

One of the most easily observed conversational patterns between intimate partners is the pursuer-distancer dynamic.[1]

As you may have noticed, pursuing distancers only makes them feel pressured and inclined to pull further away. It's a dance between one partner who moves forward and another who moves back. The pursuer-distancer dynamic is propelled by emotional reactivity—on the part of both participants. The people who pull away from us aren't just "shy" or "withholding"; they're responding to the emotionalism with which we approach them. I can almost hear the protests: "*I* don't put any pressure on so-and-so; he [or she] just won't open up."

We rarely feel the emotional pressure we put on others. What we feel is their response to it. The people who resist personal conversation with us may indeed be more reticent than most. Still, their backing off is not just habit but response.

Unfortunately, some of the people we find hardest to listen to are an important part of our lives: They are our partners, our parents, our children, our bosses, or our colleagues, and they arouse our reactivity because our need endows them with the power to distress and please us. When the frustrations of trying to speak and be heard, to listen and hear get to be too much, we may be tempted to give up and pull back into ourselves.

Facing anxious encounters tests your maturity, strengthens you if you have the courage to stand fast and let matters unfold, or weakens you if you fall back into reactivity and defensiveness. Making contact, letting others be themselves while you continue to be yourself, and learning to resist automatic reactions strengthens you and transforms your relationships. Staying open and staying calm—that's the hardest part. You do the best you can.

If all of this seems like obvious common sense—to listen well, you have to resist the urge to overreact—it's only obvious from an objective distance. Up close, when you're caught up in the pressure to get the words out or the aggravation of listening to someone saying something provocative, objectivity is in short supply. Emotionality takes over.

[1] Thomas Fogarty, "The Distancer and the Pursuer," *The Family*, 7, (1979): 11-16.

GETTING THROUGH
TO EACH OTHER

CHAPTER SEVEN

"Take Your Time— I'm Listening"

HOW TO LET GO OF YOUR OWN NEEDS AND LISTEN

Effective listening requires *attention, appreciation,* and *affirmation.* You begin the process by tuning in to the other person, paying attention to what he has to say. Put no barriers between you. Turn off the TV, put down the newspaper, ask the kids to play in the other room, shut the door to your office. Look directly at the speaker and concentrate on what she is trying to communicate.

Practice listening whenever your partner, family member, friend, or colleague speaks to you, with the sole intention of understanding what that person is trying to express. People need to talk—and be heard—to feel understood by and connected to you.

PAYING ATTENTION

You can take the first step toward better listening by making a conscientious effort to set aside whatever is on your mind long enough to concentrate on hearing what the other person has to say.

Listening to each other never seemed to be much of a problem for Tony and Joan before the baby was born. They always had lots to talk about and, maybe more important, plenty of time to do it in. Then

the baby came along, and the pressures of parenthood seemed to squeeze the intimacy out of their relationship. They got out of the habit of going out together, and somehow neither of them seemed to have much energy for conversation in their brief and hectic evenings at home.

Tony made an effort to ask Joan about her day, but when she responded only perfunctorily, he stopped asking. Anyway, he was so tired when he came home that he didn't really mind getting off by himself with the newspaper. They weren't angry or upset with each other, but they were drifting apart.

When Tony sought my advice about the lack of intimacy in the marriage, he described his failed attempts to talk to Joan at the end of the day. I could see two mistakes he was making in trying to get Joan to open up. The first had to do with timing. Trying to have a serious conversation when he first came in the door, while Joan was cooking supper and the baby was winding down like a little clock, just didn't work. The second thing was that Joan didn't respond well to global questions like "How was your day?" Such questions may work when someone is relaxed and ready to talk, but they aren't effective when someone is wound up or distracted. Joan needed him to ask more specific questions, like "How did it go at the pediatrician's?" or "What did the baby do today?"—questions that were specific enough to trigger a response *and* show that he was aware of what was going on in her life.

I did not, however, say any of this to Tony. Instead I turned to Joan and asked if she felt lonely. She said yes. Then I asked if she felt that Tony was really interested in hearing what was going on with her. "Maybe . . . ," she said softly, "but I don't feel it."

All I said to Tony was "I guess you better try harder."

Better listening doesn't start with a set of techniques. It starts with making a sincere effort to pay attention to what's going on in your conversational partner's private world of experience.

My challenge to Tony—"I guess you better try harder"—turned out to be a one-session cure. He did try harder. It didn't occur to him to ask more specific questions; he just didn't give up so easily. Instead of offering Joan a brief moment's attention, he started showing real interest in her feelings and heartfelt concern for her well-being. In response, she began to feel once again loved and cared for—and much more like being intimate with Tony in return.

When you're trying to create a dialogue with someone who isn't revealing much of her thoughts and feelings, it may help to make

empathic guesses about what's going on inside her. Comments like "Tough day?" or "Are you worried about something?" or "Is something bothering you?" if they're on target may show enough awareness to make the other person feel that you're really interested in her. But it isn't any particular comment or any technique alone that will get someone to open up. It's taking a sincere interest in what that person has to say.

Listeners who pretend interest don't fool us for long—even though they sometimes fool themselves. The automatic smile, the hit-and-run question, the restless look in their eyes when we start to talk—all these are giveaways to the fact that they're more interested in being taken for good listeners than in really hearing what we have to say. Real listening means setting all that aside. Good listeners don't act needy. They don't charm, flatter, provoke, or interrupt. None of that *look at me, listen to me, admire me, appreciate me.* None of that. They suspend the self and listen.

APPRECIATING THE OTHER PERSON'S POINT OF VIEW

Understanding one another is a give-and-take process. The best way to get the listening you need is to make the other person feel listened to first.

———◆———

Most people won't really listen or pay attention to your point of view until they become convinced that you've heard and appreciated theirs.

———◆———

Even when you're the one initiating a discussion about something of concern to you, the best way to ensure that you'll be heard is to invite the other person to explain his viewpoint before you present yours. Suspending your agenda so as to hear the other person out enables you to understand what he thinks, helps make him feel understood, and clears the way for him to be more willing to listen to you.

Let the other person know you're interested in what he has to say by inviting him to say what's on his mind, what his opinion is, or how he feels about the issue under consideration—and then giving him your full attention.

"Can we talk about . . . ? What do you think we should do?"

"I'm not sure I really understand how you feel about. . . . What *is* your point of view?"

"I'm sorry we had this misunderstanding. I'd really like to hear what happened as far as you're concerned."

"You seem upset with me. Am I right about that?"

Elicit the other person's thoughts and feelings about the subject at hand by asking specific questions that show your grasp of what she's said and encouraging her to elaborate.

"So what you're saying is. . . . Is that right?"

"I think I understand what you're saying, but I want to be sure. Do you mean . . . ?"

"I'm not sure I really understand what you mean. You're saying . . . but I wish you'd say more about your position so I can get it straight."

"I think I understand where we disagree, but I'm not sure. Did you mean that . . . ?"

If you feel yourself getting impatient or defensive while the other person is speaking, it's important to restrain your urge to respond until you've heard her out. Just keeping your mouth shut and pretending to listen may be better than interrupting, but it isn't the same as really listening. To really listen, try hard to appreciate what the other person is feeling. Imagine how you'd feel if you were in her shoes.

———◆———

Anytime you demonstrate a willingness to listen with a minimum of defensiveness, criticism, or impatience, you are giving the gift of understanding—and earning the right to have it reciprocated.

———◆———

Suspending your needs long enough to hear the other person out is part of willing yourself to listen. But suspending your needs is not the same thing as becoming a nonself.

Sometimes you need to recognize that you can't suspend the self effectively until you fulfill its needs. So while it might seem selfish, in fact telling your spouse that you do want to hear about his day but you have to get your own problem off your chest first may not be. By the same token, there are times when the most considerate and honest thing you can say to someone who wants to talk when you aren't up to listen-

ing is "I really can't concentrate on what you're saying right now. Can we talk in about twenty minutes?" Trying to listen when you're really not up to it dries up your capacity to empathize.

Some listeners are so fearful of exerting their own individuality that they become nonselves, tucked into others, embedded in a safe framework of obligations and duties. These people find it easier to accommodate than to deal with conflict, threats of rejection, arguments, or signs of distress in others. Their anxious, demanding partners are frequently unaware of how much their mates accommodate to preserve harmony. They take it for granted and want more. Such compliant people may seem like good listeners, but you aren't really listening if you're nothing but a passive receptacle, a reluctant sponge.

Listening well is often silent but never passive.

Instead of listening passively, and maybe feeling a little trapped, get involved actively by asking specific questions that help the other person express his feelings or elaborate on what he's thinking.

"What does he do that bothers you the most?"

"What do you think she should do?"

"It sounds great. What was the best part?"

"What did you feel like saying to her?"

"What would you *have liked* to hear him say?"

Real listening means imagining yourself into the other's experience: concentrating, asking questions. Understanding is furthered not by knowing ("I understand") but by investigating— asking for elaboration, inquiring into the concrete particularity of the speaker's experience. The good listener is not a passive receptor but an active, open one, attuned and inquiring.

AFFIRMING YOUR UNDERSTANDING

Once in a while we all pretend we're listening when we're not. In spite of this, we're genuinely taken aback when someone accuses us of not listening when in fact we were. One reason people wonder if we're listening is that we sometimes fail to let them know that we heard them. Silence is ambiguous.

Without some sign of understanding, the speaker begins to wonder if what she's saying makes sense, if it's worth talking about. Doubts surface. *Maybe I'm boring him. Maybe I shouldn't be complaining like this.* Without some reassuring evidence of empathy, people don't trust us enough to tell us the simple truth about their feelings, much less to reveal potentially dangerous truths. Everyone is vulnerable in this sense, and everyone holds back in many ways.

Ordinarily we take turns talking. The roles of speaker and listener alternate so naturally that it may be artificial to call what one person says "the listener's response." Responding turns listeners into speakers. But listening well is a two-step process: First we take in what the speaker says, then we let him or her know it. A failed response is like an unanswered letter; you never know if you got through.

Repeating the other person's position in your own words is the best way to show that you understand. But effective listening is achieved not by summing up what the other person said as though that should be the end of it but as a means of inviting him to elaborate so that you can *really* understand.

---◆---

Effective communication isn't achieved simply by taking turns talking; it requires a concerted effort at mutual understanding.

---◆---

The best way to promote understanding is to take time to restate the other person's position in your own words, then ask her to correct or affirm your understanding of her thoughts and feelings. If you work on this process of explicit feedback and confirmation until the other person has no doubt that you grasp her position, she will feel understood—and she will then be more open to hearing from you.

"So you're saying that you don't think Kevin should join Little League because it will put a lot of unnecessary competitive pressure on him and because you'll be the one who gets stuck driving him to all the games?"

"Let me make sure I understand what you're saying. You feel that you're always the one who calls when we get together, and that makes you wonder if I really want to spend time with you. Is that right?"

"OK, I want to make sure I understand. You're saying we should hire Gloria but that we should make it very clear to her what we ex-

pect, and we should be very serious about the probationary period, and if she doesn't do the job we should let her go at the end of six months. Have I got that right?"

"So all this time you've been feeling that I'm mad at you, and that's why I've stopped being affectionate. No wonder you're upset. You must have been feeling hurt for a long time."

"You Just Don't Get It, Do You?"

When one person says, "The world is round," and the other replies, "No, it's flat," it's clear that the second person got the first person's point and disagreed. But when the subject is more personal, disagreement—without some acknowledgment of the other person's point of view—can come across as invalidating the speaker's feelings and opinions. If people spoke like self-help manuals, they might say "I see what you're saying, but I don't agree." But since most of us not only don't speak like self-help manuals but often react in heat and haste, many conversations take on the form of two-part disharmony.

———◆———

The simple failure to acknowledge what the other person says explains much of the friction in our lives.

———◆———

The more heated the exchange, the more important it is to acknowledge what the other person says. When two people are talking about something important to them, each feels an urgent need to get his or her point of view across. But without some acknowledgment, each may continue to restate his or her position, thinking *If only he [or she] would see what I'm saying, we wouldn't have to keep arguing like this.*

One Friday night, after an especially long and tedious week, Sheila said to Rob, "We never go out." Rob, feeling attacked, said, "That's not true! We went out last week." This just upset Sheila more, and she renewed her attempt to get Rob to understand what she was feeling. "You mean when we went out with Linda and John for pizza? I don't call that going out. You never want to do anything but sit around in front of that stupid TV set." Now Rob was pissed. "Listen, I work hard all week, and if I want to relax on the couch, what's so wrong with that?" By this point Sheila felt completely invalidated. "You just don't

get it, do you?" she said. Then she went upstairs to the bedroom and slammed the door.

Maybe you can identify with Sheila. Or Rob. Or both of them. The choice between going out and vegging out is one that most of us have feelings about. But what was especially unfortunate in this quarrel that left both Sheila and Rob feeling so misunderstood and unappreciated was that neither one took the time to acknowledge the other's point of view.

———◆———

You don't have to be *responsible* for someone's feelings to be *aware* of them—and to acknowledge them.

———◆———

When Sheila said, "We never go out," she was expressing a feeling— she's bored and a little lonely—and making a request: she wishes that she and Rob could have a little more fun, do something together, maybe be a little closer. But something about the way she said it (or he heard it) made Rob defensive. Instead of showing that he understood what she was feeling by acknowledging what she was saying, he just felt criticized. He heard her saying that he was lazy, selfish, uninvolved—just the things he worries he might be—and so he didn't listen to her feelings, much less respond calmly to her request.

Dueling Points of View

When two people keep restating their own positions without acknowledging what the other one is trying to say, the result is dueling points of view. One is tempted—especially if one is a therapist—to think of two people involved in dueling declarations as simply lacking a communicational skill, that of paraphrasing what your conversation partner says before responding. The trouble with this communication-as-skill perspective is that it leaves out conflict and anxiety, precisely the things that make understanding each other so difficult. The partners who don't acknowledge what each other says are afraid to. They're afraid that to acknowledge what the other one says means surrender—"You're right and I'm wrong." Unfortunately, as in many vicious circles, their efforts to break through to each other by restating their own positions just locks misunderstanding in place.

When the subject isn't too emotional, the result is a mildly unsatisfying sense of at least having said what you mean, even if the other

person didn't acknowledge it. But when feeling runs high, dueling declarations escalate into painful misunderstandings.

Professional advice givers often talk as though couples could get along fine if only they'd learn "to communicate"—making "I" statements and all the rest. That's nice, but it overlooks the existence of real conflict.

Although they hadn't really discussed it, Charlotte assumed that once Hugh finished his Ph.D. they would move back to the city they were from. But Hugh liked where they were living, and when he announced that he might take a teaching job at the university, Charlotte felt betrayed.

Because the question of where to live was so important to both of them, they found it difficult to talk about it without disparaging each other's point of view. When Hugh presented his arguments for staying, Charlotte would try to discredit them or say that he had a responsibility to make up to her the sacrifice she had made in leaving the city for the sake of his career. He'd respond by talking about the sacrifices he'd made for her. Later, after months of estrangement, Charlotte said that if at any point in the process Hugh had acknowledged that she had given up a lot for his schooling or had said that she would get her turn later, she could have agreed to stay. But instead of listening and acknowledging her right to feel the way she did, Hugh responded by saying that his career was more important than hers.

In another couple that faced the same issue, both wanted to move; the problem was where. Raymond was an accountant and Joyce was the dean of women at a small college. Both agreed that since he would be able to find work more easily, her search for another deanship should be given priority. Raymond, however, felt strongly about *where* he wanted to live. It wasn't so much a regional preference as wanting to live either in a big city or well out into the country—anything but suburbia, where Lawn Doctor was king. And so half the time when Joyce told him that she'd read about a job opening, he'd respond by saying "I'd never live *there*." She'd feel defeated and angry and think he was being totally unreasonable.

Why did Hugh find it necessary to put Charlotte down by saying that his career was more important than hers? And why did Raymond have to reject so many of Joyce's possibilities so quickly? What made it so hard for these two husbands even to acknowledge what their wives were feeling?

Hugh was apparently afraid that acknowledging Charlotte's feelings would automatically lead to giving in and acting on their dictates.

Likewise, Raymond didn't seem to have the confidence that he could still say no to a potential new place after he and Joyce had visited it. Otherwise, why wouldn't he agree to at least take a look? Why weren't these two men able to listen better to their wives? Is it simply "selfishness" or "masculine insensitivity" or "immaturity" that prevents people from hearing each other? Maybe Hugh and Raymond had trouble listening to their partners because they felt anxious and insecure about their own ability to assert themselves. Maybe we—men and women—always have reasons for not listening, not understanding one another.

————◆————

Listening is hard because it involves a loss of control—and if you're afraid of what you might hear, it feels unsafe to relinquish control.

————◆————

He Says, She Says

He says, "You should have said something." She says, "You should have asked." And neither one feels heard. She talks about the things she'd like to do around the house, and he talks about being tired. He never hears what doing these things means to her, and she never hears that he wishes they could have more fun. Arguments escalate, feelings go unrecognized, and minds don't meet as long as we fail to acknowledge what the other person says before we respond with what we have to say.

————◆————

He says, she says—but neither acknowledges what the other one says.

————◆————

Behavior therapists teach married couples to paraphrase what their partners say before going on to give their side. This is a device to interrupt the cross-complaining that keeps couples in conflict from ever feeling understood, much less actually doing anything about each other's complaints. If a husband tells his wife that he wishes she would cook something different for supper, and she gets angry and complains that he's impossible to please—and he gets defensive and withdraws to brood over how unfair she is—neither one of them will feel understood. This misunderstanding—and many others like it—has less to do with being unable to resolve conflict than with being unable to tolerate it. If instead of

getting defensive and attacking, either person would simply acknowledge what the other said, it might not prove so difficult to come together.

Even when conflict is serious, we all feel better if we can at least say how we feel—what bothers us and what we wish—and have the other person say those reassuring words "I understand how you feel."

Here's an example. The vast majority of people I talk with have less than happy sex lives. Maybe mine is a biased sample, but many of the people I see who've been married for ten years or more have sex maybe once a month or every six months or even less. Even when they bring themselves to consult a therapist, few people mention this issue. Not only are they embarrassed (most people assume that most other people are successful parents and have happy sex lives), but also they've given up hope. Why talk about something so personal and painful when all their previous efforts have only made them angry and ashamed?

Once they do find the courage to talk about problems in their sexual relationship, some couples are able to make changes for the better, while others aren't. But they almost all feel better for talking about it. What makes them feel better, even if nothing changes, is being able to say how they feel about it, what they don't like, what they wish, and to admit feeling guilty and inadequate—something each partner inevitably feels and inevitably doesn't realize the other one feels.

Why do people need a therapist to have these conversations? They don't. *If* they can each say how they feel about the situation, *and* the other can *hear and acknowledge* these feelings before going on to say how he or she feels.

Most of us are reactive when it comes to sex, but some people are reactive to so many things that they fail to acknowledge what anyone else says about anything. If you complain to such people that they always argue and don't listen, they may protest that you're only asking them to agree with you. They're not aware that it takes some kind of acknowledgment of what we're saying for us to feel not agreed with but heard.

THE IMPORTANCE OF RELINQUISHING CONTROL

As I've said, I don't care to be interrupted in the middle of talking about an experience, by someone either giving advice I didn't ask for or "sharing" a similar experience. Interruption is interruption. What's missing in both cases is some kind of expression of understanding and ac-

knowledgment, something like "Gee, that's lousy." What's going on in both cases—and others—is that the listener just won't relinquish control over the exchange. Many of us are convinced that we're good listeners because we do and say all the right things. But do we? Often the speaker ends up feeling unheard, because what we're really doing is going through the motions, serving our own purposes.

"Why Don't You Just . . . ?"

A wise supervisor once told me that my treatment of a shy, overweight young man was bogged down because I was trying to change him before he felt understood and accepted by me. To me it seemed so simple: if the young man would only make a little effort to initiate conversations with people, at the same time we explored the roots of his insecurity, we could work toward change on two fronts. He, however, felt that my suggesting that he simply start doing what he found so difficult proved that I didn't understand how painfully self-conscious he was. The supervisor's technical recommendation (which had to do with transference and countertransference) was "Shut up and listen."

A Gaping Silence

If everyone followed my supervisor's advice, the world would be a better place. But if listening were only a negative accomplishment, we could concentrate (as many therapists and people playing therapist do) on restraining ourselves and not interrupting. Speakers may be gratified at being allowed to say what's on their minds but frustrated by the absence of curiosity and appreciation. This means that, taken too literally, "shut up and listen" isn't enough to convey understanding. If you're telling someone at a party about what kind of work you do and she's listening without interrupting, but her eyes are wandering around the room, you hardly feel listened to.

Whether or not someone is really listening only that person truly knows. But, on the other hand, if someone doesn't feel listened to, he doesn't feel listened to. We judge whether or not others are listening to us by the signals we see. Are they showing that they're paying attention by setting aside distractions and turning toward us?

Before they comment on what we're saying, people show interest and attention by maintaining eye contact, smiling with pleasure or frowning with concern, and making little interjections like "uh-huh" and "real-

ly?" Head nods also show attention; larger and repeated ones show agreement. You don't have to take Elementary Clinical Methods to learn these responses; they follow from taking an interest.

The Leading Question

Questions also convey interest, but sometimes the interest they convey is tangential to what we're trying to say. Sometimes the distraction is obvious. If you're trying to tell a friend about the inconsiderate things your husband did on your vacation, and she interrupts with a lot of questions about where you stayed, you certainly don't feel listened to. At other times people seem to be following but can't help trying to steer. These listeners impose their own narrative structures on our experience. Their questions assume that our stories should fit their scripts: "Problems should be denied or made to go away"; "Everyone should be together"; "Men are insensitive"; "Bullies must be confronted." By finishing our sentences, pumping us with questions, and otherwise pushing us to say what they want to hear, controlling listeners violate our right to tell our own tales.

HOW TO GET THE LISTENING YOU DESERVE

(The devil just whispered in my ear that maybe I should make that ". . . The Listening You *Want*." Maybe we already get the listening we deserve. But I'm not going to listen to that old devil.)

How to Ask for Support without Getting Unwanted Advice

One way to get the listening you need is to tell people what you want.

"I'm upset and I need to talk to you. Just listen, OK?"

"I have a problem that I need to discuss, but I'm not ready to decide what to do, so it would be helpful if you could just listen to me."

If you don't want a reactive or intrusive response, anticipate your listener's expectations.

"I'm not asking you to agree with me, but can you understand where I'm coming from?"

"I want to tell you something and I don't want you to get mad at me. Just listen and think about what I'm saying, will you?"

"I want your opinion about something, but then I'll have to figure out what I want to do. Will you give me some advice, even if I don't end up following it?"

If someone gives advice when you just want to be listened to, by all means say so. But put the emphasis on what you want, not on how intrusive she is: "Thanks for the advice, but right now I just want to tell you what happened and have you understand how I feel" works better than "I didn't ask for advice. Just listen, will you?" or "Can't you just listen for once, without always having to tell me what to do?"

How to Handle Interruptions

If you're driving down the road and someone cuts in front of you, there's not much you can do about it. Oh, you can hit your horn and call the other person a certain member of the canine family if you wish. But you pretty much have to yield unless you want your car smashed up. The same is not true when somebody cuts in when you're talking. You can't be interrupted unless you allow it. When you're talking, you have the right of way.

If someone starts to interrupt, you can:

- Hold up your index finger.
- Say "Wait a minute, I'm not finished."
- Just keep talking: "What I was trying to say is. . . ."

If someone does cut you off:

- Instead of getting upset (or instead of *just* getting upset), practice saying, "I wasn't finished; please hear me out." Then go back to what you were saying and finish saying it.
- Comment on feeling cut off, but without lecturing or attacking:

  "I wish you'd let me finish what I was saying."

  "I'm sorry, but I can't pay attention to your story because I wasn't finished telling mine."

"I was trying to tell you something that's important to me. When you start talking about something else out of the blue, I feel like you're not interested in me or what I have to say."

"I was listening to that story on the news. I wish you'd wait a minute before breaking in."

HOW TO LISTEN TO PEOPLE
WHO AREN'T EASY TO LISTEN TO

If you're unlucky enough to have someone in your life who's always talking about himself or herself, you might appreciate some advice about how to change that person. The best I can offer is the suggestion to think systemically.

People who talk too much are difficult to endure, but their need for our attention is genuine. Their neediness is a burden, but they shouldn't be made to feel ashamed of it. Shaming people for their needs makes them feel worse and intensifies the need. Even if we don't criticize someone for talking too much, our not listening to them has an isolating effect, which only increases their yearning to be heard.

When we describe someone as self-centered or say that he's always talking about himself, we are in fact describing only half of a relationship. In twenty-five years of counseling couples, I have rarely met a spouse who doesn't think he or she does an unequal share of listening in the relationship. This isn't to say that there aren't people who talk about themselves more than others, but if we turn away from the needs of those we love, we are part of the problem.

One of the secrets to dealing with the difficult people in our lives is to figure out how to play the hand we're dealt, rather than fretting and moaning about what that hand is. The reason some people in our lives remain one-dimensional is because that's as far as we go with them. Part of the reason your father-in-law always wants to talk about himself is that you rarely listen, or listen only halfheartedly. As long as he feels unlistened to himself, he's not likely to have much real interest in what anyone else has to say. If instead of stewing in the trapped anxiety of someone with nothing to do but flinch, you listen a little more to someone who talks too much, you might find the balance of the relationship shifting. Even a small shift can make a big difference.

RESISTING THE TEMPTATION TO TURN AWAY

At times when we want to control others' access to us, we may avoid looking at a person who is seeking our attention. A man watching television who doesn't wish to be interrupted may avoid looking at his wife when she tries to speak to him. Similarly, a waitress may prevent a customer from catching her eye to prevent his initiating an order or another request she's too harried to fulfill at the moment.

A paradoxical example of this responsive unavailability occurs in psychoanalysis, where the analyst sits behind the recumbent patient and out of view. The result is disconcerting. Unable to see how the therapist is responding, the patient is unsure of being understood and sympathized with. Unable to provide visible evidence of interest, the therapist may feel equally uncomfortable. Eventually, however, this constrained arrangement turns out to be liberating. The patient, who gets to trust that he won't be interrupted or prompted, learns to follow his own thoughts more fully and to express them more freely. The therapist discovers that looking off into space with no pressure to demonstrate interest enables him or her to listen more freely and to think about what's being said.

What is to be learned from the analyst being liberated to listen by not having to appear attentive? We've noted that listening well means suspending our needs, including the need to *do* something—to solve problems, to say the right thing, even to act attentive. Better to *be* attentive. Be interested. Listen hard. And overcome the need to get credit for listening.

It may not be possible in everyday life to offer that perfect and silent listening in which analytic patients are encouraged to reveal and reconstruct themselves. If people have learned not to expect careful listening from us, we may have to reassure them of our interest. But if we listen carefully, people will learn to trust us. Just listening, without interrupting or turning away, goes a long way toward establishing that trust.

CHAPTER EIGHT

"I Never Knew You Felt That Way"

EMPATHY BEGINS WITH OPENNESS

Among the unhelpful expectations we bring to listening are preconceived notions about *what* the speaker is going to say and *how* communication should take place. Assuming you know what someone is going to say means you don't have to bother to listen.

Assumptions about how people should talk to each other aren't usually conscious; they're part of the way we were brought up. Assuming that your way of communicating is the only one means you'll have trouble relating to people with different conversational styles and sensitivities. Interestingly, such assumptions come in pairs of opposites, such as: polite people make requests indirectly versus honest people ask directly for what they what; explanations should be short and sweet (rambling on is boring and pushy) versus explanations should be thorough and complete (make sure the other person understands exactly what you mean).

The listener who settles for confirming his expectations, like the museum-goer who looks at paintings only long enough to confirm the name of the artist, is in danger of never getting closer to another person's experience. There is no bridge of understanding, no touching. The listener who remains open, on the other hand, experiences from time to time surprise and delight as his assumptions topple and he discovers the speaker—child, spouse, friend—in a deeper, fuller way.

The essence of good listening is empathy, achieved by being receptive to *what* other people are trying to say and *how* they express themselves. Empathy takes an open mind to other sensibilities.

Although most people would vastly improve their listening by setting aside preconceived notions and remaining open to what the speaker
is trying to say, total innocence of assumptions is neither possible nor
desirable. Anticipation is useful. Anticipating how someone might react
can help you express yourself more effectively; anticipating a speaker's
needs and style of communicating can help you hear all levels of messages being sent. So, what am I saying? Are expectations a help or a
hindrance to good listening?

Expectations hamper communication when they take the form of
fixed assumptions and egocentric perspectives. Such expectations (1)
are unexamined and (2) close us to other points of view. Expectations
promote communication when they take the form of sensitivity to our
own and other people's styles of communicating. Such sensitivities make
us aware, thoughtful, and open, not biased.

CREATING A CLIMATE OF UNDERSTANDING

One of the most common expectations we bring to our conversational
encounters, especially at home, is that we will be able to communicate
just by doing what comes naturally. Unfortunately, the listening we
do on automatic pilot is often perfunctory, precisely the kind of half-
hearted or indifferent listening that makes our relationships less fulfilling than they could be, should be. If you want to make any relationship
more rewarding, practice *responsive listening.*

Responsive listening means hearing the other person out, then letting him know what you understand him to be saying. If you're right,
the speaker will feel a grateful sense of being understood. If you didn't
quite get what he intended to say, your feedback allows him another
chance to explain.

Responsive listening can be practiced like any other skill if you're
willing to put in the effort. If.

Think of how many situations where familiarity, tension, or distraction, has made you get out of the habit of being attentive,
considerate—concerned. The next time your partner comes home at
the end of the day, or your child runs to tell you something, or someone at work wants to talk, try making an extra effort to be attentive.

Paying attention goes a long way. Your effort to listen a little longer and more carefully to others will, if you stick to it, initiate a positive spiral in all your relationships.

"I KNOW WHAT YOU'RE GOING TO SAY"

"Like hell, you do!" Have you ever felt like saying that when someone cuts you off? Unfortunately, jumping to conclusions is something we all do at times. You may not actually make the remark I've used as a head for this section, but one of the bad listening habits we all need to break is making too many assumptions about what people are going to say.

Rachel gets home at six-thirty instead of six as she'd promised and says, "I'm sorry I was late, I . . . "

"That's OK," Patrick breaks in to say, "the kids and I made spaghetti. It's all ready."

Rachel is grateful not to have to cook supper but still feels cut off. She was about to tell Patrick that she was late because her boss dumped a last-minute assignment on her, but his assumption that she was about to apologize for inconveniencing him made her feel that he didn't care. All he was interested in, it seemed to her, was his supper.

She could have told him anyway, right? Maybe. But if he's in the habit of cutting her off, she may get tired of trying to force him to listen to her.

Cutting someone off to take over conversational control can certainly be annoying, but so can jumping in before a speaker is finished with words of encouragement, agreement, or to tell a similar story.

At first Hank appreciated Sharon's habit of interjecting little expressions of support when he talked to her. Her *wows*, *gees*, and *what a shames* made him think she was tuned in to his feelings. But after a while these expressions seemed effusive and predictable. They began to make him feel that she was more interested in coming across as supportive than in really listening to him.

Being supportive means neither anticipating nor exceeding a speaker's own expression of feeling. I knew a woman who was so supportive that waves of compassion radiated from her like hot air from a clothes dryer. She may have been trying to be sensitive, but after a while I was

reminded of the Al Franken refrain: "You're good enough, you're smart enough, and doggone it, people like you!"

"Oh, I know what you mean!" Celia said. "My principal treats me the same way." Though she intends to establish empathy, Todd is annoyed. He doubts that her principal really does give her as many last-minute assignments as his boss gives him. Besides, that wasn't his point. He never got to make his point because Celia cut him off to demonstrate that she understood.

The best way to avoid cutting people off is to concentrate on what they're trying to say. Give them a chance to make their point, acknowledge it, and *then* say your piece. Don't pounce at the first pause. Let the other person finish. Inhibit the impulse to switch the focus to you and what's on your mind. Don't tell every story that crops into your head. (I wince as I write this.) Stop and consider whether your comment would contribute to the conversation or disrupt it.

If you make a habit of talking out of turn, people will consider you intrusive. If you get excited and do jump in before the other person has finished, try to catch yourself and back off politely. Say "Go ahead" or even those magic words "I'm sorry."

Even if you *do* know what somebody is going to say, he or she still needs to say it—and have you listen and then acknowledge it—before feeling understood. If conversation were an aerial dogfight, maybe it would be expedient to anticipate the other person's moves so as to shoot them down as fast as possible. But conversation needn't be like that. The person who has something to say wants to express both an idea and a feeling. Listening with an open mind gives you a chance to discover what's on her mind and gives her a chance to clarify her own thinking and feeling. The gift of your silent attention allows you to understand—and the other person to *feel* understood.

HOW TO MOVE BEYOND ASSUMPTIONS
TO OPENNESS AND EMPATHY

The psychoanalyst Wilfred Bion[1] said that to listen well we must "set aside memory, desire, and judgment." This admonition is a formula for openness, calling as it does for listeners to suspend preconceptions, as-

---

[1] Wilfred Bion, *Transformations* (New York: Jason Aronson, 1983).

sumptions, needs, and wishes. Real listening is an act of self-transcendence.

However much the people we live with, work with, or just hang around with care about being with us, they're still largely preoccupied with their own agendas: worries, problems, projects, grudges, hopes, dreams. Even (or especially) if unspoken, such personal agendas are compelling and absorbing. As long as they remain private, these preoccupations have a tendency to separate us from each other. Shared thoughts and feelings, on the other hand, are a step toward each other. Empathy is the bridge.

An empathic friend or family member inquires and acknowledges what we're thinking and feeling, and thus confirms our experience. In this way the empathic listener vitalizes us by emotional participation and reflection—feeding back to us—what we sometimes experience as inchoate.

People live in their own personal and subjective worlds. To meet, truly meet, means that they must open up this part of themselves, feel it, and share it. And it must be received. Much of the time we hide away our real feelings, sometimes even from ourselves. As a result our conversational encounters, like our relationships themselves, often consist of shadows dancing with each other.

Empathy bridges the gap between us, but it requires a real effort at openness. Too many assumptions are inimical to understanding. You can hardly listen and take in anything like the full richness of someone else's experience if you're only waiting for your turn to pounce. Empathy takes restraint; it takes work.

The empathic listener offers a bond of understanding in a deep sense. It's more than the friendly sympathy you might get from your Aunt Rose; it's a deeper resonance of understanding. Perhaps you remember a time when you were hurt or scared and a friend put a hand on your shoulder. Empathy is like that.

Empathic listening means working a little harder at understanding the other person before asking him to do the same for you. It means demonstrating your understanding with comments that draw out thoughts and feelings: "Uh-huh," "I see," "Yes." Simple empathic comments express understanding and help reach something unexpressed in the other person's experience. This helps break down the denial of feeling that keeps us apart. Denial is unnecessary with someone who cares and understands.

The empathic listener celebrates the naturalness of what is felt—

"No wonder you were mad!"—against a person's need to deny what he or she feels.

Empathy is achieved by suspending your own preoccupations and assumptions and placing yourself attentively at the service of the other person, being alert to what he's saying and to the emotional subtext. It means listening without being in a hurry to take over.

Empathy requires two kinds of activity. The first is receptivity and openness, like a moviegoer who allows himself to be absorbed in and moved by the actors and their stories. The second is an oscillation between thinking and feeling. This requires a deliberate shift from feeling *with* a speaker to thinking *about* her. What is she saying? Meaning? Feeling?

Suppose your mate comes home and says he's had a bad day and is upset. You know what that feels like. You're sympathetic. So you ask what happened. He says he's going to have to go out of town again next week. His boss wants him to represent the agency at a big meeting in Buffalo, and he's not looking forward to it.

You know how he feels. All that travel. And Buffalo of all dreary places! Maybe that's how *you'd* feel. You don't look forward to business travel because you don't like to be away from home.

Your own feelings make you sympathetic. But empathy, real empathy, requires a second step: thinking *about* the other person. How does *his* "not looking forward" feel?

Maybe he's excited about being chosen to speak for the agency. It's a chance to show the boss he can handle more responsibility. But maybe that makes him nervous. Speaking in public is a lot harder when your agenda is trying to prove yourself.

Whether or not your partner gets to talk about these issues, to discover and share *his* feelings, depends on how empathically you listen. If you want to know how someone feels, ask, and then listen.

———◆———

Do you rely on sympathy and presume you understand, or do you use empathy and work at it?

———◆———

Suspending preconceived notions and remaining open to what the other person has to say is easier in the absence of conflict. Being at odds with someone means that you have your own agenda and the pressure of the situation makes you anxious to press your point of view. But since two force fields can't occupy the same space at the same time, even if your only objective is to get your point of view across, the most

effective way to do so is to set aside your assumptions and hear the other person out first—make him feel understood and taken into account. Here are a couple of examples:

A few years ago someone who was editing a book on psychoanalytic therapy changed jobs and asked me to take over for him. I was delighted—until I saw that most of the chapters weren't very good. It was hard for me, a young and relatively unknown psychologist, to convince the authors, who were big shots, to do the necessary work. One of the authors, however, who was junior even to me, called every week, asking how the book was coming and offering to be my co-editor. Then I read his chapter. It wasn't the worst, but it was weak. Trying to be diplomatic, I returned the manuscript, praising its strong points and asking for a few minor but essential changes. Three months went by. Then I received a letter thanking me for my "suggestions" but saying that a couple of his friends had read over his chapter and agreed with him that it was perfect the way it was.

Argh! After counting to ten (about twenty times), I wrote saying that he seemed to be upset about something and I was interested in hearing about it. He called the day he received my letter and told me with a lot of feeling how hard he'd worked on his chapter and how much rewriting the previous editor had already put him through. I didn't really have to say anything. He was so appreciative of my listening to him that as soon as he finished complaining he thanked me for being understanding and said he'd be glad to make the changes I'd asked for.

Frankly I hadn't really been interested in this man's feelings, but to be able to negotiate with him—all I really wanted—I had to hear him out first, or he never would have been receptive.

With someone you do care about, empathic openness is more than a useful strategy. It's the essential means of discovering what things look like from inside that person's world.

Linda *knew* Andrew didn't want to spend time with her. He was married to his career. That's why she'd developed so many outside interests over the years. Now that the children had gone off into the wide world, Linda began to sense the marriage entering its second death. Maybe it was time to turn off the life supports. She dreamed of freedom. What had she expected when she married? Attention, shared interests, affection, conversation. What she had was what she did on her own.

And Andrew? After years of career success, he was becoming a failure at loneliness. He longed to be closer to Linda, to share something more

than domestic arrangements. He dreamed of love. Unfortunately they'd gotten out of the habit of talking. He went about his business in the armor of indifference.

When Linda came to talk to me—maybe a therapist would tell her what she wanted to hear—I tried to point out one reason she felt stuck: she wasn't open to the possibility of trying to talk to her husband, trying to rekindle some basis for staying together other than sharing children.

Linda had assumed that nothing would change and so it would be a waste of time talking to Andrew. When Linda tried to open up and talk to Andrew, she found out he had just assumed she no longer wanted to be involved with him, so he didn't say anything.

Such assumptions are protective. They keep us from getting our hopes up and our feelings hurt. But they also keep us from getting through to each other.

———◆———

Most of our assumptions about why communication breaks down are about the other guy. We take our own input for granted.

———◆———

After their talk Linda and Andrew did get a little closer. Not a lot, but enough to make a difference. Shared understanding was the first step.

———◆———

You can get through to most people, even on difficult subjects, by first listening to their side of the issue and then, in a low-key but firm manner, insisting that they at least listen to your side of things.

———◆———

Openness may be the key to listening, but not total openness, as in a blank screen. Real receptivity must be informed by sensitivity to the other person.

SENSITIVITY: EXPECTATIONS AT THEIR BEST

One of the things we learn after a while—sometimes a long while—is that different people have different emotional needs. If, for example, you need time alone when you're stressed out, it might be hard to remem-

ber that in the same circumstances the first thing your partner wants is to talk. Different people also have different ways of communicating.

To listen well, and be listened to in return, we have to develop some sensitivity to other people's conversational styles. The automatic rhythms and nuances of a person's conversational style include such things as whether descriptions are detailed or summarized, whether the pace of speaking is fast or slow, and whether who-said-what-to-whom or what-I'm-working-on-now is the preferred topic.

To Naomi, loud, overlapping talk is a sign of enthusiasm and mutual involvement. To Wardell, it's a sign of rudeness and not listening.

Hannah asks for details; Ivan feels interrogated.

Rick wants Sherry to get to the point. She feels that he isn't interested in what she had to say.

Veronica likes to talk things over at length. She complains that Chet is always leaving the room. Chet replies that Veronica says something and he responds, then when he's on the way to finish what he was about to do, she gets mad.

Listening between intimates often erodes over time because the only way they know to solve problems is to talk things out. But when different styles of communicating cause problems, talking doesn't help. Trying harder, if it means doing more of the same, only makes matters worse.

People who try to communicate indirectly feel that someone close to them should know what they like and dislike without having to say so. Direct communicators feel, "We should be able to tell each other what we want."

Being sensitive to other people's conversational ways doesn't mean you have to have them all figured out. It means you should be attentive and tolerant. If you're used to a New York City pace and you're listening to a languid southern speaker whose conversation is like an old hound dog that stops at every tree, relax. Be patient. You might even get to enjoy your differences.

Unfortunately, when conversational styles differ, misunderstandings multiply. It's difficult to straighten out such misunderstandings if each one is convinced of the rightness of his or her position and the wrongness of the other's.

Belinda and her husband were at a New Year's Eve party at his parents' house. Halfway through the evening, Belinda's mother-in-law

came over and whispered, "Loosen up, have some fun. Don't be so formal!"

Belinda was cut to the quick. She had been having fun. She'd had several enjoyable conversations with her husband's cousins and aunts and uncles. She wasn't being formal; she was being herself.

Belinda was pissed. *Who does that woman think she is? Did I say anything to her about cackling hysterically whenever anybody made the slightest joke?* In fact, Belinda found the mother-in-law's loud show of emotion and high-pitched, relentless chatter quite annoying. It wasn't her style.

Both of these people were behaving in self-evidently appropriate ways, the ways they were brought up to talk and listen.

Some people consider their restrained style of speaking to be "polite." They may find people with a more expressive style to be "crude," "loud," "coarse," "histrionic," "vulgar." More emotive speakers may think of themselves as "open and honest," "warm," "friendly," "unaffected," while they think of the more restrained speakers as "aloof," "standoffish," "unfriendly," "distant," "emotionless."

(Notice, incidentally, how Belinda and her mother-in-law each addressed their differences in character. The mother-in-law was "honest" or "rude," depending on your point of view. Belinda was "polite" or "insincere," as you see it.)

Sensitivity means being responsive to the feelings of others. It doesn't mean assuming you know what they're going to say, but rather being interested and open enough to find out. On the other hand, sensitivity does mean using your knowledge of other people to understand their perspective and respect their individuality.

Some of the ways you can show sensitivity are:

- Paying attention to what the other person is saying
- Acknowledging the other person's feelings
- Listening without giving an opinion
- Listening without offering advice
- Listening without immediately agreeing or disagreeing
- Noticing how the other person appears to be feeling—and then asking
- Asking about his or her day, both before and after
- Respecting the person's need for quiet times
- Respecting the person's need to address problems
- Listening to but not pushing too hard for feelings

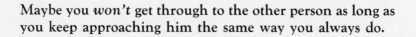

Maybe you *won't* get through to the other person as long as you keep approaching him the same way you always do.

We're Most Insensitive to Those We Love

What makes someone insensitive to what others are saying? To figure out why a listener becomes reactive instead of listening, consider where the anxiety might be coming from. It's always something specific. Sometimes the anxiety comes from stress—real or imagined. People resist both actual and threatened change. We think of powerful people as dominating relationships and perhaps therefore as not willing to listen, but in fact it's often the powerless who have trouble listening. The man who feels that he can't get his point of view across about the children may resist his wife's efforts to talk about them. The woman who doesn't feel entitled to say what she wants (or doesn't want) may resist her husband's attempts to talk about sex. Most people begin to listen better once they realize what power they do have in a relationship.

On the other hand, sometimes a person who clearly seems to have power in a relationship—a parent, say, or a dominating spouse— habitually doesn't listen to the other person. When a dominant person doesn't listen it's usually because some hidden emotional agenda is at work, making him anxious.

One afternoon Tommy came home from a long day at school with so much restless energy that he decided to mow the lawn. The machine plowed into the deep grass, releasing its familiar sweet smell. But Tommy hadn't gone ten feet when the mower stalled, its blade clogged with high, wet grass. After several frustrating starts and stops, he shoved the insubordinate machine back into the garage, stomped into the house cursing and banging, went up the stairs into his room, and slammed the door.

By this time Tommy's parents were home and heard his outburst. When his father asked him what was the matter, Tommy told him about his lousy day at school, then coming home and the lawn mower not working. He was frustrated and angry.

Instead of empathizing, his father gave him a lecture. "When you have a problem, it doesn't do anybody any good to lose control and start yelling. You have to stop and be calm. Nothing gets accomplished

when you get upset." As his father went on, Tommy's head sank slowly toward his chest.

"You can't cut grass when it's a foot high and be in a hurry. You've got to go through it very, very slow. You can't bull your way through anything—including life."

Tommy tried to explain. "Yeah, but when you've had a bad day at school and you come home and everything goes wrong, your anger keeps building. You've got to let it out somehow."

"Remember what we talked about last night? About problems? What did I say?"

"You said you've got to swallow your tongue." Tommy had stopped looking for sympathy. Now he was just trying to hang on to some of his pride.

But his father wasn't finished. "I also told you that problems when they're compounded make bigger problems. But if you take that problem and break it down, and make individual problems out of it, you can usually solve them very easily. Remember we talked about that?"

Tommy finally gave up trying to explain himself, and the conversation was finished.

This is a story of a father's failure to listen. The father asks his son why he's upset and then, when the boy tries to tell him, instead of listening, gives him a speech on the futility of anger, a lecture for a course the boy didn't sign up for. Tommy attempts to explain his feelings because he's looking for understanding. Instead he becomes a captive audience forced to listen to an account of his own inadequacies.

What's so hurtful in this encounter (and others like it) isn't that the father has a different perspective from his son; it's that, because of the feelings his son's behavior arouses in him, he tries to allay his own anxieties by pushing his perspective on the boy. In this scenario, Father knows best; Tommy's perspective carries no weight at all. It's never even acknowledged. The real impact of Father's lessons for living may be that Tommy grows up to be one of those people, like his father, with didactic views on everything—and unable to listen.

But *why* was Tommy's father so unable to listen to him explain that he was upset? What was so threatening? Anger.

Anger is a huge impediment to listening. Some people, like Tommy's father, are so reactive to anger that they can't tolerate even normal, healthy amounts of this basic human emotion. Other people are just the opposite: at the slightest provocation they flare up like a lit

match. In the next chapter we'll see how to cope with anger and how to keep it from spoiling listening.

Sensitivity to Other People's Inner Voices

One of the most common consequences of failing to be sensitive to other people's motivating expectations is giving them unwanted advice. When you're tempted to give the obvious types of advice mentioned in Chapter 5, remember those conflicting inner voices. Doing so not only might stop you from wasting your breath (and credibility) but also may give you a fresh perspective on the person's motivations and how to approach him or her about a touchy issue.

What if the issue has already touched off a tirade? The ideal response to the partner who goes into a rage about something is to acknowledge what he's feeling. Something's bothering him, and he's trying to tell you that. But there are times when most of us find listening to someone who's shrieking at us almost impossible. And so the question becomes not how to defuse the blowup but how to repair it afterward. That's when thinking about the other person's rage and your reaction in terms of subpersonalities can help you gain a little empathy and insight. Thinking of your partner's tirade as a childish tantrum may help you figure out that he feels weak and helpless, not powerful. Powerful people don't scream. But if screaming scares you (welcome to the club), when you calm down, if you consider what kind of person the screaming reduced you to (a scared kid, say), that in itself will help you recover your objective adult self when it comes to addressing the incident later.

"Have You Got a Minute?"

One way to use your sensitivity to *get* better listening is by not jumping in without considering whether or not the person you want to talk to is busy or preoccupied. People signal their openness to conversation by their posture. The person who looks up expectantly when you enter the room or walks right up to you with a greeting is probably open to talking. The person with her head down, looking away when you approach, or reading, intent on the TV, or otherwise distracted may not feel like chatting. If you really want to talk to such a person, use an orienting question. "Have you got a minute?" "Can I interrupt? There's something I'd like to ask you." It's like knocking to enter.

Recently Seymour started getting home from work an hour earlier. On the first day of the new schedule he looked forward to having a

chance to talk to his sixteen-year-old son before dinner. He came in the door and called hi, but there was no answer. Too bad, Jeremy must have stayed after school. But then a few minutes later, he heard Jeremy's radio on upstairs.

Seymour climbed halfway up the stairs and called out, "Hey, Jeremy, it's me, Dad. Come on downstairs. I want to talk to you."

A few moments later Jeremy came into the living room and said, "What did I do now?"

Seymour felt bad. Is that what their relationship had come to?

No, not really. Jeremy just felt off guard and misconstrued what his father meant. So now on days when he expects to be home early or wants to spend some time with Jeremy on the weekend, Seymour says something to him in the morning. "I'll be home by around five-thirty. Maybe we can visit before supper."

Expectations about how and when communication should take place work not when they're right or wrong but when they're shared.

"I HEARD YOU THE FIRST TIME!"

As we've seen, some of the assumptions about different ways men and women communicate have more to do with roles they play in relation to one another than to anything intrinsic to their sexes. Still, few complaints are more common from men than that the women in their lives nag.

Whenever a woman is perceived by a man as nagging, it probably means she hasn't received a fair hearing for her concerns in a long time. When our feelings are listened to sympathetically, we experience a sense of understanding and release. But if no one listens, we feel alone with our feelings and angry and unsupported in the relationship.

"He never notices how much I do around here. I never get any help without having to beg for it."

Not being listened to makes people feel ignored, frustrated, and resentful. No wonder they come across as nagging.

"She acts like she's my mother. Doesn't she know I always get my share of the chores done?"

Lloyd *hates* Cathy's nagging.

Stop leaving the bedroom window open; don't turn the heat up any higher than sixty-eight degrees. Do this, do that. She's always bitching about something. This he says to himself, and he gets no argument.

Cathy's bothered by the fact that Lloyd never listens to her. "Why do I have to tell you the same things over and over again? Why can't you listen to a simple request?" This she has said to him—often. To her friend Samantha she complains, "I try to tell him something, and he just goes underground, with no warning—and I'm left there, all alone."

If You're Considered a Nag

In a series of conversations between the same people, each encounter bears the burdens as well as the fruits of earlier ones. Persistent criticism or constant repetition of the same request creates a negative atmosphere and eventually results in the other person tuning the nagger out. I'm reminded of the Gary Larson cartoon in which a man is explaining something to his dog and all the dog hears is "blah-blah-blah."

The nagger becomes a nuisance. But what do you do if your persistent pleas to put dirty clothes in the hamper or clean up the mess in the bathroom go unheeded?

You're caught in the role of nag if even though you know somebody isn't going to remember to do something, you keep bugging him anyway; you never ask for anything just once; you come at the other person in a critical or complaining way; you get annoyed by lots of things the other person does *and* you keep letting him know it; you appeal to what "should" be done rather than what you want; the other person flinches when you make your request. You may not think of yourself as nagging, but if that's how the other person feels, he or she isn't likely to listen.

Here are some turnoffs that turn you into a nag: trying to improve your partner's behavior; offering unasked-for advice; trying to manipulate or punish; not acknowledging what he does, only complaining about what he hasn't done; expressing upset indirectly with an accusation that the other person should know how you feel.

———◆———

Nagging is in the ear of the beholder.

———◆———

Cut down on the number of things you ask people to do and the number of times you remind them. No fair, you say? You have a right to gripe? True, but asking less results in getting more. Pick out your most important concerns, make your requests clearly and directly, and make them sound like requests.

Listening is hard because it involves a loss of control, and if you're afraid of what you might hear, it may not feel safe to listen. Among the things that someone who feels nagged (even though he didn't listen the first twelve times) doesn't want to hear are blame and requests he doesn't think are open to discussion.

In all our communications we struggle to maintain our independence, to resist being controlled by others without sacrificing our involvement or losing their love. If someone hears your requests or complaints as implying power over him, he may resist—not because he's unwilling to do what you ask but because he's unwilling to accept the metamessage (implied or inferred) that you're the boss.

To avoid sounding controlling or dogmatic, add "What do you think?" after making a request or giving an opinion. This helps keep the airways open and the dialogue going. Also, emphasize how important the request is to you and be sure to understand the other person's perspective—"What do you think?" Then make sure that an agreement is really an agreement. If you aren't willing to accept "no," you can't trust the "yes" you do get.

People other than our intimates are more likely to listen to us airing our frustrations because they know it isn't their fault. If you want to get heard around the house more, try telling your partner "I know it's not your fault" or "I'm not blaming you." Then if he (or she) does listen, let him (or her) know you appreciate being listened to. "I feel relieved that I can talk about this. Thanks for listening."

Saying "I really appreciate when you listen to my feelings; it means a lot to me" encourages other people to listen more.

Finally, if you want to get out of the role of a nag, try listening to the recalcitrant other's side of things. Maybe the teenager who never cleans her room doesn't think it's fair to have to. After all, it's her room, isn't it? The husband who persists in running the washing machine with less than a full load may feel that he has a right to do so if he wants. Perhaps the wife whose husband always has to remind her to buy beer

when she gets groceries doesn't want to bring her husband beer—either because she wishes he would drink less or because she's resentful about something else.

Even if you don't agree with someone's reasons for not complying with your requests, he or she will feel a whole lot more like compromising if you listen to and acknowledge that point of view.

If You Are Nagged

Those who feel nagged are often people who have trouble saying no. If a woman asks her husband or teenage son to take out the garbage, but it doesn't get done unless she issues several reminders, probably there was a false sense of agreement to do it in the first place. Some people should say no more often.

HOW TO GIVE CRITICISM WITHOUT STARTING A FIGHT

Directly related to nagging is criticizing. The problem is that your expectations, often quite legitimate, that things should be different may provoke an unwanted flare-up if the other person feels demeaned by what you say.

First decide if what the other person does that bothers you has a direct effect on you. Leaving dirty dishes around the house does, especially if you're the one who has to clean them up; your partner's ten extra pounds doesn't (unless you happen to own his or her body).

Consider your relationship to the person you're criticizing. It's one thing to tell your twelve-year-old that you want the lawn mowed more often than twice a month. Telling the same thing to your husband (or wife) may make him react with *Who does she think she is, my mother?*

Partners who expect to be treated like adults may not take kindly to being told how to fold the laundry, load the dishwasher, or park the car. If you want these things done differently, maybe you should do them yourself.

If you do decide you have a right to complain, consider whether or not the person is likely to change. Research has proven that, if properly motivated, people can learn to put their dishes in the sink. But few people lose weight or start exercising just because someone else thinks they should.

If you've told your son a thousand times not to leave his dirty dish-

es in the living room, maybe you should let it go. Maybe it's better to give up on some things—even if it's "not fair," "not right"—than continue to play out the role of constant critic, a voice against which the husband-in-training learns to deafen himself.

How you express criticism is also important. Alert the person that you want to talk.

"Something is bugging me, and I need to talk to you. How about tonight after work?"

"I have a problem and I need to discuss it with you. Can we go for a walk after supper?"

Advance notice allows a person to realize that something's coming and she'd better be prepared. Be sensitive to time and place. The best time to talk about difficult issues is when both of you are calm and relaxed. And alone.

That criticism is best given in private may seem obvious, but many parents continue to humiliate their children by mentioning their faults in front of their friends or siblings. Another version of the same mistake is praising a child's friends (with implied invidious comparison) in front of the child. Using personal comparisons to make criticisms ("Why can't you be more like . . . ?") makes a person feel judged, usually unfairly.

Some spouses take advantage of being out with another couple to criticize their partners. Often they make a joke out of their comments. It isn't funny.

Telling someone "I have a problem" and "I need your help," even if your problem is about something he or she is doing, is far more likely to be heard than direct criticism. Least likely to be heard is criticism framed as blame, put-downs, moralizing, or invidious comparisons.

"Why must you always . . . ?"

"You never. . . ."

"You should. . . ."

"Why can't you be more like . . . ?"

Emphasize your feelings, not the other person's shortcomings: "I feel bad that you don't get more dressed up when we go out. I feel more special when you wear your good clothes." This approach works better than, "Why do you always have to be so grungy when we go out?"

Describe how the situation is affecting you rather than being accusatory. Stick to behavior and make it clear that you're talking about what you like and don't like, not what's right and wrong. Focus on how the other person can help rather than on what he or she is doing wrong.

Even if you're the one with the complaint, remember to give the other person a turn. Mention your concern, but before elaborating, ask her how she feels about it. Don't get reactive even if the other person gets defensive. Remember, you've just told her there's something wrong with what she's doing.

If you ask someone to make a change, and he agrees without saying much, he's less likely to follow through than if you ask about and acknowledge why he may not want to change or why changing might be hard for him.

Wendy told Hank that she needed more help chauffeuring the kids to all their activities. He agreed. But Wendy went further and said, "I know you don't feel like it; otherwise you'd volunteer more often. When do you feel *least* like driving?"

Hank really appreciated this consideration of his feelings. (Feeling like it's OK to say no made it a lot easier to say yes.) He said he didn't mind taking the kids places on weekends or early in the evening, but he hated going out after nine on work nights. He also mentioned that it's a lot easier for him if he knows a day in advance that he has to drive them somewhere.

Then Wendy went one step further and asked, "Anything else?"

Hank paused. Then he said, "Yes, there is. Frankly, I think you drive them far too many places. I don't think we should drive them wherever and whenever they want to go."

Wendy, who hadn't know Hank felt this way, said that the next time he disagreed he should say something. If she's willing to take them anyway, even if he isn't, she'll do the driving. "But," she added, "maybe you're right. Maybe I do drive them around too much."

On the way out of the movie theater, Ralph turned to Carmen and said, "Wow, that was really a stinker, wasn't it?" He went on to describe a basically good idea ruined by Robin Williams's overacting and the director's sanctimonious moralizing.

Carmen didn't say anything. She'd enjoyed the movie. She loved Robin Williams. Now Hank's running the picture down was ruining it for her.

Since Carmen was the one who wanted to see this picture, she felt as if Hank was criticizing her taste and that while she was enjoying herself he had been having a lousy time.

In fact, Hank hadn't thought of this movie as Carmen's choice. She may have mentioned it first, but he too had wanted to see it. And he hadn't had a lousy time. Far from it. He enjoyed laughing with parts of the movie, and he enjoyed laughing at some of its excesses.

What should you say on your way out of a movie you didn't like, when you're with someone who apparently did? Nothing.

If two people both hate a movie or concert, their saying so brings them together. Shared experience, shared sensibilities. But if you enjoyed the performance, hearing someone else pick it apart spoils your fun.

Criticism of the movie or restaurant we liked feels like criticism of our taste. If you thought the food was lousy or the play was boring but sense that your companion liked it, let him savor his enjoyment. Save your criticism for later. Much later.

SELF-REFLECTIVE OBSERVATION

Tolerance and consideration of others help make you sensitive enough to be a better listener. But even more important is developing some capacity for self-reflective awareness. When you have trouble hearing someone or getting someone to hear you, step back and try to see the process of communication between the two of you as just that—a *process* of communication between the two of you. You'll need to get beyond thinking about personalities to thinking about specific behavior. And you'll need to get beyond the linearity of thinking that the other person *makes* you respond the way you do to seeing the process as circular.

Say that your teenage son never talks to you. Oh, he'll let you know when he needs new sneakers or a ride to a party, but you miss the talks you used to have when he was younger. Now he's so sullen. You can write your son's uncommunicativeness off to adolescence if you like, or you can try to think of it as part of a circular process.

To reflect on your part in the process, ask yourself what might stimulate reticence and what might reinforce it. Do you bug him about things that every teenager keeps private, like which of his friends smokes marijuana or drinks beer at parties? Do you bombard him with questions when he wants to retreat to the sanctuary of his room? And when he does

open up, do you listen respectfully to his opinions, or do you argue with everything he says?

How Well Do You Listen to Yourself?

The respect for other people's feelings that makes you listen to them can be turned around to yourself.[2] How well do you respect your own right to think and feel what you do? How well do you listen to yourself?

Kate suffered from chronic headaches but had given up going to doctors because it never did any good. None of them ever figured out what was wrong, and few of them even bothered to listen carefully to her complaints. Finally, at her sister's urging, she decided to go the headache clinic at a leading hospital in Boston.

One of the tests they did was a CAT scan of her brain. Afterward, Kate waited anxiously for the radiologist who would explain the results. When he finally arrived, it was clear that he was rushed. He introduced himself, but Kate didn't catch his name. Then he showed her the pictures from the CAT scan, and she pointed to a small white spot on the film. "That's just a normal calcification of your pineal gland," he said, "nothing to worry about."

As the doctor was preparing to leave, Kate felt unsatisfied and wished the conversation could have gone on a little longer. But she wasn't sure how to frame her questions and was embarrassed that she didn't remember the doctor's name.

Halfway out the door, the doctor turned and said, "Any other questions?"

Kate answered in a subdued voice, "No."

Kate heard the doctor's anxiousness to leave. But she was far less well tuned in to her own needs. Her fear and uncertainty, combined with the doctor's rushed manner, had created a cloud of fog surrounding her own needs.

If you don't listen to yourself, it's unlikely that anyone else will.

---

[2]And vice versa.

Listening to yourself means not only respecting your own feelings but also getting to know something about your own ways of communicating. This isn't always easy, and it isn't always pleasant.

I, for example, have learned that I have a penchant for making jokes and wisecracks in social situations. Maybe some of my jokes are funny, but they're often distracting. Joking around may be a defense against social anxiety, but it's also a convenient outlet for fast-paced, restless energy. Whatever the reasons for it, though, there are times when I have to make an effort to suppress the wise remarks that pop into my head.

You may find it easier to think of other people's conversational habits that you wish they would become aware of. But the effort to understand your own ways and habits will enable you to relate much more effectively to other people, regardless of what they do.

CHAPTER NINE

"I Can See This Is Really Upsetting You"

HOW TO DEFUSE EMOTIONAL REACTIVITY

We come now to the number-one reason people don't listen: reactive emotionalism. As we saw in Chapter 6, when someone says something that triggers emotional attack or withdrawal, understanding goes out the window. If listening without acknowledging what the other person says turns discussions into conversational Ping Pong, overreacting can turn them into the Battle of the Bulge. If the war metaphor seems melodramatic, take inventory of your emotions next time an escalating series of attacks and counterattacks leaves you feeling wounded and bleeding in a dozen places.

Some people are so provocative that it's almost impossible to listen to them without getting upset. But after a while you may begin to discover that regardless of what other people say, your real problem is how you react.

And what about those thin-skinned individuals who fly off the handle at the slightest sign of criticism? Sure, they're overreactive, but unless your relationship to them is expendable, your challenge is finding a way to get through to them.

EMPATHY TURNS DEFENSIVENESS AROUND

Defensiveness is a paradox of the human condition: our survival and security seem to depend on self-assertion and defense, but intimacy and cooperation require that we risk being vulnerable. All human communication—whether in business dealings or personal relationships—reflects this tension between self-expression (talking) and mutual recognition (listening).

Nearly everyone is insecure to some extent. Therefore, when we feel threatened, even (or especially) emotionally, we tend to react defensively rather than opening ourselves to the other person's point of view.

One reason people pay thousands of dollars to psychotherapists is simply to be listened to. (Good therapists may do more than just listen, but they certainly do no less.) When people talk to a therapist about their troubles, the therapist doesn't (usually) feel blamed and therefore doesn't get defensive. When we talk to the people we're close to about our upsets, they feel implicated. That's why the response we get is often reactive, "No! Don't feel that way." An accepting, nonreactive response feels like "Yes? Is that how you feel?" or "Tell me more" or "What's that like for you?"

Empathy and tenderness are permission giving. Receptive, nondefensive listeners allow us to get our feelings out. They welcome unpopular parts of ourselves to speak (which allows us to do the same for ourselves). They know that even on those occasions when what we're saying about them may not be true, our feelings are.

Feelings are facts to the person experiencing them.

The simple—and often enormously difficult—act of not becoming reactive has a tremendous impact on relationships. It enables difficult people to be heard—and it empowers us to remain in control of ourselves no matter what the pressure. So let's consider how to reduce reactive emotionalism, in ourselves when we're doing the listening, and in others when we're doing the talking.

HOW TO RESIST REACTING EMOTIONALLY WHEN PROVOKED

Every so often Nadine takes out her frustration in the form of an emotional outburst about Tim's many failings:

"You're selfish and inconsiderate."

"You *never* think of anyone but yourself."

"You don't care about me; all you ever want to do is fuck me!"

Tim can't stand these outbursts. *If she's so unhappy, why can't she just say so without calling me every name in the book? If she wants something from me, why doesn't she ever ask for it, instead of expecting me to read her mind?* He tries to listen to her complaints, but by the time she's through dumping on him he just wants to go away and hide.

When Gordon complains about her handling of the kids, Jane gets furious. First he leaves everything to her, then he criticizes her for doing what she thought was right. He's always right, and she's always wrong. So she let's him know just how she feels.

All four people in these two examples have a right to their feelings. The trouble is, no one is listening. To listen without flying off the handle, you must develop the ability to tolerate a certain amount of anxiety—and to resist the "fight or flight" urge.

Don't Jump to Respond—Listen Harder

The trouble with the famous advice, "Don't get defensive" is that it's a lot harder to *stop* doing something than to *start* doing something else. If you're trying to cut down on coffee, it's easier to pour yourself a cup of tea than to sit there not drinking coffee. If want to cut down on junk food, it's easier to grab a carrot than to try to avoid the urge to rip open the potato chips. If want to cut down on emotional reactivity, concentrate on listening harder.

If either or both of the examples just given sound familiar, you probably know how it feels to be berated in an angry, assaultive way or found fault with by someone who's better at criticizing than helping. But getting reactive only makes things worse. Tim thinks his problem is Nadine's breathtaking exaggerations, one-sided view of things, and emotional explosions. But a fuller description of the problem would be that when Nadine feels ignored she tries not to say anything until she can't stand it anymore and then her feelings come pouring out—*and* Tim isn't able either to pick up her signals of unhappiness before she explodes or to listen when she does blow up without getting hurt and angry and pulling away. Likewise, Jane's problem isn't just that Gordon leaves the children to her and then complains about her handling of them. Her re-

action—getting mad and counterattacking—is part of what keeps Gordon from getting more involved.

A full description of any listening problem always includes both parties. Ultimately, what defeats us isn't the provocative speaker but our own defensive response.

The best way to develop awareness of and control over your emotionality is by having the courage to engage emotionally intense situations and tolerating the anxiety and internal emotional reactivity associated with that engagement. Avoiding such encounters affords only an illusion of self-containment.

Ginny didn't call her mother from college after being a passenger in a car accident because she didn't want to have to deal with her mother's frantic questions and exaggerated concern. So she burdened herself with another secret and further reinforced her own inability to deal with other people's overconcern.

Learn to resist the impulse to act out your automatic and habitual response—arguing, blaming, rebelling, dominating, or accommodating to achieve peace at any price. These automatic responses are driven by anxiety and designed to mask it by avoiding issues and defying, controlling, ignoring, or appeasing others. The courage to engage people and situations you might prefer to avoid, and learning to contain your own particular reactive reflexes, leads over time to a reduction in your level of chronic anxiety.

Even if you work on lowering the level of your emotional reactivity, sometimes the burden of listening becomes difficult to bear unless you find a way to become actively involved. The ideal way to become engaged in listening is to concentrate on the task, to be attentive, curious, and concerned. I'd call this *active* listening except that shopworn expression suggests a kind of chatty show of interest, a pretense of concern, as sincere as a car salesman's smile.

Really listening means taking interest, not showing it.

You can go a long way toward improving your ability to listen (and be listened to in return) by simply making a concerted effort to concentrate on what the other person is trying to communicate.

In Chapter 6, I used the example of hostile questions to illustrate how emotional reactivity escalates when an exchange starts out with provocation. Something the speaker says (or maybe it's just sitting there being lectured to) makes someone in the audience restive, and he attacks the speaker in the sublimated form of a question.

"Excuse me," said the eminent French deconstructionist, Claude Nasal-Passages, who just happened to be in the audience, "but isn't everything you've just said total blather and you're full of nothing but helium?" In big words, of course.

Unfortunately, having just stood up in front of an audience for an hour or so pouring out their ideas, some speakers get a little touchy at such moments. And I've noticed (in other speakers, you understand) a certain unfortunate tendency to respond in kind.

"Well, yes, Professor Nasal-Passages, that's an intriguing point. But you're a complete ass, and so is the horse you rode in on." Big words, again.

A better way to respond to hostile questions is to apply Formula Number One for Resisting Reactivity: hear the other person out. Instead of agreeing or disagreeing, invite the questioner to say more. Hostile inquisitors aren't really asking a question but just want to say something. So let them. The same strategy works to keep reactivity from escalating in everyday conversations.

Here's how a friend of mine used this advice to reduce the antagonism that was starting to poison his second marriage.

When Rob married Carla, they got along wonderfully well except when it came to Rob's daughter, Melanie. According to Carla, Rob spoiled her, among other things lending her money and letting her have the car whenever she wanted, even though she didn't always bring it back when she said she would. But whenever Carla raised any objection, Rob felt she was attacking his child, and so instead of listening (not necessarily agreeing, just listening), he fought back. Many second marriages are broken on this very issue.

When Rob realized that the situation had reached the point of crisis, he resolved at least to listen to Carla the next time she complained about Melanie. Two days later he got his chance. Melanie promised to have the car back by eight so Carla could go shopping, but she didn't get home until nine-thirty, after the stores were closed. When Carla complained to Rob, he felt his stomach knotting and the counterarguments surging in his mind. But instead of getting defensive, he said what

he'd prepared himself to say: "Tell me more." Carla said that overindulgence wasn't doing Melanie any good. Rob, sticking to his resolve not to judge or interrupt, kept listening, and Carla went on. She talked about how hard it was feeling like an outsider in her own house. She knew that Rob and Melanie had a special relationship, and she respected that. She had no wish to play Melanie's mother or tell Rob what to do. She just wanted to be able to talk to him when she felt concerned.

Having determined not to defend himself or argue, Rob found it remarkably easy to listen—that is, after he checked the rising emotions that Carla's first few sentences triggered in him. He stopped hearing in Carla the overbearing voice of his ex-wife, who was always so critical of the children, and started hearing how left out his new wife was feeling. Moreover, because he really listened this time, he was able to hear that Carla wasn't insisting that he change anything, just asking him to listen to her point of view. After that, things changed. They didn't always agree about how to respond to Melanie, but now that Rob knew that he could listen to Carla's opinion without necessarily following it, their differences ceased to divide them.

Anticipate and Plan for Tense Encounters

The best way to defuse reactivity is to avoid becoming reactive yourself, something more easily said than done. One thing that helps is planning, as Rob was able to do once he realized how serious his breach with Carla was becoming. You can anticipate many of the conflictual conversations in your life. If you stop to think about what the boss or your teenager is likely to say that triggers your anxiety, you can plan not to flare up in defensive fight or flight. Anticipation frees you from overreacting.

One way to remain calm is by schooling yourself to ask questions instead of reacting emotionally to the usual provocations. This is a variation of the "tell me more" strategy. Another effective way to tone down emotionality is to practice responding to rhetorical questions and sarcasm literally, instead of being provoked by their inflammatory implications into a defensive retort.

"Don't you ever think about anything but sex?"
"No, it's kind of a hobby with me. Like woodworking."

"Must you pick on every little thing I say?"
"Yes, all in the service of helping you become the perfect person I know you're capable of being."

How to Understand a Speaker's Anger

When those we care about start to cry, we have an urge to comfort them so they'll stop. Somehow, we equate the crying with the pain. In fact, crying isn't pain; it's the way people express and release that pain. The same is true with expressions of anger (even if it's a little harder to keep that in mind).

I once watched a therapist interviewing a middle-aged couple five years into a second marriage. They were having a hard time deciding how to balance their obligations to ten children and twenty grandchildren and an even harder time keeping the discussion from turning into a shouting match. They were so volatile that neither one could say anything without the other one losing it. As the wife was saying her piece and starting to go on and on, rehashing the past and finding fault, her husband's foot started twitching ominously. Sitting behind the one-way mirror, I felt apprehensive and helpless. I could see an explosion building but couldn't do anything about it.

Then the therapist, bless him, did exactly what needed to be done. He acknowledged what the wife had said and then let the husband speak—being careful to direct the husband's response to himself, who could listen, not to his wife, who at that point couldn't. Even so, the husband exploded. With hot emotion he refuted what his wife said and explained the truth of things as he saw it. But as he talked—with his wife blocked from responding—he calmed down noticeably. His jaw relaxed, the tension went out of his shoulders, and his foot stopped twitching. Not having a chance to express his anger made it build. Expressing it, *even in an angry way*, released his anger.

The hard part will be teaching this couple to hear each other out without flying off the handle so that they can learn to diffuse their own anger. It's one thing to understand that expressing anger helps detoxify it; it's another thing to be on the receiving end and try to remain calm.

The wife in the couple I observed is angry because her husband doesn't understand her point of view. She thinks one of the children, who happens to be her son, needs some financial assistance. Her husband is jealous of the attention she pays this son and feels she's neglecting him. "He's twenty-three years old. He can take care of himself." But it isn't disagreeing that causes their problems; it's getting reactive and shouting at each other. If he would concentrate on understanding what she's *feeling* and not allow himself to react defensively, he'd understand that she's worried about her boy. She might or might not actually decide to give him some money; that's just an idea, a way of expressing

her concern. Her husband's not really upset about the money but about not getting as much attention as he used to. Unfortunately, instead of talking about his feelings, he blames her for them.

◆

When feelings of not being understood come out as anger, hearing them, not shutting your ears or fighting back, is the key to calming things down.

◆

To defuse angry confrontations, don't blame the other person for upsetting you. Start by trying to understand his feelings. (Save yours for the moment. Later, after the other person feels heard, express your feelings *as your feelings*, not as something the other person is doing to you.)

Feelings don't always make sense right away, and they may come out in global and critical ways at first. It's easier to hear feelings that don't come out this way, *but if they do*, remember that they are *feelings*, not scientific statements of fact. Don't yell back, call the other person names, or bring up old issues.

◆

Don't tell angry people to calm down. Doing so only makes them feel like you're denying their right to be upset.

◆

You don't have to agree to understand your angry partner's point of view. And you don't have to understand completely to be able at least to listen and try. The harder you try to listen and acknowledge what the other person is saying, the more likely you are to understand how he or she feels.

Remember: You aren't responsible for what other people feel. Even if they blame you, what they really need is to be understood.

If someone snaps at you in an angry, assaultive way, how do you get beyond listening with a clenched mind? The obvious answer is to listen through the emotional static to what the person is trying to say. But some things are bigger than they look from a distance. When the level of frustration and anger that some people live with spills out into the relationship, our natural response is to become anxious and defensive. Learning to listen to someone who comes at you in such an intense, urgent way isn't easy. One thing that may help free you from withdrawing into a defensive posture is to hear in the anxious speaker the voice of an unhappy child demanding to be heard. That, after all,

is the part of ourselves where our most urgent feelings come from. Even though the person trying to get through to you may come off sounding nasty, he or she is hurting and needs desperately to be heard.

If, instead of focusing on the speaker and how difficult he or she is, you can focus on your own efforts to listen and avoid overreacting, the anxiety in the relationship will begin to abate. Anxiety is like electrical current. It requires conduction and amplification. If you listen and endeavor to stay cool, the angry person will feel heard and begin to calm down.

In heated discussions, repeating the other person's position in your own words shows that you understand and interrupts your own defensive response. If the heat gets so intense that you start to boil over, try squeezing your thumb and index finger together, hard. This is nothing but a momentary distraction (less hazardous to your health than "biting your tongue"), but it does allow you to channel and release tension in a way you can control.

If that doesn't work, or an emotionally reactive speaker is dumping on you and it's too upsetting, you may have to protest. Doing so before you get too upset, and without attacking, keeps your anger from boiling over: "I'm sorry, but I can't listen to this right now. I'm too upset. We'll have to talk later."

How to Take Criticism without Overreacting

He says, "You're always late."
She says, "You're always rushing me."
One point for him. One point for her. Total score: zero.

Allowing the other person to spell out his or her point of view before responding with yours is especially important and especially difficult when that someone is criticizing you. If you start to get reactive, ask yourself, Does the other person have a sincere concern about this issue? If the answer is yes, keep listening.

If your spouse complains about where you park in the driveway, you might consider that he or she has a legitimate stake in the matter. If, on the other hand, he or she criticizes how you talk to your boss, you might remember that how you decide to talk to your boss is your business. Come to think of it, remembering that might make it easier to at least listen to your partner's point of view.

If someone has a criticism of you, stay with that concern; don't switch to a different criticism of your own. Avoid cross-complaining.

"Oh yeah? Well, what about you? You never take out the garbage when I ask you to."

"I don't care if you don't like what's for supper. Maybe if you cleaned up your room once in a while like I asked, I'd feel more like cooking something you like."

After you've allowed your critic to spell out his or her complaint, agree with whatever you can or at least show appreciation for his or her concern.

"Yes, I have been a little grouchy lately. I'm sorry."

"So you think I've been favoring Cindy over Joshua?"

"Yes, I did run over your prize Pomeranian in the driveway. I'll get you a new one."

OK, so I'm saying that when someone starts to criticize you, the best thing to do is to hear him out and acknowledge his point of view before defending yourself. But isn't that a little like saying that losing ten pounds is easy—all you have to do is cut out sweets? When someone starts in on you, especially someone close to you, it isn't easy to smile and nod and say, "Oh, so you think I'm a selfish and insensitive species of barnyard animal? I see. Could you say a little more about that?"

Listening to criticism is one of the hardest things any of us ever has to do. Unfortunately, erupting, although it may be understandable, only makes things worse. To prevent yourself from doing so, train yourself to listen responsively—pay attention, appreciate what the critical other is saying, and acknowledge it. This takes practice, but in time it can become a habit. The positive effort to listen helps prevent you from becoming reactive.

Focus on the issue. Try to hear in the criticism something the other person is asking you to modify rather than a rejection or condemnation of your self. One way to help you focus on the distinction between a request and an attack is to invite the other person to explain how it bothers her.

When Sid told Nancy, "I wish we didn't have to have fish every week," she started complaining about how picky he is. "You're always

complaining," she said. "For a while there you wouldn't eat meat; now that's *all* you want."

Sid was stung. He *never* complained about what Nancy cooked. He just hated the fish she served. *Didn't he have a right to say what he liked? Wasn't it better to be honest?* This kind of internal dialogue is precisely what prevents us from appreciating the other person's point of view and what fuels the likelihood of a reactive response.

If Sid could listen to Nancy for a minute, instead of to his own hurt feelings, he might realize that it's a big job figuring out what to serve for supper every night. Add in the complication of having to accommodate spouses' and children's preferences, and that those preferences change over time, and he might begin to understand what his wife was up against. If she expresses herself with "excessive" annoyance (Sid thinks: *All I said was I wish we didn't have to have fish*), that's a sign of stored-up resentment.

What if, despite all your efforts to be a good, empathic listener, the criticism comes out as a vituperative attack?

If criticism is given in a nasty or offensive way, you have a right to react to the manner in which the message was expressed. If you can't listen to someone who berates you in an assaultive way, simply state what put you off.

"I don't appreciate being called stupid" (or compared to my mother or called a bitch or a son of one).

"I'll try to listen to your suggestion if you can say it in a less nasty way."

Actually, the word *nasty* is name-calling. Better to be concrete: "I'll try to listen to your suggestion if you can say it without telling me how selfish I am"—or "if you give me some idea of what you want instead of saying what a terrible person I am."

Will such remarks calm things down and allow the two of you to understand each other? Probably not. But sometimes you have to recognize your limits and let other people know what they are too. Even if telling someone that you can't hear him when he screams at you only makes him angrier at the moment, maybe he'll think about what you said later.

"Why Does He [or She] Have
to Talk Everything to Death?"

Jackie wishes twenty-four hours would go by without Fred's complaining about how nobody appreciates him at the office. Sometimes she feels like screaming. If he wasn't so preoccupied with himself and his precious career, maybe he'd get a little more appreciation from her and the kids. She doesn't say so, of course. He'd only get mad and sulk for a couple of days. So whenever Fred starts in on topic number one, Jackie just sits there in pained silence.

Sam wishes Cheryl would stop launching into a diatribe every time she feels overwhelmed by taking care of the house and the kids. It isn't that she doesn't have a right to complain, he thinks; it's the way she goes on and on about everything. Sometimes he tries to be sympathetic, but it isn't easy. She'll say the house is a mess or the kids are a pain, and then she'll just keep talking and talking, covering every little detail without ever really getting to the point. The worst of it, as far as Sam is concerned, is that she's always complaining about the same things. " 'Suzie doesn't have any friends,' 'Suzie wasn't nice to so-and-so,' 'Suzie this,' 'Suzie that.' Why can't she leave the poor kid alone?"

The issues that come up over and over again represent people's core concerns. (*Their* core concerns, not necessarily your greatest shortcomings.) The more understood and accepted a person feels, the safer she feels to go deeper into these issues. The mechanical and repetitive feeling of some complaints stems partly from the fact that they rarely get a sympathetic hearing. Concerned and empathic listening is the greatest gift you can give to help the other person soothe her feelings. Fred's feeling that nobody appreciates his accomplishments and Cheryl's worries about the children will never be completely healed. That's why they need to talk about these issues again from time to time.

When someone close brings up a recurring issue, some people get upset and say something like "How many times do we have to go through this?" Such retorts make sense if you feel that the speaker's complaints mean that you're responsible or that it's your job to solve whatever problem the person is complaining about. But is it really your job to resolve your mother's complaints about your sister or your partner's complaints about the children? Once you understand that other people's talking about what's bothering them makes them feel better simply for

being listened to, you can relax, knowing that just listening without becoming reactive can make both of you feel better.

Sharing problems makes people feel better. Listening is how we help them soothe themselves and how we build closer relationships.

For those who can get beyond blaming others for "making them upset," discovering what triggers their sensitivity leads to the questions "Where does my emotional reactivity come from?" and "What can I do about it?"

GETTING TO THE ROOT OF REACTIVITY

Reactivity originates in anxiety over self-expression and the need to be understood. The more our parents listened, took us seriously, and respected our opinions and feelings, the more secure and self-possessed we became. The less they listened, the more intolerant and critical they were, the more insecure and anxious we became. The more conditioned we were to expect attack or argument, the more we learned to become defensive. What makes us defensive more than anything else are the things our parents did that made us feel criticized, argued with, or ignored.

What happens in your family when people get anxious? Do they get into shouting matches? Break off relations and avoid each other? That's your legacy.

As long as your parents are still alive, there's still time to revisit and revise your relationship with them. Making peace with your parents (and calming the part of you that still goes around ready for war) means being in emotional contact with them, being yourself, and letting them be themselves. Changing your relationship to them doesn't mean changing them; it means changing the way you react to them. Notice what they do that drives you crazy. Notice how you respond. That you can change. The more you learn to resist the urge to flare up in the face of their provocations, the more self-possessed and unflappable you'll become in all the rest of your relationships. When it comes to emotional reactivity, your parents are the final exam.

Systems are tenacious, resistant to change; or to put it in more human terms, your parents have a long history of relating to you in a cer-

tain way. If you try to change that, you will be tense and their reaction will be intense. Have a plan when you visit them. Remember that when you reenter the family's emotional force field, your ability to think about what's going on is impaired. So do your thinking beforehand. Formulate reasonable goals. When you do test a new way of behaving, start with small steps.

Remember Peggy from Chapter 5? She was the woman whose mother's negativism provoked her into shouting matches. If you recall, Peggy learned to see how her mother's negativism triggered her own rage—and how expecting it made her hypersensitive. Seeing this pattern was one thing; changing it was another.

When Peggy decided to stop trying to change her mother and learn to accept who she was, she began to realize that her mother wasn't really a mean person, just someone who prized family togetherness so much that she was threatened when people decided to go their own way. This simple shift in Peggy's view of her mother made it a lot easier for her to listen the next time she heard her mother criticizing someone in the family for doing something different. However, she also found that simply remaining silent only made her seethe. So instead of either holding her tongue or criticizing her mother (for being critical!) she started to say, as calmly as possible, that she could see how her mother saw it but that she didn't agree.

At first Peggy's effort to clarify where she stood, rather than criticize her mother, was lost on her mother. "Oh, so you think I'm all wrong, do you?"

Much to Peggy's credit, she was able to maintain a calm, nonreactive position, even if her insides were churning. She listened until her mother was through and didn't contradict her or fight back.

When Peggy finally did speak, she said, "No, Mom, you're not hearing me. I'm not saying you're all wrong. I don't think that at all. You have a right to your opinion. I'm just saying that my opinion is different, that's all."

In the ensuing months, as Peggy made an effort to continue to speak up calmly when she disagreed with her mother's violent opinions, she tried to make it clear that she was declaring her independence but not any lack of love or respect. On the contrary, as she learned to overcome her inability to tolerate her mother's criticism, the two women began to get much closer. Peggy still occasionally slipped back into blaming and distancing, but not for long, and when this happened, instead of thinking of her mother as impossible and herself as helpless, she real-

ized that she was just getting reactive again. That made it easier to control and easier to let go of.

She and her mother still argued from time to time, but now Peggy spoke up before her emotional intensity reached the boiling point. That and the fact that instead of criticizing her mother she made a point of simply clarifying where she stood made the arguments much less toxic.

After things calmed down between her and her mother, Peggy decided to work on communication with her father. Growing up, she'd thought of him as a distant and unapproachable presence, a large and benevolent shadow at the edge of the family circle. She remembered him sitting silently behind the newspaper while she and her mother fixed dinner or chatted at the breakfast table. Now she longed to be closer to him but didn't know how to go about it. How do you talk to a shadow? After she'd married and had children she made a concerted effort to get closer to him. He'd listen politely when she told him about the children's latest doings, but as soon as she said anything about her job or her friends, his eyes would drift in the direction of the television, or he'd suddenly remember something he had to do. As far as Peggy was concerned, he might as well have slapped her in the face.

What Peggy interpreted as rejection from her father was in fact anxiety about intimate conversation. Her efforts to get closer to him took the form of pursuing a distancer, a pattern she also played out with her husband.

Intimacy has levels of intensity, from simple contact, to chitchat about neutral subjects like the weather, to semipersonal topics, to personal conversations about things that are important to you, to talking about your relationship. Everyone gets anxious at some point on this scale; precisely where depends on you and whom you're with. Peggy's father just happened to be one of those people made anxious by even mildly intimate conversations with almost anyone. It wasn't that he didn't love his daughter; he just didn't know how to talk about it.

To get closer to her father, I advised Peggy to spend a little time alone with him—which meant gently pulling him out of hiding behind the television or newspaper and away from the grandchildren—and moving the conversation only very slowly from one level of intimacy to the next, stopping as soon as either one of them started to get anxious. Pushing her father past his comfort zone would only trigger his distancing reflex and leave Peggy feeling like a fisherman after the big one got away.

Peggy lowered her expectations and decided simply to spend some

time with her father, during which she would keep the conversation light. Her primary concern would be to avoid becoming anxious or making her father feel that way. She found her father remarkably receptive to this new nondemanding approach and on her next visit hoped to move the conversation to a slightly more personal level. She had complained that her father showed no interest in her life, but she now realized that she hadn't demonstrated any interest in his, either. I suggested that she try an opening that most people will respond to: "What are you working on these days?" or "What are your worries these days?"

Peggy's father welcomed his daughter's interest, and he reciprocated by showing more interest in what was going on in her world. Once or twice when she tried to talk to him about something that made him uncomfortable—like how his retirement money was holding out—he did his old disappearing act, and Peggy once again felt rejected. But now she no longer dwelled on this feeling, and it didn't last long. Her father never did become the kind of man she could really confide in, but he was after all her father, and she loved him. What's more, now that she'd come to terms with his nature, she realized how much he loved her.

The people close to you don't have any tricks up their sleeves. Their actions surprise you only because you keep looking for them to do what you wish they'd do or what you would do. They do what they do. Once you learn this, you can stop being surprised and upset. You can let them be who they are. You might as well; they will anyway.[1]

A relationship matures when you can allow the other person to be who he is. If your mother criticizes everybody *and* you can't accept this, your life may be dominated by your attempt to stop her (and everybody else, for that matter) from criticizing anything or anybody. Once you can let your mother be a person who's critical—in other words, accept that she is who she is—you don't have to fight it or organize your life around it.

———◆———

Once you accept that the people who push your buttons are who they are, you can stop trying to change them—and stop overreacting when they do *what they've always done.*

———◆———

[1]One of my patients, a 34-year-old married woman, once told me, without irony, that her father "could be a wonderful person, if only he were different."

Peggy's more relaxed approach to her parents didn't stop her mother from being critical or her father from being withdrawn, but it did make her a whole lot less reactive to them—and to the other people in her life who touched the same raw nerves.

Making peace with your parents moves you closer to them, enables you to listen without trying to change them, and helps you overcome habitual patterns of overreaction by addressing emotional reactivity at its source. You aren't going to change your family, but you can change yourself in relationship to them.

Learning to listen without overreacting is an exercise in accepting that each of us is different and separate. You can even learn to enjoy the differences. Formerly "difficult" and "disagreeable" people begin to soften perceptively as soon as you let them be who they are.

HOW EMOTIONAL REACTIVITY INCREASES AS RELATIONSHIPS EVOLVE

In the early stages, most relationships are fairly relaxed and balanced. The two people can talk and listen without disruptive emotionality; otherwise the relationship wouldn't have gotten this far. Such circumstances, however, are time-limited. Relationships, like unstable chemical compounds, tend to deteriorate. Once they become heated with emotional reactivity, they may have to be cooled down with emotional distance—avoidance of one another or at least of potentially upsetting subjects. But if the two parties are closeted together or try to discuss emotionally charged issues, one or both of them starts spilling over with anxiety.

One person may act to preserve harmony by adapting to the other's needs and end up doing all of the listening (though not necessarily hearing). The other person is frequently unaware of the disparity. But both of them act to preserve this inequality. The mistake the placater makes is to confuse self-abnegation with self-restraint and openness to the other. The latter strategy allows both people to win; the former makes losers of them both. But as long as one person is cowed by the other's emotionality, and the second keeps trying to express himself in the same old reactive way, both of them act inadvertently to preserve the unhappy equilibrium.

The emotional climate in a relationship varies from hot to cold, turbulent to stable, and safe to unsafe to risk being vulnerable. The

presence of unresolved conflict makes for storminess. Some relationships, for example, are dominated by dissension over togetherness versus autonomy. In this case, anything that either partner says to the other
that's even vaguely related to who's going to do what with whom can
trigger the anxiety that surrounds this core conflict.

When someone opens up on you with a mean mouth or listens with
only feigned interest, it's natural to blame it on his personality. When
someone reacts with sudden, rancorous eruptions to something you say,
it's impossible not to feel this emotional backlash as coming from her.
But reactivity, like everything else that happens in a relationship, is
interactional. The only part of the equation you can change is your part.

Try analyzing for a week the amount of your communications that
are (1) critical or instructional, (2) avoidant, or (3) affectionate or lauda-
tory. To change the climate in a relationship, just shift from (1) or (2)
to (3) and see what happens.

***

Trying to avoid or control people doesn't resolve reactivity.

***

A listener's invisible sensitivities fester and flourish with preoccupation about giving too much and getting too little. Unfortunately, their
reactivity makes other people avoid them, which increases their sense
of alienation and isolation, which increases their reactivity. As emotional maturity and self-reliance decrease, people look more to one
another to provide a sense of well-being. This need raises expectations,
increases sensitivity, and contributes to emotional reactivity.

***

**To cut down on reactivity, respect your own right to be your-
self and other people's right to be themselves.**

***

Mature and autonomous people aren't easily threatened by loss of
their own emotional integrity, and so their relationships can be flexible. Periods of closeness and distance are tolerated. Each is free to be
close or involved elsewhere—and to have the other person move close or
pursue outside interests. Neither is particularly threatened by the other's
needs and expectations. Denying one's own emotional reactions, blaming
those reactions on others, and avoiding or pursuing others to reduce
anxiety are emotionally governed processes that undermine flexibility
in relationships. The point is not to deny one's feelings but to think
about them, then choose how to react rather than responding reflexively.

Mature listeners are responsible for their own reactions. Instead of automatically thinking, "So and so is impossible," they hear what is said, feel their reactions, and then decide how to respond. "Hearing" someone who doesn't readily open up means recognizing that he doesn't want to say much. If the reticent person is someone you care about, you may feel shut out. But if you act automatically on that feeling and pressure the other person to open up, you are projecting your own anxiety and making him feel threatened.

Pressuring someone to open up isn't listening. You may sincerely want to hear what's on his mind, you may think you can help, you may believe it would be good for him and the relationship if he talked more; but pressure is pressure.

The best way to approach emotionally reticent people is to make contact without becoming intense. Your openness without pressure helps relax the assumption that it isn't safe to open up. Respecting the integrity of the emotional boundary that allows you to be yourself (someone who wants to get closer) and the other person to be herself (someone who wants to go slow) keeps anxiety from escalating and allows you to get closer without pressure or criticism.

Releasing yourself from slavish and unrewarding obligations will stem the energy drain from a few expendable relationships. But since most of our relationships are not expendable, the most important thing you can do to avoid getting caught up in emotionally reactive transactions is to stay calm and be yourself. Staying open means honoring the speaker's individuality; staying receptive means not negating your own.

————◆————

The self-contained listener is not isolated or unfeeling but non-reactive.

————◆————

HOW TO TONE DOWN YOUR OWN MESSAGE AND BE HEARD

We all know how frustrating it is not to be listened to. But how many of us ever stop to think that there might be something about *the way* we express ourselves that makes others deaf to our concerns?

Several years ago my friend John tried to teach me how to tune up my temperamental English motorcycle. When he arrived on the appointed day and saw how nervous I was, he said, "The first thing you have to do is calm down." Calm down? How do you calm down know-

ing you're about to take apart a three-thousand-dollar piece of machinery on which you'll later be going over a hundred miles an hour? But he was right. The way my hands were shaking I'd never have been able to shim the diphthongs with the krenging hook. So we repaired to the kitchen for a beer and cooled off. Later I had the satisfaction of knowing that it wasn't getting all wound up that made me unable to put the damn thing back together. It's just that I'm a natural born klutz.

Why is it that when it comes to relationship problems so few of us bother to follow my friend John's advice and calm down before we start?

As we've seen, one way speakers undermine their messages is to make complaints or requests with such anger and upset that the listener becomes so anxious that he doesn't clearly register—and therefore doesn't remember—the content of the speaker's message. All that gets communicated is the upset. Suppose, for example, that once every few months a wife gets so sick and tired of her husband's always leaving the bathroom a mess that she blows up at him about it. It infuriates her that he doesn't remember—even after she's told him how upset it makes her. All he remembers is getting yelled at.

It's hard to listen to complaints—or anything else—if you feel attacked. That's why sometimes even though we've been complaining about something for years, the other person never really gets it. We've told him (or her) a million times; still he (or she) doesn't understand. Anxiety is the enemy of listening.

One message sure to give your partner's hackles a workout is your pointing out some financial extravagances, of his naturally. Here's the great humorist S. J. Perelman illustrating his technique.

> Weary of pub-crawling and eager to recapture the zest of courtship, we had stayed home to leaf over our library of bills, many of them first editions. As always, it was chock-full of delicious surprises: overdrafts, modistes' and milliners' statements my cosset had concealed from me, charge accounts unpaid since the Crusades. If I felt any vexation, however, I was far too cunning to admit it. Instead, I turned my pockets inside out to feign insolvency, smote my forehead distractedly in the tradition of the Yiddish theater, and quoted terse abstracts from the bankruptcy laws. But fiendish feminine intuition was not slow to divine my true feelings. Just as I had uncovered a bill from Hattie Carnegie for a brocaded bungalow apron and was brandishing it under her nose, my wife suddenly turned pettish.
> "Sixteen dollars!" I was screaming. "Gold lamé you need yet! Who do you think you are, Catherine of Aragon? Why don't you rip up the foyer and pave it in malachite?" With a single dramatic gesture, I rent open my shirt. "Go ahead!" I shouted. "Milk me—drain me dry! Marshalsea prison! A pauper's grave!"

"Ease off before you perforate your ulcer," she enjoined. "You're waking the children."

"You think sixteen dollars grows on trees?" I pleaded, seeking to arouse in her some elementary sense of shame.[2]

Notice how Perelman employs his knowledge of psychology. Shaming someone is a sure way to get her attention.

Here's Perelman a little later in the same story demonstrating how to handle the delicate subject of gratuities. He and his family are moving out of their apartment, and he's faced with the challenge of appropriately expressing his gratitude for the staff's service.

Heaped by the curb were fourteen pieces of baggage exclusive of trunks; in the background, like figures in an antique frieze, stood the janitor, the handyman, and the elevator operators, their palms mutely extended. I could see that they were too choked with emotion to speak, these men who I know not at what cost to themselves had labored to withhold steam from us and jam our dumbwaiters with refuse. Finally one grizzled veteran, bolder than his fellows, stepped forward with an obsequious tug at his forelock.

"We won't forget this day, sir," the honest chap said, twisting his cap in his gnarled hands. "Will we, mates?" A low growl of assent ran round the circle. "Many's the time we've carried you through that lobby and a reek of juniper off you a man could smell five miles down wind. We've seen some strange sights in this house and we've handled some spectacular creeps; it's kind of like a microcosm like, you might say. But we want you to know that never, not even in the nitrate fields of Chile, the smelters of Nevada, or the sweatshops of the teeming East Side, has there been a man—" His voice broke off and I stopped him gently.

"Friends," I said huskily, "I'm not rich in worldly goods, but let me say this—what little I have is mine. If you ever need anything, whether jewels, money, or negotiable securities, remember these words: you're barking up the wrong tree. Geronimo."[3]

Notice that even though Perelman's message might have been a trifle unwelcome, his delivering it in a calm, reasoned tone enabled him to drive off to a chorus of ringing cheers (or so it seemed from a distance).

But seriously, what can you do if someone you try to talk to becomes reactive? Perhaps whenever you say something the least bit critical, your partner gets hurt or angry and shuts down. Try getting less invested in being heard but remain open to the relationship on the other

---

[2]S. J. Perelman, *The Swiss Family Perelman* (New York: Simon & Schuster, 1950), 4–5.

[3]Perelman, 16–17.

person's terms. This can be done without compromising yourself. It's the difference between giving in (living with appeasement) and temporarily setting aside your own agenda to respond to your partner's.

For example, say that whenever a wife tells her husband, even very nicely, that he shouldn't put certain dishes in the dishwasher, he gets that wounded look and withdraws into hurt silence. Normally, she's likely to become reactive in return. She's upset and feels wronged. The same thing happens when she complains about his not making the household repairs he's promised: he sulks. She feels like she's living with a big baby. But if she can calm down enough to ask herself where her criticism comes from, she might discover that it stems from unrealistic expectations.

The people we live with have assets and limitations. If we pitch our expectations at their assets instead of their limitations, we stand a better chance of being heard. Coming to terms with the real person you're relating to, rather than agonizing over the fact that he or she isn't different, will do a lot to lower your reactivity.

Learn something about what makes certain people reactive and try to defuse it with preparatory comments. For example, "I'm not saying that it's your fault, but I'm tired of seeing the kids leave their toys all over the place." Or, "I'm not sure how to say this. . . . " If you're trying to make a request, not expressing anger or disapproval, say so. But maybe you should examine your motives a little more carefully. When you say the kids shouldn't leave their toys around, do you really feel that your partner is at fault for allowing it? Is the inference he or she reacts to accurate? Even if you don't make such criticisms explicit, they often come through.

If you want someone to hear what you have to say without getting into a snit, don't forget tone and timing. Do you bring things up at the wrong time? Do you allow a judgmental tone to creep into your voice or use accusatory language?

If someone you know gets annoyed when you offer advice, inquire before doing so. "Would you like some advice, or would you rather I just listen?" If you intend to bring up an upsetting subject, give your listener some kind of warning. What makes something traumatic is being overwhelmed. If you aren't prepared, it takes less to overwhelm you. The more reactivity you anticipate, the more important it is to set the scene. A note or phone call telling the person you need to talk to him about something will help him gird himself.

———◆———

Although to some people it seems artificial, putting difficult messages in notes is an effective way to short-circuit reactivity.

———◆———

Ultimately, of course, it's not the other person's overreaction that is your problem but how *you* react to that. It's hard not to, but you don't have to get upset when someone else does.

One thing to remember when emotional reactivity drowns out listening is that *it's always your move*. The temptation to wait for the other person to change—or keep hammering away until he or she does—is understandable but unproductive. Sometimes it makes sense to write off unrewarding relationships that aren't central to your life. The man or woman who's so touchy that anything you say can trigger an angry response may be more trouble than he or she is worth. Unfortunately, many people are more likely to write off those relationships that *are* central to their lives—spouses, parents, colleagues—because they're the hardest to manage.

"What's Wrong with *Him?*"

The next time someone overreacts to what you're saying, ask yourself, "Where does this emotional response come from?" "What exposed nerve must I have touched on?" rather than "What's wrong with him [or her]?"

Any of the following remarks add fuel to the fire:

"You're such a big baby!"

"Someone sure got up on the wrong side of the bed today!"

"Can't you take a simple suggestion?"

"You're so immature."

"What's the matter, is it that time of the month again?"

"What's eating you? Every time I open my mouth you snap my head off."

According to Claire, her son Jeffrey was oversensitive. The least little thing she said to him could make him fly into a rage. One time she told him that his teacher probably wouldn't pick on him so much if he acted more mature in class, and he burst into tears and ran into his room. "He's always throwing tantrums," Claire said.

A child who bursts into tears and runs out of the room isn't having a temper tantrum; he feels ashamed. Kids aren't stupid. If they pitch a fit because they want to bend you to their wishes, they do it in front of you. (If you want to inactivate a temper tantrum, remove the audience; leave the room.)

The way to understand reactivity is to try to understand it, not fall back on familiar judgmental labels. Imagine a little boy storming out of the room after his mother said something apparently innocuous to him. Why would a child get so upset? Often it's because what she said made him feel ashamed of himself. When a child (or adult) feels humiliated, he becomes foot-stompingly outraged; he is I-am-wronged! Injuries to self-respect are a bruising as muggings. If you asked him what was wrong, he'd probably say, "Mommy yelled at me" or perhaps "Nothing, leave me alone!"

Few of us, children least of all, label our experience as shame. Unfortunately, parents who don't recognize a shame reaction or can't tolerate a child's upset get into a tug of war that makes things worse. They demand to know what's wrong, as if a child convulsed with emotion could say.

Give a shamed person room to hide and lick his wounds. Shame is so painful that the child momentarily loses control of his feelings. He needs time alone to regain his composure. Let him have it.

If someone becomes enraged at something you said, it might be because he feels shamed. Think about how you might have offended his dignity. Did you treat him like a baby? Imply that his opinion is wrong or doesn't count? That his feelings aren't legitimate? The way to decode an "excessive" or "inappropriate" emotional response is not to blame the other person—or yourself—but to consider what the exposed nerve might be.

SOMETIMES IT'S A MISTAKE TO TRY TO CONTROL YOUR FEELINGS

Some people are afraid to get up and say something at funerals, wedding banquets, or other emotionally charged occasions because they might start to cry—as if crying were a sign of weakness and not compassion. "But," one woman protested when I tried to tell her there's nothing wrong with crying, "if I start to cry, I won't be able to finish what I want to say."

If you start to cry and tell yourself that's awful and try to stop, you may well have trouble speaking. It's hard to concentrate on two things at once. But if your heart moves and your feelings show, what's wrong with that?

A trick some people use to help them cope with their anxiety about formal public speaking is to accept and acknowledge rather than fight their nervousness. "Good morning. My name is so-and-so, and I want you to know that I'm a little nervous about speaking in front of such a large group." Such candor makes an audience sympathetic, not judgmental. Most of us know what it feels like to be nervous about speaking in public. Even more important, though, is the effort to accept your feelings as natural instead of trying in vain to fight them. (Incidentally, thinking about communicating *to* a group of people instead of "speaking in front of them" shifts your attention and helps you calm down.)

There's an even more important way that trying to overcontrol feelings leads to more reactivity. If you let someone know how angry you are by venting your bottled-up frustration in an emotional outburst, you're likely to come across as overwhelming and attacking. If, instead of hearing your complaints, the other person responds with angry counteraccusations or just walks out, you may conclude that it's a mistake to try to talk about your feelings. This conclusion leads to a control and release cycle. You hold everything in until you explode in tears and shouting. The solution is not more control but less.

Don't wait until your frustration builds to rage before talking about it. Describe clearly the reasons you're unhappy. Discuss conflicts openly as they arise. Speaking up sooner will make it easier for you to lower your voice and to eliminate accusatory statements.

Instead of "You never do anything around here," try "I'm overloaded with housework. I need you to help me."

Don't turn the discussion into a *zero-sum game*, in which one person can win (or be right) only if the other loses (or is wrong).

There is, however, a difference between expressing what you feel and venting your emotions. Recently I got into a heated argument with a woman who was tired of her father-in-law's belittling comments and planned to tell him off. When I suggested that she tone down her emotionality before talking to him, she blew up at me. "What's wrong with emotion? What's wrong with getting angry?" Good question.

This woman *did* have something to be angry about. Her father-in-law's cutting remarks were thoughtless and disrespectful. But if she allowed her upset to overwhelm her, her complaints would not be voiced

clearly and would not be heard. Unloading her anger, rather than voicing her complaints, would allow her father-in-law not to take her seriously, to dismiss her as "oversensitive," "bitchy," or "having a bad day."

I'm not advocating emotional detachment. Anger helps preserve our integrity and self-regard, but simply venting anger doesn't usually solve the problem it signals. The distinction I'm trying to draw is not between emotion and reason but between uncontrolled reaction and deliberate action. There's nothing wrong with emotion, and there's nothing wrong with telling someone off—if that's what you want to do. It's not responding with feeling that spoils listening and makes us feel childish and inept—it's losing control.

PART FOUR

LISTENING IN CONTEXT

CHAPTER TEN

"We Never Seem To Talk Anymore"

LISTENING BETWEEN INTIMATE PARTNERS

It started innocently enough. She met him at an office party, and all they did was talk. But when Maureen got home and her husband asked if she had met anybody interesting, she found herself unwilling to mention Arthur, as though he were a secret wish she didn't want to lose by telling. Arthur called the next day and invited her to lunch. One lunch followed another, and then there were drinks after work. The following week they drove up to Thatcher Park and talked, as they watched the sun setting over the valley below. Nothing happened, unless you count the brief moment when Maureen's glance left Arthur's eyes and dropped to his lips and a shiver ran through her.

It was at this point that Maureen consulted me. She felt on the brink of something that could wreck her marriage. Arthur was everything her husband wasn't: successful, self-possessed, but most of all he really listened when they talked. Telling me this, Maureen was visibly nervous. Her eyes scanned mine, looking for understanding, expecting perhaps judgment, or maybe permission to do what she longed to.

When, I asked her, did the passion in her marriage die? She looked away. Then she wiped her eyes and said that Raymond, her husband, was a good man; they'd just . . . grown apart. He never talked to her anymore.

175

My sympathies were with this woman. Life holds few choices as consequential as the one between satisfaction and security. Still, I'd seen too many stale marriages blamed on the other partner not to wonder what Maureen's contribution was.

When I suggested she bring her husband to our second meeting, Maureen was reluctant. She wasn't asking for marital therapy, she said, and she was terrified of Raymond's finding out about Arthur. What finally overcame her hesitation was her hope that if I saw what her relationship with Raymond was like, maybe I'd understand why she would consider leaving him.

Raymond agreed to come, and Maureen told him that she was unhappy with their marriage. He seemed sympathetic, as though accustomed to obliging, but not really involved and not willing to tell his side. Only when I asked about his work did Raymond open up and become animated. We talked for a few minutes until Maureen interrupted to complain that he never talked to her about these things. Why couldn't he ever share his feelings with her? Raymond didn't have a very good answer for that. I was encouraged. Here was a concrete problem, something to work on.

If two people can't talk, I said, something's wrong. Then I turned their chairs to face each other and asked Raymond to talk to Maureen about his work in such a way as to make her understand what he was worried about. I told her to listen in such a way as to help him bring out his feelings.

Raymond talked about the anxieties of opening a new law practice in the middle of a recession. Very little work was coming in, but he was convinced that if he could hang on for another year or so, things would start to turn around. Maureen broke in to say that he was being foolish. Things would never turn around until he got rid of that idiot Roger, his partner. They argued for a minute, and then Raymond shut up.

Here was one reason this couple didn't talk. When Raymond talked about what was on his mind, Maureen argued or advised; he protested feebly, then folded his tent. Perhaps she was comfortable with conversational give-and-take and he wasn't. Maybe he couldn't listen to her opinions because he didn't believe in his own power to decide what to do, and her strong views made him feel anxious and unsupported. In any case, here clearly was something to work on.

Before I could start to help these two sort out their relationship, I knew I had to talk separately with Maureen about Arthur. I would propose a trial nonseparation, a period of not seeing Arthur and put-

ting her energy into improving the marriage, so she could find out if it could be better.

Maureen was relieved that I'd seen her and Raymond together. "Now you can see," she said, "how bad our relationship is. It's never going to change." (Maureen was a great believer in chemistry, that famous force of attraction with more power to excite than endure.) Nothing I said about postponing any decision until she'd waited a few weeks to see if we could improve the marriage made any difference. She started seeing Arthur again that same week, and when Raymond found out the following week, he was as forgiving as most husbands.

Their divorce was finalized a year and a day after the one time I saw them together, eleven months after Maureen's affair with Arthur heated up, and eight months after it was over. Maureen was left with the house, two children, mortgage payments she couldn't keep up with, and the memory of that shiver.

Maureen viewed her marriage as a predicament, an entity, something with a history, perhaps, but one that after a while takes on a life of its own. Most of us feel this way at times. But a relationship is not a thing, not a static state; it is a process of mutual influence. A relationship isn't something you have; it's something you do.

———◆———

Couples who learn to listen to each other – with understanding and tolerance – often find that they don't need to change each other.

———◆———

The impulse to change things, to make them better, is a natural and largely constructive one. But anyone who thinks of marriage as an infinitely improvable arrangement is making a mistake. The ideal of perfectibility breeds hope of overcoming differences and solving problems. Many problems can be solved, but the problem of living with another person who doesn't always see things the way you do or want what you want isn't one of them. Perhaps marriage isn't necessarily about resolving our differences but about learning to live together with them.

WHAT GOES AROUND

When I was in the third grade my teacher, Miss Halloway, used a stroboscope to show us how light affects what we see. Late one winter afternoon when the shadows were long she took out a small fan with a metal

blade and plugged it in. She turned on the switch, and the blade began to spin and then whir. Then she turned on the stroboscope. As she adjusted the rate of flash, the fan blade slowed down and then stopped. The blade looked so still and harmless! How easy it would be, I thought, to reach out and touch it.

The blade looks stationary, Miss Halloway explained, because the stroboscope illuminates only one point in the cycle. As I came to realize later, this is the same way we usually see our relationships.

The first thing to understand about listening within couples is that *complementarity* is the governing principle of connection. Behavior doesn't take place in a vacuum but in the context of relationships in which we act and react to each other. In any two-person relationship, one person's behavior is functionally related to the other's. If at times we see only one point in the cycle—a friend's failure to call, for example, or a partner's lack of interest in what we have to say—that doesn't mean that relationships don't spin around in a circle.

The greatest impediment to understanding in our intimate relationships is the hurt and longing that make us look outside ourselves for the sources of our disappointment. We can't help wishing our mates would be a little more interested in what we have to say about ourselves and a little less defensive about what we have to say about them. At about this time, the romantic vision of marriage gives way to melodrama—the story of villain and victim that many unhappily married persons tell themselves and, when things get bad enough, anyone else who will listen.

Many couples expect too much of each other and then see their difficulties as more apocalyptic than they really are. The real tragedy of this tragic view is that our ability to see where we're going is compromised. Like Maureen, we fix on the hurtful things our partner does and think of our troubles as inevitable.

When all is said and done, marriage and its famous complications can be illuminated by focusing on one thing: the basic pattern of interaction between two partners. Start with the hurtful things your partner does—the avoidance or selfishness or irritability—but then ask yourself: What is the complementary other half of this pattern?

The only thing you can change is your response to the other person, and the best way to begin is by listening.

RHYTHMS OF CHANGE IN A COMMITTED RELATIONSHIP

Although the cycle of human life may be orderly, it isn't a steady, continuous march. Periods of growth and change are followed by times of relative stability in which changes are consolidated. The good news is that life isn't one long uphill struggle; sometimes we reach plateaus and can coast. The bad news is that we can't stay forever in one place. Partnership, too, has its cycles and seasons.

Courtship—what a lovely, old-fashioned word—is a time of opening up and testing for compatibility. Enchanted by freshness and discovery, the partners are absorbed and engaged with each other. Conversation flows, and listening comes easily. They find each other so novel and delightful. So attentive, so interesting, so *interested.*

Fascination makes them overlook or forgive gaps in listening. Something puts her in mind of high school, and she asks him what it was like for him. He talks eagerly about his experience, but when he doesn't reciprocate, doesn't ask her what it was like for her, she thinks it's an oversight. She'll get her turn later.

Young and in love, we take such pleasure in each other's company that sober considerations give way to dictates of the heart. Falling in love is an act of imaginative creation. Later, our hearts may shrink, and with it our attention spans and our eagerness to listen. But that's later. Now, although we might be more compatible with partners more like ourselves, nature's urge to mix genes draws us to the otherness of the other.

———◆———

The great challenge of courtship is to be together and still be yourself.

———◆———

With love at stake, we lie a little. We tell tender lies, a few self-protecting lies, and more than a few self-deluding lies. Looking back, we may wish we'd been more honest and hadn't tried so hard to get our partners to like us.

When courting couples move in the direction of their intentions, trying to discover how far they can go together, it's usually two steps forward and one step back. A dozen or so pairs over the years have sought me out for premarital counseling. What a good idea, I used to think. Unfortunately, these encounters often turn out to be quite frustrating. The people seeking help come not because they are amazingly precautious but because they are amazingly mismatched. Despite that, most

of them have passed an emotional point of no return and intend to marry, no matter what. Among the obstacles they will overcome is their own good judgment.

———◆———

If courtship were more conscious, people would pay more attention to the quality of one another's listening.

———◆———

Among the most important things to find in a mate is someone who's fun to talk to. Making friends and being able to really talk to each other is a far more reliable guide than a person's good looks, cleverness, or that dizzy feeling that people call "falling in love." (Try telling that to someone in love.)

He Needs Space, She Wants Closeness

He wants to be left alone and she wants attention. So she gives him attention and he leaves her alone.

Jack and Irene were a handsome couple, in their mid-thirties I guessed. Irene was a pretty woman, with ash-blond hair and an energetic look. The day they came to see me she was wearing a linen suit with a silk blouse. Jack, tall and slender, wore jeans. She'd dressed up; he'd dressed down. Was it just a different approach to this interview or a different approach to life?

"What brings you to therapy?" I asked, looking at both of them.

Jack answered first. "Well, I'm a little intolerant."

"What does Irene do that's hard to tolerate?"

They exchanged looks. Irene gave Jack a faint smile, and he turned back to me. "She yammers. She makes assumptions, and there's nothing I can do about it—about what she assumes—so I give up and go on about my business."

"You mean, you pull away?"

"Well . . . Yes."

He went on to describe himself as a man who isn't very emotional, married to a woman who is.

I turned to Irene. "So, Jack is learning to be more tolerant and not react to you. What would you say you're learning?"

"I'm working real hard to identify and express my feelings to him.

But he always wants an explanation of *why* I feel upset. Sometimes you don't know why; you just know that you do."

Jack's response to Irene's distress took the familiar form of an obsessional person trying to comfort an emotional one: He barraged her with questions, all based on his own approach to emotion, which was to label and compartmentalize it. (He was an electronics expert who could figure out just about any machine on earth, but with women he wished there was an instruction manual.)

Irene felt things strongly without always being able to put them into words. At these moments her husband could have comforted her by just being there, holding her perhaps, but certainly not by demanding that she stop crying and explain herself. The truth was that when Irene cried, Jack couldn't imagine it might be about anything but him, so he felt accused and guilty. His comfort took the form of asking her to reassure him. "What's the matter?" really meant "Tell me you're not mad at me."

Jack went on to talk about Irene's anger as the reason he didn't listen better. When Irene approached Jack in an excitable or nervous way, he became anxious and responded by trying to be analytic or—if that failed—by distancing himself. His distance aggravated her emotionality, which then pushed him even further away. Their failure to listen to each other wasn't caused by Irene's emotions or by Jack's anxiety; it was the combination.

Jack could see the pattern and thought Irene should break the cycle by toning down her emotional behavior. Irene thought Jack should learn to be a little more tolerant of her feelings. Even as they talked, though, they played out the familiar progression. Irene's rising pressure made Jack anxious and defensive—or, to look at the circular pattern from another angle—Jack's inability to accept what she was saying drove up her emotionality.

Finally I interrupted and told them the story of the North Wind. "One day the North Wind and the Sun were arguing about which was the most powerful force in nature. 'I can churn up the seas and drive a blizzard,' the North Wind said. 'Yes, but I can melt the snow and dry up a flood,' the Sun replied. Just then a man wearing a heavy overcoat happened by. 'I know how to settle this,' said the Sun. 'Let's see who can make that man take off his coat.' The North Wind blew hard. But the harder he blew, the more the man bundled up. Finally the Sun said, 'My turn.' The sun shone down its warmth, and the man opened his coat. The Sun shone warmer, and the man took off his coat."

Irene and Jack smiled broadly.

"Irene, sometimes you come on like the North Wind. And I don't blame you, because it's frustrating to feel shut out. And out of that frustration, you either give up or out comes the North Wind."

"You're right. I never thought of it that way."

At this point Jack, feeling relieved, opened up and started to talk about needing space. He had a lot of pressure at work, and when he came home he needed space to decompress. And Irene was afraid to give him the breathing room he needed, the freedom to read or go for a walk or spend time with his friends.

"Jack," I said, "I could tell you understood the difference between Irene being the North Wind and being the Sun. But you know, the guy wearing the coat is in the story too. It's both of them. The North Wind blows, and he bundles up, and so the North Wind blows more, and he bundles up more. He bundles up more for a lot of good reasons— he has his moods, his job is stressful, he needs his space, he likes to read . . . I respect those things. But the bundling up is part of the problem."

"I understand that," Jack said. He went on to say that he's been making an effort. After dinner, for example, he used to get up as soon as he was finished eating and go in to watch the news, while Irene cleared the table. Now he's making an effort to stay a little longer and talk with her. But, he admitted, "It's not the easiest thing for me, to be close."

By now, the atmosphere in the session had shifted. Jack and Irene had begun to see how they were locked together in a pattern in which they both pushed each other to respond in a way they didn't like.

Once Irene learns to see very clearly that coming on strong only pushes Jack away, and *he* learns that keeping his distance only makes her more anxious and persistent, they can figure out how to break their halves of the cycle. Will that magically change everything? If you kiss a frog, will he turn into a prince? Maybe not right away.

BALANCING INTIMACY AND INDEPENDENCE

In accommodating to each other, couples must negotiate the space between them as well as that separating their couplehood from the rest of the world.

When you become intimate with someone, physically and emotionally, you open up the boundary around your private self to let the other

in close. Being in love is to want no distance between you, but a wall of privacy protecting the two of you from outside intrusion. This closeness and privacy make conversation intimate, with the obvious rewards and risks.

Minimal self-reliance exists between two people when they call each other at work all the time, when neither has separate friends or independent interests, if they come to view themselves only as a pair rather than also as two individuals. Under such pressure of togetherness conversation is constrained by the threat of conflict. When two people are alone in a lifeboat, they'd better not argue.

In contrast, couples who put autonomy over connection do little together, have their own rooms, take separate vacations, have independent checking accounts, are more invested in careers or outside relationships than in each other, and don't talk much. Listening is limited because they have so many other outlets.

Most couples don't start out disengaged; the wall that grows up between them is a product of unresolved conflict. Often it's not specific transgressions so much as the not listening, the not hearing. They both feel as if the other doesn't care. That they *do* care very much but are too afraid of conflict to listen doesn't alter the feeling of being deeply unappreciated. Some people pay a lot for peace.

Typically, partners come from families with differing degrees of separateness and togetherness. Each partner tends to be more comfortable with the sort of conversational sharing he or she grew up with. Since these expectations differ, a struggle ensues over how much to talk everything over together and how much to keep to yourself. This may be the most difficult aspect of learning to listen to a new mate—developing sensitivity and tolerance to a different conversational style.

In the early stages of a couple's relationship, raging passion can mask difficulties in communicating. Sometimes both partners have broken away wrenchingly from their families, and they come together with an unchecked urgency for connection. Such fusion, such boundarylessness, the desideratum of love's young dream, is hard to sustain, especially when those in its thrall isolate themselves from family and friends. Couples who expect that all their needs for listening will be met in one all-fulfilling relationship are in for the rudest of awakenings. One reason many people get too little out of intimate relationships is that they want too much.

Tension in a couple can be resolved in one of three ways: working it out, triangulation, or distancing. When distancing between intimate

partners is unchecked by a clear boundary around their relationship, the two often drift apart.

Brendan and Gina were very much in love when they married, also very young and very much unaware of how different their backgrounds were. Hers was a large, close-knit family whose watchword was togetherness. His was a small, fragmented family in which independence and personal achievement were the highest accomplishments.

In Brendan's opinion, Gina was addicted to attachment. She always wanted to talk. Even when they were watching TV or reading, she'd interrupt every few minutes to tell him something that popped into her head. It broke his concentration and made him furious. This he tried to signal indirectly by sighing or saying "Yes?" with a weary note in his voice. But Gina didn't get the message, or did she?

Gina took closeness for granted and found Brendan's "coldness" and "detachment" selfish and punishing. Why did he have to shut her out all the time?

Brendan and Gina each had their own point of view, at best sporadically sympathetic to the other one. It's a sad and familiar story of hurt and blaming, unfortunate misunderstandings, poor choices, inability to compromise. Two young people with too great a disparity in their backgrounds and expectations to fit together easily, and too little experience to know how to work things out.

It wasn't really their differences that made the first few years together so painful; it was their inability to talk about them. Once a week or so, Gina would get fed up with Brendan's distance. At these times, Brendan was appalled by the meanness and exaggeration of the things she'd accuse him of. The worst was "You don't give a damn about anybody but yourself!" *How could she say such things?* He certainly couldn't listen. Then, feeling the frustration of not being heard, Gina would raise her voice, which only made Brendan shrink further into himself. Finally, Gina would break down in tears and sob, "Why are you so mean to me?!" Brendan only thought it, and never more than once a day.

Like a lot of ill-matched couples, Brendan and Gina gradually did learn to live with each other. After a while they had children to cushion their couplehood. Gradually they learned to accommodate to each other. Gina got used to Brendan's silences and occasional games of golf with his friends. He learned to spend more time with her and the kids. But what they never learned very well was how to talk to each other. Brendan didn't talk to Gina because he felt that she was unreasonable in

her expectations and that she didn't respect his right to his own prefer-ences. Gina continued to express from time to time her disappointment with Brendan's lack of involvement, but he never really did learn to listen. He listened well enough to pacify her—"I'm sorry"; "Yes, dear"—but not enough to understand how she felt. He wished he could change things, he wished he could escape, and these thoughts kept him from ever really understanding or coming to terms with the real person he married. Like a prisoner who thinks of nothing but freedom, he never really did adjust to the realities of his relationship.

PURSUERS AND DISTANCERS

Pursuers (like Irene) want more connection, which makes distancers (like Jack) feel pressured and pull away. The more she pursues, the more he distances; the more he distances, the more she pursues. It's a game without end, though it does have interruptions.

When pursuers get fed up with being rebuffed, they withdraw in hurt and anger. But after a while they feel a little better or start to get lonely, and then they begin the cycle all over again.

If you're a pursuer, try backing off. Pay less attention to the other person for a few days. This planned distance isn't the same as reactive distance—getting fed up and giving the other person the cold shoul-der. Snubbing isn't the same as ignoring someone; it's an attempt to punish him with silence, which of course doesn't lessen your preoccu-pation with him. Instead of getting angry and passive-aggressive, in-crease your emotional investment in other things.

When you stop pursuing, notice what happens. You'll probably find your tension rising. This is important. Consider how much of the pur-suing is an attempt to cope with your own anxiety and a lack of other avenues of satisfaction in your life.

Accept any forward movement on the part of a distancer—even if it's angry or critical. This, too, is important. Pursuers often say they want their partners to share feelings with them, but what they usually mean is positive feelings. A pursuer who experiments with shifting the pattern should try very hard to avoid getting defensive about whatever the distancer does express. Distancers have feelings, too, but they keep them locked away in tightly sealed compartments. If your distancer does start expressing his or her emotions, try to listen without getting reactive.

If you're a distancer, you know that pursuers are hard to cope with.

They put you on the defensive. It's hard to stop running when you feel someone chasing you. The first thing to realize is that it isn't just him or her chasing you; it's an interlocking pattern of pursuit and withdrawal. Instead of avoiding a pursuing partner, try initiating contact—on your terms. Call the pursuer in the middle of the day, invite him or her to go for a walk. Say what's on your mind; ask what's on your partner's.

If you shift your part in the pursuer–distancer pattern for a week, you'll discover that change is a three-step process: First you change. Second, you partner responds—usually in ways that are partly rewarding and partly annoying. Third comes your response to that response—either you change back, or you persist.

If an emotional pursuer makes a deliberate effort to stop pursuing her partner, he may not immediately respond by moving toward her. The resulting distance might make her feel cheated. She might think, *See? I changed, but he didn't.* At that critical juncture—the third step in the change process—she would either revert to her old style or persist, making an effort to remain calm, develop other interests, and give her partner space to discover his need for her.

Alternatively, if an emotional distancer decides to break the cycle of pursuit and distance by moving toward his partner, she might not immediately become calm and respond the way he wants her to. She might not, for example, be receptive to his opening up about things that are bothering him. She might be critical. If her response makes him anxious and he reverts to distancing, he might conclude, "I tried, but she'll never change." But if he *does* change back, it wouldn't be because of how his partner responded; it would be because of how he responded to her response.

Another reason the pursuer–distancer dynamic isn't so easily resolved by reversing your role in it is that pursuers and distancers tend to have constitutionally different operating styles. Pursuers have a greater affinity for relationship time; distancers prefer either time alone or activity together. (That's one reason some people are emotional distancers but sexual pursuers.) Pursuers tend to express their feelings, while distancers tend to avoid them. Pursuers have relatively permeable personal boundaries, such that they relate readily to a wide number of people. Distancers are particular and let down their defenses with only a select few people.

Although each of us has a predominant operating style as either a pursuer or a distancer, the dynamics of complementarity can trigger different roles in different relationships. For example, a man may be

a distancer with his mate and a pursuer with his mother. A woman may be a pursuer with her partner but a distancer from her father and her brother.

Distancers are unsure of themselves (in the areas where they distance); they depend on privacy for protection. Pursuing only makes them feel pressured and intruded on. (If you would approach a distancer, move slowly; don't push. Knock to enter. Give him time to anticipate company.) Distancers handle threatening issues by closing them off. Anxiety about these issues may not be acknowledged, but it is always present below the surface. The tension created by such unaddressed anxiety often triggers displaced conflict in the relationship or emotional problems in one of the partners.

Emotional pursuers handle sensitive issues by talking about them over and over again in a somewhat ritualized manner. The issues never become closed off, but the emotionality surrounding them is never dealt with. For their partners, this pseudo-communication has the effect of salt poured on an open wound.

Like other familiar complementary patterns—overfunctioning/underfunctioning, strict/lenient, fast-paced/slow-paced—the pursuer–distancer dynamic isn't static. Very little about any relationship is static.

ACCOMMODATING DIFFERENCES

Intimate partnership is a process in which two individuals restructure much of their lives into a new unit: The Couple. Friends invite The Couple over for dinner, the IRS taxes The Couple, The Couple accumulates belongings. The two separate personalities don't disappear, of course, but their relationship is now a system, their fates interactive and interdependent.

The first priority of intimate partnership is mutual accommodation to manage the myriad details of everyday living. Each partner tries to organize the relationship along familiar lines and pressures the other to accommodate. They must agree on the big things, like where to live and whether and when to have children. Less obvious, but equally important, they must coordinate daily rituals, like what to watch on television, what to eat for supper, when to go to bed, and what to do there. What's at stake is the viability of the relationship and the integrity of the partners. Unfortunately, there is a thin line between accommodation and collusion. If you don't speak up and say you don't like some-

thing, if you don't say you wish things were different, you may find your-self disappearing into your partner's ways.

Lynn was just nineteen when her mother died. After the worst of the grief gave way to emptiness, she decided to get out of New York and move to Montana. When she got off the plane, she was stunned and uplifted by the intensity of the sunlight. The last of the snow was melting, and the valley blossomed. Summer came, stretched and yawned, and then it was early fall. That's when the loneliness set in, and Lynn started wondering what she was going to do with her life. Right about then she met Travis. After all the boys she'd known in New York who couldn't stop talking about themselves, Lynn took Travis's quietness for strength. She thought he was the real deal. So when he asked her to share his trailer with him, it seemed like the right thing to do.

A year later their relationship wasn't a lot better or a lot worse. Maybe a wedding would do the trick. So Lynn gave Travis an ultima-tum: either they get married or she was moving out. But even walking down the aisle, she found herself thinking, "This is never going to last." Afterward she got drunk, hoping to numb this giant step into the unknown.

Lynn got pregnant on the honeymoon, and two weeks later Travis joined the Air Force. When Travis was posted to Korea, he went ahead to get settled, and Lynn moved in with his parents. It was not a happy time. And so, six weeks later, when she boarded the plane for Inchon, it was with as much relief as anxiety.

When jet lag wore off and reality settled in, Lynn found herself alone all day with the baby in a tiny apartment. She'd written Travis to buy a car with automatic transmission because she couldn't drive a stick shift; but he hadn't listened. Not being able to drive sealed her isolation. When she tried to talk to Travis about it, he said, "What's the matter with you? You'll get the hang of it. Don't be such a big baby." What could she say?

Unfortunately, Lynn neither insisted that Travis listen to how she was feeling nor asked how he was feeling. "I nagged," Lynn says. "I was angry and bitchy. Back then I wasn't very sure of what I was feeling, and so the frustration just built up and came out as attack. Instead of telling him how I was feeling, I'd say things like 'We never do anything'; 'You never take me anywhere.' He always put it back on me. 'What's the matter with you?' That was his answer to all my complaints." She didn't really remember Travis's complaints; all she remembered was that he didn't listen to hers.

Going into the marriage, Lynn had thought that if she did all the right things, Travis could become the man she wanted—loving and affectionate. She'd grown up with a self-absorbed father, and the main question for her always had been "How do I make Daddy happy?" With Travis, she'd played the good wife, hoping for a payoff of affection and attention. But there was no affection; just sex. Lynn put up with not having her needs met because she wasn't sure how to put them into words.

When her frustration turned to bitterness, Lynn's conversations with Travis took on the form of combat. Each felt trapped and misunderstood, and both of them led with their defenses. After suffering so much neglect, Lynn was seized with rage when she tried to talk about her feelings. When she opened up on him with a mean mouth, his stomach knotted and he stopped listening. Once or twice, when she cornered him, he'd answer her accusations with an outburst of his own nursed resentment. Then they'd go back to avoiding each other.

The proximity forced on them in Korea may have kept them together longer than otherwise, or it may have put too much pressure on their shaky alliance. In any case, when Travis was posted back to the States and Lynn started school again, the marriage fell apart. With school and friends of her own, Lynn felt stronger and no longer willing to put up with a relationship that gave her so little satisfaction. Ironically, as Lynn started pulling away, Travis asked her to stay and for the first time since the early days of the relationship tried to listen to her. But it was too late.

Lynn said: "He wanted someone to mother him, to cook and clean and all that. I was willing to do it, and so he was happy. But when I wanted more from him, he couldn't deal with it, and he hated me. Then my independence gave him the room he needed, and so he started liking me again. But now I knew it had been a mistake to begin with." And so they ended it.

Travis and Lynn might have had an easier time adjusting to other mates. Maybe not. Second and third marriages don't fail because people keep picking the wrong partners; they fail because it's not our differences that matter but how they're negotiated. Maybe Lynn tried to do too much compromising, in the process leaving too little room for herself. Maybe Travis did too little compromising. He was a young man caught up in confirming his masculinity rather than achieving love, and perhaps he was afraid he'd lose himself by giving in. The trouble was, neither of them dared to listen to the other's point of view.

Travis and Lynn might have found a way to talk about their differ-

ences if they'd managed to be less emotionally reactive to each other. Instead of holding her feelings in until they exploded, Lynn might have approached Travis calmly (it isn't necessary to *feel* calm to *speak* calmly), saying, perhaps, "Something's bothering me and I need to talk to you. Is this a good time?"

———————◆———————

The best way to tone down emotionality isn't to avoid talking about problems but to discuss them openly — before the upset boils over.

———————◆———————

Travis thought that if he didn't listen to Lynn's complaints, he wouldn't have to deal with them — and he could avoid the anxiety her distress made him feel. But he found out that feelings are like any other form of energy: if they don't find direct expression, they come out in other ways.

The way to reduce your own defensiveness is to stay calm and stay open. Don't interrupt, contradict, qualify, or change the subject. If you don't understand something, ask for clarification and examples. Otherwise, shut up and listen.

"Why Can't a Woman Be More Like a Man?"

When the differences that attract turn out to be hard to live with, we may be tempted to think that intimate partnership works best with a person as similar to us as possible. Actually, that's not true. With very similar partners there is the possibility for weaknesses to combine and create exaggerated, even destructive, imbalances. Two people with explosive tempers or who are financially irresponsible often form disastrous unions.

Lynn told herself she married the wrong person. Travis was strong and good-looking and smart, but he didn't know how to trust people with the truth about his feelings. A man dedicated to autonomy, married to a woman who prized togetherness. Travis, too, thought the mistake he made was choosing the wrong mate. He never suspected that the extravagant and desirable woman he fell in love with would turn out to be a dependent nag.

Your partner doesn't have the power to say what is and forever shall be or who's right and who's wrong. Even the person who puts things that way doesn't have the power to make it so; *you* give him that power if you react as though he did.

You don't have to agree to acknowledge that the other person has a point.

The simple act of omission involved in not acknowledging what the other person is saying before countering with your own point of view may be the single greatest impediment to shared understanding. If we don't know that we've been heard, we're not about to hear what the other person is saying. Instead, we turn away or raise our voices. Maybe if we scream at her, she'll hear.

Emotionally charged discussions should be kept as brief as possible. Don't unload everything. Doing so only makes the listener feel inundated, nailed to the wall, with just two choices: fight or flight.

Nowhere to turn. That's the way a lot of unhappy people feel about their relationships—trapped in the space of a relationship with another person who has some pretty strange ways. Accommodation means finding a way to fit together, but many couples mistake fitting together as an all-or-nothing proposition.

Wise couples accept their differences and accommodate. But they also realize that accommodating doesn't mean they must become two peas in a pod. Maybe she'll never be interested in politics. Maybe he'll never really get to like her parents. Rather than battle over these differences, or be untrue to themselves by giving in entirely, realistic partners avoid dwelling on certain subjects about which they cannot agree. But instead of drifting apart or insulating themselves emotionally from each other, they search for alternative avenues of connection.

Listening and adjusting to each other's realities requires a balance between tolerance and selective coming together. Mates may tire of hearing about each other's job, but they owe each other a few minutes of listening at the end of the day. (Asking questions may make familiar stories more interesting.) But couples must also search to discover which subjects are most rewarding to talk about (with each other). The same balance applies to activities other than talking.

When Dennis returned from playing golf on Sunday morning, Lorraine was still in bed, so he took off his clothes and crawled in beside her. When he kissed her awake, she gave him a dubious look. It wasn't what he'd hoped for, but over the years he'd learned the difference between a red light and a yellow one. When they were first married, Dennis expected Lorraine to be ready for sex without warning. When she tried

to slow him down and later said no, he felt rejected and avoided her altogether. Now he read her look as saying that she was happy to see him but not really in the mood to make love. They did a lot of talking with their eyes, but he made himself say, "Let's just hug a little." They did, and after a while Lorraine relaxed enough to become more affectionate. In the end they did make gentle love.

After lunch Dennis mentioned that he was going to watch football for a while. Once he'd expected to watch football all day on Sunday, and Lorraine, who came from a family that didn't follow the national obsession, would get very angry. For years they'd alternate between his watching and her fuming to his not watching and feeling resentful. This day he watched the first half while she had a long phone conversation with a friend, read the paper, and occasionally looked up when the crowd roared. At halftime she asked if he wanted to go to the movies. He did. Movies were one thing they never had to compromise about. They went to see *Batman Returns* but didn't go shopping afterward, as he knew she would have liked and she knew he would not have. After supper, they watched television for a while, until Lorraine went into the other room and read. It was a nice day.

As this example illustrates, listening in its full sense means taking each other into account. Dennis listened to Lorraine signaling her mood; later she listened to his wish to watch football, and between them they found a balance between separateness and togetherness.

In spite of the large emotions involved, marriage isn't about monumental issues; it's about little things, about everydayness, about knowing that tomorrow morning you'll wake up with a new chance to work at it, to get it a bit more wrong or right.

GETTING BEYOND BITTERNESS

Couples who survive the break-in period continue to go through cycles of closeness and distance. Some conflicts are resolved, others are avoided, and a few keep cropping up from time to time. Arguments still occur, but the nature of these heated discussions should change over time. They become less bitter and less violent. There is less blaming and a greater feeling that both of you are in the same boat. If arguments don't become less frequent, less intense, and shorter, partners would do well to see what they're doing to keep emotionality high and listening absent.

Successful couples learn that the methods most commonly used in attempting to induce unilateral change—complaining, cajoling, sweet-talking, nagging, inducing guilt, becoming angry, and using other forms of emotional manipulation—don't work very well. When empathy doesn't come easy, successful partners work at it—making themselves listen even when they would prefer to be heard. (You don't have to *feel* sympathetic to listen. Sometimes showing concern works from the outside in, the way smiling can put you in a good mood.)

Problems arise when partners keep too many secrets, say yes when they don't mean it, or don't tell the truth about their feelings because they're afraid of arguments. The broken promises that result from being afraid to say no are too great a price to pay for avoiding honest argument. Learning to say no enables you to say yes and mean it. If you're wishing that your partner would realize this, ask yourself, why would someone lie to you?

Trust allows partners to relax vigilance. Being honest is central to establishing this trust, as is being open, listening to and acknowledging the hard things your partner says. Love that grows out of and feeds into self-respect is love for ourselves as we are, not for a partial and carefully selected portion. The person who hesitates to speak wonders if it's safe to broach certain embarrassing or controversial issues. The person who never opens up to you has already decided that it isn't safe to speak.

———◆———

If we want the truth from our partners, we must make it safe for them to tell it.

———◆———

Unfortunately, even with the best of intentions, many couples reach a point where they get bogged down in bitterness and can't hear each other at all. Pursuers get sick of pursuing and distancers get tired of all the pressure, until one or both of them pulls back so far that they reach what family therapist Phil Guerin calls an "island of invulnerability."[1] Anger and animosity build to bitter resentment, and two people who once thrilled each other now give up on each other. Giving up on satisfaction in favor of security, retreating to the island of invulnerability, is cold comfort. But even loneliness sometimes feels better than constant conflict.

[1]Philip Guerin, Leo Fay, Susan Burden, and Judith Kautto, *The Evaluation and Treatment of Marital Conflict* (New York: Basic Books, 1987).

Mates bogged down in bitterness can take a step toward releasing themselves from ice castles of frozen hope by taking a hard look at those hopes. If you're willing to let go of blaming and look for a way back together, examine your expectations. Are your conflicts based on a desire for a partner who is fundamentally different from the one you married? If you're chronically irritated with your partner for being who she or he is, rather than about some particular behavior, then you are in the wrong relationship and it's never going to be very fulfilling. The only things worth fighting about are the things that can be changed.

People come to intimate partnership with an interesting and self-contradictory pair of expectations. They expect their partners both to duplicate the good aspects of their own families and to make up for the bad. To make matters worse, these expectations are often directed toward a partner's limitations rather than his or her strengths. ("I know he could be a really sociable person, if he only tried.")

Don't judge your partner by measuring him (or her) against your strengths; measure him by his strengths. Everybody wants to be appreciated for their contributions.

———◆———

No one benefits when weaknesses or shortcomings become the principal focus of attention in a relationship.

———◆———

To move away from bitterness, concentrate on your partner's strengths. See if some of the things you find objectionable are actually the downside of attributes you appreciate, that even attracted you in the first place. If your partner were different in ways that you'd like, he or she would also be different in ways you wouldn't like. Request changes of certain behavior, but don't punish your partner for what you consider misbehavior. Find your way to forgiveness and acceptance. Tenderness and appreciation will follow.

With maturity, the human quest moves from the outside in, from conquering the world and subduing others to struggling with ourselves—to be who we are and to be connected to others. Looking for love that will simultaneously recreate and undo the past, we latch on to someone and hope for the best.

New couples are ripe with possibility. Over time they become progressively structured as a system, organized by the demands of living together and perhaps raising a family. As we've seen, the process

that transforms two people into a pair is based on accommodation and boundary making.

At first the patterns of behavior a couple establishes are free to vary; later they may become entrenched. But even then, change is possible. The key is complementarity. Those who would remake their own luck must learn to see the annoying things their partners do as one part of a pattern, a pattern that connects two people together in cycles of action and reaction. Look to your part.

CHAPTER ELEVEN

"Nobody Around Here Ever Listens to Me!"

HOW TO LISTEN AND BE HEARD WITHIN THE FAMILY

As we've seen, the quality of understanding between people isn't fixed in character but depends on the *process* of their interaction. The great advantage to understanding the process of relationships is flexibility. What can be seen as a pattern of mutual influence can be changed. But there's a catch. Patterns of communication in families are often resistant to change because they're embedded in powerful but unseen structures.

FAMILY STRUCTURE

Families, like other groups, have rich possibilities for relationship and satisfaction. (Don't we marry and later bring children into the world with clear and simple hopes for happiness?) Walt Whitman said, "I contain multitudes." The same could be said of family relationships, though, sadly, many soon congeal into limited and limiting molds.

Listening is an art that requires openness to each other's uniqueness and tolerance of differences. The greatest threats to listening in the family are rigid roles, fixed expectations, and pressures to conform.

As they are repeated, family transactions foster expectations that establish enduring patterns.[1] Once these patterns are established, family members use only a fraction of the full range of behavior available to them. The first time the baby cries or the in-laws come to visit or a child misses the school bus, it's not determined who will do what. Will the load be shared? Will there be a quarrel? Will one person get stuck with all the work? Soon patterns will be set, roles assigned, and things take on a sameness and predictability.

When a mother tells her child to put away his toys and he ignores her until his father yells at him, an interactional pattern is initiated. If it's repeated, it creates a structure in which father is the heavy and mother is the overburdened listener.

Family members tend to have reciprocal and complementary functions; the more one parent does for the children, the less the other is likely to do.

The Possibilities in Every Pair

The family system differentiates and carries out its functions through *subsystems.* Every individual is a subsystem, and dyads (such as husband–wife or mother–child), as well as larger groups, make up other subsystems, determined by generation, gender, common interests, and functional responsibilities.

Individuals, subsystems, and whole families are demarcated by interpersonal *boundaries,* invisible barriers that regulate the amount of contact one has with others. Boundaries protect the autonomy of the family and its subsystems. A rule forbidding phone calls at dinnertime estab-

---

[1]Salvador Minuchin, *Families and Family Therapy* (Cambridge, MA: Harvard University Press, 1974); Salvador Minuchin and Michael P. Nichols, *Family Healing* (New York: The Free Press, 1993).

lishes a boundary that insulates the family from outside intrusion. When small children are permitted to freely interrupt their parents' conversations, the boundary separating the parents from the children is weak.

Subsystems that aren't adequately shielded by boundaries limit the development of understanding achievable in these subgroups. If parents always step in to settle arguments between their children, the children won't learn to fight their own battles.

These days when work and school and after-school activities consume so much of our lives, most of us have less personal time and less family time. In the little time we have left over for our families, many of us are reluctant to exclude some members of the family so that others can do things together—such as a father taking a daughter to a basketball game or a mother and son taking in a movie together. This is unfortunate.

——◆——

Time alone together allows every pair in the family a chance to talk and freedom to listen.

——◆——

The most obvious example of a relationship that suffers without time alone together is the one between wife and husband.

Lewis complained that he'd lost his wife to the children. Once Iris was his wife and his friend and his lover. Deciding to have kids and the pregnancy and the birth and those first few wonderful, exhausting months of babyhood brought them closer together. Then, as Lewis saw it, Iris just kind of pulled motherhood over her head, and that was that. They were still friends, sort of, but they were more parents than anything else. They rarely listened to each other because they rarely talked. When Lewis decided to move beyond cursing his fate and casting blame, he found that the simple act of spending time alone together with Iris was the first step in revitalizing his marriage. (In the process he discovered that two people who aren't spending time together aren't just busy; they're also anxious about the quality of their listening.)

Parents also need time alone with each of their children. One of the best ways for parents to listen to their children is to arrange little outings with each one. Once a week isn't too much to aim for. Even if a child has a good relationship with a parent, conversation and intimacy are easier away from everyday distractions. The time a parent spends taking a child out to dinner or for a hike or on a bus ride into

the city may well be the best time in both of their lives. Every pair has possibilities.

Now let's look at how some familiar structural flaws create problems in listening.

When Boundaries Are Blurred

The two biggest mistakes parents make in listening to their children both involve a blurring of boundaries: failing to establish control over their children's behavior and interfering too much in their lives.

The most important thing to keep in mind when listening to children is the difference between allowing them to *express* what they want and allowing them to *do* what they want. When a young child says "I don't want to go to bed," he or she is expressing a feeling and making a request. A wise parent distinguishes between the two and acknowledges the feeling before ruling on the request.

Of course children don't want to go to bed! They might miss something. Staying awake is their way of clutching at life. Parents who blur the distinction between expression and action get into foolish debates with their children. They say "I don't care what you want, you're going to bed anyway." Or they try to convince children that they're tired, as though obeying the rules depended on agreeing with them.

Parents who confuse love with leniency often fall into a pattern of not setting and enforcing rules. Mistaking permissiveness for understanding and democracy for respect, such parents confuse their children about who is in charge and end up too anxious about controlling the children's behavior to be able to listen to their feelings and opinions. The dichotomy between strictness and understanding is a false one; actually, they go together.

The most common alternative to effective discipline is nagging. Constant bickering with children wounds their pride and does more to engender insecurity than to establish parental authority. Effective parents take firm control early in their children's lives and use it sparingly. They make clear and consistent rules *and* back them up. Children learn from consequences. Whenever possible, parents should let them learn from the natural consequences of their behavior. If the consequence of every third or fourth thing they do is that their parents nag them, children learn that their parents are nags and that they themselves are a nuisance.

The boundary that helps parents listen to their children because they know they're in charge is related to one of the crucial elements

in listening: acknowledging what the other person says before responding with what you have to say.

Remember Tommy, the boy whose father lectured him on the futility of anger? If only his father had first acknowledged what Tommy was feeling, the boy might have been less upset and more open to his father's message. Seeing Tommy storm upstairs and slam his door, his father might have said, "It's frustrating when that mower doesn't work, isn't it?" or "Sounds like you had a bad day."

Being a parent in charge doesn't automatically make you a good listener, but it does release you from some of the anxiety about control that gets in the way of listening.

If you listen in on conversations between parents and children, you'll often notice how little each listens to the other. The conversation sounds like two monologues, one consisting of criticism and instruction, the other of denial and pleading. Parents anxious about authority are too easily aggravated to listen to many things children have to say.

Suppose a little girl runs into the kitchen saying, "Look, I caught a caterpillar!" The mother who responds with "Go wash your dirty hands!" is obviously deflating the child's enthusiasm. Saying, "Yes that's nice, but go and wash your hands" isn't good enough either.

"Yes, but . . . " is insufficient acknowledgment. Like adults, children need to feel heard before they can be open to a new thought. If a mother were to take a minute to acknowledge her child's enthusiasm, she might say, "What a lovely caterpillar," or "Hey, wow! Good for you." The little girl, feeling heard and appreciated, might then wash her hands without needing to be told, especially if she knows that that's the rule.

Even when they make an effort to acknowledge what the other person is saying before replying, many people don't make *enough* of an effort.

"Yes, but . . . " is never enough. The *but* drowns out the *yes*.

Emotional Triangles

When he came downstairs, Marshall was surprised to see his teenage daughter sitting at the breakfast table sipping hot chocolate. Before he could ask why she was still home, Paula jumped up and threw her arms around his neck: "No school!" Looking out the window, Marshall saw the yard blanketed in white.

Assuming that the driving would be bad, Marshall decided to wait until after nine before going to work. By that time the roads would be

clear and the worst of the traffic would be gone. While he boiled water and ground the beans for coffee, Paula built a fire in the fireplace. When the coffee was ready and the fire blazing, they sat on the couch to watch the flames and share something that had gone out of their relationship: spending time together.

Just then the front door flew open, and in walked Paula's boyfriend, Jerry. "Guess what? School's canceled!"

"Hi, Jerry," Marshall said, none too enthusiastically. Then he went upstairs to his study. He didn't exactly slam the door, but he didn't close it very gently either.

Paula and her father, who had been so close, were growing farther and farther apart in this, her last year of high school. As Marshall sat there brooding about how Paula seemed to drop everything, including her homework, when Jerry was around, he knew he was wrong. Daughters grew up and had boyfriends; a father had to accept these things. He knew he was wrong to be so irritated by Jerry, and now he had that bitterness as well to swallow.

When Paula was born, Marshall vowed never to be one of those fathers who said, "I'll play with you tomorrow." What a remarkable thing it was to be a daddy, gifted and burdened with the power to bestow moments of total delight. As Paula grew older, they still did special things together, but he noticed that her pleasure in his company was no longer entirely spontaneous; he knew that at least part of the time they spent together now was only to please him.

Two weeks later Jerry broke up with Paula. She cried but showed no sign of real grief. These things happen. Marshall couldn't help being secretly relieved and said so to his wife, Elaine.

On Monday Paula said she couldn't face going to school. Couldn't she stay home, just for one day? It seemed little enough to ask. That afternoon Elaine decided to come home early and cheer Paula up with a little shopping expedition. Finding Paula asleep in her room, still in her nightgown, was no great surprise. After all, it wasn't easy being seventeen and having your heart broken. Elaine never knew what made her go into the little bathroom, where she found the empty bottle of aspirin in the wastebasket.

Paula spent four weeks at Twin Oaks on the adolescent unit, where she learned the importance of giving voice to her feelings. When she discovered her anger, she started raging at her mother for always wanting everything to be "nice" and for thinking that going shopping could possibly be the answer to her problems. Her mother then did a surpris-

ing thing: she listened. But when Paula directed her anger at Marshall, telling him that he'd been unfair to blame her for growing up and having a boyfriend, Marshall lashed back at her. Nothing hurts like the truth.

During the last week of Paula's stay in the hospital, Jerry came to visit her, and after she was discharged they started seeing each other again. Marshall was not happy.

Aside from his earlier objections about Jerry, he didn't think it was a good idea for Paula to put herself back into a dependent and vulnerable position. His mind filled with bitter thoughts—about this callow boy who'd hurt his daughter, and might do so again, and about Paula's unforgiving anger at *him*. Well, maybe bitter thoughts were easier than wondering, achingly, how a father lets go of his daughter.

Now when Jerry came around, Marshall was barely civil. He wanted to talk to Paula about not becoming dependent, about the importance of having many friends, but he was afraid of her anger and his own. So he started complaining to Elaine.

Paula, too, started complaining to her mother. "Why is Daddy so unfair?"

Time passed, and the crisis—for that's what Marshall called it; he couldn't bring himself to say "suicide attempt"—began to seem unreal and long ago. Routine reasserted itself, and the only truly tense moments were occasions on which Paula wanted to go somewhere with Jerry, and Marshall looked grim and said nothing. If Paula pressed him, he said sarcastically, "Ask your mother." He felt angry and bereft, but increasingly less so.

Winter passed, and then it was spring. After graduation Paula broke off with Jerry, saying she wanted to have her last summer at home free to be with her friends. Men, she had learned, can be pretty jealous and possessive.

In D. H. Lawrence's *Sons and Lovers*, Paul Morel, the young artist, doesn't feel free to become his own person until his adored mother releases him from her possessive love by dying. In the last scene, when Paul's sweetheart, Miriam, asks if he is now free to marry, he says no. He's become free to go his own way.

One of the great themes of literature is the oedipal conflict—a child's passionate attachment to one parent and rivalry with the other. In real families, children fall in and out of love with each parent many times. We expect fathers to become antagonistic to their sons—and hope they will grow out of it. But when a father becomes alienated from his daugh-

ter, as Marshall did, we seek explanations in character and circumstance. Maybe Marshall was too attached to his daughter to tolerate a rival. Maybe he was too stubborn to let go. Or perhaps we can be more generous and say that it was only natural for him to worry about Paula's relationship with Jerry, considering what happened.

The trouble with these explanations is that they may account for the conflict but not why it wasn't resolved. Most family conflicts eventually get worked out—*if* the parties involved are willing to listen to each other.

When Paula felt the innocent indignation of being misunderstood by her father, it seemed only natural to turn to her mother. Likewise, when Marshall found himself troubled but uncertain about Paula's seeing Jerry again, it seemed reasonable to complain to his wife. In turning away from each other and detouring their dispute through Elaine, Paula and her father created a triangle, one of the great roadblocks to listening.

Take a minute to think about your most difficult relationship in the family. Chances are you thought of the one between you and your spouse, or maybe one of your parents, or a child, or perhaps one of your in-laws. Actually, the relationship you thought of is almost certainly between you and that person and one or more third parties.

Virtually all emotionally significant relationships between two people are shadowed by a third—a relative, a friend, even a memory.

The most notorious triangle is the extramarital affair. An affair might compensate for something missing in a marriage, but as long as one's emotional energy is invested elsewhere, there's little chance of improving the primary relationship. Similarly, if a young husband or wife remains overly attached to his or her parents and runs to them with complaints about the new spouse, the couple in formation may never work out their difficulties. Unlike infidelity and interfering in-laws, many forms of triangulation seem so innocent that we hardly notice their destructive effect. Most parents who have pretty good relationships with their children can't seem to resist complaining to them once in a while about their spouses. "Your mother's *always* late!" "Your father *never* lets anyone else drive!" These interchanges seem harmless enough. Someone who's upset about something has to talk about it, right?

When you hear a story in which one person is a victim and the other is a villain, you're being invited into a triangle.

If something's really bothering you and you're afraid to talk about it—afraid you won't be listened to—the urge to confide in someone else is overwhelming. The trouble with triangles isn't so much that complaining or seeking solace is wrong. The problem is that many triangles become chronic diversions that corrupt and undermine listening in our family relationships.

Mary Lewis was a twenty-year-old single mother who came to the clinic because she was having trouble controlling her three-year-old. After I'd listened to her unhappiness and frustration for about forty minutes, Mary confessed that she'd been hitting the baby and was afraid she might hurt her. I was alarmed but not content to think of the problem as located only in one person, so I asked Mary to bring Tamara to the next session.

Mary, who was alone and isolated, related to her little daughter like a playmate. When the baby was building a tower with blocks, Mary grabbed away some of the blocks to make her own tower, insisting that the baby "share." Later in the session, when I was trying to talk with Mary about her life as a single mom and Tamara started throwing blocks at the door, Mary yelled at her—"Quiet down, OK? I'm talking to the doctor"—but she didn't follow up. Tamara looked up and then continued throwing blocks. She seemed used to ignoring her mother.

Over the next two sessions I helped Mary understand and practice what it means to be a mother-in-charge. Parents take charge by being parental, which consists of two things: nurture and control. (The latter makes the former easier.) Mary learned not to try to control everything the baby did but that when she did need to enforce a rule to do so with a clear, direct message and then follow through with consequences. Becoming more in charge made it easier for her to be more tolerant of Tamara in play. The language of small children is a language of action; "listening" to them means letting them take the lead in play.

Mary was a receptive learner, and her relationship with Tamara improved rapidly. They started getting along better, but in the fifth session Mary reported that she was still having trouble controlling Tamara at home. It was only then that she told me that often when Tamara

was punished, she'd run down the hall to her grandmother's apartment. Instead of supporting her daughter's authority, Mrs. Lewis tried to comfort Tamara by telling her not to worry, "Grandma loves you."

Mrs. Lewis's interference with her daughter's mothering may strike you as too obviously misguided to be of much relevance to the problems of listening in your own life. But aren't we playing the same game whenever we take one person's side against another?

Most family problems are triangular. That's why working only on a twosome may have limited results. Teaching a mother better techniques for disciplining her son won't resolve the problem that she's over-involved with the boy as a result of her husband's emotional distance from her.

Are triangles always a problem? No. Sometimes you just *have to* talk to someone else. For example, when I complain to my friends about my wife nagging me to take out the garbage, it's just because my wife doesn't understand why I don't always feel like doing it. Besides, if I tried to discuss this directly with her, we might get into tedious and unnecessary issues, like fairness and inequality and so on.

When Rigid Boundaries Keep Us Apart

Some families (or individuals or dyads) establish rigid boundaries, so restrictive that they permit little outside contact, resulting in *disengagement*. Disengaged individuals or subsystems are independent but isolated. On the positive side this fosters autonomy, growth, and mastery. If parents don't hover over their children, telling them what to do and fighting their battles, the children will be forced to develop their own resources. On the other hand, disengagement limits warmth, affection, and nurture.

Being listened to by parents who are a reliable presence in their lives is how children build confidence in their powers of communication. Parents may not always listen, but for a daycare worker in charge of eight toddlers at once it's almost impossible to listen more than very briefly.

A visit to your child's school might result in the sober realization of how little our children are listened to, might inspire you to reoccupy center stage in your children's school-dominated lives. Spending time with your children—in whatever way you can without struggling for control—helps displace peer pressure and pedagogy that pressure your

children to conform or rebel, both of which undermine their efforts to discover themselves. The best way to help children figure out who they are is to listen to them.

Disengagement is a behavioral description for lack of involvement—spending time together, sharing activities, talking. People who are disengaged aren't necessarily uncaring, even if they do seem to spend all their time pursuing their own interests. Often these people are using distance and displacement to protect their own conversational sensitivities.

Suzanne and Rick were worried about their small son's difficulty making friends. The boy's lack of friends, as it turned out, was nothing serious, little more than a ticket of admission to therapy. Actually, Suzanne was far more concerned with lack of tenderness between her and Rick. She complained of his distance and of his not thinking about her needs, but she talked in an anxious, vague way, circling her feelings, never really saying flat out what she meant.

Rick tried to listen but wasn't very good at it. Perhaps he heard and recoiled at the underlying whininess of Suzanne's complaints. Suzanne also mentioned—"by the way"—that she was seeing an individual therapist. When I asked why, she said she needed someone to understand how she felt, and she wasn't getting that from Rick. (*Oh, great,* I thought. *She's using a therapist as her confidant at the same time she's trying to create a more confiding relationship with her husband.*)

The hard core of Suzanne's and Rick's problem with intimacy wasn't that they were busy or that the wild happiness they once knew had faded or simply that they'd gotten out of the habit of being close. It was that they had trouble talking and listening to each other. Her contribution was holding back her complaints and then making them in a nebulous but blaming way. His contribution was neither listening hard enough to penetrate Suzanne's metaphors to hear her loneliness and need nor speaking up about his own complaints. He made a typical unconscious bargain: if he wasn't satisfying her complaints, he'd better not make any of his own, lest that obligate him.

After a while they did start getting through to each other. Suzanne was able to be more direct when she realized how she'd learned to be indirect to avoid her mother's stinging remarks. Rick worked harder at listening and harder at speaking up. Then Suzanne made what felt like a confession. For years she'd spent hours every day confiding in her journal. She spoke of it almost like a child's invisible friend. This, then, was Rick's rival.

Is it wrong to complain about your spouse to an individual therapist? Is it wrong to keep a journal? Of course not. But the more we confide our wishes and dissatisfactions to other than the people we want to get closer to, the less pressure we feel to work directly on those relationships.

Disengaged relationships don't exist in a vacuum. To close the distance between yourself and someone you love, keep two things in mind: You catch more flies with honey than with vinegar. And if you want to close the distance in a disengaged relationship, be prepared to hear some complaints. Disengagement isn't just distance; it's protective distance.

When Closeness Smothers Intimacy

Sometimes the boundaries separating the family or a pair within it from the rest of the world are so rigid that the relationship becomes enmeshed, offering closeness at the expense of independence and autonomy. Isolation from outside contact—from conversation, broadly speaking, with the rest of the world—puts too much pressure on any relationship. Intimacy grows with time together and time apart.

Enmeshed relationships can comfort like a warm blanket on a cold night or chafe like a warm blanket on a hot night. Children enmeshed with their parents become dependent. They're less comfortable by themselves and may have trouble relating to people outside the family.

In the back of most people's minds is the unquestioned assumption that parental involvement with children is a good thing: if children are having problems, their parents must not be sufficiently involved or caring. In some cases this is true. But in other cases the problem is a parent's anxious overinvolvement, robbing children of room to be themselves—to have problems, make mistakes, and learn to chart their own course.

A clear boundary between the generations puts the parents in charge, allows them to claim their own rights and privacy, and helps them respect the children's freedom and autonomy within their own orbit.

When family therapists encounter mothers enmeshed with their children, they certainly don't want to blame mothers for this arrangement (as though a family's structure were the unilateral doing of one of its members). Oh, no, they wouldn't do that.

Enmeshment, unfortunately, *is* usually blamed on mothers. Who else? They're the ones smothering their children, aren't they? (Most of

us still harbor ancient grudges against the hand that rocked the cradle.) Blaming mothers for a family structure that leaves them underinvolved with their husbands and overinvolved with their children is like saying that a car without spark plugs won't go because the pistons don't fire. Infants and mothers engulfed in the blissful intimacy of new baby love need paternal involvement. They need a supporter and a confidant, not a frustrated competitor.

Children need attachment? So do their parents, not just to their children but to each other.

Some people are togetherness oriented. They value closeness and connection, but these values can sometimes actually reduce intimacy if they result in pressure to conform. To achieve genuine closeness, you must respect all family members' sovereign individual experience, their right to their own feelings and their own point of view.

Forming a United Front

To forge an alliance that works, both parents must yield some separateness to gain in belonging. *Accommodation* is the process by which people adjust their differences to come together. It is the mechanism of compromise, sometimes a deliberate matter of agreement and cooperation, sometimes the result of instinctive mutual adjustments. Unified family leadership is based on communication, compromise, and agreement between the parents and then presented to the children as one policy. Most parents discover how important it is to accommodate their differences about nurture and control to present a united front.

––––––◆––––––

When a child's misbehavior persists, you can bet that one parent isn't backing the other up.

––––––◆––––––

If you don't feel supported by your partner in parenting, if you end up doing all the driving or always have to be the one to enforce the rules, don't start blaming your partner. Maybe he or she disagrees with what you're doing. Try asking.

"I get the feeling you don't really agree with my way of handling this. Maybe you don't think I'm interested in your opinion—but I am. I'd really like to hear what you think."

Parenting is also an excellent place to observe the other face of complementarity—polarization. Instead of coming together on certain

issues, parents move further apart. If one is too strict, the other may react by becoming more lenient. The more one harps at the children, the more the other tries to compensate by being indulgent.

Polarization is like what happens if the controls on your dual-control electric blanket accidentally get switched. The first attempt by either of you to make it warmer or colder will set off a cycle of mutual maladjustments.

Small differences drive some couples to antagonistic opposites. A mother whose threshold for telling the kids to quiet down at the dinner table is only slightly higher than her husband's may never get the chance to admonish them if he always shushes them before she feels the need. Every time he reprimands the kids she'll feel that he's being too harsh. If she complains about his impatience, he'll feel betrayed and angry. The dinner table then becomes a tense battleground, where instead of sticking together, two parents become adversaries in a game where everybody loses.

Why do couples accommodate on some issues and polarize on others? Because we accommodate where we're able but polarize in response to our own inner conflicts.

The engine that drives conflicts within us to become conflicts between us is projection. This dynamic comes into play when an ambivalent inner balance between pairs of conflicting impulses (dependence–independence; emotional expression–restraint; desire–anxiety; privacy–companionship) is resolved by projecting one's own motivation onto the other person. A man (or woman) who's afraid of anger may express it through passive control that provokes his (or her) partner. When they fight, she gets angry and he gets hurt. The man who feels only hurt may be seething with rage but can remain unaware of those feelings as long as he has a collusive, obliging mate who will act out his anger for him. In the process, the partner who shows anger may be able to avoid facing inner feelings of weakness and helplessness.

———◆———

Polarized mates fight in each other denied and repudiated aspects of themselves.

———◆———

Projection and polarization turn couples into antagonists and prevent partners from integrating latent possibilities in the self—because these are played out by the other. The tough man may be unable to integrate his softer side to the extent that his wife acts emotional and helpless. His dependent wishes and vulnerability are repudiated because

they're seen as her domain. She then becomes a dependent and demanding wife. This is one reason men take revenge for their dependency—that bottomless need for mother-love—by bullying and criticizing their wives for openly exhibiting the needs they themselves don't dare express.

In our day, gender differences have permeated the consciousness of the middle class. No longer do we believe that men are strong and women weak. Yet what is the current vogue of celebrating women's and men's uniqueness if not stereotyping updated? It's hard for husbands and wives to work at partnership when all around they are told that women speak in a different voice and men have strange ways of communicating.

Are we once again to believe that anatomy is destiny? So many husbands and wives run out of patience with each other that they sometimes lose hope of ever reaching understanding. This haunting feeling of despair is something that comes to all of us from time to time. If it helps some people to blame failures of understanding on irreconcilable gender differences, and if doing so seems to armor some people against their own despair, fine. But if stereotyping serves to abstract members of the opposite sex, to turn them into categories, and to avoid genuine encounter, that I think is unfortunate. Exaggerating gender differences is a weapon and a shield favored by those who fail to find understanding—no, fail to *reach* understanding.

The wounded narcissism and boundless ambition of our time also militate against self-sacrifice, compromise, and partnership. In hard and troubled times like ours, loyalty, tolerance, cooperation, and complementarity—the values necessary to create and sustain family harmony—are greatly undervalued. Too often we hear what once might have been thought of as teamwork described as codependency.

We tend not to see complementarity. Instead, we see control and submission, power and weakness, villain and victim. In trying to create more flexibility for both men and women, we are in danger of forgetting that complementarity can be mutually enhancing. Individual self-actualization does not require constant self-assertion. The sturdy self can tolerate difference and thrive on it.

LISTENING TO YOUNG CHILDREN

From two to seven months "listening" to a child boils down to paying attention and responding to the baby's moods. When new parents leave

the hospital and bring home their first baby, that smiling miracle of their own creation, they wonder, *What now? How will we know what to do?* They soon find out. The baby's needs are simple, and the crying that announces them is simply overwhelming.

Once the baby is fed and changed and has had enough sleep, parents convey their responsiveness through cuddling and play. "Listening" at this early age consists primarily of reading the baby's mood—rather than imposing the parents' moods, as though the baby were an extension of themselves. Lucky babies have parents whose temperamental styles match their own. You get a sense of this fit when you ask a mother about her baby, and she beams. "He's an easy baby, so sweet and cuddly." "He's so enthusiastic, he just loves to play!" Mismatched parents complain that theirs is a difficult child—too demanding or not responsive enough.

More reliable than luck is a parent's willingness to tune in to and follow the baby's rhythm. Long before the baby can talk, his parents demonstrate the degree to which they're able to listen. Here as elsewhere, flexibility and responsiveness demonstrate willingness to tolerate the otherness of the other. Call it sensitivity.

Being listened to creates a sense of being understandable and worthwhile. Not being listened to fosters insecurity. In practice, however, not being listened to may take forms that aren't always obvious. Here are some cues that you're not listening to your young child—despite the fact that you do indeed care very much.

"Watch Out! Don't Touch That!"

Some parents who seem attentive are more concerned with the external environment than their children. They hover over their babies and make sympathetic noises, but they don't listen. They pay attention to the hard edges of a table, sharp things on the floor, cold drafts, and hot food. Because they worry a lot, we sometimes think of them as very involved with their children. But because they're preoccupied with trying to make the world safe, they remain too anxious to share the baby's experience. These hovering "child-centered" parents provide almost no experience of intersubjectivity. The impression of closeness they convey is an illusion. Hovered-over but not-listened-to children may become "dependent," in the sense of being uneasy on their own—not because they're used to intimacy but because they suffer from a pervasive sense of aloneness, an intolerable feeling from which they use superficial relationships to distract themselves.

"Quiet Down, Go Wash Your Hands, and for Goodness' Sake Don't Touch Yourself There!"

More common than this general lack of attunement is the selective attunement by which parents convey to their infants what is shareable. In this way the parents' desires, fears, prohibitions, and fantasies affect the basic wiring of the child's self-system, leaving the child with the conviction that he is or is not a self worthy of respect.

The power of parents' selective attunement determines what behavior falls inside or outside the realm of acceptability. Is it all right to bang toys hard and noisy, to get real dirty, to masturbate? It includes preferences for people: is it all right to get mad at Grandma or sometimes to prefer to play with her rather than with Mommy? And it includes the extent to which degrees or types of internal states—joy, sadness, delight—can be experienced with another person. Is the child whose parents invariably try to jolly him out of it when he's frightened likely to come to them with his fears when he's older?

It is in the breadth of attunement—from generous to cramped—that parents help determine whether their children will feel OK about themselves and whether they will have a broad or narrow range of acceptable experience.

Suppose a one-year-old listening to *Peter and the Wolf* is happy and excited. He's moved by the music and wonders if his mother feels it too. He looks up, and she smiles back at him; her eyes are bright and she's nodding. *Yes, she feels it too!* With this attunement, the child knows that he feels something that can be shared—rather than something that's somehow not supposed to be and thus should thus be kept secret. His feeling is validated; and since the feeling is part of him, he too is validated. Being moved by music becomes part of the universe he expects to share with others.

"Don't Brag, Honey. It's Not Nice."

In addition to the lessons parents teach deliberately, they shape their children's experience and behavior with negative affective responses. When a little child proudly shows off to a parent who responds with disgust or disinterest, it's a slap in the face of the child's healthy narcissism. This is shame.

What children show off for their parents' approval isn't simply who they are and what they can do; it's also their grand fantasies of who they wish they were and what they dream of doing. They're not little

and weak—oh, no, they're big and strong. If parents squelch that wonderful wish to make an impression—for whatever reason—the child may decide that he's worthless or unlovable or that he has to achieve really big things for anybody to notice him.

Before you let negative reactions slip out, think about why you're tempted to be so critical or disapproving. Is it really a prohibition your child needs, or are you more concerned about what other people might think of your child (and yourself)? Sometimes, in an attempt to instill social graces too early, we crush a child's self-respect. Again, *listen* to what your child is saying and react to that. The little girl who shouts, "I can jump higher than Robbie" isn't putting down her toddler pal but asking for your approval of her accomplishments. Why not give it to her?

Or is your instinctive admonition based on a desire to force the child to live up to your own expectations? A little girl runs to her mother and says, "Mommy, Mommy, guess what! I got an A in spelling!" "That's nice, dear," the mother responds, sounding pleased, but not very. The daughter tries again. "There's *twenty-nine* kids, and *I* got the second highest score." "That's good, honey." The conversation continues another couple of minutes, with the little girl proud and excited, trying to drive up her mother's enthusiasm, and the mother pleased that her daughter did well but not wanting her to get hooked on achievement (like her father is). When the little girl persists, the mother finally says, "Don't brag so much. It isn't nice."

One minute the little girl is throbbing with excitement. Getting an A was wonderful. She rushed home to tell the good news to her mother in order to complete her experience. You could say she met with misunderstanding, but it was worse. Because a child seeking an empathic response is reaching out, exposed, a failed response is like a head-on collision.

Empathic failure can come out sounding mean: "Don't be such a baby!" "Stop showing off!" But even indifference or a simple lack of enthusiasm can hurt a child who's excited and eager for attention. When our children make the mistake of daring not to be invented by us, when they reveal, perversely, minds and wills of their own, we are put to the test.

THE PARENT'S GIFT OF EMPATHY

A parent's empathy—understanding what the child is feeling, and showing it—builds a bridge of understanding, linking the child to someone

special who listens and cares, thus confirming that the child's feelings are recognizable and legitimate. The sharing of emotional experience is the most meaningful and pervasive feature of true relatedness.

How do you empathize with a child who won't stop pestering or complaining or showing off, as though he were the center of the universe and you had no concerns of your own? The solution is not to mistake sympathy for empathy. Sympathy means to feel the same as rather than to be understanding of. It's an emotion that makes parents suffer *with* unhappy children, and that feeling motivates them to talk children out of their feelings or to do *for* them rather than to empathize with them.

Foremost among the obstacles to listening are those that stem from our need to "do something" about what someone tells us: to defend ourselves, to disagree, or to solve whatever problems are being described, because hearing about them makes us anxious. Parents are particularly prone to offer advice; it comes with the job description. But if a father's first response to his son's complaining about a sunburn is that he should have used sunblock, the boy will feel blamed rather than commiserated with. Likewise, if a little girl complains that she doesn't have any friends and her mother tells her that if she were more friendly to other children they'd reciprocate, the girl might conclude that even her mother doesn't like her.

Psychologists use the term *empathic immersion* to describe the intense and focused listening that helps therapists understand their patients' experience. It is an apt and evocative metaphor, but it is of course hyperbole. Perhaps a better metaphor for empathy would be taking someone's hand.[2] Two clasped hands are still two hands—but they are also two hands touching, the warmth and pulse of one in contact with the other.

To be better listeners parents should lead less and follow more. If a child shows signs of distress, a simple statement like "You feel bad, don't you?" is more likely to make him feel understood than pressuring him to define exactly what he feels or telling him. If an exasperated child indicates that she wants to be alone, let her. She may need time to pull herself together. If someone is having a hard time putting something into words, it's often more empathic to say something like "It's hard to explain, isn't it?" than to guess what the person is trying to say.

[2] I am indebted to Alfie Kohn for this metaphor. Alfie Kohn, *The Brighter Side of Human Nature: Altruism and Empathy in Everyday Life* (New York: Basic Books, 1990).

A parent who finishes a child's thoughts for him is the opposite of empathic.

Listening well is more midwifery than dentistry. In the presence of an empathic parent, children are able to discover their own minds rather than having to resist or succumb to what their parents expect them to feel.

There's no way of calculating what constitutes sufficient empathy or how much misunderstanding a child can tolerate without being damaged; but, clearly, children are remarkably resilient. The empathic failure that saps self-regard isn't as often the kind of dramatic abuse that completely rejects the child as it is a silent, invidious lack of responsiveness. Empathic failure doesn't "batter," "bruise," or "injure" children; it deflates them.

Empathy is energizing. Being listened to releases us from self-concern and mobilizes us to actively engage the world around us. Children lacking empathy grow up preoccupied with themselves, as though attention were a need that, unmet, keeps growing. The unlistened-to child remains locked in silent conversation within himself, too anxious and unavailable to enter the freedom of the moment.

Parents Are Human Too

Why do parents so often fail to acknowledge what their children tell them? Question their accounts in a way that makes them feel not taken seriously? Criticize them for feeling bad? Tell them they're lazy when they find something difficult? Say they talk too much when they only want to be heard? Because children are a trial.

Parental guilt over failures of patience and empathy isn't just foolish self-reproach. Kids *do* drive us crazy, and sometimes we *are* mean to them.

One day when my son Paul was two, I was right in the middle of screaming at him, "If you don't shut up *right now,* I'll give you something to cry about!" when Bob Pierce, my first and favorite psychotherapy supervisor, walked in the front door—he from whom I'd learned about the hurt and harm parents inflict by trampling their children's feelings. It was not my finest moment. Nor as it turned out was it the last time I would get ugly with my children for having inconvenient feelings.

Every parent has felt that blind fury, and most of us have yelled at our children, screamed at them, blistered them—and seen them

stricken. When memory stabs us with our failures, we think of these outbursts of unkindness, the times when we lost our tempers and flayed them with our anger. But it isn't these sudden storms of emotion that rob children of the listening they need; rather, it is an everyday atmosphere of unresponsiveness.

Sustaining Empathy

Thinking about sad-faced children, hurting but afraid to reach out, it's hard for us not to be touched. We want to put our arms around those little kids and love them. We know how they feel. But here's where it's possible to get confused. Empathy is generous, and so it is easy to slide into thinking of it as just another way of saying loving kindness. Empathy is loving, but it doesn't mean being affectionate or supportive or helpful or a lot of other nice things. Some parents are loving but the love they express is so intense and suffocating that it smothers a child's initiative and is anything but empathic.

It's easier to listen to children's wants when parents are firm with their own wills.

Other parents mistake sympathy for empathy, as we've discussed, and that often goes hand in hand with confusing lenience and love. The often overindulged children of today's harried parents don't feel appreciated; they feel anxious, uncontained by parents who are themselves floundering in a social environment that doesn't support or sustain them.

Parents who allow the boundary between generations to erode become not grown-ups-in-charge but peers and playmates, without the authority to enforce boundaries or the credibility to comfort and protect. "No" is less palatable than "yes," and so it's often served up with a lot of verbal sauce, the way some people try to get kids to eat vegetables by smothering them in butter and salt (the vegetables). These parents won't magically take charge if someone teaches them to use gold stars and time-out chairs. Setting limits and enforcing rules—beginning when the children are small—follows naturally from maintaining a clear boundary between the generations. It also permits and facilitates empathy.

When children are little, the greatest impediment to empathy is a parent's not being in charge. When children get a little older, the

most difficult part of empathy is letting them be themselves. Many parents have an easier time empathizing with children when they're little. They're comfortable with closeness. But sustaining empathy means allowing children to differentiate, to have their own wishes, their own interests, their own feelings. Children aren't merely cute or needy or headstrong; they're people, and they yearn, like you and me, to be acknowledged and taken seriously. This is the hard part: loving children not only because they're ours but also because they aren't.

"You Make Me So Mad!"

It starts with the "terrible twos," that period in the career of novice parents when they first reveal their frustration and intolerance of the fact that their small fry want to become little persons in their own right. Imagine getting worked into a temper just because a tiny child is practicing autonomy! Parents who aren't constantly anxious about controlling their children listen with pride to their children's self-assertion—even if it means hearing "No!" at sonic boom levels a thousand times a day.

The understandable but misguided ambition to raise perfect children tempts parents to cross the line between the child's rights and the parents' responsibility. Mutual respect is fostered by allowing children a voice and, where possible, a choice in matters that affect them. Notice the distinction between voice and choice. Some decisions should be left to children. Other decisions that affect the child's welfare are the parents' responsibility. In such matters, children should have a voice but not a choice.

Even a two-year-old can be asked whether she wants a half a glass of juice or a whole glass. Asking very young children what they want for breakfast may be granting too much latitude, but you can show respect for their right to choose by asking them if they want their eggs boiled or poached or their cereal hot or cold.

Perhaps the most important shift a parent can make is to move from wanting their children to be successful to being pleased with them, right now, loving them, enjoying them, and accepting that they are who they are. They are separate from us; they are themselves. Parents can begin to really hear their children only when they set aside thinking of them as unfinished products, clay for the parents to mold. None of this is meant to say that we should not control and limit our children's behavior—for our own convenience as well as for their own good. But once we accept that they are who they are, for better or worse, we can

worry less about them, relax our attempts to control and reform and manipulate and improve them, and concentrate on listening to them.

LISTENING TO TEENAGERS

One reason being a parent remains an amateur sport is that as soon as you get the hang of it, your children get a little older and throw you a whole new set of problems. Successful parents learn to shift their style of parenting to accommodate to their children's development.

As children grow, parents should allow them more volitional control and show increasing respect for their ideas and opinions. "Because I said so" may be the best answer to a small child who wants to know why he has to do something, but older children deserve an explanation. This shift conveys respect for the child and helps build self-respect as well as responsibility.

Avoiding Battles for Control

There's a lot of talk these days about how children don't respect authority. They argue with their parents and speak rudely to their teachers. Who teaches children to argue? Parents who get into needless battles of control.

"You're Right."

Most people understand that adolescent rebellion is normal and that it serves a purpose, but as adults we tend to misunderstand the child's experience by seeing it primarily in relation to ourselves. We listen to ourselves but not to our children. Parents who think of their teenagers as "defiant" confuse autonomous strivings with stubbornness. Most teenagers are strong-willed, not oppositional. They struggle not to defy their parents but to gain respect and acknowledgment, and they struggle as hard as they have to. How far they carry that struggle, how extreme their behavior, is determined largely by how tenaciously parents resist recognizing their voice in an effort to retain control.

Too many parents are afraid to say "You're right." They're afraid that letting their children be right makes them wrong and afraid that letting the children win means that the parents will lose. In fact, the opposite is true.

A girl who can't win control of how to dress for school may seek to express herself by putting on dramatic makeup after she leaves the house. If she cannot win that battle, she may escalate the conflict further, deliberately coming home late or getting into shouting matches with her mother. Or she may defy her parents by smoking cigarettes or shoplifting or experimenting with drugs. Reckless experiments, chancy relationships—all for the honor of proving she has some say in her life. Wouldn't it be easier to listen to her?

"No, because. . . ."

Some parents are willing to grant freedom but cannot tolerate rudeness. Like everything else in family life, adolescent rudeness is a function of interaction.

A frequent complaint of teenagers is that their parents don't listen to them. Teenagers are exquisitely sensitive to disrespect; they demand to be treated like people with a right to their opinions. Often without realizing, parents provoke adolescents by talking to them from the same one-up position they used when the children were small. The "rude" response is a protest against what feels like a shameful put-down. Parents can avoid escalating arguments into power struggles by tolerating the children's right to *say* whatever they think, even if it means using language parents don't like.

Parents who struggle to listen to their children even when it's hard are best able to handle the inevitable battles with their teenagers. Explain the "no." "No, I won't drive you to the concert on Sunday night, because I don't want to drive that far, and I don't want you out on a school night." But don't argue. Don't debate. And don't escalate: "And if you dare to take the bus, I'll ground you for a month." Finally, and most important, don't insist on having the last word.

Recognizing the Need to Break Away

A major reason for lack of communication between teenagers and parents is the parents' failure to recognize and accept the inevitable: if their children are to grow up, they must break away from the older generation. Translation: it's a teenager's job to criticize his parents. The same children who once looked up to Mommy and Daddy as giants who can do no wrong now look down on them as impossible old fogies who can't do anything right. This disdainful attitude is a natural stage in the evo-

lution of the family system and the development of the self. It's a necessary part of pulling away and becoming your own person. When parents are threatened and fight back, they fuel an escalating series of conflicts, which in many cases are never settled, only broken off when the children leave home.

It may not be pleasant to hear your teenager criticizing everything and everybody, but it's part of the process of building self-esteem. Parents who criticize their children for being critical are fighting fire with gasoline.

The more inflexible the parents are, the more defiant teenagers will be. Too many put-downs wear away at children's self-esteem and prompt them to reject everything about their parents. Some people are so ashamed of their parents that they spend their whole lives trying not to be like them. They're so busy *not being* their parents that there's no room left for them to be themselves.

In the process of looking for new models of how to be, teenagers often glom onto someone outside the family—it can be almost anyone, just as long as he or she is different—and perhaps more willing than the parents to take the child seriously, to listen. When this happens, their ability to hear their parents is compromised, though they may have a fairness channel that remains open. If a parent can listen calmly and demonstrate openness to what a teenager is trying to say, but the child doesn't reciprocate, the parent can say, "You're not being fair to me." The child may then listen. Teenagers respect fairness, especially if it is reciprocal.

You might say something like "Now that I understand your point of view, would you be willing to let me explain mine?" The point about fairness isn't to demand tit for tat, but that really listening to someone frees her from being preoccupied with her point of view and makes her more willing to listen to you.

"I understand that you're upset with me. But is it fair for me to have heard your opinion and then you not be willing to listen to mine?"

Breaking Out of Mutual Antagonism

One reason parents and teenagers have trouble listening to each other is that each side hears the other only as objects in relation to themselves. When teenagers, who want respect and freedom, come to expect only criticism and control, they shut their ears to what their parents are trying to say and respond reflexively with either resistance or passive compliance.

Teenagers who notice only their parents' criticism and control forget that they themselves aspire to certain grown-up achievements, such as an education and a good job. And parents who hear their children only in response to their own worries forget that *they* also value much of what their children want—self-discovery, pursuing one's own path in life. When the narrative of control and rebellion comes to dominate the relationship, these shared values are forgotten in the ensuing strife.

When oppositional perspectives take over, parents and children fail to register inputs that don't fit with the dominant theme. An angry father may not notice or acknowledge the times his son volunteers to help his parents out. The son may not appreciate or remember the times when his father has encouraged his freedom.

Breaking out of mutual antagonism is difficult but not impossible. Listen hard and acknowledge exceptions to the dominant concern—times when your youngsters act responsibly, show restraint, and listen to your point of view. Adolescents can learn to recognize and appreciate the occasions when their parents don't push or criticize.

If a parent concerned about the dangerous attraction of smoking or drinking is lucky enough to have a child who admits or even alludes to this kind of experimentation, he or she has a rare opportunity to refrain from giving the expected lecture. Candor is built on trust.

It's also important to acknowledge your teenager's right to see things differently from you—not just because that's true but also because that's imperative to having him or her listen to your point of view. To make this explicit you might say something like "I'm not saying that I'm right and you're wrong. I'm simply trying to get you to understand how strongly I feel about this and why." When you do get the privilege of attention, it's best to start by describing what you're afraid of, not why your teenager is wrong.

Striking a Balance between Autonomy and Connection

Teenagers are still children. For all their opposition to their parents and their breathless enthusiasm for the adventures of adulthood, they still need their families. Autonomy is important, but so is connection.

Adolescents need their parents to listen to their troubles, their hopes and ambitions, even some of their farfetched plans. The more tolerant parents are, the more they remain open to hearing their children, the more possible it is to preserve connection. Talking and sharing increase when divergent ideas are admitted into the family's values and habits.

In realizing that they can disagree and argue with their parents,

adolescents come to differentiate between conventional views of relationships—as nonconflicted—and a more realistic view, namely that disagreement, conflict and confrontation, and working though differences are part of a healthy, intimate relationship.

Teenage boys still expect to be supported and understood by their parents, but perhaps more than anything else they want the freedom to be independent. Teenage girls, on the other hand, often have more complex and ambivalent relationships, especially with their mothers. As a member of Carol Gilligan's study of the relational world of adolescent girls, Sharon Rich found that mothers' dependence on their daughters troubles the daughters and makes it harder for mothers to accept daughters' independence. Daughters want mothers to be there for them, but also to trust them, accept their independence, and honor their choices. Over and over, girls reported being unhappy with mothers they described as poor listeners.

"These girls depict themselves as receiving two messages when they feel their mothers are not listening: Their mothers do not care and are not 'there' for them; and their own opinions are not important."

As one girl in the study reflected: "I sort of feel that I don't want her to know too much about me. I mean not that I'm trying to keep everything a secret, but just that I want to be more myself and less her trying to mold me. And so there are lots of things I don't tell her because I just know what she would say . . . and I don't feel like hearing it."[3]

Adolescents who don't feel listened to flare up in angry resentment, and later retreat into silence and secrecy as the best way they know to protect their vulnerable, distinct voices and themselves. In attempting to protect themselves from feeling "terrible," teenagers may cut off the primary means for changing the relationship: communication.

Unheard adolescents who flee their families are seldom really free. Protective distance affords them the illusion that they are grown up, but it is only an illusion. Adolescents who find it necessary to break off relationships with their parents remain frozen in adolescent patterns, forever vulnerable to overreaction.

Not enough discipline and too much intrusiveness make parents poor listeners, and so does failing to lead full satisfying lives of their

[3]Sharon Rich, "Daughters' views of their relationships with their mothers." In Carol Gilligan, Nona Lyons, and Trudy Hanmer, eds., *Making Connections: The Relational Worlds of Adolescent Girls at Emma Willard School* (Cambridge, MA: Harvard University Press, 1990), 268.

own. The boundary between generations that puts parents in charge and enables them to listen is also related to what's on the other side of that boundary—the parents and their relationship with each other.

It's possible to celebrate and enjoy family life without denying the pain and boredom that families inflict on their members. But it may not be possible to resolve those vexations that creep into our lives and break our hearts without recognizing the patterns that unite us.

Most families have problems not because there's something inherently wrong with them but because they've gotten stuck. Families resist change even more than individuals do because the structure that holds them together is supported by the actions of every single family member. That's why systems are stubborn. What we mustn't forget, though, is that even though families act like systems, it is still individual persons who do the acting—and they, as you may have noticed, can sometimes be pretty courageous.

CHAPTER TWELVE

"I Knew You'd Understand"

BEING ABLE TO HEAR
FRIENDS AND COLLEAGUES

Friends make the best listeners. They may not love us quite as much as our families do, but then they don't need quite as much from us either, and that frees them to listen better. No matter how close we are to our friends, we retain a certain autonomy that enables us to listen without needing to control them or protect ourselves.

WHY FRIENDS MAKE THE BEST LISTENERS

Sandy had just come from a terrific workshop on counseling high school students when she met her friend Roberta for lunch. If she didn't trust Roberta's unselfish support so completely, Sandy might have hesitated to tell her that she was thinking about doing something that would mean an end to their lunches. The two of them had been teaching French at the same school for nine years, and now Sandy had decided to go back and get a master's in guidance counseling. It was a big decision, scary and exciting, and she needed someone sympathetic to talk to.

Roberta was startled and dismayed by Sandy's plan. Giving up tenure and going back to school seemed a rash and risky thing to do. How did Sandy know she would like counseling? Wasn't she taking an awful chance? Besides, Roberta couldn't imagine getting along at work

without Sandy. Sandy was the only sane person in the place. It would be awful if she left. But Roberta didn't say any of this. No matter how much she questioned Sandy's decision, it was Sandy's decision, and Roberta could see how excited she was by this new dream of hers. So she listened.

It took Sandy two more days to get up the nerve to mention her idea about going back to school to her husband, Gordon. "I can't believe you'd even think of doing such a thing!" was his answer. "Are you crazy? You've *got* a perfectly good job. You *love* teaching French. How are we going to pay for you to go back to school?" Sandy started to protest, but she was really too hurt to bother, and so they finished supper in silence.

Sandy's friend's ability to listen to her was the mirror opposite of her husband's inability. Roberta could listen because she wasn't threatened—or at least not *as* threatened.

Clearly Gordon had a direct stake in whether or not his wife went back to school. He had a right to his concerns and his opinion. At some point the decision may become a joint one. But his inability even to listen to Sandy's plan not only deprived her of the chance to play with it out loud but also made her *less*, not more, likely to consider his feelings in the final decision.

Whether it's money, the kids, or your mother-in-law, there are unsafe subjects in all family relationships. A woman doesn't talk to her Catholic relatives about having an abortion. The same woman may not risk telling her husband that she might be able to sleep better if they got separate beds, if she's afraid he'd be too hurt and angry even to entertain the possibility. He might not tell her about a problem he's having at work if he's afraid she'll respond with criticism or unwanted advice. He might not want to burden her with financial worries (or share the decision making). It's not necessarily a question of keeping secrets, though most family members have a few. Rather, it's simply hard to live with someone and tell that person everything. With friends, few subjects are off limits.

In conversations between friends, little misunderstandings can be passed over or allowed to be forgotten between breaks in contact. Such differences between people who live together are harder to ignore or forget.

The relationship between friends is voluntary and optional; you can leave if you want to, and therefore it's safer to be honest and take risks.

You can talk over painful and embarrassing subjects, reveal self-doubts, try out different sides of yourself, and be who you are.

People show interest, caring, and respect by the quality of their listening. Friends who listen make *us* feel interesting, and their interest inspires us to say more interesting things. Their receptivity is transformative: by listening intently to us, our friends make us feel larger, more alive. That's the glory of friendship.

A close friend is someone with whom we can talk about almost anything. With such friends we take turns as selfobjects, caring listeners willing for a time to submerge ourselves and be there without strings for the other person. Friendship grows with mutual disclosure. So do we. The compassion and empathy friends share when they listen to our triumphs and worries deepens us; their understanding and acceptance keep us from feeling alone—and help us understand and accept ourselves.

If friendship deepens us, it also broadens us. Friendships expand our definition of ourselves and awaken unrealized possibilities in us, possibilities that weren't part of the roles we were scripted to play in our families. With many friends we can express many sides of ourselves. The intimacy of friendship, the selfobject function, strengthens us. Mutuality, the sharing function, stretches us.

With friends we are easy, but, sadly, it isn't always easy to find time for friendship. When I asked people what interfered most with their talking and listening to friends, by far the most common—and wistful—response was "I'm too busy." In crowded and hurried lives, competing obligations often squeeze out anything optional, like spending time with friends. But even though many of us are terribly preoccupied these days, it's more than lack of time that undermines our friendships.

WHEN FRIENDS TAKE SIDES

After her divorce Maggie turned to her friends. They saw her through the shock of separation and the months that followed. Though she felt somewhat adrift, at least she was not alone.

Maggie's friend Liz was also divorced and disillusioned; she understood what it was to be single again, having to start all over, the indignities and misunderstandings. The two women had known each other for nine years, ever since they met at a conference for real estate brokers (ever since, in fact, they both skipped the afternoon session and ran into each other at a local art gallery).

Liz made friends easily. She had embraced Maggie with her warmth and held her with her intelligence and her keen eye for the pretentious and foolish. They both liked to cook and have friends over, but the best times were when it was just the two of them. They met often, for lunch or breakfast or for a drink after work, reveling in endless spirited conversations about work, families, friends, what they were reading, how they felt—if any subject was off limits, they hadn't come to it yet.

Maggie met Dominic three years after her divorce. As chance would have it, he lived in Liz's building, and on several occasions she actually ran into him in the elevator or downstairs lobby. She found him attractive but couldn't imagine speaking to him; he seemed so self-possessed and unapproachable. It came as a surprise, therefore, when he started talking to her one Saturday afternoon and, after no more than five minutes, asked her out. To her equal surprise, she found herself accepting.

If opposites attract, it might have been the perfect match. Maggie had the ruddy complexion and emotional reserve of her Scottish ancestors, while Dominic was Greek, with dark hair and olive skin and an openly expressive nature. She liked the way his mind worked, all intuition and confidence. What a relief after all those pale, shadow men her friends had fixed her up with!

The passion Maggie felt with Dominic stunned her. Unfortunately, as she soon found out, the price to be paid was a series of passionate quarrels. Dominic was jealous: of her time, her friends, and just about everything else. Though he himself might sometimes be busy for days, he expected her to be available whenever he wanted to see her. When she wasn't, there would be storms, scenes, and shouting matches.

When Maggie told her friends about all the trouble she was having with Dominic, they were sympathetic. Liz got angry. She considered Dominic's possessive jealousy abusive and thought Maggie was wrong to put up with it. "I'd never let a man treat *me* that way," she said. Liz too had had expectations of men and had been disappointed. Men had come to represent an absence, an absence that they could not or would not fill.

After one particularly Vesuvian outburst, Maggie decided not to see Dominic for a while. As long as they'd been going together, Liz had held back the worst of her criticism, but now that Maggie was considering ending the relationship, Liz spoke up. Maggie would be better off without him, she said. In this opinion, Liz was not alone. All of Maggie's friends felt the same way: if Dominic was causing her so much unhappiness, she should dump him.

Unfortunately, sympathy can get in the way of empathy. Unable to suspend their own emotional response, which was to rescue Maggie from the anguish she communicated to them, her friends urged her to put an end to what was making them as well as her unhappy. That's what friends often do when we complain about another person: they take our side and push us to retaliate.

It's one thing to honor a friend's right to happiness, but far more difficult to respect her right to suffer unhappiness if she decides to go to war for love.

Maggie was buoyed by the sympathy of her friends but felt pressured by their urging her to break off with Dominic. While it's comforting to have someone to share your feelings with, it's not always comforting to be told what to do about them. Dominic's rages might be reason to leave him, but she wasn't sure. It's called ambivalence.

So after a while Maggie stopped talking to her friends about Dominic. She wasn't just angry at Dominic; she also loved him. While it's OK for you to criticize your lover or spouse or family member, it's a mistake for friends to agree. Your griping expresses one side of your ambivalence—and leaves you free to do whatever you decide about the relationship. But a friend's agreeing that someone you're close to *is* a terrible person is a judgment and a rejection. It's a boundary violation.

There is certainly no formula for an empathic response, but it may help to remember that there are two sides to every dilemma. Understanding — empathy—therefore usually means acknowledging conflict. If a person hasn't acted to resolve a problem, there's probably a reason. Statements of understanding recognize this. Liz might have said something like "You sound pretty unhappy, but I guess you're not sure about what to do?" Instead she said, "Dominic's not good enough for you. If you go back to him now, you'll hate yourself for it."

There are things that have no place in friendship, and judging is one of them.

Showing empathy to friends doesn't mean just caring about them; it means listening to their point of view, whether or not you agree with it. Friendship doesn't require total acceptance or neutrality; but before they disagree or give advice, good friends listen.

Here is an example, from Paul Auster's novel *Leviathan*, of a friend struggling to be empathic. Peter's friend Sachs is telling him about the accident in which he fell off a four-story fire escape, trying to explain

that he feels responsible because he wouldn't have been out there if he hadn't been flirting with a woman.

> There were questions I wanted to ask him then, but I didn't interrupt. Sachs was having trouble getting the story out, talking in a trance of hesi-tations and awkward silences, and I was afraid that a sudden word from me would throw him off course. To be honest, I didn't quite understand what he was trying to say. There was no question that the fall had been a ghastly experience, but I was confused by how much effort he put into describing the small events that had preceded it. The business with Maria struck me as trivial, of no genuine importance, a trite comedy of man-ners not worth talking about. In Sachs's mind, however, there was a direct connection. The one thing had caused the other, which meant that he didn't see the fall as an accident or a piece of bad luck so much as some grotesque form of punishment. I wanted to tell him that he was wrong, that he was being overly hard on himself—but I didn't. I just sat there and listened to him as he went on analyzing his own behavior.[1]

It might be argued that men and women bring different expecta-tions to friendship, that women have a basic commitment to attach-ment, men to independence. Thus it may be difficult for some men to listen to themes of dependence and attachment, while some women may have trouble accepting a woman friend's choice to go her own way. This may be true in general, but relationships don't exist "in general." Relationships take place between unique individuals. While those in-dividuals may have been conditioned to have certain expectations, the fate of our relationships doesn't depend on conditioned traits of character, but on how we choose to act toward one another.

To be with other people authentically—that is, to respond to them as they are, not as we need or imagine them to be—is no easy feat. This ability depends on an awareness of ourselves as unique and autonomous individuals who relate through listening to other separate and distinct individuals.

Maggie and Liz's attachment was built on sameness and commiser-ation. When Maggie began to feel differently, the friendship waned. The two friends didn't know how to change or tolerate the differences that were emerging between them. Maggie felt she was betraying Liz whenever she was happy and fulfilled. Neither of them knew how to talk about the kinds of feelings they were experiencing. Liz felt aban-doned by Maggie. The differences and their inability to talk about them

---

[1]Paul Auster, *Leviathan* (New York: Viking, 1992). 131.

formed a widening gulf. As in so many situations where differences between friends cannot be talked about, the friends drifted apart.

When Maggie eventually worked things out with Dominic, she stopped seeing Liz altogether. Years later she would say to someone, offhand, "Oh, we just lost touch."

Resolving Conflict between Friends

Why, if Maggie was able to work things out with Dominic, her demanding and critical boyfriend, wasn't she able to resolve the conflict with Liz, her like-minded and appreciative friend? Here is the irony of listening in friendship:

The same elective quality of relationship that enables friends to speak freely about so many subjects makes them less likely to speak openly about serious problems between them.

The binding and imperative nature of romantic and family ties makes it more urgent to speak up about our unhappiness in these relationships. While friends do sometimes voice complaints to each other, they are less likely to talk about serious negative feelings, like envy, jealousy, and resentment. Because the boundary around friendship is less fortified than that around family, there's a greater fear that friends will abandon us if we voice serious complaints to them. Sadly, when such feelings are strong, friends often drift apart.

People who hesitate to speak when something is bothering them often imagine that those brave souls who do simply have more confidence and self-respect. Perhaps. But most of the people I've known to tell friends that something is bothering them were just as worried about speaking up as those who keep silent. What enabled them to take the risk wasn't only respect for themselves and their right to their feelings, but also respect for the relationship—and for their friends.

The longer you avoid telling a friend that something's bothering you—say, that you wish your friend wouldn't make a habit of bringing along a third person when you get together—the more preoccupied you become with your grievance. In your internal debate about whether or not to complain, you probably imagine phrasing your complaint in such a clear and forceful way that your friend will have to hear you. In fact, the most effective way to address an impasse between friends is to take into account what you imagine your friend's position to be.

Acknowledging your friends' position releases them from brooding about it and opens them to hearing your side.

Let's say that you always seem to be the one to call a certain friend about getting together. You're not the sort of person to keep score, but her never inviting you to do something troubles you. It's not that you mind calling but that you're starting to wonder if she really likes you. You hesitate to say anything because she might feel attacked and get angry. What to do? Tell her all of that. Use your ability to empathize to anticipate how your friend might feel about what you have to say. "Something's been bothering me, but I've hesitated to bring it up because I didn't want you to think that I was blaming you. Actually, this probably has to do with my own insecurity. . . ."

Sometimes an honest complaint can save a friendship.

Chris got tired of Arlene's constant complaining—about her jerk of a boss, her numerous aches and pains, and her awesome repertory of boyfriend troubles. But Chris didn't want to say anything. She didn't want to hurt Arlene's feelings. So instead she just stopped being available when Arlene called, and the friendship withered and died.

When friends don't speak up about negative feelings, grievances can eat away at the relationship. Even if it doesn't completely resolve the conflict, hearing each other's position makes a big difference. The best place to start to address an impasse between friends is not to state your position but to consider what the other person might be feeling and try to acknowledge that in a way that invites your friend to elaborate.

Few friendships last long if all one person does is complain to the other. We all have troubles in mind, and we can all use some sympathetic attention to our complaints. But remember that listening, especially to complaints, is a burden. If you have a friend who takes advantage of your willingness to listen, without reciprocating, you can absorb this emotional burden passively until you get fed up—like collecting enough brown stamps to trade in for the right to walk out on a friendship. Or you can say something about it.

A running friend of mine used to complain about all the trouble he was having with his stepson. I'd listen sympathetically and occasion-

ally offer advice (it's OK, I have a license). But if my friend talked for more than a few minutes, he'd get self-conscious (maybe partly *because* I have a license) and apologize. When he did, I'd remind him that in our relationship complaining was a two-way street. I didn't mind hearing about his problems because I was grateful for all the time he spent listening to mine.

When two people are locked in silent grievance, the best way to break the impasse is to elicit and acknowledge the other person's feelings. This applies especially to cases of mutual misunderstanding. Don't be too quick to tell your side. In cases of major misunderstanding, concentrate first on listening to the other person. Save your feelings for later. Of course if your friend has hurt or annoyed you and doesn't know it, saying something about how you feel may be the only way to keep your resentment from poisoning the relationship.

Alice and her husband were quite independent and regularly did things like go out to dinner or to the movies separately. Alice's friend Marie, on the other hand, had a more traditional marriage and rarely felt comfortable socializing without her husband unless he was busy at work or out of town. So the two friends sometimes got together alone, but more often they did things as couples, as Marie preferred. They both understood their different situations, but each came to feel that she was doing more of the accommodating. Gradually, they saw less and less of each other.

Marie was hurt. She envied Alice her greater freedom but was disappointed that Alice wasn't more sympathetic to her feelings. The less they saw of each other, the more Marie brooded over how hurt she felt; and the more she brooded, the more she imagined confronting Alice. Could Alice's feelings conceivably mirror her own? It was a possibility she hadn't considered, but she decided to take a risk in the interest of recovering the friendship.

Marie called and said she imagined Alice must be pretty frustrated by her having trouble getting together except as couples. Alice, greatly relieved to have her own feelings acknowledged, said yes that was true, but deep down she worried that Marie didn't really like her enough to want to do things with just the two of them.

Once Marie had broken the ice by demonstrating her concern for Alice's feelings, the two friends were able to talk about their envy and resentment—feelings that often seem too ugly to talk about. The basic conflict didn't disappear—Alice still preferred to get together alone with

Marie, and Marie still had trouble going out without her husband—but it no longer festered. The two friends now understood each other. They both felt listened to, and their friendship endured.

WHEN AND HOW TO OFFER CONSTRUCTIVE CRITICISM TO A FRIEND

Real friends are honest. There are times when just listening to a friend you feel is making a mistake is less than honest. If you feel like offering criticism or advice, it's a good idea to first ask your friend if he or she wants to hear it.

"Would you like to hear a suggestion about this?"

"Are you interested in a second opinion?"

"Have you definitely decided to . . . ?"

Even well-intended criticism can backfire. You may have been trying to be honest or simply have been thoughtless; either way your criticism may make your friend feel put down or let down. If you criticize a friend for something he or she isn't interested in changing (or likely to change), your comments, however well-intentioned they may be, can leave the friend feeling emotionally deflated and resentful.

Sometimes when we give our opinion, we feel rejected if our friend doesn't follow it.

"Why did you ask my advice in the first place, if you weren't going to take it?"

Taking your advice means considering it, not necessarily following it. The best kind of feedback has no strings attached. A good listener allows friends to accept or reject suggestions without acting slighted.

See how your friend responds to your first comments before going on. Don't become so attached to convincing a friend of the rightness of your assessment—of *her* decisions—that you are insensitive to her right to decide what to do. If your friend seems defensive about your advice, pull back and let her talk.

The time to press your point of view is when you disagree with a friend's advice about what *you* should do, not the other way around.

If you're not sure how your friend feels about your advice, ask.

"What do you think?"

"Do you want me to say more about this or not?"

"Should I go on, or have you pretty much made up your mind?"

DO FRIENDS OUTGROW EACH OTHER
OR JUST FORGET HOW TO LISTEN?

For all too many people the story of their friendships is a history of severed or eroded connections. The divorces and separations of friends
may not be as wrenching as those of people who live together and share
destinies, but the process is similar. We make friends in one set of
circumstances—in college, say, or starting a new job or, like Maggie
and Liz, as wounded veterans of divorce. Then one or both of us changes;
we move on, and the points of connection are harder to sustain.

The reasons we marry at twenty aren't the same reasons we stay
married at thirty or forty; but friends, who have fewer ties to bind them,
are less likely to do the maintenance it takes to sustain a relationship
through major life changes. A lot of that work involves respecting each
other's differences and learning to listen when it doesn't come easily.

Gil and Roy were friends in high school. Both were basketball players
and good students, both intensely competitive and known for their acer-
bic wit, and they gravitated together naturally. It was a friendship based
on shared interests and the kind of wisecracking that teenage boys use
to test themselves, experimenting with insecurity. Their listening to
each other, if you can call it that, took the form of taking turns showing off.

As they grew older, Gil found Roy's constant ribbing exasperating
but often invigorating too. Others just found it annoying: Once, when
they were in their thirties, they were at a basketball game and Roy had
had a few beers. It was just after the great Kareem Abdul-Jabbar had
changed his name from Lew Alcindor, and for some reason he became
the target of Roy's abrasive humor. Every time Jabbar missed a shot,
Roy would holler, "Hey *Lew*, nice shot, *Lew*!" He was really starting
to bother the people around them, but Gil didn't say anything. After
the game a couple of guys confronted Roy, called him an asshole, and
knocked his glasses off. Later, when Gil teased him about the incident,
Roy got very upset, and the two friends stopped speaking to each other.

A couple of years later Roy called Gil, and the friendship was

renewed, only now it seemed more superficial, at least to Gil. Roy still seemed so adolescent. He was always posturing, looking for an angle, a spin, a take. By this point in his life Gil expected friends to talk and listen, not to continue showing off.

Together the two friends attended their twentieth high school reunion. Gil remembered how the waves of emotion and memory washed over him but that Roy remained his old wisecracking self. Afterward the two of them went out for a drink with Gil's old girlfriend.

Janice, who was still sensationally pretty, brought out the old competitive edge between the two friends, who spent an hour in the bar tossing barbed comments back and forth. Gil didn't think Janice was very impressed by their performance, and later he felt a little embarrassed.

Much later Gil learned that Roy had taken Janice home that night and the two of them had had an affair. The way he found out was that Roy called him, all upset, to tell him that Janice had broken off with him. Gil was furious. It seemed like such a devious and hostile thing for Roy to have done—not just to score a conquest with his old girlfriend, but to keep it secret. Why, if there was nothing sneaky in what Roy had done, hadn't he said anything to Gil about it? Still, when Roy turned to Gil to nurse him through his hurt, Gil was forgiving, the way friends are.

The next time the two friends got together was when Gil invited Roy to his annual company picnic. Roy, who'd again had a few beers, started making loud jokes about private things Gil had said to him about various members of the company. Gil was acutely embarrassed and tried to shut Roy up but wasn't very successful. The following week, Gil wrote a letter to Roy saying that he didn't trust him anymore, that he didn't plan to see him again, and that he didn't want Roy to contact him.

Gil (who would later outgrow and shed his first marriage) found this act—deliberately severing a tie that had become a burden—quite liberating. It felt like a declaration of self-respect. Thinking about the end of the friendship, he remembered Woody Allen saying that the things that mean the most in this world, the things that are the most enjoyable, come naturally. You can't work at them.

That's how we sometimes feel, but that doesn't make it so. Maybe when we're kids friendship comes easily, but as we get older we may have to work at it. Working at making friends and keeping them may go against the grain, but that's true of a lot of things worth doing. Gil's friendship with Roy may have become one of those relationships that

persist out of habit even though they are fundamentally unrewarding. But many friendships, based on a more solid connection than the one between Gil and Roy, may require repair from time to time. For friendships to grow with you, you may have to put in some effort.

One important ingredient in getting the listening you deserve is cultivating relationships based on caring and mutual exchange. This means remaining open enough to form new relationships and selective enough to drop those that are basically unproductive. Deepening relationships requires a balance between self-disclosure and reciprocal listening. But then, inevitably, many of us find ourselves stuck in a variety of relationships with people who have trouble listening. Instead of remaining bitter or fatalistic, it's possible to teach them to listen—by setting an example and, if necessary, asking for reciprocation.

Having friends means making time for them. If friends come second, if you're too busy working to be with your friends, what are you working for? Keeping friends means being willing to work at the relationship. Not all the time certainly, but listening sometimes when it's hard and speaking up sometimes when it's necessary.

For friendship to flourish the relationship must be given priority. That means finding time for each other, and it means making a real effort to listen to each other. At work, however, there are more important things than relationships. Aren't there?

GETTING YOUR POINT OF VIEW ACROSS AT THE OFFICE

Bradley Duke and Bill Nowicki were thoroughly charming to Marianne when she applied for a job at the small publishing firm where they were respectively publisher and senior editor. They asked the usual questions about her training and experience but spent more time talking about the company and the books they published, telling her what a great place it was to work. Marianne needed little convincing. Any small publisher, she felt, would be a better place to work than the huge corporate firms where editors were drowning in profit and loss statements and books of substance were considered with suspicion and irony.

Marianne felt she could learn a lot from Duke and Nowicki. She knew she had the makings of a good editor, but her experience at the large firm where she'd been a valued assistant hadn't prepared her to negotiate contracts or conduct other such business matters with ease.

Marianne was thrilled when she received a letter offering her the

job a week after her interview. She'd worked a long time for this moment, and she finally had what she wanted.

Marianne was surprised at how quickly her responsibilities built up. Who would have thought that so many of the bright young authors she was attracting to the firm (and some older ones as well) would need so much hand holding?

Duke and Nowicki seemed happy to have Marianne around. But she soon discovered that they considered themselves chiefs and her an Indian. They were friendly enough, in a superficial way, but they never thought to really include her. Between meetings and appointments they would talk to each other and not to her. They'd discuss people she didn't know and exchange inside jokes. Their constant showing off, meant to entertain and impress, made her feel that all they wanted from her was an audience.

When Marianne discovered that they went out to lunch together every Wednesday without inviting her, she felt a humiliating shock of alienation. Later she learned that the firm's small board of directors had forced them to hire a woman editor and that Duke and Nowicki resented this intrusion into what they considered their fiefdom.

Another reason Marianne felt shut out was that Duke and Nowicki were such great friends. So close were they that people invariably referred to them as Duke-and-Nowicki, as though they were inseparably a pair, a single hyphenated unit. People invited Duke-and-Nowicki to parties, the booksellers asked Duke- and-Nowicki to serve on committees, and authors and agents referred to Duke-and-Nowicki as the savviest and most devoted people in the business. The fact that they were both enormously popular with authors, literary agents, and other industry people only underscored Marianne's sense of isolation.

One reason they were so well liked was that they were so accessible. They loved publishing, they loved books, and they loved the way their authors looked up to them with the total, trusting eagerness that people whose identities are invested in their writing reserve for those who appreciate their work. So Marianne was perplexed by their response when she approached them about the manuscripts she was having problems with. Duke and Nowicki made a pretense of listening, their brows furrowed in concern like state-funded bureaucrats on autopilot, but they asked no questions. When she was done they told her just to continue to do her own good work.

These encounters left Marianne not just disappointed but humiliated. But instead of getting angry, she felt ashamed of asking for help.

She didn't really need much help; what she really wanted was simply a witness to her work. More than advice, she needed collegiality, that comforting sense of shared enterprise that had sustained her through the hard years of school and publishing apprenticeship.

Shut out socially, then judged inadequate just because she'd asked for feedback, Marianne became cold and hostile. Not wanting to give her antagonists the satisfaction of exposing her real hurt and anger, she took refuge in contempt and punished them with silence.

The atmosphere in the office became so unpleasant that Marianne thought about quitting. But she was a single mother and didn't have that luxury.

It was at this point that Marianne started dating a publishing executive at another firm, a tall man with gray eyes and a large spirit. Quinn was a man of patient sweetness, but he too was divorced, and at first he and Marianne were somewhat tentative with each other. Then love took over and work became less important.

The trouble was, as Marianne now began to see, that from the beginning she'd expected a lot from Duke and Nowicki. When she'd interviewed for the job she mistook their friendliness for an offer of friendship, and when that promise wasn't fulfilled, she became hurt and bitter. Then, too, she wanted both to be appreciated as competent and given the guidance she needed as a beginner. That these motives are somewhat contradictory doesn't make them unreasonable. Marianne's bitterness was due partly to the frustration of her own inflated expectations and partly to her colleagues being too caught up in their own lives to be open to a new person.

Things changed at work when Marianne stopped worrying so much about Duke and Nowicki. Now that her personal life was full, she was less interested in their friendship or even their approval. And now that she felt better about herself, she was no longer willing to put up with blatant unfairness.

When Duke, who was filling out the annual review, rated her "mediocre," Marianne refused to sign it. "I want to talk about this," she told him evenly. When Duke said he didn't have time, she insisted. "You *have to* talk to me. Make time." He sighed theatrically but agreed.

"You *know* I deserve a good evaluation," Marianne told him when they finally met. "What's the problem?"

"I call it as I see it," Duke said, getting up to leave.

"Please sit down," Marianne said. "We have to talk about this." And talk they did. Marianne acknowledged that she may have ex-

pected too much when she arrived, but she also pointed out that she'd been treated from the beginning like a second-class citizen and that she was tired of it. They didn't have to be friends, she said, but they did have to get along. She spoke with dignity, but also with intensity.

When Marianne finished saying what was on her mind, Duke apologized. He changed the evaluation, and after that both he and Nowicki started treating her with more respect. In return, Marianne dropped her own belligerent attitude; but she was no longer willing to put up with not being listened to.

Why were Marianne's bosses so unresponsive for so long, and why now all of a sudden did they start to listen to her? Could it really be that all she had to do was speak up?

Duke and Nowicki had allowed their resentment about being pressured to hire a woman to turn into a grudge. Unwilling to confront *their* bosses, they took out their frustration on Marianne, shutting her out and treating her as someone to be seen but not heard. What they didn't realize was that grudges have no place at the office.

———————◆———————

Holding on to resentment of people you have to work with punishes you as much as it does them.

———————◆———————

It may be a cliché, but people who work together are a team, and sometimes it's necessary to set aside or get over personal feelings that interfere with the smooth functioning of the group.

Although Marianne had tried to complain, her expectations got in the way. Like many of us, she wanted to be liked, hoped to be friends. That's fine if it happens, but Marianne had allowed her wish to have a good relationship to take priority over doing her job and insisting on being treated fairly. It's harder to confront your boss if you need him or her to like you than it is if you just want respect.

Anxious and uncertain about speaking up—lest Duke and Nowicki not like her—Marianne spoke to them in a nervous, tentative way. At the other extreme, speaking up in a shrill voice doesn't get you much respect either. No one coached Marianne on exactly what to say or how to say it, but the greater assurance she drew from her relationship with Quinn resulted in her lowering the pitch of her voice and speaking in a firm and direct way. She didn't just want to vent her feelings; she wanted things to change.

On Secretary's Day, Duke and Nowicki gave the receptionist a dozen

white carnations with a card signed from the two of them. Marianne was furious. They responded by saying that this was a social gesture and they could do what they liked. She told them that this was an office, not a social setting, and that she wouldn't be excluded like this. The next day they apologized.

Keep in mind the difference between dissent and defiance as a response to being treated unfairly. *Defiance* means attacking the other person's position and making him wrong. *Dissent* means having the courage to stand up for what you think and feel. It's the difference between saying "You're wrong" and "This is how I feel."

Defiance is reactive, a counterphobic response to the temptation to deference. A dissenting message is much easier to hear than a defiant one.

Marianne now realized that she was entitled to be listened to, and when important issues arose, she insisted on it. Knowing she could fight back effectively made her more relaxed, and so there was less often a need for it. No longer anxious for Duke and Nowicki's approval, as though she were a child and they parents, Marianne lost her dependence, her need to please: she was an independent person. The company, as usual, published some very good books that year, and an author Marianne had brought in had a great success, both critical and commercial. She and Duke and Nowicki had a wonderful celebration with him one evening, and their gratification was genuine and shared.

Marianne's unhappy experience at the office is instructive for two reasons. First, her colleagues' extreme lack of consideration illustrates one of the greatest mistakes senior people make in work settings: not listening to their subordinates. Second, the same insensitivity placed Marianne in the kind of situation that tempts us to feel and act like victims, wearing our suffering as a rebuke to the villains we hold responsible. The fact that Marianne was a woman suffering at the hands of two men also permits those who care to to see this as an example of men as tyrants and women as martyrs. Let's look at these issues one at a time.

A GOOD MANAGER IS A GOOD LISTENER

Managers are expected to lead and direct the people under them. Unfortunately, people are promoted because they were good at the jobs they were doing, not because they've proven themselves as managers.

In fact, according to the Peter Principle, people tend to advance until they reach their level of incompetence. As a result, many principals and vice presidents and supervisors pay more attention to the product than to the people producing it—to the detriment of both.

Effective managers are proactive listeners. They don't wait for members of their staffs to come to them; they make an active effort to find out what people think and feel by asking them.

The manager who meets frequently with staff members keeps informed and, even more important, communicates interest in the people themselves.

An open-door policy allows access, but it doesn't substitute for an active campaign of reaching out and listening to people. The manager who doesn't ask questions communicates that he or she doesn't care. And if he or she doesn't listen, the message is "I'm not there for you." Even if a manager decides not to follow a subordinate's suggestion or not to give that person a raise, listening with sincere interest conveys respect and makes the employee feel appreciated.

When Duke and Nowicki hired Marianne, they were impressed by her maturity. They thought of her as a self-sufficient person who would share the load. You might think that as experienced people they would have been more sensitive to a new colleague's need for support. But the truth is, they did their best work outside the office. When they sat down to court an agent or an author, they were very sensitive.

Duke and Nowicki didn't offer Marianne any supervision because *they* never got any. What didn't occur to them was that their close friendship had sustained their own needs for support when they'd first started out. The mistake they made in dealing with Marianne was thinking about her only as a worker and not as a person. Interest in peers may come easily; but even if it doesn't come naturally, senior people must take an interest in junior people. They're the ones who get the work done.

———◆———

Communicating by memo—however witty or informal— doesn't substitute for personal contact, because it closes off the chance to listen.

———◆———

Simply going through the motions of meeting with people doesn't work. The fake listener doesn't fool anyone. Poor eye contact, shuffling feet, busy hands, and meaningless replies, like "That's interesting" and "Is that right?" give them away. The insincere listener's lack of in-

terest in the conversation betrays a larger problem: lack of interest in the person with whom the listener is communicating.

Most people don't listen with the intent to understand; they listen with the intent to reply. Even at work, where performance takes priority over relationships, listening carefully to understand the other person's point of view, before you even think about replying, is the key to productive communication.

It's important to realize that failure to listen isn't necessarily a product of meanness or insensitivity. Anxiety, preoccupation, and pressure can undermine the skills of even a good listener. The point is, really, that at work, as in every other arena of life, listening is important and may require a little effort.

Effective managers develop a routine in which communication time is an integral part. They meet with their staff and ask questions. They don't react before gathering all the facts. If they don't know what their people are thinking and feeling, they ask—and they listen.

WHAT IF YOUR BOSS DOESN'T LISTEN?

If at this point we were to leave the subject of listening at the workplace, we would have fallen into the easy habit of reducing a complex subject to a simple formula: thoughtful managers listen to what their employees have to say. Where does that leave those who don't get listened to at work? Feeling sorry for themselves.

When we don't feel heard by our superiors, few of us give up right away. We write memos, we ask to meet with them, we try to communicate our needs and convey our points of view. Then we give up. Frequently we do what Marianne did: we complain to other people.

Once Marianne came to the conclusion that her senior colleagues were uninterested and unavailable, she started griping to the receptionist.

Gossip, something we all indulge in, is a form of consciousness lowering. The rules of the game are simple: players are free to run down anybody who's not in the room. (Hint: If you play this game, don't leave the room.)

Triangulation—ventilating feelings of frustration with third parties rather than addressing conflicts at their source—takes on epidemic proportions in work settings. Letting off steam by complaining to sympathetic listeners about other people is a perfectly human thing to do. The problem is that habitual complaining about superiors locks us into

passivity and helplessness and mean-spiritedness. We may have given up trying to get through to the sons of bitches, but by God we don't mind saying what we think of them—as long as they aren't within earshot.

I once worked in a clinic with six other psychotherapists, where everyone except the director went out to lunch together. Guess what the main topic of conversation was? The director and what a rigid guy he was. And guess what the group did about it? Complained regularly among themselves, as though they were a resistible force and he were an immovable object.

But, some of you might be thinking, my boss *really is* insensitive! I've *tried* to talk to him, and he just doesn't listen.

I don't doubt it. People aren't promoted because they're good listeners. They get promoted because they're good workers, or maybe good talkers. Moreover, positions of authority encourage the directive side of human nature, often at the expense of receptivity. The mistake people make in trying to get through to unreceptive superiors is the same mistake most of us make in dealing with the difficult people in our lives: We try to change them. And when that doesn't work, we give up.

You don't change relationships by trying to control other people's behavior but by changing yourself in relation to them.

Instead, start by examining your expectations. What do you want, and how are you programmed to go about getting it? Are you, as Marianne was, expecting to have your personal needs met at the office? Do you work hard and wait patiently for the boss to tell you that you're doing a great job, like a good little boy or girl? Have you learned to try to get responded to by being clever rather than competent or by being pleasing rather than productive?

No matter how fondly we may remember the Mary Tyler Moore show, the workplace is not a family. Yet many of us relate to our bosses as though we were children and they were our parents. The alternative is to think of yourselves as two self-respecting adults who happen to occupy different positions at the office. Marianne wanted Duke and Nowicki to take her seriously, but she hadn't taken herself seriously. Trying too hard to be liked by our bosses and waiting patiently for them to recognize our worth are common examples of not taking ourselves seriously.

The chairman of the department of psychiatry once complained to me that certain faculty members responded to him as though he were their father. I had to laugh. Of course they did. One of the things that comes with a position of responsibility is becoming the object of people's attitudes toward authority. (I think it's called transference.) Supervisors should remember this when they meet with their subordinates. When employees are summoned to meet with the boss, many of them expect a reprimand—why else would the boss call you in?—rather than an open forum. Supervisors must break through this anxiety by asking questions that show interest. And listening to the answers.

LISTENING WITHIN LIMITS

Leslie was sympathetic when her secretary complained about the problems she was having at home. But once Donna discovered what a willing listener Leslie was, she started taking up more and more time talking about her problems. Donna's troubles were beginning to interfere with work getting done, and Leslie was getting annoyed. She wanted to be understanding, but she didn't want to be Donna's mother. What to do?

If you have a good relationship with someone at work and that person is burdened with a personal problem, your willingness to listen helps lighten the burden. But some people are so full of their problems that they take advantage of anyone willing to listen.

When personal conversations start keeping you from your work, cut them off, firmly but gently.

"I'd like to hear more, but I have to get back to work."

"This all sounds pretty painful. I hope you have somebody to talk to about these things?"

Listening is important at work because it enables people to understand each other, get along, and get the job done. *But:* Don't get too personal. Don't let your compassion (or desire to be appreciated) allow someone to let talking about their personal problems interfere with work. This may be happening if you're the only person he talks to or if she uses your sympathy as more than an occasional excuse for taking time off or for not getting work done. A good supervisor keeps channels of (business) communication open—and keeps them focused on the task

at hand—by asking for frequent feedback about how things are going (at work).

"What do you like and dislike so far about working here?"

"Is there anything you think we should change to make things smoother?"

"How do you feel about. . . ?"

"What's your reaction to. . . ?"

Remember that it can be intimidating for subordinates to give criticism or make suggestions. If you want them to feel safe enough to open up, reassure them that you appreciate their ideas.

"I'm glad you spoke up."

"Thanks for letting me know. . . . "

"I didn't realize . . . I'm glad you told me."

Listening to the people we work with isn't the same as becoming friends with them. Many people worry that if we allow ourselves to get personal at the office, things might get sticky. But those who think that effective teamwork isn't about listening (it's about getting things done) are wrong. Without being heard we are diminished, as workers and as people.

◇✦◇

Epilogue

The epilogue is where an author can be expected to wax philosophical. Here, for example, I might tell you that better listening not only transforms personal and professional relationships (which it does) but can also bring understanding across the gender gap, the racial divide, between rich and poor, and even among nations. All that may actually be true, but if I'm going to indulge in the unearned right to preach, maybe I should confine myself to matters closer to home. After all, I'm a psychologist, not a philosopher.

Having read this far, you've probably been reminded of some things you already knew about listening but perhaps also come to see that careful listening is even more important and difficult than most people realize. The urge to be recognized is so compelling that even when we do listen, it's usually not with the intent to understand, but to reply. And, as if that didn't make careful listening hard enough, at times of heat and conflict we must make a heroic effort to overcome, or at least restrain, the reactive emotionalism that jolts us into anxiety and out of sympathy with each other.

As I hope you'll come to see, few things can do as much to bring mutual understanding to your relationships as reflective listening—hearing and acknowledging the other person's thoughts and feelings before voicing your own. You can make reflective listening a habit, but—like developing any new habit—this takes work, takes practice.

One of my least favorite remarks comes from some people who are in therapy to improve their relationships. They've complained about their difficulties; I've listened and sympathized; then I've suggested some

things they could do to start giving and getting the understanding they say they so urgently long for. Then comes The Comment: "Why does everything have to be so artificial? Why can't we just talk to each other naturally?" I hate it when people say that! They *are* talking naturally, and it isn't working.

I get annoyed when people say that it's unnatural to hold back their reply until they've acknowledged what the other person has to say, because this protest seems so stubborn and resistant. But the thing that really annoys me about this comment is that it's based on the truth: good listening *doesn't* come naturally.

Listening is a skill, and like any skill it can be practiced and improved. But although listening can be looked at this way—as a performance—it can also be looked at another way, as a more or less natural outgrowth of an attitude, an attitude of caring and concern for other people.

Caring about someone doesn't require a great deal of deliberate thought; it's something you feel. Caring about a person almost automatically impels you to act with consideration for him or her. This consideration isn't wholly unselfish, because to care about someone means that your well-being is tied up with theirs. When a bad thing happens to someone you care deeply about, something bad happens to you as well. But *showing* that you care, suspending your own interests and making yourself available to the other person, takes some effort. It means devoting alertness to another's well-being.

Listening a little harder—extending what we do automatically, extending ourselves a little more—is one of the ways, one of the best ways, we can be good to each other. Attending a little harder to the other person—enough to discern his feelings, enough to consider her ideas and point of view—this takes a little effort.

Caring enough to listen doesn't mean going around selflessly and automatically available to everyone you encounter. Rather, it means being alert to those situations in which the person you're with needs to be listened to.

Ironically, our ability to listen is often less flexible with our inner, intimate circle. We love, but our love gets frayed. Conflict, habit, and the pressure of our own emotions makes us listen least well where listening is most needed. As we move outside the family circle to those for whom we have personal regard but less emotional intensity, we tend

to be more open, more receptive, and more flexible. It's not—as we're sometimes accused—that we "care more about our friends than we do about our family" but that these relationships are less agglutinated with conflict and resentment.

So. We don't get far with our efforts to listen better without running into the problem of our own emotionality and reactivity. Listening better requires not only a greater openness to others but also a greater reflective awareness of ourselves. Do we express ourselves in an emotionally pressured way that makes our listeners anxious and defensive? If so, what can we do about it? (If the answer is nothing, then that's the improvement we can expect in the listening we get.) Under what circumstances do we become reactive and give advice or interrupt or make jokes instead of listening?

Concern for other people is an instinctive expression of the best part of us. Unfortunately, frustrations at home and a sense of powerlessness in the wider world mean that we don't always feel or act with generosity and concern.

Everywhere around us we're encouraged to claim our victimhood and our right to bitterness. This widespread feeling of injured entitlement can be understood as a product of insufficient emotional nourishment. The people in our lives who are hungry for attention are suffered, shunned, or shamed. We let them know in some way that their great need to be heard is excessive and selfish. And where does that leave them? Hungry for attention. And so the problem of listening, like all human problems, is circular: inadequate attention and understanding make us insecure in ourselves and less open to others. The listening we don't get is the listening we don't pass on. In this sense, the blatant clamoring for attention of the narcissist is a caricature of us all—which is why these needy, demanding people make us so uncomfortable.

Their inability to get the attention they crave leaves them feeling powerless—a feeling that's reinforced by living in a world marked by economic decline, poverty, AIDS, crime, pollution, and bureaucratic ineptitude. So it's not surprising that we've lost faith in our own capacity to make a difference. Public disillusion and private disappointment deplete and discourage us. We feel put upon and let down, and so, naturally, we turn our resentment outward and our sympathy inward.

When we're feeling beleaguered and insecure, it's natural to think about looking out for number one rather than reaching out to others.

Unfortunately, preoccupation with the self is self-defeating. Trapped in excesses of self-consciousness, men and women become polarized and resentful. Sadly, anger and despair have fueled a decline in concern and a retreat to the dead end of preoccupation with the self.

We cannot simply reverse the process of misunderstanding, but we can realize that relationship problems are circular, not linear. And circular patterns can be broken—if someone is willing to make the first move.

The great reward of making that move is that listening well allows us to be open, generous, and connected, to touch others' lives and enrich them and us in the process. Effective listening—empathic listening—promotes growth in the listener, the one listened to, and the relationship between them.

That generous listening enhances our own well-being is the natural perspective of psychology, in which all human behavior is seen as motivated by the agendas of the self. But when you narrow down human relations to a collection of selves, and the self to the early conditioning of the child, what you have left is fixed characters, and you're stuck with them. The problem with such explanations is that, in explaining the status quo, they tend to undercut our autonomy and responsibility to do something about it.

It's a dogma of American life that all actions are motivated by self-interest. But this dogma is false. The tendency to view our lives on the planet from the perspective of individualism obscures the larger view that we are part of systems within systems: the family, the extended family, the community, vast networks of associations. The truth is that looking inside ourselves can show us only part of the reason for our feeling empty and unfulfilled. Viewing the self-created world of our relationships entirely from within our own egos locks us in to a very limited view of the human condition.

Should the idea of benevolent self-interest include benevolent interest in others? Yes. Benevolent self-interest does go hand in hand with interest in others. But is it only a matter of enlightened self-interest to take an interest in others?

Trade-offs have their place in the conduct of life. But it would leave too much out of the story of human affairs to give an account of relatedness to others only in terms of narcissistic utilitarianism.

Caring about other people, which takes shape in political justice, the relief of suffering, and the love of family and friends, is fundamental to our sense of who we are and what makes our lives hang

together. Pressures that block or obscure this impulse reduce, even mutilate us.

A universal respect for human dignity doesn't mean only feeling sympathy for others or doing for them. It means respecting them enough to listen to them, to hear and respect their voices—to view them as subjects, worthy of a hearing, not just objects of our needs.

Listening to others is an ethical good, part of what it means to have just and fair dealings with other people. Listening is part of our moral commitment to respecting each other.

Learning to listen better to those we're closest to is easier when we remember that we are separate selves. Openness and autonomy are correlated. If we're to have the courage to be ourselves, to stand squarely on our own two feet, then we must accept and acknowledge that other people are themselves and entitled to their own unique points of view. The idea isn't to distance ourselves from others but to let them be themselves while we continue to be ourselves.

Learning to listen involves a paradox of control: controlling yourself and letting go of control of the relationship. It's like letting the other person drive. To listen, you have to let go.

Trying harder to understand the other person's perspective takes effort, but it isn't just a skill to be studied and practiced. Hearing someone out is an expression of caring enough to listen.

One of the things I've hoped to do in this book is to help restore a sense of balance to the way we think about relationships. First because seeing our relationships as mutually defined enables us to change what we get out of them by changing what we put into them. And second because recognizing that we live in a web of relationships, which give meaning and fullness to human life, may inspire us to a little more generosity and concern for other people.

Does talk of rebalancing relationships and rediscovering concern sound a little pious? After all, you probably picked up this book to learn a little more about listening, not to read a sermon on universal benevolence. Sorry. But maybe the natural sympathy for other people that we're born with is something we have to remind ourselves to express from time to time.

We all believe in fairness and respect for the rights of others. We believe in compassion and justice and that everyone has a right to be heard. Of course these standards are regularly violated. Of course we subscribe to them better in principle than in practice. It remains that

they are valid standards. And they do from time to time galvanize us to action—as when we somehow manage to listen instead of arguing in the midst of a heated discussion or when we remember to take a little extra time to hear what's going on in someone's life.

The obligation to listen can be experienced as a burden, and we all sometimes feel it that way. But it is quite a different thing to be moved by a strong sense that the people in our lives are eminently *worth* listening to, a sense of their dignity and value. One thing we can all add a little more of is understanding—respect, compassion, and fairness, the fundamental values conveyed by listening.

As I said at the beginning of this book, the reason we care so much about being listened to is that we never outgrow our need to communicate what it feels like to live in our separate, private worlds of experience. Unfortunately, there is no parallel need to be the one who listens. Maybe that's why listening sometimes seems to be in short supply. Listening isn't a need we have; it's a gift we give.

DATE DUE			
FEB 12 96			
SEP 0 1 1997			
DEC 0 2 1998			
NOV 1 9 2001			
DEC 3 0 2009			